Capria Rodalia

by
Sidney G. McPhail

Illustrated by Jessica Mulles

Copyright Page

Capria Rodalia-Copyright © 2013 by Sidney Grace McPhail

Illustrated by Jessica Mulles

All rights reserved. Published in the United States by Deep Sea Publishing LLC, Herndon, Virginia.

ISBN-13: **978-1-939535-32-0**

ISBN-10: **1939535328**

E-Book ISBN-13: **978-1-939535-33-7**

E-Book ISBN-10: **1939535336**

www.deepseapublishing.com

Printed in the United States of America

Dedication

This book is wholeheartedly dedicated to my Granny and Poppy, who have taught me so much about learning from our struggles, unconditional love, and seeing the grace of God everywhere in our lives.

Table of Contents

Prologue

Chapter One

If you were among my people, you knew the one thing that could get you out of most any situation in life: running. And you had to know it fairly well if you wanted to survive. *In and out, in and out,* I told myself. No, I'm not talking about my breath. I had become so used to barreling through the streets every night practically since I could walk, all before I left home, and all just to be there before the death hour. Running a terrifying mile without any sense of direction was the easy part. The streets, however, could easily become the end of you. *In and out, in and out, try to lose them in the alleys, in the crowds, in the side roads.* But they were just as fast, if not as nimble, as I was. The pleasure of running for my life from the latest band of good-for-nothing-except-eating Guard was a privilege I hadn't been granted in years. It was no question who they were after, but for what? What crime did I commit that could possibly be worthy of such a dramatic pursuit? I had watched my family slowly deteriorate in bad seasons, and never stolen a piece of bread. I was and always had been a lanky stick, and couldn't hurt someone if I tried. But there was no dancing delicately around the compelling evidence that I did, in fact, exist. At eight o'clock sharp, that's a big enough crime to be met with my execution.

I dove into an alley, desperate, and stumbled down further, nearly colliding with a solid brick wall at the end. Their deafening clamor echoed up the street, and I took what I thought was my last option, stepping on the several loose stones in the wall. I try and cannot remember what, besides adrenaline, was running through my mind, but just reaching out and touching the cruel monument that used to rule my life made me feel as if I was already dead. Taking a classic, blind leap of faith, I managed to clutch the corner and haul myself up onto the roof of a stumpy building backed to the wall. One of the Guard below barely missed when he reached up to grab my ankle. If my sprint for life didn't grasp people's attention before, I certainly had it now. Knowing I was stranded with no direction but down, the Guard surrounded the base of the house. Staring horrified into the murky, dark, starless presence above us, I thought it truly a shame I didn't teach myself how to fly.

Damn, they've caught me.

Part One

Chapter Two

A group of three boys, none of them any older than ten, sat on the corner. Their light hair had long since passed their eyes, but I could still see the dirt their faces hid behind. All three were related. I didn't have to know what they looked like to know as much. No sane person would take the risk with anyone else.

Begging was illegal. Technically, they weren't, but sitting on a street corner watching people pass by could still be treated the same way. The Guard was nowhere in sight, but it wasn't unheard of for other people to go condemn a bunch of clueless, probably homeless children for occupying their space. Just by sitting there, the boys were taking the ultimate risk. They had to be ready to get up and run at the first dirty look.

The oldest one seemed to study me as I walked by. I tried to find something less pitiful to look at, but never could. Staring back at him, and at the two younger boys crouching behind him, I thought they were all rightfully afraid of me. I lowered myself in front of the three, pushing my broad-rimmed, awkwardly large glasses higher onto the bridge of my nose, and holding the thick book in my lap, both arms firmly over the cover as if worried someone would walk by and snatch it away.

"It's alright," I tried to lighten my voice for these children. "I'm one of you, see?"

I looked over my shoulder twice before daring to pick at a single thread on my shirt, revealing a sliver of bright yellow beneath the blue sewn overtop. If I didn't cover it up, that stark, yellowish-gold would broadcast I was a Stoleh to the world. I had hidden and skirted around my birthplace since before I was old enough to even comprehend exactly what the yellow patch meant, rarely speaking to people while passing through what I referred to as enemy territory. As the three boys gawked at me, I carefully replaced the fiber, regretting ever approaching them.

"Where did you get a book?" the smallest one finally asked in an even smaller voice.

Smiling for a moment, I held the book closer to them so passersby wouldn't see the inside. I cracked open the cover to reveal a large rectangle in each page all the way down, forming the small compartment that carried my family's lifeline. Currently, a piece of bread more than filled it.

"What the Guard doesn't know won't hurt them," I hastily closed the book, taking a tin coin from my pocket. It'd been what Uncle Graham gave me to buy most of our dinner. In our borough, it might have purchased a cheap, partially stale loaf. But out here, what we viewed as currency was used to make dispensable cans. If I tried to buy anything with it, they would know immediately I was not who my patch said. But I always brought home what I left for, my methods aside. A jar of tin coins sat buried in the top drawer of my dresser; left over from when my uncle sent me out to what he thought was a center of town in our borough. When I was younger, I fantasized that this virtually valueless metal I was saving could bail my dad out of jail within the next decade. Even though that dream faded with the years, I still kept my stash in case something ever happened with Uncle Graham's job, and we needed an emergency store of money. After staring through the coin for a while longer, I decided the boys needed it more, and held it out to the oldest one.

"Don't waste it. If you run, you might be able to find a sympathetic Nemiren, and you should be able to make it back to the Wall before they close the gate. Be careful. And seriously, run."

The three of them didn't thank me. They took the coin, and sprinted together into the crowds.

I stood slowly, and glanced down at my patch. The sloppy blue threads still read the lie I was a Haritite: the upper-middle class that inherited all the decent paying jobs by birthright, most viewing those below them as unfit to live. Locally, if one were to say a ten year old from a lower class violently assaulted them, the Guard would ask no questions. As a result, everyone scurried about like mice, trying to keep their heads down and avoid them at all costs. But after I determined that couldn't help me, I thought I might as well blend into their ranks for just those couple hours every day. Somehow, for seven years, I'd passed for a particularly dirty, cautious, and strange-looking Haritite.

Four classes led to the chasms running through our yards and streets, but believe me, those at the top were not feeling anyone's misery. Nobody was quite sure what criteria were used when selecting the thirteen families that made up the Etaira. Though they were the stuff of legends to my people, so distant they basically didn't exist, I could guarantee you they never worked for what they had. We had to specialize in something to stay alive, all within our own little world behind the Wall. The only talent they had developed over the centuries was a refined expertise in the field of ass-kissery. Their technique paid well. They lived almost exactly like Lebon, without any say in their corrupted politics. Just under them, the Haritites worked every important job, their children attending the only credible schools in the area. ; They were the qualified physicians, the best teachers, and blue patches solely made up the Guard, or anything else considered esteemed or influential. There was a significant gap between them and the Etaira, but they still had every reason to be content by the looks of their large, stone houses. The Haritite State was their center of activity, but there was no shortage of exclusive and comfortable neighborhoods around, either.

The Nemirens followed them, forming a good portion of the population. They produced literally everything: all the food, all the products, all the new innovations came from Nemirena. They were free in the sense that they had few restrictions on where they could go and what they could do. I, however, still believe the only reason they weren't treated like slaves was because everyone, even and especially the Lebon, needed what they made. Passing Nemirena, it looked like one, giant industrial district on the southern side, and to the north, miles and miles of rolling hills and flatlands evenly dusted with crop. My friends and I regularly visited them to grab something to bring home. I justified myself by reasoning that they weren't going to miss a husk of corn when your uncle, who didn't even have to raise you, works like a dog every day and still can't make enough to support his family.

The bottom tier was a cold, dismal place where it seemed people were born, struggled, and died in an unfeeling cycle. We had our celebrations, our joys, our friends and family, but it felt as if a malevolent presence hovered over any and everything among us. Rare, brilliant minds in my class were not appreciated. If they dared to be vocal, they were executed in silence under the scapegoat of threatening the system. Even though that was typically not worrisome due to the law that decided we were also forbidden to attend any form of school or work beyond the Wall, there were still no human rights, and very little freedom. Waiting for someone to show us sympathy hadn't worked, and over time we learned to live with the disgraceful conditions, skillfully rationing the leftover, often spoiled food the Nemirens gave us monthly to supplement what we could grow. Still, constantly being called an 'it' walking through the streets carried a heavy toll. For the Lebon, it was ideal to keep us behind the Wall our whole lives. But, in an effort to paint themselves as compassionate benefactors in front of their people, they decided to let us out of our giant prison at eight in the morning, as long as we returned before eight at night. The Guard gained a new excuse to arrest and murder, and we gained nothing aside from the freedom of walking around. We still weren't allowed to buy anything outside of the Wall, and were easily the victims of everyone's abuse and ridicule. The first time I ventured away from the Wall alone, I came home having been beat up by a group of Haritite boys. I was nine. That night I made my fake badge.

In order to routinely remind us of their authority and keep our population down, the Haritite Guard also has full consent to raid our scattered boroughs behind the Wall, raise hell and kidnap or even kill people who strike them the wrong way. When Rose was just a toddler and I was five, the Guard marched into our borough. Our mother had never done anything to them, Ellamae told me a while ago. She remembers the day vividly, she was eight when it happened. When they dared try to take Rose and me, our Dad pulled a short knife on one of them. I couldn't understand why he wound up in an Etairan prison instead of on the scaffold the following morning, but by sneaking around stealing with a Haritite patch, providing what I could for Rose, I thought I was somehow avenging my parents' memory and purpose. We heard Mom was found dead a week later close to the mountains, and Dad was still rotting for saving Rose and me. I could only wonder how long they would let him live. I'd heard of Stoleh being in jail for shoplifting for twenty years before their death sentence came around.

After all the fires had been extinguished, after all the smoke had lifted, after all the living had been accounted for, my Uncle Graham and Aunt Clarissa took me, Ellamae, and Rose into their home. A little over three years later, there were suddenly five kids in the house. Us three, and my then newborn cousins, Oakley and Niles. Ellamae turned nineteen last month, got up, and left us. She told us she moved in with a friend, and I didn't even know her name, or where they were. All Ella left was a note. We hadn't seen or heard from her since.

Traitor, I thought bitterly to myself, continuing down the streets, through the narrow alleyways, and back up and around the brick crossroads. By that point in my life, I had learned how to subconsciously avoid people, and was shocked to feel a hand coil around my forearm in a gap between buildings.

"We know what you're up to. You're coming with us."

A panic unlike anything I'd ever felt took control of my leg, and it kicked backwards. A painful *oof* responded, the hand released me, and I moved to take off running in the opposite direction.

"What's your problem?" she said before I could stumble back into the street. I looked behind me to see Stella, standing hunched over with her hand on Barney's shoulder.

"You okay?" she asked him. By the way he stood half bent and grimacing, I knew I could have easily kicked him in the gut.

"Swell..." Barney looked back up at me with a degree of harshness. Neither one of them appeared overly accusing, but I instinctively began defending myself.

"You scared the living daylights out of me! I thought you were the Guard or, or Lebon!"

Shortly after I'd said it, I realized how stupid I must have sounded. Barney and Stella only stared dubiously at each other, and then at me. They were unaware of the recurrent nightmare, another lovely consequence of the constant, terrifying rush of running about as a Haritite, which kept me staring at the ceiling all night at least three times a week. No matter how unrealistic it was to even think about being snatched off the streets by a Lebon, the dream kept permanent dark circles beneath my eyes.

"I think maybe you should go home and lie down," Barney regained his composure and stood straight again. I had to look up at him, and the demoralizing worry now ridden in his face. "The Lebon couldn't and wouldn't show their faces 'round here. You know that."

Lebon were the distant tyrants that invaded the island centuries ago, separating us into the four classes for their own convenience. Over in Imperiam, they lived and ruled like miniature kings and queens, all under the Imperial. I thought his name was Aloysius. That was all I knew and cared to know about him.

"Don't do that to me," I shuddered.

"We've got to move on before someone sees three Haritites whispering in an alley," Stella dismissed the topic, staring first back into the street, then at her own fake patch as if to ensure it was still there. Walking around too long wearing those things was bound to turn heads at some point, namely, the heads of the Guard. If we were caught, we would surpass the infinite wait for death row.

The three of us blended back into the road home, a state of silence surrounding us. We never removed our patches until we approached the Wall. But it was still a long walk, and we stuck close together, carefully carrying our three 'books.' As the bustling of crowds faded into a low hum behind us, people began to appear less happy, less clean, and less full. Soon the only presences besides our own were the stumpy, disfigured homes and empty dirt path. Barney, Stella, and I stopped for a minute to take off our fake patches in the shadows of an abandoned building. Before I touched mine, I heard the voice behind us, and simply died internally for a couple seconds.

"Stop."

Drawing in my breath, I turned around and saw them approaching us. The six men were intimidating by themselves. The embroidered blue patch of Haritite Guard only added to their moving visage.

"Yes, sir?" I asked in an innocent voice, gingerly touching my glasses and squinting like I could barely see them. When in fact, it was the glasses making their presence blurry to begin with.

"Now, what would three young Haritites be doing so near these slums?" The same man asked, and I automatically began running a list of reasonable excuses I could give through my head.

"We're doing an assignment for school, sir. On the extent of the rounds of the Guard so that we may better appreciate the lengths to which they go to ensure our community remains safe."

He was suddenly less accusing. I may have been a Stoleh, but I certainly had the Etairan art of apple-polishing down to a science.

"Well, it is unsafe for a couple of young people to approach the Stoleh Wall. These louts might attack Haritite children if they get too close. That is why it was built; to protect those of us on the outside from the likes of them."

"We will head home after we finish the project, sir," I barely kept the distaste out of my voice. "We won't be long."

"May we at least get your names?"

Despite the 'may', it was not a request. But this was not the first time Stella, Barney, and I had found ourselves in a similar situation, and the three of us already had appropriate names for the imaginary people whose identities we had stolen.

"Arnold," said Barney. "Arnold Hiram."

"Ada Fuller."

"And I'm Delilah Owen," I smiled uneasily again, praying the men wouldn't have enough sense to follow us. They bought our story without hesitation..

"Then be on your way."

I adjusted my glasses again as Barney thanked them, and we turned around, making horrified faces at the dirt. After we rounded the corner, Stella and Barney allowed themselves to breathe raggedly, while I lifted my face, glancing under the frames and over my shoulder for any sign of movement until the looming outline of the Wall rose into view. The three of us stopped again at a safe distance, and easily picked apart the loose, messy stitching that preserved our fictional lives. I stuffed the patch in my pocket along with my worthless glasses, which I had found half broken and for sale in my borough years before. I suspected their previous owner had died, but was eager to protect myself behind some kind of mask while my name was Delilah. As the short spurt of migraine leeched away, I sleepily made out the grimaces plastered across the faces of two Guard at the gate.

"Cutting it close," one looked at us as if thoroughly disgusted. "Names?"

"Barney Luther."

"Full names, kid," the other man growled, preparing to flip through a thick, deadweight of a book balanced on his knee.

Barney scowled, knowing it shouldn't have mattered either way. He also hated his actual name. It typically took all my strength not to smile when he mumbled,

"Barnabas Luther."

"Stella Harland."

I paused for a moment as if trying to remember my real name.

"Amaryllis Carter."

The man holding the book made three marks on three different pages, and then motioned upward at the two main watchtowers operating the heavy gate. Dirt roads connected all the boroughs. About a quarter mile away, ours was the first one. We said goodnight without any discussion over the day's trophy enclosed in our books. I had no more money to give, and had to look away when my eyes met another group of young children sitting in the streets.

Chapter Three

"Where have you been?" was my greeting as I closed the front door and bolted it shut. "It's almost eight o'clock. I was worried!"

Aunt Clarissa was on her hands and knees, the entire top half of her body hidden inside our hopelessly decrepit stove. She at least called it a 'stove.' It was just a tall, semi-circle shaped opening built into the wall. She piled some rotting logs into it, managed to start a fire on them, and we magically acquired a stove to heat the house and boil discolored well water. Aunt Clarissa backed out of the hole. By the look of sweat on her brow and black soot all over her arms, she'd been scrubbing the misshapen inside with her bare hands. As she stood up, she carefully wiped her hands on the front of her once white skirt. I remembered what it looked like three years ago, when it was fairly new. Just a long, white thing with little cutesy pink flowers and green leaves printed on it. Now, the white had been tinted a sickly yellow, and only a few flowers hadn't faded. There weren't holes in it yet. This skirt of hers was the one thing she owned that she cherished. She'd actually bought the yellow button down shirt she was wearing so the golden Stoleh patch was less obvious, even though she hardly ever emerged from the house. It was relatively thin, and cuffed at her elbows. I thought she looked cold, and suddenly felt bad about taking her coat the other day.

People who didn't know us often thought Aunt Clarissa was my mother. We looked somewhat alike, I guess because she was my mother's sister, but I still didn't see it. Her brown, now streaked with gray, hair fell mostly straight, though she usually had it pulled back into a loose bun. Our neighbors said we had the same shaped nose and ears, whatever that was supposed to mean. I felt let down and bitter when people related us closely, and began to resent her swaddling nature as I grew older. Aunt Clarissa had always been good to us, but I thought her much like a child herself, her home being her only world. Whenever she tried to advise or scold me, I often wished I could scream what I actually did during the day loud enough the rattle layers of dust from the high beam.

Aunt Clarissa moved around the table, and looked me up and down a couple times.

"Where have you been?" she repeated.

"I just met up with Barney and Stella. We went outside, and stopped by the market on the way home."

Her anxious reaction to the term 'outside' was uniform every day, though she had learned by now that no horror story she told could keep me behind the Wall during our allotted hours. "Did your uncle give you money to buy bread?"

"Yes, ma'am."

"Did you get it?"

"Yes, ma'am."

She stopped, and looked at me strangely.

"Where is it?"

You idiot, you forgot to take it out of the book before you walked in. She already asks you every other day why you carry the book around everywhere. Can't exactly take the bread out now, that'd be just as suspicious.

Niles and Oakley saved me by chance as they tore past us, and straight onto the single, lonely sheepskin bench that rested in the left corner. Oakley tackled Niles, and they fell screaming from the seat onto the floor. While Aunt Clarissa was distracted, I quickly opened the book and snatched the bread out, crumbs falling to the floor from the pages.

"Boys!" she shouted over their senseless squabbling, pulling the two apart. "What in the world?"

"It's mine! Give it back!" Oakley was almost in tears.

"No, it's not. I found it!"

"Well, I saw it first!"

"What are you talking about?" I interrupted from the sidelines of the war.

Niles produced a smooth, gray stone from his pocket.

"A rock?" my mouth dropped open. "Y'all are going at it over a rock? What's next? The dust bunnies?"

"Amaryllis," Aunt Clarissa said in a reprimanding voice, and I cringed like the tone itself disgusted me. "If it's important to them, then you will respect that, understand?"

"Yes, ma'am," I grumbled, considering rolling my eyes so she'd send me upstairs and I could get out of there. Niles and Oakley were twins: seven *and a half* years old. If I never got caught by Guard, I was convinced their constant bickering like little girls would be the death of me. For as long as I could remember, they were either fighting with each other or with other people. The scenarios got stupider and stupider by the hour.

As Aunt Clarissa worked out the latest apocalyptical happening, I waited, holding the bread on top of the book. With the boys shuffling off to the corner to *share*, she turned back to me. I handed her the bread, and she turned it around in her hands in shock, so much so that she didn't question where it had come from.

"How did you get a loaf so fresh?"

"I think the ladies in the stand down the street felt sorry for me or something... they gave me the best one they had."

Her eyes narrowed as if I'd just cursed in front of her.

"Amaryllis Carter, how many times do I have to tell you-"

"We don't take charity," I finished her sentence in monotone. I never understood the point of that lecture, no one in their right mind would hand something to us. "It wasn't charity. I still paid full price. Why can't we just take the bread and enjoy it? We don't get something like that every single day."

She frowned at my tone, but still looked happy, even excited, and dismissed me with a slow nod. I eagerly skirted up the winding stairs, ducking as always to avoid the wooden, protruding beams.

Rose and I shared the only upstairs room. Beforehand, it belonged to Aunt Clarissa and Uncle Graham, who were forced into what would have been Niles and Oakley's room, leaving only a spare area the size of a large closet for them when they were born three and a half years later. I don't know how they stood it now. Our room had a large window, and still got unbearably suffocating in the warmer months. There were three mattresses, one sticking out from the wall by the window, one pressed against the opposite corner, and Rose's cupboard bed. The one had been abandoned and untouched since Ellamae left. Other than that, the only other thing in the room was a chest of drawers. Just that overfilled the floor space.

The quilts strewn carelessly across our beds provided the only color. We each had one, though Ellamae left hers behind. Our mother made them when we were each born. Aunt Clarissa said she and Dad would spend a small fortune just to get material to sew various patches of cloth together. The stitching was neat, but the unmatched rags made them look like the maker was colorblind. Uncaring, we buried our faces into them every night as if we might catch a breath of her scent.

17

Rose laid in the middle of the floor with her quilt beneath her, staring at the ceiling as if watching birds on the other side.. It was a relief to see her out of bed after the latest fever had gripped her so tightly. I remembered how sickly she had been as a younger child, so much so that I lived in fear of losing her. Rose had gotten healthier with the passing years, and she hadn't relapsed since age ten, but I couldn't help but slip into a panic every time she was warm to the touch.

"What's so interesting about million year old shingles?" I asked as I threw the empty book down on my mattress, and joined her on the floor. Her face was still drained, making her smile appear weaker, though it was an improvement on the day before.

"There's nothing more exciting to do around here than watch the mold grow all over them," she nudged me teasingly. Rose looked exactly like what little I remembered about Mom, and what Ellamae described her as. Her hair was bright, bright red, with a soft, innocent wave when freshly washed. She had few freckles, like me and unlike the rest of the family, and couldn't smile without proudly showing her major overbite. I had been told I took more after my father: my hair the same length and texture as Rose's, but a bland, rusty color. Our borough identified us, the 'Carter girls,' by our hair, blue eyes, and other mannerisms they insisted we shared with our parents. Ellamae, with a jet black, straight head of hair and teal-green eyes, was the odd one out when it came to that rule. She had told us, in a huff, that Mom said that's what Grandma looked like.

"Where'd you go?" she continued as she made room for me on the quilt. We both lay back, folding our arms behind our heads, and stared absentmindedly at the ceiling.

"Up in the Nemiren markets where they sell stuff to Haritites. Got fresh bread."

"Fresh bread?" She sat up again and looked down at me, feigning total surprise. "There's no way you could buy that with one tin coin, you fell-on."

I laughed, delighted Rose remembered that. Several years ago, in between her spells, I took her with me outside the Wall just to get her into the fresh air. We didn't come back with anything we didn't have before. But the Guard still randomly stopped me at the gate, and made me turn the pockets of my clothes inside out to prove I wasn't hiding anything. He called us *little maggots, felons, all of them*. On the way home, Rose asked what a felon was. I told her, and up until recently she pronounced the word exactly like it's spelled: *fell-on*. To this day, she has to say two separate syllables to say it correctly.

"I am no fell-on, little miss. I gave the coin to a couple of boys on the streets. They didn't have an aunt and uncle to go to. They needed it more."

Rose took the corner of the quilt closest to her, and I brought the one beside me to form a safe cocoon on the floor, the two of us huddled inside.

"Good. I know you're not a felon. I just worry that whenever you guys go out, you're never going to come back."

"Of course I'm always going to come back. No one ever sees me in Nemirena, and people don't pay attention to a Haritite kid with glasses and a book coming down the street."

"What about three years from now when you're older like Ella?" Her voice turned bitter. "Are you going to leave me behind and never come back?"

Rose's eyes weren't teary; she was past that. She was thirteen now, she insisted. Not ten. But I could see the hurt from Ellamae leaving the way she did in her expression, hear it in her voice, and feel it sitting there beside her. *What did we expect?* I asked myself. *She was nineteen. Was she supposed to live with Uncle Graham and Aunt Clarissa for the rest of her life?* But she didn't even tell us she was going, or where to, or for how long. And then she never came back. I had always been under the impression that kind of behavior meant you couldn't stand your family, and of course Rose took it personally. It killed me to see how she thought every loss in our lives was somehow her doing.

"Tell you what," I put a dangling strand of oily hair behind her ear. "I am going to leave someday. But I'm not going anywhere without you; I promise. I would never take off and leave you behind without a word, Rose. I definitely wouldn't leave a dumb letter to announce I was leaving after I'm gone. You're gonna leave someday, too. Not so sure about our little cousins at this point, but they might grow up in their thirties and meet somebody. We all have to find a life for us someplace out there. We wouldn't be here if there was no reason."

I paused and licked my lips, trying to think of something else I could say.

"Maybe one day we'll all get together and topple the Wall."

"Yeah right," she shifted her gaze back up to the ceiling. "They kill us if we're two minutes late. I hate to think what they'd do if we so much as touch a stone in the Wall."

I shrugged, trying to pretend her comment didn't strike me.

"You're probably right. But it doesn't hurt to build a castle in the air, I guess."

A sound of disbelief sounded from the back of her throat, and we sat there in silence for a few minutes until the first shot came. Our borough was so close to the Wall, we heard each and every one. It echoed through the window and into the room, leaving the taste of iron and blood in my mouth. The shots usually came consecutively, but sometimes Rose and I would hear the ringing early in the morning. One. A couple seconds later: two, and three. Three shots fired meant three Stoleh dead or dying on the dirt road that led up to the Wall. They were late.

Rose's breathing grew shallower as she took a few steps toward the window, staring hopelessly at the looming Wall.

"It's never coming down," she said through her teeth. I felt compelled to hug her. Like if I blocked her view, then she would always be shielded and we could make believe nothing ever happened. Rose's face hardened, but there were still no tears. I wasn't used to little Rose reacting this way to what we knew were the deaths of three

19

more people. She was becoming too much like me, and that wasn't a good thing. I didn't want my life for her. Haritite or even Nemiren girls might teach their little sisters how to sew, to cook some things, or impress a man. I would sooner turn myself over to the Guard than show Rosalie how to avoid them while stealing.

Uncle Graham came home from his job at the marketplace. He was a clerk: the person who keeps records of all the buying and selling within his little area. I used to go with him when I was younger. People would sell something such as clothes that were too small for their kids or the occasional homemade craft or medicine, and then turn around and buy what they needed right there. I wasn't any older than eight, but even I knew his boss cared nothing for him, only the fact that he could read, write, and perform calculations. It sickened me to think about how much Uncle Graham let that man take advantage of him, too afraid to speak up for fear of getting released.

It was nine. Rose, Niles, Oakley, and I were all downstairs sitting around or on the bench, waiting for Aunt Clarissa to finish heating the bread and a murky liquid she passed off as soup. The door clicked open as she sat there stirring. He approached the bench without taking off his collared jacket, and Niles scooted to the other side so he could sit down. Uncle Graham was about thirty five, yet half of his chocolate brown hair was gray. He'd recently cut off most of his beard, leaving only stubble. He looked at the four of us intently, his gaze repeatedly stopping at me to affirm I was still there. I only stared at his whitened knuckles and the gathering sweat stain on the collar of his plain tunic.

"Promise me," he said. "You all will always be early. Always. Amaryllis?"

"I'll come back earlier, Uncle Graham," I told him just so he'd relax, knowing I would always be risking it for the chance to walk to the Nemiren markets. The five of us waited in silence for several minutes until Aunt Clarissa called us in. An hour later, Rose and I sat on my bed in our nightgowns. I was behind her, slowly combing her hair with my fingers, and missing the feeling of Ellamae behind me doing the same. For once, we didn't speak. When I knew it was almost ten, I kissed her forehead good night, and she scuttled off to her cupboard bed. I lay there under Mom's quilt for another twenty minutes before I fell asleep.

I had my doubts about seeing those three homeless boys on the street corner again.

Chapter Four

Barney, Stella, and I crouched low in the brush. Though the sun beat down on us, I wore a thick, dark jacket. It was Uncle Graham's, and several sizes too big. I only wore it to protect my skin from the jutting thorns on nearly every shrub and bush that encircled the area for miles.

Most would think the best time to sprint into an open field to steal crop would be under the cover of darkness. Precisely the thinking of the Nemirens. It'd be child's play for them to catch you at night, when they had people patrolling the fields at all hours. During the day is when they got lazy and left everything sitting there: unguarded, and for the taking.

They would probably never even know it was gone, but a nagging voice inside my head always condemned me for stealing from the same field, from the same person. Sweat lingered on my brow as I peered over Stella's shoulder at the field. We were what most would consider uncomfortably close, but had gotten used to it. The only thing that separated us from the field, from Nemirena in general, was a poorly constructed, wooden fence. The rain had already rotted out its logs, and half of the remaining upright posts leaned against each other. I continued to repeat our premeditated plan under my breath.

"Ready?" Barney looked back at us. I gave a single, slight nod, gently folding my glasses and leaving them with our books so I might see where I was running. Still half bent over, we moved from behind the brush. Slowly picking up our pace as we went along, we were in a full sprint by the time I saw a good, clear shot. I hopped the three foot tall fence and tore across the field, realizing I was already lagging. Barney and Stella had jumped sooner and were far ahead. Terrified of the time it would take to catch up, I focused narrowly on the ground until I found a patch of what appeared to be some kind of orange squash. I skidded to a halt and dropped to my knees to pluck one large, ripe one from the most mature plant I saw. Looking over my left shoulder once, I tucked the vegetable in the crook of my arm like a ball. I couldn't see Stella or Barney in the panicked blur around me, and assumed they were already waiting for me in the surrounding woods. Only after I began blindly running for the fence did I realize I was much farther away than I first thought, and way beyond my comfort zone. *Almost there*, I told myself. *A few more seconds and we're home free.*

In the next moment, home free became an unattainable memory.

I was nearly lurched off my feet, and dangled for a couple seconds until they threw me on the ground. They loomed high over me--one pointing a particularly sharp pair of hedge cutters at my head. The squash tumbled from my arms and out of reach. It was so ripe, it split open the moment its skin made contact with the densely packed dirt.

The sun shined directly in my face, making the people unclear. I couldn't even tell whether they were men or women. Still flat on the ground, I shielded my eyes with one hand and squinted up at them. If it was possible, they were covered in more filth than I was. Their plain clothes suggested they were people who worked the land for a living. If these middle aged men and woman weren't glaring at me so harshly, then they would have just looked like a group of nice, normal Nemirens.

"Another thief," the woman half sighed, half snarled at me as one of the men grabbed my arm and hauled me to my feet again. He and the other one pinned my arms behind me and put pressure on my back. If I tried to move, I'd collapse under the weight. "Look alive, kid," her eyes moved from me to the two halves of squash on ground. "We aren't going to call the Guard. I'll be sending for your folks, though, let them deal with you. Where do you live?" I looked up at her as if I couldn't understand her dialect. She glowered at my face, not at my fake patch. She was assuming I had come from someplace else in Nemirena.

"We're going to figure it out, anyway. Would you rather go home or spend the night in jail where you belong?" she folded her arms across her chest, frowning. I continued to simply stare back at her. Anything I said would some way or another end up with them figuring out I was a Stoleh. My only chance was to get away from these men, which didn't seem physically possible.

"This is your last chance to speak up," she now seemed more impatient than anything else. "Don't think we won't turn one of our own in. If we send someone, the Guard will pick you up by the end of the week. And for a Nemiren, you will be in prison for months over that squash."

"I-I-"

"She is a Haritite," one of the men apparently saw my blue patch, crumpled and all but unravelling. The woman blinked several times as the two slowly released my arms. I instinctively dove past them and ran for the woods. I felt their eyes on my back as I left, but no footsteps pursued me. I looked once over my shoulder, about to hop the fence again, and saw them still standing there, unsure how to react. I thought I might return home with little more than a red mark on my side, turning my head forward again in time to plow into a giant. This man towered over me by at least a foot and a half, and, judging by his size and composition, he did some of the heavy lifting involved in the farm work. He grabbed both of my arms and forced me back to the three. When he began walking, I managed to look beyond him, and saw them faintly. Stella was in tears, Barney holding her beside him to keep her quiet. They then ducked lower in the brush, and disappeared. Knowing they would return to the Wall without me that night was enough to make my eyes burn and cry.

"This girl is most certainly not a Haritite. I've seen young people of her kind pull this trick. I don't understand how the Guard falls for it," the man gripped my blue patch and ripped it clean off my shirt. "Honestly, why would any Haritite be stealing food? A Stoleh, probably an orphan."

"Get off me!" I shouted, twisting around in his iron grasp to absolutely no avail. When that had no effect, I lowered my voice and tried to appear as fragile and innocent as possible, insisting I would never return to his fields and throwing in a couple 'my poor sister' tears, all in an equally pointless effort to strike a nerve in him somewhere.

"Don't waste your breath. You're only going where all thieves belong until the Guard comes for you. They do not take too kindly to Stoleh, particularly Stoleh who abuse their privilege to be let out from behind the Wall on a regular basis."

I looked at him horrified, my mouth practically agape.

"You think I do not see you? You are a regular around here, are you not? Perhaps next time we will be fortunate enough to catch your little friends." He turned his attention to the three. "I would tell you to take her to the jail. But after you almost let her get away, I am not sure I believe you are capable. Just send the boy to inform the Guard. I doubt they will come before the week is over, but she will still wind up where all criminals of her kind do."

He stooped over and spoke hauntingly beside my ear. His voice sent chills up my spine, and made my breath come in crippling gasps.

"At least until they get around to your execution date in the crossroads."

As I was marched from the fields kicking and fighting with every last shred of strength I had left in my weak legs, looked back at the bush I knew, or thought, Barney and Stella hid behind.

"Rose!" I shrieked multiple times as their image faded into hers. I could see her face and feel her presence as if she walked willingly beside me. Even after I had no more strength to resist against the man, I could still shout her name at his deaf ears. "Rosalie!"

Chapter Five

The walls, the locked door, the bars, everything made me feel deeply nauseous. I couldn't bring myself to stand, and stayed on my knees, huddled in the corner like a beaten dog. Quiet, tearless breakdowns overtook me several times before the sun went down. Inside the jailhouse, it was near black, the tiring glow of three oil lamps creating a narrow radius of discernibility around me. The cell was built of a kind of strong, non-corroded metal, and I could just fit my hand in between the bars.

After night had settled in, my legs ached, having long since fallen asleep. I stood shakily and began walking in circles in an effort to find feeling. Once I could stop limping, forcibly moving each leg, I continued pacing around with my face buried in my hands. Eventually, the panicked churning settled in my stomach became too much. I sat against the wall and cried into my knees. Without me to bring home half our dinner and to talk her through the harsh times, Rose might not make it through her next fever. I had already given up all hope of ever reaching the Wall again. A Stoleh caught stealing was considered lucky if their execution date arrived within fifteen years.

I never thought it was possible to literally sit awake all night. I cringed almost every time I blinked, holding my eyes open wide at the laughing, uncomfortable air. It was another hour before I heard the loud creak of a door opening. I didn't realize how violently I shook until the footsteps stopped in front of my cell. My mind immediately shut down and crumbled under a renewed sense of grief, and I retreated to the wall as if I could hide myself in the darkness.

It was another kid who stepped hesitantly into the light. He stood taller than me by a margin, and looked like he came from a relatively well-off family. The boy stood there holding one of his elbows in his hand, staring at me as if not exactly sure what to think. He seemed like a bigger version of one of the boys I'd given the money to the day before, but with coarse brown hair, and rounder eyes. I couldn't see much more than that in the dimly lit aisle.

"Hey," he said shortly. I looked at him for a few seconds, startled, and averted my gaze to the floor, harshly wiping the tears on my cheeks away.

"What do you want?"

"I have twenty minutes left in my shift. Figured I'd come meet the kid the field supervisor's been complaining about for six months."

I didn't even look up. His voice was casual, like we'd known each other for years, like it was just a normal conversation in the middle of the marketplace. I decided I couldn't cower in the corner like I was afraid of these people, and moved to the front of the cell, trying to raise my voice above a whimper.

"What do you want?"

"You said that already."

"If you think you can come back here and act friendly because your field supervisor wants information, then forget about it."

He frowned. "I'm not trying to get any information for him. If you're going to be like that, then the only reason I came back here is because I thought you ought to know I didn't tell the Guard."

I blinked. *Like that? You'd be 'like that' if you were going to get picked up to spend an eternity in prison until you were publically hanged or just shot like an animal.*

"You're the kid they sent to tell them about me?" I held my tongue.

"Yeah. I didn't. I just left, walked around, and came back. It should buy you some time."

"Some time to do what?" I snapped. "Sit in a cell?"

"I was going to try to talk him into letting you go," he looked at me as if exasperated.

"He's not going to let me go," I glared at him, weakly leaning against the wall and sinking to the floor. If the boy thought he could pull such a feat off, then he must have spent his entire life under a rock. Society simply didn't work that way.

"My dad's not as heartless as most people think he is," was his answer.

I was silent, hoping he'd take that as his cue to leave me alone.

"...What does your dad do?" he leaned against the wall opposite the cell. I considered turning my head away and not saying anything. I couldn't help but get increasingly suspicious the more relaxed he made this setting. For all I knew, the Guard was waiting on the other side of the door.

"He's in prison," I blurted out before I realized I was talking, staring at the floor as if infuriated by its presence. Since I'd been in the cell that was the first time my father came to mind. If he truly had been in a similar place for eleven years, I couldn't imagine his mind was still remotely intact.

The boy was quiet. "What about your mom?"

"She's dead."

He swallowed as if trying to select his words carefully before speaking. "Mine too. She got very sick all of a sudden and passed away last year while I was spending a couple weeks with my grandparents."

I looked up at him, not expecting anything like that to come from a Nemiren. For some reason, I had always thought that kind of suffering dwelled solely behind the Wall.

"No parents... who do you live with?" he eventually changed the subject, deeply bothered by speaking of his mother in the past tense.

"My aunt and uncle took me and my sisters in."

"I heard you screaming Rosalie. Is she one of them?"

I felt my face flush. *I was supposed to bring home dinner and then help her wash her quilt after her fever,* I said only to myself, almost offended that the boy kept listening.

"Why do you steal stuff from here?" he asked, something sounding like personal hurt in his voice.

"I wouldn't if I didn't have to, okay?" I said bitterly, nearly spitting. "But if it makes you feel any better, I'm going to be stuck in a prison for half my life and then executed for trying to get Rose a stupid squash."

He shifted uncomfortably. "They aren't going to kill you."

"I'm a Stoleh."

"I know. They're not going to kill you."

"Do you have any idea what they do to us?!" I shouted. He shot me a look like I had lost my mind. "They come and raid our boroughs and burn our homes and slaughter people! They killed my mom when I was five, and they would've killed me and Rose if my dad hadn't stepped in. That's why he's in prison! We have to stay behind that stupid wall and if we're ever caught outside after eight o'clock, we usually get shot where we stand. Or if the Guard's feeling generous, we might get shipped to prison to be executed later. They murder people, kids, for just being late. Of course they'll kill me for stealing! They won't even think twice about it!"

My voice was high and shaking by the time the last sentence left my mouth. I turned my head away so I wouldn't have to see his reaction, wondering why this kid couldn't just leave and let me have two days of peace before the man figured out what he had done.

"I didn't tell the Guard. They don't know."

"Eventually the field supervisor, your dad, he's going to find out. Then he'll tell them. And he won't skip the fact that I was wearing a Haritite badge."

He half smiled. "I heard about that. That's pretty good."

"Pretty good? Would you like to switch places right now?"

Before he answered, the door opened again. The field supervisor's glare shifted from me to his son, alarmed to find him talking to me.

"What are you doing in here?"

"Nothing," he started toward the door, red-faced. "I was just leaving."

The field supervisor moved to let him by, and then turned his attention to me. "Don't try anything stupid, girl."

His unfeeling voice snatched any remark from my throat as he turned around and left me again. I continued to sit there for the rest of the night, periodically pacing around as if I could clear a path home for myself just by walking far enough. In the early morning hours, I gave up and slumped into a pile on my back so I might see the stars through the high, barred cell window. As much as I tried not to consider it, it seemed clear I could never see Rose again, and was marked to be mindlessly slain at the hands of the Lebon acting through whichever prison I was sent to.

But I still would've relived the morning if it meant I could have had my mother's quilt that night.

Chapter Six

The next several hours were painstakingly long, and the cell miserably humid even though we weren't into what people considered the warmer months yet. I removed Uncle Graham's jacket, the closest comfort to that of Mom's blanket, and lay on top of it. Hunger kept me conscious through the morning, though I finally drifted off in the early afternoon.

I woke after what appeared to be several hours. The first thing my eyes focused on was a simple roll of bread lying just within the bars of the cell. Without thinking, I peeled myself off the floor, and scrambled to it. Taking the bread in both hands, and barely dusted it off before eating quickly enough to make my chest burn afterwards.

"I'm sorry I couldn't get more. Someone would notice if I took anything else."

I stumbled backwards upon hearing this voice, and managed to stifle my shriek only after it had penetrated the silent air.

"Are you insane?" the boy lowered his own voice and looked daggers at me. "It's evening. People are still out and they might have seen me come in here. They hear you, and we're both in for it!"

"You startled me," I answered lamely, refusing to say he scared me. The boy let out a deep sigh and shook his head to dismiss the topic. I still couldn't decide whether he was in the jailhouse talking to a random petty thief out of pity, curiosity, or boredom, and managed to temporarily convince myself this kid was not a spy for his father. I actually started answering his good-natured, if not intrusive questions with more than one sentence, but I still couldn't shake the strange feeling. I didn't even know this boy, and his red Nemiren badge didn't help my lacking faith. If nothing else, he seemed to be the first outsider who genuinely cared about my life, and we sat there under a dangling oil lamp talking about harmless topics: our childhoods, our families, what we did during the day. I was surprised by how much I wanted to trust him and how little I held back from saying. I told him about Rose, about Ella, about Uncle Graham, Aunt Clarissa, Niles, and Oakley. I told him about Barney and Stella, too, about how we always worked in a group and had well thought-out methods for avoiding the Guard. I ventured out and told him a little about what went on in our world, but that discussion quickly turned stale and dismal, and was short-lived. He told me he was an only child, and spent most of his time in the fields with his dad. The only real time besides working he spent with his father was playing and losing at several games of cards every morning. All this, and never once did either of our names come up.

"How old are you, anyway?" he eventually asked.

"Sixteen."

"You're *sixteen*?" he didn't even try to conceal the shock in his expression.

"Next month. Close enough."

"I thought you were maybe thirteen at the oldest," was his answer, though he quickly caught himself. "I guess it's just because you're really small."

I didn't know how to interpret that.

"Most of my family is. How old are you?"

"The same. My birthday was several months ago. Not that Dad or anyone around here cares. He'd probably tell you I'm twelve."

"The only things your dad has said to me are how the rest of my life is going to pan out from here, and..." I deepened my voice. "Don't do anything stupid, girl."

He looked like he was trying to laugh, but only one note made it out.

"Sounds about accurate. I still don't know your name."

I opened my mouth to answer, not even considering giving a fake name until after I pronounced the *A*. I cut myself off when we heard several voices passing by. They didn't stop or pause, but the boy appeared frantic upon hearing them.

"Those are the people from the last shift. Mine was the one before them. I skipped it." He swore. "I've got to go."

"Just make it look like you left for some important reason," I offered, feeling guilty that I was going to cause him to get in trouble with both the field supervisor and his father.

"I'll come up with something."

I heard him lock the door from the outside, and stared at it for a long time. Only after he'd been gone for a while did I come to terms and realize I'd just halfway opened up to a stranger. That's all he was: a complete stranger, and I told him things I'd never even said to Stella and Barney, or Rose. I kicked myself over it for hours before I could let something so drastic in my mind go. Without him to distract me, the same, piercing fear that gripped me before returned, and I curled into an uncomfortable ball within my uncle's jacket to separate myself from the filth and insect carcasses littering the cell floor. The little, now bittersweet happiness of having someone to talk to imploded. This was my second night away from Rose, and the longest time she'd ever not been with me. She, Uncle Graham, Aunt Clarissa, and Niles and Oakley must have thought I was already dead since I'd missed the gate the night before.

I lay there thinking about what Rose was doing until dark, and couldn't help but childishly wonder if she somehow knew I wasn't dead. Rolling onto my side and huddling inside the jacket, I closed my eyes in time for the door to open. Assuming it was the boy again, I didn't even bother to move until I heard the jangling of keys.

Instead of a towering member of the Guard, I barely made out his anxious, frustrated face as he forced the unwilling key into the hole, jerking it to the side until the entire cell door groaned loud enough to wake the dead.

"Get out, go," he finally looked me in the eye, his face mirroring my own disbelief. Still watching him over my shoulder, I took a long while to stand and gather Uncle Graham's jacket in my arms, moving at a snail's pace as if waiting for him to call the rescue a practical joke and slam the door on me. The boy said he was going to try to talk his dad into letting me go, though we both knew that wasn't going to happen. He was here having stolen the keys. As I slowly walked into the aisle, we only stared at each other as if waiting for an extreme reaction.

"I can't get over the Wall. I'll get shot."

The boy's eyes momentarily grew wide as if just realizing what he had done, and he swore again.

"I forgot about the Wall." He paused, running his fingers through the side of his hair, and then gestured at the rear door leading outside. "There's a tiny shed. It's been abandoned for the past five years. You could hide in there and I'll come get you out tomorrow."

"Wouldn't it make more sense to just wait here until tomorrow?" I looked inside the cell. I dreaded going back in, but knew I'd have no chance if I left then, even if I could hide in the woods all night.

"My dad keeps these keys with him constantly. I'd never get them. It was a big risk for me to come in the evening. If someone saw me walk in here in broad daylight, they would be watching for when I came out. But the shed is out of the way. I could get you out and on your way by nine."

I took several steps away from him, loudly colliding into the outside of the cell. It was easy to make small talk, yet placing my life in his hands went beyond trust, it meant I had to have some kind of amity with someone from another class, someone I would usually profess to hate. I convinced myself in seconds that following his instruction could place me in an even worse situation, though I couldn't imagine one at the time.

"Would you rather stay here until the Guard finally wises up or get home to your sister?" he picked up on my doubt, knowing after only two conversations what would get through to me.

He was right. In my eyes, that seemed plenty of a reason, and I followed behind him out the back door. Although I trailed him closely, I could barely keep up. He must've known something about where he was going, because we walked in dead silence and there was no trace of people. Within a few minutes, we approached a ramshackle shed. The only thing even halfway sturdy about it was the door. Everything else appeared ready to collapse. The wood was beyond rotted, the shingles of the roof nearly falling off. I wasn't overly ecstatic to go in there. It reminded me of a place only a ghost would enter.

The boy stopped when we reached the reddish door, fiddling with the lock for several seconds until it gave. Once within the dark, moldy, damp protection of the shed, I turned around.

"I'll come back, I swear," he said, reading my face again. He moved to leave. And he plowed into a giant.

"Hello, Bennett," the field supervisor folded his arms and looked down at him. "Now what would you be doing out here so early with my keys?"

"I, uh... there was this, I..." he stammered, almost trembling. It was sad to see how afraid he was of his own father.

"I see you, girl. You might as well come here."

I shook much more violently than Bennett, and could think of nothing I might say that would save our skins.

"I understand you did not tell the Guard about her," the field supervisor continued, placing his hand on the doorframe of the shed, forcing Bennett to take steps backward and barring either of us from running.

"I, she has a sister and a family who need her there and she-"

"How do you know she isn't lying? She is trying to get away, and she will come back to steal again."

"I'm not lying," I snarled, my steady voice startling me. "Hold a grudge against me if you want. But if you send me off to die, you're also killing Rosalie. And I'd rather be shot trying to get back to her than be killed at the hands of the Lebon."

He seemed surprised I was confronting him like that. I expected him to grab me again, and march me back to the cell. I half expected him to throw his son in there with me. But the man watched me for a long time, his face slowly loosening from anger, to surprise, to interest. Finally, he sighed, and dropped his arm to his side.

"Both of you follow me," he moved away from the door for us. I looked beyond him and into the cover of the surrounding woods. There was a clearing, and I thought for a moment I might be able to make a run for it until I accidentally caught Bennett's gaze. His eyes were dismal, clearly telling me not to try.

"And do not try to run because then I will go to the Guard immediately. I did you a favor not telling them today, girl," the field supervisor repeated his son's expression in words.

Bennett sucked in his breath and began walking, and I followed at as far of a distance the man would allow. Once we were in the open, he placed a hand on each of our backs, making us move quicker. His touch seemed to be reiterating exactly what he had just said about not trying to run, though it made me want to even more. Passing the jailhouse, we came upon another building. It was built with the same stones and shingles, but was taller and much larger. Despite its sinking foundation apparent even in the darkness, it was still in better shape than anything behind the Wall.

The man took us past several crates of produce, and into a dimly lit area separated from the rest of the storehouse by four walls and a heavy door. He didn't lock it once we were inside, but motioned to the table and rickety chairs in the room's center. As Bennett and I slowly sat down, the chairs creaking under our weight, the man joined us on the opposite side of the table. He turned a small brass knob on an oil lamp, and the flame inside grew and danced, illuminating the room a bit more. The man moved the lamp to the floor so it wouldn't shine directly in our eyes. Before he spoke, his hand reached over the table, dropping two large rolls of wheat bread in front of me, from where, I didn't know. All that mattered is they were fresh, and I didn't have to steal anything.

"Eat."

Despite my renewed gnawing hunger, I was suddenly afraid to touch the bread.

"Is this not the reason you came here to begin with? Eat them."

I continued to stare as if I didn't understand. The man seemed frustrated now, and slammed his fist on the table, sending the rolls tumbling in opposite directions.

"Bennett, bite one."

"What?" he quickly echoed my expression.

"Your little friend thinks we are trying to poison her. Go ahead, bite one."

Bennett painfully picked up one of the rolls and took a miniscule bite out of it. Several minutes of silence ticked by, and he wasn't writhing on the ground. I took the other one, and once again forgot any manners I'd ever been taught. I bit into it ravenously and inhaled more than half of it in fifteen seconds. Taking note of the man's

33

disgusted look, I shamefully tried to slow down. He waited until I had finished, and leaned forward in his chair, staring at us intently. His voice was just above a whisper.

"So, what were we talking about last night and all evening?"

I looked at Bennett, already shifting his weight in his seat and anxiously cracking his knuckles.

"Stop fidgeting," his father told him sternly, and he froze, staring at him as if caught with blood on his hands. "Speak up. What were you doing talking to her?"

"I thought she could use someone to talk to," he said without looking at me or him.

"That is interesting. You never went to talk to any of the other thieves we've arrested."

He didn't answer.

"What is your name?" the man turned in his chair and looked at me. I was surprised he cared, and this time, I strongly considered lying. "Unless you would prefer I continue to call you girl."

"Uh, Delilah-"

"Do not give me the fake name you give the Guard."

I stumbled over the two syllables in my Haritite last name, and then sheepishly admitted, "Amaryllis Carter."

"I would like to hear you elaborate on what you said outside. About being killed at the hands of the Lebon."

I averted my eyes to the other side of the room, unprepared, and spoke in a quiet, matter-of-fact tone.

"That's what it is. That's what they do to any Stoleh they can get their hands on. It seems like it's all about making it look as if they're slowly getting rid of us. But we're just the scapegoat. If one day we were all gone, then it'd be only a matter of which class to go after next. They don't worry themselves about any of us. They created the whole idea of Etaira, Haritites, Nemirens, and Stoleh to lessen their own workload. Now they have us going after each other instead of rebelling against them."

"Too many things, too many people, are scapegoats. You mean what you say?"

"Why would I say it if I didn't?"

The man stared off into nothingness, past our heads and at the wall as if something out of the ordinary had just appeared on it. He then heaved another sigh, and rubbed his forehead.

"I will not tell the Guard," he looked back at me. What should have been overwhelming relief was a deeper anxiety as I believed, by the tone of his voice, to be trading one evil for another. "But I won't let you go for nothing. You must run an errand for me."

"What is it?"

"You may leave in the morning to go home and tell your family goodbye. But you cannot talk to them about what you are doing, and you must be back here early the day after tomorrow."

Say goodbye? I didn't like the sound of this. But instead of asking what could be so dangerous that he'd give me a day to be at home, or why he trusted me to come back, I found myself saying,

"I can't get here early. The Wall doesn't open until eight."

"I know when the Wall opens. You will be here by eight thirty."

"It's a two hour walk."

"Then I suggest you run. Don't think you can simply never come back here, because if you aren't here on time, I will turn your name over to the Guard." The man paused as if to allow his threat to sink in. "You couldn't slip out unseen if you stayed in the cell. It is exposed land from the jailhouse to the fence. As much as I would like to offer you a room, we would have the same problem in the hallways. Bennett, take her to the supply closet."

"Are you serious?"

"It's the only place. Now both of you get out and be quiet going down the hall."

"Wait," I said as Bennett stood. I hated the sound of fear in my voice again. "What am I doing that's so bad I have to go say goodbye to my family first?"

"You'll find out soon enough, won't you?"

I sat there staring at him, him staring at me, knowing it was my only option. Refusing resulted in death without a goodbye. Accepting meant a gray fate and I could see Rose at least one more time. I finally forced myself to nod and joined Bennett.

"I want your word on this," the man also stood and extended his arm for a handshake. "Do we have a deal, Amaryllis?"

I shook his hand briefly, timidly, and without looking at him.

"Yes."

He smiled a subtle grin as if to approve of my decision. When he wasn't staring at me so harshly and calling me *thief* and *girl*, he seemed like one of those people who cared, but didn't want others to know that. The kind that had hardened themselves against most emotion, turned bitter, but still had a tiny sliver of compassion somewhere deep inside. For some reason, I thought I saw all this in just his thin smile. I then remembered Bennett telling me his mother had passed away at the drop of a coin. This man had lost his wife without any warning only last year. Even though I'd spent hours upon hours loathing and blaming him for basically ending my life, I couldn't help but feel both indebted and guilty as Bennett and I left into the dim hallways. We walked lightly and in total silence past an uncountable number of identical doors until he stopped in front of one. It was out of the way, with nothing around it besides the exit outside. Bennett gestured me over to the window. I looked at the shadows of where he pointed.

"You can't really see it right now, but the fence is right there. There's only a little exposed land, and nobody comes around the building that way. I'll come and get you tomorrow. Don't try to leave."

"What is your dad making me do?" I whispered, almost afraid to know. Bennett shook his head passively, and I thought he might have felt shamefaced for how his rescue attempt had turned.

"I honestly don't know," he opened the door. Instead of a damp, muggy shed, it was, as the name suggested, a small closet. The only things I could see within it were several empty crates stacked on top of each other, a broom and mop each with several abandoned spider webs attached to them, and a few torn up, soiled livestock blankets. "I'm sorry about this," he continued. "But we can't risk someone seeing you out of the cell."

"How long do I have to stay in there?"

"Depends on when he tells me to come get you out. I guess around ten. If you show up at the Wall only a little after eight, then they'll be suspicious, to say the least."

I reluctantly stepped backwards into the closet, though Bennett didn't say anything. He closed the door almost in my face, and I heard it click locked. Turning around, I looked at everything now surrounding me, settled in the total darkness. Minutes passed as I sat huddled beneath the arm of the broom, praying a spider would not descend onto my head, and I was powerless to do anything besides agonize over what I had just agreed to.

Chapter Seven

I chose the least smelly and stained livestock blanket and tucked it behind my head. *It's not that bad,* I said under my breath in an effort to convince myself it wasn't. I planned to pick another one to cover myself with, but couldn't even bear the thought. Who knows around what time in the morning, the doorknob began to jiggle violently. It shook me from my state of limbo: not asleep, not awake. I thought it was Bennett, or the man to let me get out of there. I placed the reeking blanket on the folded pile and walked to the front of the room. The unfamiliar voice frightened me, and I stumbled backwards, barely missing the broom and mop.

"Why is this door locked?" it was a man's voice, but not Bennett's father. He raised it down the hall, shouting, "Come here, boy."

"Yes, Mr. Ethon?" he answered in an uninterested, flat yawn.

"Go get your father. We need the cattle blankets."

"Uh, w-why?" Bennett sounded much more alert. I heard him moving casually, or attempting to, in front of the door.

"Because it's thirty five degrees out, looks like rain, and we have no space for them inside," he answered. The last part was meant as a joke, and Bennett chuckled slightly, smoothly, the nervousness once in his voice completely gone.

"I just saw him, actually. He just went outside. He's taking care of it."

I expected at least some small talk to take place. But there was nothing, the man only made a small sound of surprise, and walked away. I almost shrieked when Bennett's hand came under the door.

"Slide me the blankets," he hissed urgently. I managed to get them under the door only when folded in half. They barely fit, and the door jerked back and forth as he tried to pull them out. I was surprised no one heard and came to see what was making the noise. The moment I slid him the last one, Bennett took off running in the opposite direction.

The little section of hall was quiet afterwards. I leaned against the empty wall where the blankets used to be, staring off into space with burning eyes until the door clicked and opened over two hours later.

"Come on, it's ten."

Eager to get out, I scrambled upright and into the hall. The brightness made me blink and shield my eyes with my arm as Bennett quickly ushered me in the direction of the door. I expected his father to be there, and finally tell me what I was doing. But it was only him.

"You are going to come back, right? I know he means it. He will turn your name over if you don't."

"I'm coming back" I said shortly. It would be at least noon by the time I got home, I wanted as much time as possible with Rose, with Stella and Barney. "I gave him my word, didn't I?"

"Not that many people will keep it."

"I'll be here, okay?" I nearly snapped, and he motioned out the door as if granting me permission to leave.

"I guess I'll see you, then."

"Thanks for trying," I blurted out without thinking, immediately wishing I could take it back.

"I'm just sorry I couldn't get you out before this happened. But don't mention it, I guess. To anyone."

I smiled at what also sounded like a joke. But Bennett looked serious, and I quickly wiped it off my face. Without a backward glance, I kicked up dust running and stumbling back to the fence. I climbed over it and continued running deeper into the heavy woods, Uncle Graham's jacket protecting my skin from the thorns. I felt Bennett's eyes on me until I knew I was gone.

I didn't slow to a walk for over five minutes, feeling as if blood trickled down my throat with every erratic breath. There was no path. The only thing I could do was walk until I found a street, and then at least I would know exactly where I was. I followed a winding, indeterminate road for a long time, breaking through the trees in the middle of a quiet area. A couple kids kicked a ball back and forth in the middle of the narrow street, unmindful of the adults trying to weave around them. When I passed, a young girl picked up the ball and, along with the other three, backed away to the grass beyond the road. They stared at me as if not sure what I was, and I briefly glanced at them, struggling not to pay attention. Bennett's father had stolen my fake Haritite patch, and now, the bright yellow stood out like a sore thumb against my dark jacket. I knew I'd be dealing with this, with sneers, with rude comments all the way to the Wall. Sure enough, it was much worse. I had almost forgotten how bad it was to walk around this far from home as a Stoleh. It's technically legal for us to go anywhere. But the further away you dared to venture, the worse it was to be around so many Haritites, and even so many Nemirens. You would figure they'd have some compassion. But while they didn't say much about us, we usually weren't treated any better. They only brushed us off, unsympathetically telling us to move along should we linger too long in their territory.

The streets got busier, but were never truly crowded. In a way, the impending Wall came as a relief, as much as I hated it. I was walking among only other Stoleh within half a mile. There was one woman and two men standing at the gate. The two looked at me as if disgusted, though she seemed indifferent. This was all a boring routine for her.

"Name?"

"Amaryllis Carter."

She hauled a huge, binder-like book from the ground, leaning against the Wall and resting it on her knee. I knew everyone was alphabetized, but it was also common knowledge they never looked for our real names. We all had numbers, and she would know by *Carter* mine began with 3118, *3* for *C*, *1* for *A*, and *18* for *R*, my entire number being Am311820518. Stella was St8118121144. Barney was Ba1221208518. When the bureaucrats in the top tier of the Guard realized how families could skirt around their rules by pretending to be another person, they decided adding the first two letters of our first name would be easier than rearranging their entire system. The Guard were all skilled at locating us quickly, and she found me in a few seconds despite the list of thousands. The woman paused, frowned, and I knew that could only mean something was out of order.

"It says here you went out two days ago and never came back. You've been marked dead."

I shifted uncomfortably and looked down, trying to formulate some legitimate explanation under the men's accusing stares.

"There must be some mistake," I answered lamely to stall for time.

"Layne was here the night this one was recorded as unaccounted for and presumed dead the next morning. Of course he forgot to mark her down." She angrily crossed out something with her pen. "Let her in."

One of the men signaled at the two watchtowers, and someone began to spin the wheel. The gate opened its creaky, powerful jaws, and I scuttled inside, continuing to run to my borough.

I was greeted by several blank faces. Slowing to a walk, I continued on, trying not to pay attention to them. Several of the older women who worked with my uncle stopped me, looked me up and down, and gathered me into their fragile arms before I could even remember their names.

"They told us you were dead, my dear," one said. "We heard several shots that night, we were sure one was you. Have you been home yet?"

"I'm heading that way now, ma'am."

"Good girl. Don't scare your poor uncle like that again. He didn't even come to work yesterday."

That meant much more than most people would think. If he didn't work, he didn't bring home any money, which in turn meant no dinner. There was no such thing as a day off in his mind unless he was, in his own words, *sick and dying*. It normally took a couple minutes to get to my home in the beyond overcrowded outskirts. But this time, it took at least ten because of how often I was stopped. When I finally reached the house, I only stared up at it. The stone base stood strong, and the shingles of the roof were still intact, but the wood was beginning to decay like teeth after the rainy season had passed. I breathed heavily, trying to think of anything I could possibly say, and resorted to knocking on the door. There was no response, and I worked myself up to hesitantly pushing it open.

It was unlocked. Aunt Clarissa was at the table with a rag in her clammy hand, her face red, and her eyes swollen. Uncle Graham sat beside her with a hand on her thigh, almost the same state. Niles and Oakley were on the floor, for once silent, and Rose was nowhere to be seen. When the door slammed behind me, all of them

40

shuddered, and stared. Aunt Clarissa was the first to recognize me. She forced Uncle Graham off of her as she stood, still clutching the rag, and seemingly cautious to believe I could have miraculously come home.

"Amaryllis," she passed Niles and Oakley and the floor, and lifted my chin so I looked her in the eye. She started crying in seconds, holding my head against her and stroking my hair with her other hand. I was almost her height, but she still hugged me there and refused to let go of me. "Amaryllis, sweetheart, are you hurt?"

That was the first time I remembered Aunt Clarissa ever calling me sweetheart.

"Come here. Sit down," she didn't give me a chance to answer, leading me over to our sheepskin bench. She sat beside me and continued to rub my back as if expecting my bright red face to give way to tears. "What happened?"

"I don't want to talk about it," I buried my face in my hands in hope they would take that as their cue to not push the topic.

"Did you miss the Wall?"

I nodded.

"Did you hide all night?"

I said nothing, and she hugged me beside her again. Normally I would have pushed away from her and hid upstairs, but now, I wanted more than anything to hear her voice. The more I thought about lying to her and then breaking her heart again the next morning, the more I fell apart.

"I got caught," my voice shook, but it was still a pathetic cover for fact I was making this up as I went along. "I knew it was past eight. I knew better than to get near the Wall. I hid in an alley, and the Guard found me. They chased me into the woods. They shot at me, but they kept missing. I lost them far, far away, and they stopped following me. I stayed in the woods most of yesterday... because I needed to make sure the Guard who were after me wouldn't be at the gate. I started heading back last night, and walked the entire time. The Guard didn't find me again, and the ones at the Wall didn't recognize me. They thought it was a mistake the record said I never came back."

She was quiet. Uncle Graham took the time.

"Amaryllis, you promised me you would always be early. How could you be so careless as to miss the Wall? Your little sister went out to the gate yesterday and asked the Guard. She spoke up and asked those people if you came back, and a woman told her you were dead."

"This isn't the right time for that, Graham," Aunt Clarissa scolded him like Niles or Oakley. "Go upstairs," she pushed the hair away from my eyes and wiped the tears to the sides of my face. "Go upstairs and get some sleep. I'll make you something to eat."

"Don't make anything in the middle of the day for me. It's a waste."

"I'll hear none of that. Go."

41

With the two chunks of bread, I'd eaten just as much as they had yesterday. I had no strength to argue as Aunt Clarissa walked me to the stairs with her arm lightly around my back. I forgot to duck with the first wooden beam on the stairwell, and smacked my head hard enough to get a grip. I surfaced into our room, and saw Rose huddled by the window, wrapped tightly in her quilt even though the air was already stale and hot. She also held a corner of mine, staring wide eyed into the middle distance and across the room like I was right in front of her.

"R-Rose?"

She looked through me as I joined her by the window, and slowly lowered myself to the floor.

"How could you?" her voice shook more violently than her body. She dropped my quilt and pushed hers away. I knew it was only my paranoid imagination, but I could've sworn she was relapsing into her past fever. "How could you scare me like that?! They told me they shot you!"

Though she had just screamed at me, Rose stood on her knees, leaned forward, and nearly knocked me over. I did the same thing to her as Aunt Clarissa had done to me. She still didn't cry, and slowly calmed down, pulling on my arm until I stood up. We sat together on my bed. Rose looked at me intently, but now as if concerned.

"Why didn't you come back?"

"I got caught in Nemirena trying to bring something home."

She now looked at me like she was in the presence of a ghost, like I should have promptly vanished upon my explanation. "You got away?"

"No. They put me in jail for two days. Then the man who nabbed me let me go."

"He did?" she seemed just as surprised.

"Not without a condition, Rose," I nervously milked my hair over my shoulder. "I have to go back. He's making me do something for him... an errand. He didn't tell me what it was. That's the deal I had to agree to."

"Why did you agree to anything? He'll just turn you in to the Guard, Arlie. Don't go."

"If he was going to turn me in, he wouldn't have let me go and trusted I'd come back. And if I stay here, he'll give my name over to the Guard. They'd find me. But after this is over, I'll be back here with you, Uncle Graham, Aunt Clarissa, and the boys, and it never happened."

"He wouldn't have let you come say goodbye if it wasn't really bad."

I was silent, in unstated agreement. We couldn't bring ourselves to speak of it for the rest of the afternoon. Rose eventually got up, and retreated to her cupboard bed. She lifted the corner of her mattress at an awkward angle, and pulled her journal, falling apart at the spine, from beneath it. It was her gift when she turned seven, because Aunt

Clarissa knew I was trying to teach her how to write. That was what the book I hid the bread in used to be: instructions on letter forming, probably intended for a Nemiren four year old. After she didn't need it, I found my other uses. She still wrote in that journal, poems, mostly. She had become much better than me at handwriting. Rose said it was because she had a lot more time and practice. That was then, and I hadn't picked up pen and paper in years. There weren't but so many Stoleh who had ever held a pen in their hand.

I lay back on my pillow with my arms pressed over my stomach, as if physically holding myself together. The same sickness as when I was first thrown in jail returned. As I was falling asleep, I felt Rose wordlessly pick my quilt off of the floor and drape it over me.

I had never been happier to force down Aunt Clarissa's soup. I drank it quickly, and then left to see Barney and Stella. She didn't want to let me go until Uncle Graham finally convinced her that crossing the street wasn't dangerous, saying that I owed them an explanation as well. I went to see Barney first, assuming if he and Stella weren't out sneaking around in the Nemiren markets, they would both be there. His mother answered the door, and immediately held me just as tight as Aunt Clarissa. She kept both her hands on my forearms, the wrinkles in her face, making her look older every time I saw her, struggling to let her smile. Mrs. Luther must have sensed how eager I was to see Barney and Stella, and led me only past her infant son's makeshift crib, and to the bottom of the staircase.

They sat on the floor in a heavy, sad silence, balling up paper and throwing it into a dented pail. Barney and Stella didn't bother to look at me, probably assuming I was Mrs. Luther, until I slowly lowered myself in between them. Stella didn't say anything, and neither did I as she dropped her projectile. We only held each other tightly as if in fear of letting go again. Around this time, Barney would typically have some form of a sarcastic comment. But he just waited for Stella and me to separate.

"I don't hug," he said the moment I looked back at him.

"Heaven forbid after I was dead for two days."

"How'd you get away?"

I stopped, the relief of seeing them running stale. They knew just by my expression something was suddenly wrong.

"That man who grabbed me at the last second let me go. But I have to go back."

"No," Barney answered flatly, his stare cutting through me. "He'll kill you, or turn you in. He was stupid to think you'd actually make a deal with someone like him."

"If I don't go back, he'll turn my name over to the Guard. They'd come find me even if I stayed behind the Wall for the rest of my life. But he'll stay quiet if I do this."

"What is 'this'?" Stella asked.

"He wouldn't tell me."

"Now I really don't like the sound of it," Barney frowned deeper. "What do you know about this guy, Arlie? He could be some psycho or pervert. And he's a Nemiren."

"I don't think he's a pervert or a psycho; he has a kid. He called it an errand, so I'm going someplace. But I'll be home soon. We'll be back out in the markets by next week."

They refused to answer. I took a balled up piece of paper from the floor, and missed the pail.

"I don't think you should," Stella took the other one and aimed it. It sunk to the bottom without touching the rim.

"It's either don't go and die, or go and... whatever happens."

"Then do it." Barney nodded. Stella glared at him like he was out of his mind. "But if he hurts you then I'll go up there myself and-"

"Stop it. You're not helping."

"I'm serious."

We sat there throwing old, useless paper until dark. From the start, I was nervously sickened by the thought of leaving to an unknown destination on my own. But after Stella and I left Barney's house, I was detached, generating an image of the absolute worst scenario. I almost ran into the doorframe as the image of getting picked up by real Guard crossed my mind.

Chapter Eight

It was no earlier than midnight when I snuck downstairs. I paused at the last step, and nearly screamed when I felt a presence behind me. Rose earnestly shook her head in response to my order that she go back to bed, and walked glued to my back as I stalked to the door, knocking quietly.

"What?" answered a wide awake voice.

"As much as it pains me, I need your help. Let me in."

"No way! Girls aren't allowed in here!" Niles retorted as if such a rule was mounted in stone outside their windowless, closet-sized sanctuary. Oakley promptly shushed him.

"Let me in, guys," I also lowered my voice.

"I told you girls aren't-"

"Then I'll break down the stupid door and whip both your sorry, identical butts! Open it, now!"

A soft *click* sounded, and the door lazily creaked inward after less than five seconds of debate. Rose and I shuffled past the boys and into their hazy, dark room. I'd never been inside it before. It didn't seem much of a loss considering the overwhelming stench of unwashed clothes and matches. There were two tiny mattresses stuffed with straw, each pressed against the opposite corner. One of the bed sheets was tied across the room, dividing it in half, and leaving virtually no space to walk. Niles pulled the sheet to the floor, and the two sat against the wall, side by side. Without the light, I struggled to distinguish who was who. The only reason I ever knew was Oakley's narrower face. Rose and I sat on the floor in front of them. Though we were on the other wall, we were still almost right on top of each other. Niles took something from behind him. It abruptly caught fire, and Rose and I jumped. I saw the candle in his left hand, and the match in the other.

"Where in the world did you two get matches?" Rose asked, though her voice made it sound like she truly didn't want to know. I could tell the unsettling thought that our seven year old cousins had a way to access fire made her nervous.

"We have our ways," Niles answered diabolically, holding the candle directly beneath his head and allowing the flame to light up his creepy expression.

"Outta the drawer in the cabinet. Momma thinks we can't break the lock," Oakley clarified. "Yeah, yeah, we'll put 'em back."

The same sound of disbelief came from Rose as she folded her arms and leaned back against the wall.

"So how may we be of service?" Niles gave a half, mockingly courteous bow.

"I need a distraction, or more specifically, a way to get your mom and dad out of here tomorrow as early as possible. Discretely. They can't know we're trying to get rid of them, you know?"

"So you can go finish the deal you made with the guy who arrested you?"

I shot him a piercing glare like he had just shouted it from the middle of the street.

"How do you know about that?"

"First, your attempt at lying to Mom and Dad was pathetic," Oakley shook his head as if disappointed, his long, dirty blond hair flopping across his eyes.

"Yeah, you're quite the skilled bullet dodger," Niles shared his expression. Despite the darkness, I saw Oakley roll his eyes and sigh.

"I can't believe they bought it. Second, we were listening to you on the stairs because we knew you were keeping somethin' from 'em. But don't hit the ceiling. We're not gonna tell 'em."

"So, the runaway fugitive needs a distraction so she can slip out an' go run this *errand*." Niles tapped his chin with two fingers as if deep in thought, making quotation marks with his free hand around the word 'errand'. I still didn't know Niles or Oakley knew words like fugitive, or several of the others used in the past five minutes. "So the adults have gotta get out, but not know they're being got rid of..."

"Precisely."

"Leave it to us, cousin," Niles smiled with excitement. "Now both of you be gone!"

The three of us shushed him. In spite of his annoyed, childish protests, I roughly ruffled Niles's hair as we left the room, hearing their whispers until Rose and I reached the stairs.

Morning arrived too quickly. I was still wearing clothes from the several days before, and decided I needed to wear something smelling a bit less like cattle blankets and sweat. The Stoleh patch was neatly sown near the hem of my green, shrinking shirt, and also brightly asserted its power against the dark color. I had only two pairs of pants: the tan ones I'd been wearing, and another that looked something like denim. The real thing was way too expensive, and clothes were a hard thing to steal. I left the room wearing those, along with Uncle Graham's half-zipped coat and a tight pair of boots from a year or two before. I nervously pulled my hair into a messy ponytail in hope nobody would question my appearance as Rose and I sat together on the bench, pretending like we were reading something from her journal. It didn't take long for Aunt Clarissa to glance up from her painstaking crocheting and stare strangely at me.

"Why are you dressed like that?"

"Dressed like what?"

She dropped the subject, and went back to whatever she was making. Uncle Graham, unaware, continued to poke around with the logs in the stove, trying and failing to start a fire for warmth. The boys weren't around. We were all interrupted when a breathless Oakley theatrically burst through the door.

"Papa!" he looked like he was going to cry. "Niles tripped over somethin' near the center of town and he can't get up. He says his leg's broke."

Uncle Graham retreated from the opening. "Is he sure?"

"I don't know. I'm not him!" Oakley nearly jumped up and down. "You and Momma have gotta go help him!"

Oakley remained in the doorway as Uncle Graham moved past him, Aunt Clarissa trailing in his shadow. He waited until they had vanished down the street, and then pointed at me.

"They'll be a while. The gate opens in, like, five minutes. Now's your chance."

47

I nodded, the fact that I had to leave them all again returning to haunt me. Just considering how Rose, Niles, and Oakley were going to explain themselves once Uncle Graham and Aunt Clarissa figured out what had happened was sickening. The feeling worsened when my little sister hugged me as if she would never see me again, and I had to practically pry her arms off.

"I'll be back real soon," I kissed her forehead. She nodded, though it was obvious she didn't believe me. Stepping into the fresher air, I tried to shake the image of her pleading eyes as I walked quietly down the street with my hands digging into my pockets.

"Hey, Arlie," Oakley's voice stopped me just as I neared the street corner. "Don't die again, okay?"

I smiled, retraced my steps, and gathered him into an unwilling bear hug. Though Oakley squirmed, saying *get offa me* several times, I knew there had to be something beneath his frown. I felt tears behind my closed eyes as I forced myself to turn around and walk away, bowing my head until I could look back up with a clear face. It took a few minutes after I'd left the Wall before I realized I'd told Bennett's father I would be there in half an hour despite how long of a walk Nemirena was. I didn't even know if I could find his fields again. I could only locate the nearest spot that let me slip into the woods unseen, and proceed to run in short bursts until the live trees gave way to a rotting fence. It was either subconscious memory or complete, dumb luck when I stumbled across my book and glasses, still hidden neatly in the brush outside of Bennett's father's fields. It at least told me I was in the right place, and I left it there, knowing I was almost an hour late.

I didn't know how to just walk up to the door and knock, or even which door to go to. Swinging myself over the fence, I ambled toward the building where I had spent the night in the supply closet. I hoped I looked normal enough that anyone watching from a distance wouldn't bother to come investigate. Before I knocked, Bennett's father opened the door.

"You're late. You're lucky I didn't already go to the Guard. Get in, get in," he harshly gestured me into the hallway.

"Are you going to tell me what this errand I have to do for you is anytime soon?"

"Olivia," he ignored me, calling down the hall.

The same middle-aged woman from the fields came around the corner, seeming equally jubilant about the situation. Then she actually recognized me, and became even more so. Our arguments commenced together, her questioning of the man's sanity in unison with my stiff refusal to go anywhere with a woman who threatened to turn in one of her own. If she would do such a thing to another Nemiren, I had every reason to believe she was not concerned over my neck. Though the man didn't seem to particularly care about either of our reserves, and forced us down the hallway with little more than a harsh, warning stare at both of us, for our different reasons.

She led me into a small, box room hidden away in a corner of the large farmhouse, where no more than a trundle bed, rug, and side table lay. As the woman stood hunched over, digging around in a musty closet, she told me in a subtle voice that I *was literally covered in filth* and smelled from over there, like the fact was so obvious that it required no sugarcoating.

"I have to pass you off for a Haritite," she momentarily backed out of the closet, sitting on her legs and studying me with a harsh eye from over her shoulder. Her voice more than suggested that she already thought such a transformation was laughable.

"I've passed for a Haritite before," I grumbled under my breath, stuffing my hands deep into my pockets in an effort to hide my clenched and shaking fists.

"Well, the Guard is not as gullible in the Haritite State itself. You must look like one of them and play the role flawlessly. And would you take your hands out of your pockets? I could give you ten Haritite patches, but if you act like a dirty thief, then it doesn't matter. Now go on," she pointed me toward an adjacent room, only partially hidden by the closet's door. My expression alone seemed to infuriate her.

"Don't you cop an attitude with me, girl. I could have just turned you in first thing, but now here I am trying to make sure you will not run off and get yourself killed. In light of what he's doing for you, I wouldn't keep Mr. Johansson waiting, either."

What he's doing for me? I thought bitterly to myself. I wouldn't exactly have considered this blind errand a favor. Under the woman's glare, I shuffled past her, defeated, and into the other room. A copper tub already filled to the brim with water and some kind of excessively sweet-smelling oil waited for me, and I felt myself furiously blushing at the idea of not even having a door to separate the strange woman and me. I gently dragged my fingers along the lower part of my arm, wondering if it was truly as bad as she made it out to be, and realized I had dirt all but growing on my skin, and had no choice if I wanted to put this senseless errand behind me and get back to Rosalie.

It took so long for her to drag a comb around my head, my hair was mostly dry by the time she was done. I tenderly removed my nails from my palms, realizing I'd nearly made myself bleed in the twenty minutes of torture. I watched from my seat on the corner of her hard mattress, wearing a silky, black dress that fell to my knees. The top half was divided into sections by thin, horizontal, white stripes, and the bottom kept the same, but flipped pattern, making the stripes vertical as if pointing at the slightly heeled sandals that I could scarcely force my feet into. The dress hugged my body from the waist up, even though I was small for my age. It was clearly made for a younger girl, maybe someone a little older than Rose. I admitted that I liked the feel of the silk as opposed to how uncomfortable my normal clothes got. But I already felt so fake, almost like I had betrayed my family just by dressing myself in not only a Haritite's clothing, but a Haritite's skin.

Another sharp pain traveled through my hair and into my scalp as the woman abruptly dragged the comb once more through my hair, apparently not quite satisfied with her earlier work. I impulsively turned away, crying out in pain. Minutes later, the man, Mr. Johansson, was on the other side of the door, demanding to know what in the world Olivia was doing to me.

"She's perfectly fine," the woman retorted, yanking the comb through one last section of hair before deciding to put the tool down for good. "She will be ready in five minutes."

"Tell her to keep it down. If someone finds her here, we're all next in line for the gallows."

I heard him walking away.

"Got that?" she asked, unaffectionately pulling me to my feet. I nodded, not trusting myself to open my mouth. The woman reached into the dusty, cardboard box that had contained the black dress, and turned a delicate, bright blue shawl over in her hands. She held it out to me, watching as I slowly pulled it over the dress and picked the ends of my hair out of its collar. As I did so, the woman pointed to the subtler, light blue patch covered in black markings near the top, centered almost over my heart as if imprinted upon it.

"Do not," she said sternly, looking me straight in the eye. "Lose this. This is your lifeline. If the slightest imperfection gets on it, you are a corpse. Understand?"

I blinked a few times, startled by her sudden change of tone, and agreed.

"Is this my Haritite patch?"

"Don't be ridiculous," she returned to fiddling around in the box. "Yours was acceptable. But it was wrinkled and if one were to look close enough, it would be discovered a fake in a moment. This is one of ours. It is real. Surely now you do not need me to tell you what your so-called errand is."

"I'm going to the Haritite State."

"Smart girl. You catch on quickly. That will be key to your survival. Do not underestimate the people there. It may look like a utopia in comparison to what you are used to, however, it could quickly become a nightmare if you so much as misstep. The person who receives you and Bennett once you arrive will tell you nothing different."

"Me and who?" I asked, having already expected to be hiding alone somewhere in a dark alley of the Haritite State. "He's coming with me?"

"Actually, you are going with him. Mr. Johansson has been meaning to send his son for a long time, but needed to find someone he could trust to help him. Someone resourceful and sincere, he put it a while ago. So he chose a Stoleh."

She shrugged, the concept well over her head, and instructed me to turn around again, pulling my hair into a single ribbon. Annoyed, I picked several strands out as I faced her again.

"How do you feel?" she asked.

"Like a stupid dress-up doll."

"Very good. Now, what you are wearing is a typical school uniform for the largest school in the entire Haritite State. The classes are divided between boys and girls there, so literally everyone who surrounds you will look exactly like you. Observe what the other girls act like and imitate them in every possible way. Do not speak unless you are spoken to."

"Wait, why do I have to go to a school in that hellhole, too?"

"Watch your mouth," she snapped, recoiling as if horribly offended. "Mr. Johansson has reasons for you being there. He is much more generous than I. I would have just turned you in and been done with you. Be thankful you have this chance."

Olivia silently unlocked the door, and steered me like cattle through the halls, turning around and telling me to stop making so much noise each time my shoes tapped. By the time we reached another locked door, she was in a panic. The woman fiddled with the bolt for at least thirty seconds, and then roughly shoved me inside. She followed, and quietly closed the door as another, oblivious person came around the corner.

"You did well." I jumped about a foot in the air upon hearing Mr. Johansson's voice. He and Bennett stood there in a tense silence, far apart from one another, waiting for us. The woman nodded in thanks, or maybe agreement, taking my arm and forcing me beside Bennett. He looked at me, and I returned his gaze for only a couple seconds. We were both too unnerved by the two of them as they scrutinized us from head to toe.

"They will pass for Haritite children, assuming they can behave like it."

"This is ridiculous..." Bennett grumbled under his breath, staring harshly at the heavy, matching blue sweater and Haritite patch he wore. His dark brown hair had been cut slightly on one side to level it out with the other, and combed back flat to his head. Bennett continued to shift uncomfortably as his father and that woman took us in. I didn't realize I was doing the same until she spoke, talking to me.

"What is your name?"

"Amaryllis Carter."

"Wrong. What is your name?"

I looked at her for a few seconds.

"You are not speaking to me, you are speaking to the Guard. Three of them, and they are questioning you. If you tell them your name is Amaryllis, they will know something is wrong right off the bat. No normal Haritite family would name their daughter after a flower, or after anything in nature. It is too, as they say, primitive. I ask you again, what is your name?"

I didn't pause. "Delilah Owen."

"Very good. Common, but not unbelievably so, and could belong to someone from any part of the Haritite State."

"Your turn. What is your name?" the man asked his son.

"I presume it's not Bennett?" he seemed totally clueless. Mr. Johansson's eyes narrowed.

"Don't be a smartass. I want you to leave here at least knowing what your name is."

Bennett sighed and looked down at his own Haritite patch. "I don't know anything about Haritites or what they name their stupid kids. The only thing I think I've heard somewhere is Levi."

"Bad idea. Levi is usually a Stoleh name," I began before I could stop myself. "My friend took Arnold... the only other one I know is common is Nicholas. As for the last name, you can probably make something up."

I stopped for a moment, and remembered a Haritite name from the back of my mind. "I know one from the Guard named Layne."

The three of them only stared at me, like they had thought I knew absolutely nothing beyond the Wall.

"How do you know this stuff?" Bennett asked.

"I've never gotten anywhere near the State itself, but I hear a lot when I get close to the Haritite neighborhoods around here."

"You see, this is why she's going with you," Mr. Johansson cut in, eager to push the conversation along. "You can come up with your stories in depth on the way. You must go if you are to reach the State by tomorrow afternoon."

"You still haven't told us why you're sending us to the Haritite State to begin with. It's sort of illegal for us to fake this." Bennett pointed out, for what sounded like a multiple time, as the woman began to lead us down the hall. Mr. Johansson only ushered both of us out the door along with her.

"I told you. You are delivering something. There are two people waiting for you outside, they will explain everything you need to know for now."

I noted how he ignored Bennett's second sentence. The three of us were back in the empty hallway, and as Mr. Johansson began to close the door, the woman escorted us away.

"Bennett," he said quietly. "Be safe. Don't do anything stupid."

At that, he disappeared back inside the room. Within a minute, the woman was mumbling a goodbye, and practically pushing us outside near the same sad-looking fence. She pointed at two horses attached to a cart and the people attending to them, and closed the door in our faces. I made myself look at Bennett, and found he was already staring at me. I could tell we were both thinking the same thing.

Chapter Nine

A makeshift cart waited just on the other side of the fence, attached to two large, indifferent horses. The dark one ate an apple directly from a woman's hand as a man in the back of the cart sifted through a low mound of bags, unmindful of us. When the two finally looked up, they only waited until we reached them, seeming to study our every move.

"Very nice to meet you both," the woman piped. As she searched for something other than wariness in our faces, I tried not to stare at her sharp, beady, ember-colored eyes, in deep contrast with her black hair. The man next to her seemed normal enough, with a stubble beard that immediately reminded me of Uncle Graham, though this man's hair was much lighter. I was sure the two were only trying to be friendly, but the way all the features of their faces smiled unnerved me. "We know Mr. Johansson has been meaning to send you for a while, Bennett. And he must have chosen a special young lady to go with you."

We refused to look at each other. *If special young lady translates into runaway fugitive who's only doing this to avoid execution, then I'm special, alright.*

"May we get your name?" the man asked me. I debated whether or not to give my usual alias.

"Oh, I'm sorry, your real name. You can both trust us. We work for Mr. Johansson. We've been making these runs for over ten years."

Neither of them appeared much older than twenty five.

"Amaryllis," I answered hesitantly, unused to saying it to strangers.

"That's a beautiful name," the woman said, leading us to the back of the cart. "It doesn't sound Nemiren."

"It's not. I'm a Stoleh."

They nearly halted in their steps, staring at me as if in total shock.

"Forgive us, my dear," the woman tried to dismiss the topic, but I could see how much it bothered her. I kicked myself for telling them anything. "It is simply that Mr. Johansson has not involved or worked with a Stoleh in eight years."

"Why?" Bennett glanced briefly at me, like he could find some physical feature that made me vastly different from any Nemiren, a third eye or tail.

"The only other was betrayed by her partner after they were together for nearly four years. She was arrested and killed, and he was never discovered. As far as we know, he remained in the Haritite State."

I must've looked more scared stiff than I thought, because she quickly added,

"But don't worry about it, Amaryllis. Bennett would never do anything of the sort, would you?"

"Of course not," he looked insulted she would even ask such a question. Now aside from distrusting Mr. Johansson and the people who supposedly worked for him, I started to question my unsupported confidence in him again.

The man slipped around to the horses as the woman motioned us into the cart. Bennett effortlessly stepped on the back and swung himself over, though I couldn't even bend after Olivia had laced my dress so tightly. I stood straight again as if bound to a solid metal pole, grimacing.

"Poor thing," the woman took my shoulders and removed the thin, blue shawl. She unlaced the dress all the way down my back, redoing it only half as tight. I felt my face burning red under her and Bennett's stares, and gripped the side of the cart until my hands were white and shaking. When she returned my jacket, I shortly nodded in thanks, keeping a distance between me and Bennett once inside the cart. Unaware, she followed, and the man swung himself onto the driver's wooden perch. A startling pitch struck fear into me, which only worsened as he steered us down a cobblestone road away from Nemirena, away from my routine, my way of surviving, and everything I had hope of knowing. Out there, on nothing more than a narrow dirt road, there were few signs of life. Eventually, the rhythmic pounding of axes echoed from a distance, the tree stumps telling us what to expect. In a once heavily forested area, a large group of men mindlessly took heavy axes to ancient trees, taking their turns hacking away at their foundations. They paid us no attention as we passed by, though we arrived in time to see one imposing tree fall, supported from the ground only by the dying arms of its neighbors. There was something in the sight that seemed like a blaring ill omen to me.

"My name is Serah, and that is my husband, Vince," the woman dared to speak in the overbearing silence, smiling at us again, only trying to distract from the fading progress behind us. She apparently expected us to begin carrying on a nice, happy conversation, though neither of us commented on it.

"Do you have any children?" I felt obligated to ask just to fill the space.

"Goodness, no. This is our job. Children would be too distracting."

I'd figured. Bennett had nothing to say, so the quiet continued.

"Come on, now," she reached out and placed a hand on my knee. "Don't be so upset. Everything will be alright. Mr. Johansson would not send either of you if he thought you were incapable."

I wondered if Mr. Johansson had told Serah and Vince how I came into this situation, scooting away from her touch, and slightly away from Bennett. But the cart was packed to its breaking point. I had no choice but to stay close to them. Hours ticked by slowly as we travelled through an untouched, grassy area. I could just make out the hazy mountaintops in the distance. Beyond there was home to the distant, almost fabled Etaira. According to the Guard, somewhere on an abandoned trail not too far away from where we were now, my mother had been killed. What haunted me the most about the entire story, and being so close to where it might have happened, was that I would never know if the Guard had chosen her at random, she had rubbed one the wrong way, or if she had purposely defied them in hopes of escaping half a lifetime of miserable isolation.

As late morning turned into afternoon, a comfortable breeze relieved some of the unbearable humidity. I became narrowly focused on turning my face against the wind, only coming back to reality as Serah placed one of the burlap sacks in front of each of us. I figured carrying around such a plain and rough sack with no handle would make us look like criminals in privileged place like the Haritite State. Sifting through the bag, I found a small pouch of real coins, among other generic things, none of which caught my eye until small notebook and attached pen. Serah watched as I removed them and turned them over in my hands like I had never seen anything like it before.

"I picked one up for the each of you. I thought you would like them. You can write, can't you, dear?"

"Yes, I can write," I snapped before I realized the tone my voice was going to take. I struggled to change it. "I know how to read, too, and basic math. I taught myself and my sister."

"I-I'm sorry. I didn't mean to hurt your feelings. I just thought that-"

"Serah," Vince interrupted without turning around. "Just let it go."

She reluctantly held her tongue and reached into another bag, pulling out a thin, black book with no title. I wondered how she could read with the constant, jarring bumps in the rocky dirt, and the noise of grinding pebbles beneath the cart's wheels.

"We should come up with our stories in case we're questioned like my dad said," Bennett said long after the two seemed to have forgotten our presence. He'd never done anything except try to help me, but after Serah spoke of the last Stoleh's partner betraying her, the only thing I saw when I looked at him was how his eyes were a color like dried blood. "And I don't know anything at all about the Haritite State. Can you tell me what you know?"

I agreed, pushing the irrational thought away. We spent hours upon hours trying to build entire life stories for ourselves with our little compiled information. After a while, the conversation had lost its seriousness, and turned into just tossing about our ridiculous ideas of how our betters thought. I told Bennett things I'd heard them say to each other, and things they'd said to me as a Stoleh child before I made myself one of them with a coarse strip of blue fabric. It was dark by the time the first long pause settled between us, the stars brighter and easier to see out in the middle of nowhere. Unmindful of Bennett, I laid back and looked up at them as if mesmerized. The night had always seemed so frightening and deadly at home with the nearby Wall and ringing shots. Stars themselves were almost foreign, but nevertheless one of the most beautiful things I'd seen in a long time.

"Thinking about your sister?" Bennett interrupted my thoughts, and I began quickly thinking of a cover for my embarrassing position.

"My sister and cousins. They've all been in for it tonight. They had to help me slip out this morning."

"I'm sure they're fine."

"I know that. But still, I've always felt like I needed to be there for Rose.... The nights in jail were the longest time I'd ever not been with her."

"You said she's thirteen?"

"Yes, but she used to be sick all the time, and she still gets bad fevers every once in a while. It scares me."

"I'm sure it does, but babying her won't help in the long run. Maybe it's time for you to stop treating her like a little kid."

I was quiet as the cart abruptly halted off road.

"We'll make camp here," Serah said, closing the book without ever looking up from it or at us. "We can't travel during the night. It would attract attention the closer we get to the State."

Bennett and I jumped from the cart with our sacks, set them on the ground, and returned to help Vince and Serah unload. They only waved us away, taking two more bags each and adding them to the pile. Vince chose an area in the darkened shadows beneath a large oak tree, lighting the fire a safe distance away from any excess brush.

"Couldn't someone see the smoke?" Bennett asked him as he added more twigs to it and leaned back, joining his hands around one leg.

"No, not out here. We don't need to worry until we're a few miles out."

Serah took an old, well-used skillet from one of the bags, and began frying some sort of overly salted meat preservatives. The silence continued throughout a meal of pork and cornmeal biscuits. Serah must have attempted to give me another helping two or three times, wanting to ignore me as I continuously refused it. I knew the only reason she offered, and fidgeted uncomfortably under her kind stare. After she finally resigned, I never looked up from my plate.

The blankets they gave to Bennett and me were much thicker than my mother's quilt. I folded it in half and lay on top of it, away from the fire despite its inviting warmth, and away from Bennett, Serah, and Vince. At least half an hour crept by, and I still couldn't find sleep, or even say I was tired, still entranced by the sky as I tried to position my head to see the stars through the tree's weaving branches. Stoleh didn't have much written folklore, but spoken tall tales were passed through generations. I knew of several where some form of this scene occurred: the hero or heroine is inspired by the stars and knows exactly what to do or where to go next. Or maybe he or she makes a wish, but it doesn't come true until the end of the story, which would be told the next night despite the crying protests of sleepy children. It was always a marvel to see so many kids drawn to the same exact story, told by the exact same storyteller, and never grow bored of it. I couldn't remember Ellamae ever attending as anything more than our chaperone, but Rose and I often joined the other children before Niles and Oakley were born. The two loved our borough storyteller just as much as we did as children, and only stopped attending the year before. My cousins would have kept gathering around that small oil fire in the middle of the street to hear Mr. Dabrowski's stories for many more months, if he hadn't caught pneumonia during one harsh winter and died.

"Amaryllis?" Serah's voice startled me from my trance. I sat up, but couldn't bring myself to say anything, still feeling like my state of limbo was reality and this

57

entire situation was a vivid, terrifying figment of my imagination. "Aren't you cold? Don't you want to come near the fire?"

"I'm alright, ma'am," I mumbled, looking away. "Thank you."

Serah slowly lowered herself in front of me, her arms wrapped loosely around her knees. I couldn't sit in many different ways because of the dress, and stayed as if both of my legs were glued flat to the blanket, wringing my hands in my lap.

"*Ma'am* isn't necessary. Why don't you tell me what's bothering you? Are you nervous about going to the State?"

"I want to know exactly what happened to that girl who last came here. The one whose partner betrayed her," was my answer. I immediately felt foolish for asking, but I couldn't ignore how much the incomplete story ate away at me. In turn, Serah's supportive, accepting smile went completely away. I could tell this conversation had taken a turn she wasn't expecting.

"I told you not to worry about that. It's not going to happen to you."

"But she was still the last Stoleh who sat here and she's dead. I want to know about her."

Serah swallowed, refusing to look me in the eye, and spoke like she was trying to recall a painful memory she had buried deep years before.

"Her name was Ruth Backenstose. I believe she was barely seventeen when she and Jason first went to the Haritite State. They lived there with the same correspondent you and Bennett shall stay with for well over six months, and became the camp's local eyes and ears until the Guard intercepted one of her letters. They came for her and Jason, but they knew, and were gone before they arrived. The two returned to the camp and lived there together for another year. They were the best of friends. No one was surprised when they became a couple. I remember how respectful and loving they were toward each other, and how they took care of one another. It seemed there could be no better match. They were both only nineteen when they became engaged. Before the marriage, Jason was sent back to the Haritite State to retrieve something. It was his first time leaving the camp without Ruth, and he never came back. The poor girl was so heartbroken, and rather detached from reality. She would not speak to me, to Theo, to hardly anyone, and it was normal for her to disappear at night for walks in the woods by herself. No one thought much of it. I suppose she must have strayed much, much too far from camp one night. The Guard found her and chased her into the streets. Ruth was caught, and first sent to a prison in the Haritite State, assumed to be Stoleh found outside of the Wall after eight o'clock. Jason was in fact not dead, but working in that prison, and so of course he found she was there. He not only didn't offer a reason for his absence, he told the Guard she was working with us. Ruth was shipped to Imperiam along with others from our camp and executed by bullet." Serah paused, and wiped her face with her fingers although there were no tears on her cheeks. "There is strong suspicion that the reason Ruth was found in the woods to begin with was because Jason tried to help the Guard find our camp. We almost moved multiple times, deeper into the Wilds, because of the rumors. There's now a memorial service for everyone we've lost to the Lebon once a year, but Ruth has her own just at the start of spring. After Theo learned about her execution, he put the puzzle pieces together from what our other correspondents had said, and sent many people to the State to try to hunt down that wretch Jason. Calling off the search with no results or proof was one of the most painful things he ever had to do. We assume Jason still lives somewhere in the State today."

Serah forced herself to her feet, covering her face with her hands.

"But as I said, that will never happen to you. Try to get some rest. Tomorrow is going to be very busy for you and Bennett."

Serah quickly scuttled over to Vince, and lay beside him on the other side of the fire.

"I remember when I was seven there was a girl who came to visit my mom and dad on the farm a couple times, and they always seemed happy to see her. That was probably Ruth," a voice spoke from almost beside me. I jumped as I spun around and saw Bennett's barely illuminated form. He leaned against the side of the tree facing away from the fire, only a few feet away, but not looking at me. "I don't know what she's talking about with the camp, though."

He barely paused, shaking his head. "What a bastard."

"The world is full of people like that," I answered softly, still absorbing the story, and trying to deny the surreal connection I suddenly felt to Ruth simply because of our shared birthplace.

"Still, it truly does take a special kind of lowlife to abandon and then basically oversee the execution of your wife-to-be. Not that I guess he had any intention of marrying her after all," Bennett seemed to hold his tongue, and changed the subject, catching me off guard. "Why after hearing about this Ruth girl do you seem so much more panicky than you were before we left? Do you think something like that's going to happen to you?"

I lowered my eyes back to the ground, then glimpsed at the sleeping horses still attached to the cart as I tried to avoid giving an answer.

"I know you don't trust me at all now that you've heard about that," he continued without my input. "I guess neither of us have a reason to trust one another, anyway. It's not as if we've known each other's existed for more than three days. But you still need to know that I would never dream of doing something like that to you, Amaryllis. That's sickening."

He stood up and began to return to where he had set up his blanket, over on the side of the fire between me and Serah and Vince.

"My friends call me Arlie," I said as he passed me.

"I like your name the way it is. If you don't care, I'd rather call you Amaryllis."

Chapter Ten

"Everything's going to be alright. I won't let them do anything to you."

"Theo sent for you so many times. You never responded; we thought you had been captured. But you're here working in a prison. Better yet, you're working in a prison that executes my people! You left me for this?!"

"Be quiet. They can't hear us or we're both dead," he took my hand, moving to push my hair behind my ear, like he'd always done. Then he realized that, in his absence, I had cut almost all of it off. "I wanted to come back. I know they were sending for me. But I've been here for months, now. They trust me and I'm getting information. We're so close, Ruth."

"Get me out of here, and come back. I need you to come home with me, and you can tell Theo what you know."

"Okay," he said. I was surprised at his immediate agreement. "Okay, that's what we'll do. I promise."

I felt his other hand on the back of my neck. He pulled me into a kiss, our faces pressed against opposite sides of the rusty bars. After so long, he was practically a stranger to my eyes. But after that, he had never left. It lasted until voices echoed from the hallway.

"I'll come get you once the Guard leaves," he whispered, gently stroking the side of my face. I feel nothing but shame for allowing all the alarms in my head to silence at the familiar, comforting, slimy movement of his hand. "Then we'll head to Nemirena. Gerald Johansson's wife will have something you can wear, and they can help us get home."

Jason stood up, and looked down upon me, my believing eyes, and desperate face. He couldn't smile or frown, appearing deep in thought. I assumed he was trying to formulate a plan for sneaking around the Guard and returning us to the camp, almost a hundred miles away. He remained there for several seconds until I finally asked him what he was doing.

"I still want to marry you, Ruth," was his answer. I laughed for the first time in months. "If you'll still let me."

"I'll think about it," I teased.

This time he did smile, and started for the door. Jason nodded once as if to avow his promise to come that night, and was gone.

At his departure, I remembered that we had not been alone, the other people in the cell now staring at me with wide eyes. The eleven of us were crowded together, the smell of neglected, unwashed bodies unfiltered by normal air drifting in from the single, barred window. There wasn't one area of the wall that was undressed by mold or mildew, and the hay scattered around had long since rotted from the inside out. One would think even prisons must have a standard. But we were told this was built for us, and they tried their absolute hardest to replicate our society behind the Wall. If this didn't live up to it, then we shouldn't have missed the gate. They were actually quite accurate with the conditions I remembered from my childhood. But the part that made us all so silent as the hours passed is the fact that we all knew we were on death row. That kept me from ever speaking to my cellmates, as I spent each day trying to convince myself of what Jason had first said. Now, I was smiling. I believed him. Everything would be alright, for us. There were children here, and elderly people. I didn't know the first thing about them, but it would be worse than selfish to leave them here to accept their punishment while I got off free. After all, as far as the Guard knew, we'd all committed the same crime.

"You... know that man?" an old woman asked. Her voice was broken, and not only due to her age. It sounded like she hadn't spoken in years.

"We were- are. We are engaged."

"A Stoleh girl betrothed to a Haritite man?"

"He's not a... it's more complicated than that."

The woman's pained eyes opened fully, seeing me in an entirely different light, and boring into me until I felt pressured to look away.

"No, no, child. You are too young to be with the Idrisans."

Shocked didn't cover it, and I only watched the woman, horrified as if she had just shouted the name from the rooftop. I lived for nearly four years under the safe belief that no one knew about the camp, or Theo, or any of us. Only an Idrisan would know another

Idrisan, and as long as we were careful to keep it that way, we could have people posted throughout the entire island living as ordinary citizens. The Guard would never know the difference so long as they were discrete. All Etaira, Haritites, and Nemirens knew of a figure called Idris, but no one understood what he or the people surrounding him truly did. But Stoleh? Stoleh were kept so separate from the rest of the population, they shouldn't know what in the world an Idrisan was. That, and the only static law across all classes was the strictly proscribed mentioning of the name.

"What are you talking about?" was all I managed.

"Do you realize what they will do to you when that boy tells the Guard who you are?"

"He's with us, too. I told you, we're engaged," my voice nearly shook in a blinded anger. I couldn't accept the notion that Jason would do anything to hurt us. In a tense, lingering silence, it took a while before I came to realize what I had just admitted to a group of complete strangers.

"He is not a spy. Not for the Idrisans, anyway," a middle-aged man shook his head. He stared at me like I was already lost, like I might as well hang myself before Jason returned. "He's with them, now. He will tell them you are here."

"HE IS NOT WITH THEM!" I impulsively shouted, and a harsh pound on the door followed. I took it as the Guard's way of telling us to shut up. Apparently, they couldn't hear the actual conversation.

"Listen to me, child," the old woman continued in a low voice. "I know you do not understand it. But that is the way our land works in regard to the Lebon and the Idrisans. People switch sides when they are caught and offered a deal, and I fear that happened to your... Jason."

"I'm not a child," I grimaced like the word had struck me. I wasn't going to argue with her about him. "I'm twenty."

"I was a child when I missed the Wall. And I was twenty one."

The woman looked at least in her early sixties.

I couldn't bring myself to say anything else to the others. As darkness fell upon the cell for the eighty-second time since I was dragged there, I began uneasily waiting for Jason to return. When the last light from beneath the door snuffed out, I stupidly worried he had forgotten about me, or perhaps someone had found out.

The latter is the story of my peoples' lives.

The children, all of them younger than twelve, had long since huddled together and fallen asleep. Some of the tired-eyed adults leaned against the wall and uselessly tried to. They were all roughly jolted into reality when the door to the cell block opened slowly as if afraid to make a sound. A broad, excited smile spread across my face. He had come. That old woman didn't know what she was talking about. I stood to see him, but quickly fell over when, instead, four Guard marched into the room. They stopped in front of our cell, the only occupied one. I felt the old woman's arm come around my shoulders, and she pulled me close to her as though she could protect me. I still didn't know her name, yet she tried to comfort me like her own daughter.

A painstakingly long minute passed before someone unlocked the cell. He held the door wide open as if to invite us out. We were deterred from his gesture by the other three, standing in the way, comfortably resting their pistols near our heads.

A strange man followed behind them. He seemed young to be the superior of the people who ran this jail, though he wore the pin that indicated it. Not unlike every other Guard I encountered, he was broad-shouldered, muscular, and imposing; his blond hair uniformly cropped above his eyebrows all the way around his head. I couldn't see much else of this man. But I easily felt his harsh gaze scanning the cell.

"Now which one of you is..." he took a slip of paper from his front shirt pocket. "Ru21311514192015195?"

I listened to every number he said, praying that, somehow, there'd be a difference. But I did not have to count to every letter in my last name to know that paper called for me.

"I am," the old woman answered feebly, pushing me aside and away from her. She laboriously forced herself to her feet, and faced the man. He stared at her for a moment, in disbelief, yet I still watched him take the handcuffs from his belt with a deep, sickening pit in my stomach.

"Actually, that woman would be Ch12518201514. Charise Aberton. Ruth Backenstose is the young one beside her," a horribly familiar voice spoke from the dimness beyond the cell. I wished I could've argued with myself over its owner.

Everyone recoiled as the man roughly shoved Charise aside. She fell against the opposite wall, and didn't get up. The rest of the cell was too frozen stiff to help her, and I was paralyzed as the man took a fistful of my filthy shirt, hauling me up against the wall. He spoke so close to me, I felt his breath on my face.

"We've been after your camp for a while now, Ruth. My name is Hal Vern, and I will be your escort to Imperiam."

"Imperiam?" I asked meekly, and waited to be harshly reprimanded for speaking at all. But he didn't appear to care, only impatient to leave.

"Yes, his Majesty Imperial Aloysius will be glad to have your company."

The next few minutes passed as seconds. I could barely comprehend what he had said by the time I was pushed out of the cell, my hands chained behind me. When we left the room, Jason retreated toward the shadows in between the candlelight, hoping I would not see him.

"Jason!" I nearly shrieked, something inside me still holding onto a lost hope. He only averted his eyes, and Hal Vern roughly jostled me for my outburst. "Jason..."

"How does that Idrisan know you?" one of the other four Guard demanded of him as he slammed the door to the cell closed.

"I-I don't know, sir," he answered innocently. Jason then forced himself to meet my gaze, and I only cried when I looked into his emotionless eyes. "I've never seen that girl before in my life."

Chapter Eleven

We could judge the distance between us and our destination by the roads, which abruptly changed from dirt, to scattered patches of uneven cobble, to flat, stone streets that wove together seamlessly around the outer edges of the Haritite State. I thought marching into town in a cart pulled by two horses would turn a few heads, but it actually helped us blend in. There were at least three others on the same road. Vince took off his jacket, Serah removed her scarf, and their own Haritite patches became visible. As we moved a bit deeper into the State, Bennett and I pretended to preoccupy ourselves in order to avoid peoples' gazes.

Before we lost sight of the way home, Vince pulled into a secluded, off-road area. No one paid much attention as he and Serah motioned at us to get off. My back and legs ached from sitting in the cart all day, and I cracked my neck several times as the two joined us on the ground. Vince reached back into the cart, under one of the horses' feeding bags, and handed Bennett a large, faded envelope. We were only told to find the address printed upon it, and that the woman there would decide what to do.

"Hanchoré? Is that the name of the street?" Bennett asked, squinting to read the writing.

"No, Allyson Hanchoré is the woman's name. The street is under that," Vince answered. Everyone only stared at each other until Serah reached out, and hugged both of us at the same time. Bennett and I didn't react the way she expected, and embarrassed, she quickly backed away, handing us the burlap sacks. With a small smile, she insisted she would see us again soon. Vince nodded a farewell like he couldn't bear to look us in the eye, and we watched the two briefly tend to the horses before setting off again, not looking back, leaving us only with an envelope imprinted with the block letters of *7372 Ceaves, Rochonnell.*

With the anxiety from the surrounding Guard seemingly pursuing us, we slipped down the nearest street, and blindly walked for over an hour. I can't say the Haritite State was what I pictured. A couple main roads bustled with carts, either pushed by people or pulled by horses, but all the other places had plenty of space for people to walk. We passed several markets; only instead of the clustered stalls I was used to, they were large buildings sectioned off from the residential areas around them. Said residential areas spanned over a mile, and just beyond them, I couldn't believe how people flocked to everything they could need and almost anything they could possibly want. Seeing the plethora of toys they had for children to play with around here, I couldn't help but bitterly remember my cousins fighting over a rock.

We reached Rochonnell in the evening, and only knew because of a giant sign right at the side of the road. Just within its visible borders, women gathered in gossip circles stood together on the corners, older children passed balls everywhere you looked, and two men were even engaged in some sort of chess-like game at a table backed to a tavern of some kind. Rochonnell appeared to be a decent area with decent people. But couldn't help but wonder as we walked around aimlessly. How quickly would all these people become not-so decent if they discovered a Nemiren and a Stoleh were currently walking on their streets; breathing their air?

Bennett and I passed an elderly couple. I told him several times that we shouldn't speak unless we were spoken to, though he seemed to rightly believe we would never find the address unless we asked for directions.

"Can we bother you for a moment, sir?" Bennett politely asked the man. The two stopped and looked us up and down, staring strangely at the ugly burlap sacks in our hands as if they thought we'd each kidnapped a small child. "You wouldn't happen to know where Ceaves is, would you?"

"You are in Ceaves, son. Who are you looking for?"

"A woman named Allyson Hanchoré."

"We have lived here for quite some time," the old woman continued. "I don't know an Allyson. What's the address?"

She must have assumed by the envelope in Bennett's hand that we were delivering it. Though after he answered her question, they only appeared more hesitant, and more suspicious, of us.

"I do not know who sent you, but there is no such thing as seventy-three, seventy-two. All the homes here must have a first number less than or equal to the second. But seventy-three, seventy-three is just down this road here and to the right. Perhaps they will be able to help you."

Bennett thanked them, and we merged into the crowds before they could ask anything more of us. "He sent us to a place that isn't real to find a person who doesn't exist," I heard Bennett grumble under his breath, the unease obvious in his spiteful voice.

The homes on this street were all conjoined, though none of them looked anything alike. Seventy-two, seventy-nine sat directly beside seventy-three, seventy-three on the end of the line of houses. Only a wide, darkened alley separated it from the next building. The house, a number off from the nonexistent address we were given, stood a little bit taller than the one attached to it, the grayish-brown stones looking as though they had been weathered down to a pulp. Everything about it appeared old, almost like a prouder version of the abandoned shed back in Mr. Johansson's fields. What would make anyone notice this place at all was its intensely blue door, completely untouched, and even more unique from the three other homes in this one, elongated building.

"Should we ask the people here if they know Allyson Hanchoré?" I could hear Bennett better now that we had left the more active part of town.

"I don't like asking people about this lady. Obviously we aren't supposed to be here, so that means your father wasn't supposed to send us and she isn't supposed to receive us. We don't know her reputation in Ceaves."

"You have a better idea, then?"

I couldn't say I did. But we never made it to that obnoxious front door. With our feet already on the first of ten steps, a rapidly breathing figure all but catapulted from the alley. I nearly screamed, and backed into Bennett trying to distance us from it.

The seemingly crazed figure grabbed my arm and the collar of Bennett's shirt, pulling us into the shadows of seventy three, seventy three.

"Give me the envelope," a woman's panicked, but stern voice demanded. My initial thought was we were being mugged by a desperate old wench. Then I remembered this wasn't behind the Wall. There was no need. The woman snatched our envelope from Bennett before he even realized her hand was moving. Reading the neatly folded piece of paper inside, she slowly relaxed, and disturbed me with a crooked, forced smile.

"Bennett and Amaryllis... you are both very young. But assuming you can keep your mouths shut, you will be alright."

"Are you Allyson Hanchoré?" Bennett ignored the comment.

"Oh, no, Allyson fled the State several weeks ago. I'm Rowana Laurie. Come inside, my dears, we have much to discuss."

I didn't like the look of this woman any more than the other people we'd come across since we left the cart. It seemed like too big of a jump to go from her demented state to *my dears*. She was short, shorter than both of us, and at least in her late forties. I still couldn't help but feel intimidated by her appearance: her uneven, peppered hair and overly vibrant patchwork skirt. I'd seen Haritite women wear jewelry. It was just their pointless way of showing the rest of us their status. Her bronze, emerald ring, as thick as the thin pointer finger it rested on, didn't help convince me she was any different than the rest of them. As I stared at her hand, Rowana shifted uncomfortably and removed the ring, slipping it into the pocket of her skirt. She turned and headed toward the back of seventy three, seventy three, and Bennett trustingly moved to follow her. I suddenly felt obligated to protect a boy who seemed so naïve to the world beyond his farm.

"I don't trust her," I told him, knowing well enough she could hear me. "We were told to give the envelope to Allyson Hanchoré. She packed out of here, so should we."

"You have nothing to fear, honey," Rowana extended her arm toward us. It only unnerved me more to have a pet name from a person I didn't know. "I am just another correspondent. I have the same job as Allyson, and you will be safe with me. I don't want you two trying to go back, anyway. You can't possibly walk there. Even if you could, the Guard would intercept you before you reached the edge of the State and question what you were doing. Besides," she tried smiling at me. "You two are not here just to deliver a letter. If we only needed that, then it could have been sent by mail. You are here because you two were chosen to be here."

"Chosen to be here for what?" Bennett frowned. "All we were told was to deliver the letter, and that we were supposed to go to school here. Why? What's the purpose of any of this?"

The woman's smile turned downward, and then reformed, sympathetic.

"Part of your purpose here is to figure that out for yourselves."

I wanted to scream at her, to talk some sense into this 'correspondent' who only parroted the same, lacking information we'd already been told. Bennett seemed equally frustrated, but he forced an indifferent expression on his face as Rowana led us around the unit. She opened the unlocked back door of seventy three, seventy three, bolting it behind us. I wondered how she could see to do so in the dimly lit, narrow corridor leading to another door in the concrete wall. I half expected the woman to open a kind of secret passageway next, but she only led us to the living space behind the unmarked door. Bennett froze in his steps upon seeing the well-kept inside, like he thought we were entering someone else's home.

"The fake address is so no one comes knocking," Rowana explained, urging us forward. "If any information is intercepted, then they believe the address a misprint and disregard it. If everything goes normally, then I can pick up letters in the center of town like everyone else in Ceaves. I told you not to worry; that's my job. Just go upstairs and see your rooms. Make yourselves at home."

Our rooms? I thought. We were in hiding. Shouldn't we be in a dusty basement, some underground chamber? Rowana had to also be living here illegally, but her house was much nicer on the inside than the outside. There was a real stone oven and cooking pot in one corner, with a sturdy table and four chairs beside it. Several cushioned chairs and a couch scattered the floor on the other side of the room, along with a large, ornately carved bookshelf on the only unoccupied wall. Rugs and mounted shelves with various little trinkets and memories all decorated the area, brightly lit by oil lamps lying around in casual places.

"Go on," Rowana spoke gently. We simply stood there taking it in. "I want to see you both in about half an hour. We have some things to talk about."

Bennett started up the winding stairs first, and without looking back at either of us. I didn't follow until I heard his door close.

The giant window, curtained with dark blue drapes, was set in the wall the bed lay against. A tall, thin dresser rested in the opposite corner, and a little table sat right by the door. This room was also decorated with all kinds of relics. I stopped and looked at each one on every shelf as I approached the brown, leather bag strewn over the cotton mattress. It was clearly intended to replace what Serah and Vince had given me, though I only shoved it in a random drawer on top of a folded pile of clothes, and threw the burlap sack down on the floor by the window. I eventually worked myself up to peering through the curtains to see the limited view of the dark alley in between us and the adjacent building. Disappointed, I returned to the bed. It sank several inches as I sat down, staring at the large knit rug, with a lighter shade of blue encircling the cream inside. Staring absentmindedly into it, I reached into my sack and removed the moleskin journal and pen. I couldn't understand what Serah had intended us to do with them. Was I supposed to keep a diary of the passing weeks? That ship sailed when I was ten. In other words, when Aunt Clarissa kindly told me I couldn't keep wasting paper. It was too expensive.

His knocking made the cracked door drift into the room. Bennett didn't say anything, though his wavering seemed to be asking permission to come in.

71

"Yeah?"

"I found this at the bottom of that sack," he walked across the rug, and held an intricately folded piece of paper out for me to take. Bennett sat leaning against the frame of the bed as I turned the paper over and read the neat handwriting.

Bennett and Amaryllis

"Is it Serah and Vince?" I asked him. Though I knew it was no friendly *how-are-you*, I was eager to have perhaps a few comforting words.

"It's my father's print," was his answer. I lowered myself beside Bennett so he could see the words. Actually, it was probably so I wouldn't have to read out loud. I didn't expect a long, emotional story of why he illegally sent his own son and a strange petty thief together to the Haritite state, though I still thought there might be the slightest trace of concern if he'd bothered to write it and slip it to Serah and Vince ahead of time. But the tone sounded like a business deal, and I struggled to read it to myself.

If Vince listened to one word I said, you should not be reading this until you reach the Haritite State. If you are already there, you've been told by now that Allyson has 'fled'. She did not flee, she was needed elsewhere and had to leave on a moment's notice. Rowana Laurie stepped up in her absence. I don't know her personally, so I am hoping she is just as capable as Allyson. But if something doesn't feel right about her, get out of there immediately.

Finding your own purpose for being there is part of your objective. No, it is not school. That is just to give you an idea of how the Haritites are, their mindset, I suppose is the word. But I am sure that through this school, you will learn something that can help you. Just remember that this isn't a trip. If someone discovers you, then the Haritite Guard will not take the fact that you are children into account when they kill you. So watch out for each other. There is a reason why I sent you together. Within six weeks, Madam Laurie should be accompanying you back to the edge of the State, or at least to the edge of Rochonnell. Serah and Vince will pick you up and bring you back here, and then we will discuss what to do next.

Be smart about this and good luck,

Gerald Johansson

Chapter Twelve

Madam Laurie waited for us at the empty table. Before she could say anything, Bennett all but demanded to see the envelope, what we were sent to deliver. She happily passed it to us once we sat across from her.

18-15-23-1-14-1,

20-23-15 14-5-23 3-8-9-12-4-18-5-14 9-14-20-5-14-4-5-4 6-15-18 1-12-
12-25-19-15-14 14-15-23 3-15-13-9-14-7 20-15 25-15-21 13-1-11-5 3-5-18-20-1-
9-14 25-15-21 8-1-22-5 20-8-5 18-9-7-8-20 15-14-5-19 1-14-4 20-8-9-19 23-1-19
14-15-20 19-20-15-12-5-14 2-15-20-8 23-9-12-12 2-5 23-5-1-18-9-14-7 21-14-9-
6-15-18-13-19 6-15-18 20-8-5 4-18-9-5-18-9-5 19-3-8-15-15-12 1-14-4 3-1-18-18-
25-9-14-7 2-21-18-12-1-16 19-1-3-11-19 20-8-5-25 19-8-15-21-12-4 2-5 8-1-18-4
20-15 13-9-19-19 2-5-14-14-5-20-20 10-15-8-1-14-19-19-15-14 13-25 19-15-14 1-
14-4 1-13-1-18-25-12-12-9-19 3-1-18-20-5-18 2-5 13-9-14-4-6-21-12 20-8-1-20
19-8-5 9-19 1 19-20-15-12-5-8

Bennett stared at the long series blankly, and so did I for a while, until I finally realized the paper was encrypted like our numbers at the Wall. As I spent a painstaking amount of time decoding it, switching around the order of the alphabet in my mind many times and only realizing it when the final word didn't make sense, Madam Laurie seemed to get more and more nervous.

Rowana,

Two new children intended for Allyson now coming to you. Make certain you have the right ones and this was not stolen. Both will be wearing uniforms for the Drierie School and carrying burlap sacks. They should be hard to miss. Bennett Johansson, my son, and Amaryllis Carter. Be mindful that she is a Stoleh.

I slid the original note back to Madam Laurie, frowning.

"I'm sure he didn't mean anything bad by that, Amaryllis," her smile was strained. "He just... he probably feels the need to tell me that because... you see, the last Stoleh girl-"

"I know," I interrupted, not looking at her. "I'm sure he told you because he thinks my kind are more likely to snap in this place."

"You stop talking like that," she took the encrypted note and my translation, sharply folded them together, and placed them aside. "Your people are just as human as the rest of us and I won't hear you talk about yourself that way. Here, in this house, there are none of those damned classes. Do you understand me?"

Hearing Madam Laurie speak so certainly and strictly kept me quiet as she turned to Bennett, asking for our aliases. She only nodded approvingly at the names, saying they would blend nicely.

"I'm not going to make you tell me your stories and all of that nonsense," she regained her composure, and leaned back in her chair. "I'm sure you've already taken care of it. But the rest of this is important. You both attend Drierie School-"

"Dreary School?" Bennett asked, looking even more thrilled.

"It was named after the man who founded it. Drierie School: D-R-I-E-R-I-E. The entire subdivision pronounces it '*dreary*,' but the teachers insist it is '*druh-ear-re*.' Saying it like they do will get you on their good sides, anyway. Now, the school is very large. It ranges from age six to nineteen. The building itself is symmetrical, divided literally down the middle between boys and girls. You will be on the second floor with all the other teenagers, just on opposite sides of the building. I've arranged for you to have a guide for your first day. You both leave here tomorrow morning at seven. You walk back through that door at four. No loitering around, understand?"

I nodded once, wondering why she thought we would stay there any longer than what was required of us. Bennett and I both refused Madam Laurie's offer of dinner. The sky was not yet entirely dark, though she hesitantly dismissed us upstairs, sensing at least I needed time for myself. I found an oversized nightgown in one of the drawers of the dresser, and sat on the corner of the bed for a long time, dazed, and dutifully watching the alley as if expecting a drastic change at any moment. Even after only the moon's light reflected off the cobblestone roads, I couldn't imagine falling asleep in another foreign place, with another gray fate. Before I realized what I was doing, I began instinctively running my fingers through my hair, remembering the way Ella used to comb it with the gentlest touch. After she vanished, I felt cruelly abandoned in more ways than one, left to fill not only the provider role but also that of the oldest sister. I found the ribbon clinging onto a thin strand near my neck, and remembered how the three of us would sit in a line on her bed, braiding each other's hair on the nights when none of us could find sleep. It was much easier to be Rosalie's older sister when I also had a pair of open arms and ears that I could run to. Without Ellamae around, I couldn't help but feel that I was failing her. And now, miles and miles away, I knew I would literally worry her sick up until the moment I returned, if Bennett and I managed to make it back to the border unscathed. The more I thought about it, the more despicable my actions seemed. With only hours of night remaining, I forced myself to lay my head on the palms of my hands, and close my eyes. Though I was so far away, I kept waiting to hear a gunshot, cringing every time the slightest noise stirred from outside.

The sun was barely up when I dressed and crept downstairs. I walked as silently as I could, trying to avoid waking them, but Bennett was already on the couch staring off into space. I sat at the table, my back to him, and we didn't speak until Madam Laurie's voice came from upstairs. She knocked on our doors, telling us it was nearly time to leave. Inattentive, she skirted downstairs, turning her ring around on her finger, and jumped when she saw us sitting there.

"Well, I'd say you two are easier to get moving than my children were when they were teenagers. Do you have your bags I set out for you?"

I stared at her as if I didn't know what she referred to. Madam Laurie sighed, and disappeared back upstairs. When she came down again, she gently placed one of the identical, empty bags on the table in front of me, and the other on the couch beside Bennett.

"You wouldn't normally leave for ten minutes, but it might be a good idea to be on your way. Only to allow yourselves some time in case you get lost, and to not keep your guides waiting."

"Madam Laurie?" I asked as she chaperoned us to the door, my shaking hand struggling to keep hold of the leather bag. "Where is the school?"

"Follow the other children dressed like you. The building should not be hard locate, anyway," she half-smiled. "And call me Rowana. Please, Madam Laurie is what the Guard says."

Chapter Thirteen

"It looks like a prison."

After following a long, scattered line of other kids sweatered and dressed in bright blue, the Drierie School came upon us. Bennett's prison comment seemed an accurate way to put it. The entire building was constructed out of three different colored stones: gray, darker gray, and darkest gray. Walls surrounded the school itself, and they were at least twenty feet high. The only things missing were watchtowers and a couple scowling Guard.

We merged with the students that seemed about our age, and lost each other in the crowd. As I was ushered into the building by the next incoming wave of kids, I looked up at the doorframe and saw the sign: copper, and almost dangling by one screw. *The Drierie School.* Somewhere along the line, it appeared a vindictive student had replaced '*Drierie*' with '*Dreary*' in black paint, and there was little fading indicating the teachers had attempted to scrub it away. Once inside the double doors, the clustered crowd of babbling kids miraculously fell silent, and separated by gender into two of the three hallways. I found the opposite wall and stood by it, waiting for someone who knew where I was supposed to go to find me. Only after the crowd had begun to thin a little could I see Bennett standing on the other side of the room near the door. We did little more than glance at each other, and turn our attention back to the floor.

The last couple kids, little ones, ambled by into their respective hallways, leaving us alone. I figured we were probably late by now. Bennett asked if I thought we should find someone, though I was in no hurry to be forced into a room with other girls dressed exactly like me, and a teacher who might as well be speaking a different language. I shook my head in response.

"You two!" a woman, I thought, called at us no more than a few minutes later. An elderly lady walked toward us from the middle hall. She wore a long, dark green skirt that sat high on her waist, and was met with a soft yellow shirt and a tightly buttoned, sleeveless vest. Her graying hair was worn half up, and tied off near the top of her head, revealing her stern and sagging face. This woman seemed so familiar to me, though she wasn't looking at us yet, talking to the two older students at her sides.

"Hi," the girl next to her smiled when they reached us. "My name is-"

"Are you Delilah Owen and Nicholas Layne?" the older woman interrupted her sharply, finally looking us in the eye. I nodded slowly, suddenly fearful of any and everything that left my mouth revealing my inferiority.

"Both of you come over here," she motioned us toward her. Still standing on completely opposite sides of the room, we did as she said. The woman only squinted as if studying new and strange objects.

"I know you two," she wagged her finger in the air as if trying to recall something that'd happened years ago. "Stand closer."

We took a tiny step toward each other, not looking away from her. I was only trying to figure out how she could've possibly seen us before.

"Yes, now I remember," she smiled. Not at us, but at herself. "You are that boy who asked Gregory for directions yesterday. Whatever happened to you two with the nonexistent address?"

My mind was clearly still not in this place. It was the wife of that man, the elderly couple, from yesterday. Of all things I could've pictured her to be if I cared, a headmistress wouldn't have been one of them. I couldn't help the surprise that immediately spread across my face, but caught myself as Bennett spoke for us.

"Oh, yes, it was just a misprint."

"Were you delivering that? Why are you just now coming to school?"

Two different questions that required two different lies that I couldn't manifest immediately.

"We are actually moving in with our aunt to come to this school," Bennett answered smoothly. I could now tell no change in his voice as he lied through his teeth. "Rowana Laurie."

"That crazy old bat?" the woman seemed strangely spiteful toward her, and now, toward us. "I don't know why in the world you would want to live with her. So you two are brother and sister, then? Why do you have different last names?"

I nearly swore, and frantically looked around the room as if an explanation was written in the same black paint above our heads. Bennett had clearly forgotten everything we planned out in the cart with Serah and Vince.

"I was adopted, madam," I quickly picked up our explanation before Bennett could sink us deeper. "When I was about five. There was an unfortunate accident when my mother and father traveled outside of the State. When my family adopted me, I begged them to let me keep my last name so I could have a connection to my birth parents. They kindly agreed."

The girl looked like she could hug me, and the boy gave a slight nod of apology. Meanwhile, the old woman barely frowned, and proceeded to push the conversation along quickly, instructing the boy, Brice, to show Bennett to his class and the girl, Emeline, to take me to mine. She bid us a mechanical goodbye, saying how happy they were to have us, and it was all I could do to keep from smiling. *You have no idea how happy you ought to be*, I thought as Brice left with my now adoptive brother Nicholas, and Emeline led me down the opposite, left hall.

"The headmistress never introduces herself properly," she tried to smile once we reached the stairs. I knew from the look of Emeline's face she was older, yet she was still my height. "That's Madam Guise. I pray for your sake you never have to talk to her again."

Emeline explained the way the schedule and rotations operated at her school, though I only took what I deemed important to heart. In other words, the fact that there was one teacher in the morning, a different one in the afternoon, and a thirty minute break in between them. After she believed she covered all the basics, Emeline changed the topic, and began pumping me for information about Delilah's previous school, home, and family outside the state. Her questions were innocent enough, but I still felt under attack as I struggled to answer smoothly.

The second floor appeared identical to the first, with the muffled instruction of female teachers drifting in the hallway. Emeline approached a closed door, and looked at me sadly, like she had led me to my ultimate demise. The longer I returned her stare, the wider the nervous pit in my stomach grew, and I forced myself to look away. Taking that as her hint, Emeline knocked lightly on the door, cutting off the teacher's lecture.

A young woman with a plain, symmetric haircut unenthusiastically looked between the two of us, deciding which one she was the least thrilled to see. She recognized Emeline, and therefore felt compelled to wholeheartedly wish her a good day as she eagerly retreated into the adjacent hall barely after introducing me.

"Good luck. You'll need it," Emeline whispered next to my ear as she walked behind me. She didn't seem to care that the teacher had heard her.

The woman waited until after Emeline had gone around the corner to prop the door open with her back, waving me inside the classroom. My entrance was met with the stares of at least twenty girls dressed exactly as I was, with identical bags, and identical expressions.

"Girls, this is Delilah. She is joining our class today. I trust you all will help her catch up, as we cannot slow down."

"Yes, Miss Fendrel," they answered mechanically.

"Delilah," the teacher motioned me into an empty chair at the end of one of the long, polished, wooden tables. I took that as my cue to sit down and shut up.

I'd heard of school, and poked my head in its windows. But I had still never been to it, or even been informally schooled by my mother like I told Emeline. I was always under the impression that school dealt with teaching reading, writing, and arithmetic: the basic things I tried to learn myself and Rosalie so we might be able to get a job like Uncle Graham's, which, despite all its monotony, paid more than others. But if this woman was talking about any of those three subjects, then I was much rustier than I thought. She had the class write down whatever she was talking about practically word for word. The other girls were happy to give me paper, a pen, and ink, but I couldn't bring myself to use them. Every time I raised my hand off the table to write something down, it trembled. I told Serah I could write. It wasn't a lie, but I was so incredibly out of practice. When I finally wrote one sentence at the top, the letters were shaky, disfigured, and I knew every other word was misspelled. Frustrated, I stopped trying and focused instead on what Miss Fendrel was saying. As I expected, she might as well have been speaking another language.

After an hour, she began asking the class questions. The other girls answered them easily, like a second instinct. I didn't notice any pattern until the two in front of me took their turns. My heart quickly sank into my stomach. Like a divine miracle, I was next, and I had nothing but doubt in my ability to hold my identity for the following minutes.

"I don't know," was my answer. I knew they all stared at me, though I felt the teacher's eyes boring into me the most. She tried to move on, giving me a purely fake smile and reading another senseless question. The entire room emitted a groaning noise as if they were born able to solve it. I gave the same response, talking just above a whisper, and sinking deeper into my chair as Miss Fendrel frowned deeply. Agonizing seconds passed before she spoke again, saying I should have learned this alien material years ago.

"My mother taught me at home up until now. When-when she had the time," I tried my generic explanation, but I already knew it wasn't good enough to excuse my ignorance. "My brother and I moved in with our aunt and she sent us here."

"Even so. Let me see your notes."

I must have looked much more horrified than I thought, because the other girls began halfheartedly encouraging me to the front of the room. I felt like a caged animal, caught in the corner with no hope left, as I slowly took my paper to her, bracing myself.

"What is this?" Miss Fendrel demanded. I shuddered as she ripped the paper from my shaking, outstretched hand. "Are you five, or a Stoleh?"

My heart, still in my stomach, hardened into a rock.

"No, ma'am."

She only instructed me to see her before midday, and refused to return my paper. The other girls watched me as I all but ran back to the safety of my seat, wishing more than anything I could make a run for the door. Some were sympathetic, though it appeared most of them currently thanked their lucky stars it was me in the limelight. I sat quiet and unmoving until Miss Fendrel dismissed the class, contemplating how long it would take for her to validate her obvious reserves. I knew from the start I could not blend in with the Haritites. My sheer stupidity compared to my classmates would destroy my cover in a matter of days, much less six weeks.

Still, considering the look of ire in Miss Fendrel's eyes, I was happy to take a verbal beating about sassing the teacher and playing childish tricks. A *trick*, I thought as she dropped my paper on the table, violently slamming the pen on top before it had fluttered down to the surface. *My writing is so appalling, it has to be a trick of some kind to a Haritite teacher.* I swallowed and forced myself to turn around in my chair to face her, but no matter how innocently I insisted I was not intentionally disrespecting her, that I only didn't understand what she was teaching, she only scoffed,

"I see that. I wouldn't mind if you didn't understand; you're new. But this?" She pointed at my offensive handwriting. "That is ridiculous. Can you not write or spell? I expect you to at least try. And to reinforce that, you will spend your midday break rewriting your notes legibly on the back of this paper ten times."

I stared at her as if mortified, though she showed no sign of repealing her decision. She closed the door loudly, leaving me alone at the eerily empty table. I probably spent the first five minutes deciding if I would or could transpose my original hieroglyphics, sitting directly in the heat of the sun filtering through the window along

81

with the loud chatter below. I wrote very small, touching each word with my pen and trying to logically decide how each was actually spelled. Only after the twentieth repetition did my writing become decipherable, and only after forty-nine did I think it might pass for a Haritite with naturally terrible language capabilities. I left the paper on her table in the front of the room, and nearly ran out into the hallway, feeling like I was suffocating. With no idea where I was going, I could only follow a couple other kids ambling through the downstairs. But I eventually found the double back doors, and faced a sea of blue. Boys and girls shared this place, seemingly the only one on the school's property. I avoided the expansive, confusing crowd, and found a cool area under the roof. To the disgust of the couple girls around me, I sat on the ground against the wall. When I realized people were staring, laughing, I scrambled upright, and shamefully locked my eyes on the ground, never so out of place. For a long time, I thought to myself that a yellow patch might as well have been tattooed on my forehead.

She said it three times, and it took me a while to remember my own name. I jumped, but relaxed when I realized it was just another kid. I only knew she was in my class because she called me *Delilah*. The girl was almost exactly my height, with tight, almost unnaturally smooth and unmarked skin. Her straight hair and thin bangs framed her face, stopping just above her equally dark, far-apart eyes. She half-smiled at me as I studied her, searching for some visible sign of enmity.

"I'm sorry about Miss Fendrel saying that in front of the whole class," she said, looking away uncomfortably. I only then realized how wide my stare was. "She's kind of a witch. And don't worry about it, I get the lowest passing marks with her. You'll like Mrs. Cromwell much more."

I blinked, and stood with an unnaturally straight back and steely face, as if this Haritite girl could smell fear. It seemed that anything I said would break down a kind of untouchable barrier, and I struggled to put any response into words. "I-I'm sorry, who are you?"

I tried to ask the question casually, but it was already destined to make the situation even more uneasy.

"My name's embarrassing," the girl shifted her weight to her other foot.

"It can't be that bad."

She sighed, and grumbled under her breath, "Camellia."

"That's pretty," I smiled, reminded of several kindly women from my borough who shared the name. The girl appeared shocked by my reaction, like she had expected me to burst out laughing.

"The whole class makes fun of it because it's a flower, so don't call me that. I've managed to avoid the ridicule for a few months. I go by my middle name, Riley."

I couldn't make sense of it, and then I remembered what Olivia had told me. Flowers are too, as they say, primitive.

Emeline was spit out of the babbling crowd. She tried to greet us, but I could sense something bothered her as she turned her attention to me. "I heard what happened. I think that's a new record for pissing off Fendrel."

Knowing that even the most mediocre of news spread so quickly around here startled me, and as I stammered out a defense for myself, Emeline laughed at my anxiety.

"Chill. I think it's quite admirable. She hated me too. She hates almost everyone. She's the kind of teacher who makes an idol out of one student, and everybody else doesn't mean much more than scum."

"And for three years running, that idol's been little Miss Melodie," Riley rolled her eyes, saying the name in a mocking, sing-song voice. "Don't worry, you'll start hearing about her very soon. She wasn't here today, and that's the only reason she never came up. Thank all that's good in this forsaken world Mrs. Cromwell sees through her."

I pretended to relate to the situation they described, looking over my shoulder as if hoping to find an excuse to leave. Emeline and Riley were probably the most harmless people in the building, but being thrust even into an ordinary conversation with them, in my mind, had the potential to be catastrophic.

"A-D-Delilah," another, timid voice entered the conversation, interrupting them. I knew who it was before I turned around, and adjusted my face warningly as Bennett stopped beside me.

"Is that your brother?" Riley asked. I said he was. "You don't look alike much."

I told her I was adopted, and left it at that, eager to shift the focus away from me. I reasoned that it really wasn't a lie, anyway. Bennett, or Nicholas, and Riley exchanged a polite hello, and that was the end of us acting semi-casual. They didn't seem to know what to talk about, and I was simply too afraid to say something that could be considered abnormal. Bennett eventually asked why I was so late coming outside, saying he'd been looking for me, and chuckled when I admitted I had already gotten in trouble with a teacher. Bennett started to tell me a little about his pathetic excuse for one: that he couldn't care less about the students, and just gave them thick, openly biased books to sit there and read in silence. All the while, I tried to harden my stare at him, nervously glancing back and forth as he talked about the Haritites' skewed textbooks. Though Emeline and Riley didn't seem to care, almost as if they agreed with him. A strange, malevolent voice injected itself into our circle, and everyone turned in unison to see four eavesdropping kids standing over us: all of them taller than Riley, Emeline, and I, and the boys taller than Bennett.

"You better watch what you say."

"No one's going to hear anything unless you decide to snitch like a bunch of children," Emeline nearly snarled at them.

"Who's to say we won't?" the girl folded her arms, ignoring the comment. "I don't think your grandmother especially would take kindly to you and your little friends breaking her rules, Miss Guise."

"Oh, I'm trembling. I can talk circles around that woman. Go find something else to do, would you?"

The four gave all of us a penetrating, harsh glare. As they walked away, one of the girls commented,

"That's why all of her friends are at least three years younger than her."

Bennett waited until the four were gone before asking if Emeline could really be related to the indifferent, yet equally frightening headmistress.

"My skeleton in the closet," she looked down as if ashamed. "They're right. No one in this school will have anything to do with me once they know I'm Emeline Guise. But Grandmother couldn't care less about me. She would expel me just as quickly as she would any other kid, and I'm only allowed to call her Grandmother outside of school. The only reason I ever visit is because of Granddad. He makes her bearable when he can."

"And those four are just a few of the kids who think this place is a battlefield," Riley added in a much quieter voice. "The sooner they can make teachers dislike you and get you out of their way, the better. Getting kids in trouble for no reason is one of the things they specialize in around here. We're not supposed to talk about teachers at all outside of the classroom. People do it anyway, even the little kids. But they never fail to show up and to see if they can dig up any dirt on you. Because where you go once you leave here is entirely determined by your family's connections."

I looked in the direction they had gone. If I couldn't get my act together here, then they would have much more than dirt on me.

Inside, Miss Fendrel the Witch was nowhere to be found. At her desk, a much, much older woman sat sifting through brittle, yellowish papers. Her hair was gray with the occasional brown streak, sitting in an insanely curly pile barely passing her earlobes. Her nose was broad, and accompanied by a disfigured age spot just to the right of it. She didn't wear glasses, but judging from the squinting she was doing, she needed them. The woman appeared narrowly focused on her papers as we filed into the classroom. But when Riley and I passed, she glanced up at me, nodding once. I gave no sign I saw her, and continued to my seat by the window.

"Mrs. Cromwell is a good teacher, and a saint compared to Miss Fendrel," Riley spoke just above a whisper, taking a seat at the table in front of me. "But she doesn't get involved with anybody's personal life or talk much outside of school. That nod she just gave you is her equivalent of a hug. It means she likes you."

Riley sounded like she was talking about a pet dog with her last sentence. And I didn't think a nod meant I had won someone's, much less a Haritite's, approval before we even spoke. Mrs. Cromwell was probably acknowledging that I was new, or maybe she'd found the paper I left for Miss Fendrel and was thinking of all the things I could have possibly done to deserve it.

"Afternoon," she addressed the room from her chair. I noted there how she was met only by silence, and didn't seem to care. Mrs. Cromwell pushed herself up from the desk, grunting, and walked out into the center of the room with an unadorned cane.

"I will never understand why Julia feels the need to teach the kind of math she focuses on," she shook her head, referencing the papers now laden carelessly across her desk.

"Miss Fendrel says it's so we can learn how to think and solve problems."

This voice came from the opposite side of the room. I couldn't and didn't care to see who had spoken.

"Miss Vern, I see you decided to join us today," the old woman began to walk slowly toward the door. When she reached the other side of the room, her eyes locked on a single point in the six tables. "Stand up and answer me this."

A blonde-headed girl rose confidently to her feet, with a straight back and her arms by her sides. Still, her face looked totally innocent as she met Mrs. Cromwell's steel gaze.

"That's Melodie," Riley clarified to me. She didn't seem at all surprised that this girl had openly challenged the teacher.

"Miss Vern," Mrs. Cromwell continued. "Have you ever found yourself in a serious situation?"

"I'm not sure I understand."

"One that threatened your life, or perhaps the lives of others."

"No, and I don't plan to."

"Ah, well, none of us plan that sort of thing, I suppose you're right about as much. But here is the lesson, Miss Vern: something I believe very few people in this room will ever fully grasp. Problem solving cannot be taught from studying textbooks. It is taught by actually being presented with the problem itself. Not a math problem, something much more real than that. Problem solvers are the ones with the problems, Miss Vern."

I could've sworn she looked directly at me with her last sentence.

"And the greatest problem solvers come from those with the greatest problems," Mrs. Cromwell finished with a lasting air, and turned her attention back to Melodie. "Now sit down."

As she quietly did so, I expected some sort of snicker or remark from the class. But there was nothing. It was like they were all still afraid of this girl despite her being upstaged.

Pretending it never happened, Mrs. Cromwell returned to the center of the room, and the scene quickly faded away into her afternoon class. I spent more than half the time trying to decide whether or not Mrs. Cromwell had directed her philosophic guidance at me, and finally convinced myself it was just a coincidence. Once I actually started trying to follow along, I found she wasn't nearly as forceful and uniform as Miss Fendrel. Of course I still understood nothing, but her way of approaching things felt lighter. I wrote what I heard, most of it little fragments of speech as I focused on forming the letters more than anything else. Eventually, an excited buzz spread across the room. I figured that meant the day was almost over. While Mrs. Cromwell said her last few words, I examined all I'd written. It was little more than half a page, but legible, and I knew it would pass with Fendrel the next morning. But my satisfaction with my work vanished when I realized what I'd mindlessly written down: an unfeeling timeline of five events set centuries before, what would be a very basic history lesson to a much younger Haritite. Nothing could have been more biased or rose-covered regarding the Lebon, portrayed as saviors to a rapidly falling society who swooped in and solved our problems with the creation of the four classes. A nauseating feeling gripped me as I read my own notes, like I had morphed into what Stella, Barney, and I would consider 'one of them' in only a day of Haritite school. I wanted to rip the paper into a thousand pieces, but forced myself to fold it several times, stuffing my shame deep into my bag. Mrs. Cromwell instructed us to keep our papers, that we would discuss more next class, before dismissing everyone with a wholehearted *get out*. It sounded like a joke, though her tone of voice left me wondering. Before I'd even made it to the front of the room, the entire class was gone.

"Delilah?" Mrs. Cromwell asked once I was out in the hallway. I slowed down, but didn't stop walking, noticing Riley waiting for me. I decided to pretend I hadn't heard her, eager to leave. After one day, I'd had my fill of the Dreary School.

Bennett met up with us at the front door. Riley seemed like she was trying to be a friend, but I was still going to use the *I-have-to-wait-for-my-brother* excuse so she wouldn't follow us back to the house. In silence, the three of us left the school's property and merged with the students remaining in the streets. I now saw why Rowana had told us not to linger. It took several minutes to find a passable road not infested by blue. We had barely emerged from the thick of it before other children in various obnoxiously bright colors began to appear, blue becoming rare only five minutes away from the building. I figured not many Dreary School kids lived near Rowana. When the three of us were virtually the only blue around, I began to wonder if Bennett knew where he was going. I definitely didn't. Both Riley and I were following him, though she eventually mumbled a goodbye and turned down another street. The quiet between Bennett and me was more than drowned out by the noise of the area. He led us behind a row of houses to just get out of the chaos.

"You have to feel bad for the people who live on roads near the schools," Bennett spoke for the first time since we left. "They have to put up with all the kids this time every day."

"The men probably have a job of some kind and aren't anywhere near here," I answered, watching the unchanging, organized cobblestones beneath our feet. As stupid as it sounds, I momentarily thought that maybe Rochonnell paid someone to spit shine their surface. "And I really don't feel sorry for them about anything."

Bennett walked like he was heading to put out a fire, and I broke into a trot to keep up.

"How do you know where you're going?"

"I memorized the way to the school. Now we're just going backwards," he answered, stopping in his tracks. It took me a while to recognize the back of seventy-three, seventy-three.

Rowana sat in a cushioned, red chair near the front door, her arms folded across her stomach, and her face nearly white.

"Is everything okay?" I hesitantly moved toward her, slinging my empty bag across the back of a kitchen chair.

"Fine, Amaryllis. I'm fine."

I persisted until she forced herself to look at me. Comforting her like a close friend didn't seem like a line to cross yet, so I sat in front of her, pulling my dress down to cover my legs, and sat there as if expecting a story.

"It's..." she shook her head. I thought she was going to cry. "The Guard just left... it's a good thing you came through the back."

"The Guard?" Bennett asked, lingering beside the table like he was still deciding whether or not to approach us. "Do they have a reason to think...?"

Rowana held one finger against her lips, shaking her head, and leaned forward in the chair. She held her hand out for me to take, and just to appease her, I did. Her other hand warmly invited Bennett over, though he only stared at her as if he still couldn't figure out what she was asking. Only at my glare did he eventually join me on the floor. Rowana sensed his discomfort, and didn't force him to hold her hand, instead clasping mine in between her two.

"The Guard are difficult to explain. In a way, one cannot blame them for what they do. They are only acting under a higher power. But yet, you can incriminate them for doing just that. You would understand this, Amaryllis, more than I would. I cannot imagine what goes on at and behind the Wall. But they..." Rowana licked her lips and averted her gaze, staring through the shuttered window with a hollow look in her eye. "They come around to collect ordinary taxes if you did not deliver them yourself. Typically they only visit the very old or ill, and do not take kindly to coming around in person otherwise. I couldn't walk all the way to the edge of Rochonnell yesterday morning. I was preparing for you two to come stay here. The Guard does not particularly like me, either, for a number of reasons, but mostly because I am not involved in the community. Most think me a recluse, which is best. Every time they come by here, they badger me with questions. It is all I can do to not hint that I am... not supposed to be in Ceaves. I was born a Haritite, and I raised my children as Haritites, so it is not that my family is illegal here. But after my son was arrested, everything changed. I hardly ever go outside except when I must; for almost ten years, now. I do this for my son, to avenge him and fill his place, but it is still hard to live this way."

She released my hand and wrung hers together in her lap, now staring off at no particular point on the wall.

87

"Why was your son arrested?" Bennett asked as harmlessly as he could. But the question still looked as if it'd physically hurt her, and I glowered at him again.

"I don't know. If it had anything to do with our work, then he would have been sent to Imperiam, not held like a low criminal in a Rochonnell prison. They wouldn't tell me anything, and they won't let me see him. Now my daughter has nothing to do with me, either."

Rowana cupped a hand over her mouth, looking away with tears in her colorless eyes.

"My father's in prison," I said just to keep her from crying, trying to find something relatable to how she felt. Rowana slowly removed her hand and studied me. Her eyes were like those of children, waiting for an explanation. "The Guard raided our borough during a Cleansing some eleven years ago. We heard them in the streets. Dad told my sisters and me to hide. We stayed behind the sofa, and he and my mother went upstairs, purposely making noise so if they broke in, they'd go there. As they dragged my mother outside, one of the Guard must have heard my little sister crying. He moved the sofa, and tried to take Rosalie and me. But my father ran downstairs and pulled a knife on him, just barely cutting him as a distraction. More Guard came inside, wrestled him off, and took him with my mother, leaving me and my sisters there. We got word a while later that our mom was dead, but never received anything about Dad. We assume they're holding him in prison until his execution for attacking that Guard with the pocketknife."

I had to bite my tongue to stop myself, no matter how much I wanted to tell her more. She was actually listening, and caring, but I knew I'd done too much harm with what I'd already said. The damage was sealed and documented when she scooted out of the chair, and hugged me on the floor. I let her, more for her sake than mine, though Rowana held me there as if waiting for me to burst into tears. When she realized it wasn't going to happen, she let me go. It appeared she was trying to say something, but her mouth wouldn't obey.

"I'm sorry about your son, Madam-" I stopped, remembering what she'd told us. "Rowana."

She didn't seem able to respond, and only held my chin to look at her. Her warm smile echoed what I had been told so many times over the years from everybody: Aunt Clarissa to nosy neighbors. They would say that somehow, there was still a chance Dad could make it home again. I bought right into the encouraging, meaningless rubbish when I was eleven and needed something to keep me from forfeiting my life as a quiet thief, though it was now just a slap in the face. No amount of tin coins could get me to the Etairan Mountains, or bribe the Guard there into releasing a Stoleh marked for death. I knew that now, but for some reason, I still needed to believe I was working for something in order to keep my sanity, especially after Ellamae left. I thought for a moment that was what Rowana lacked, having already accepted she had no control in her son's fate. When she looked at Bennett and me, I wondered who she was really seeing. The thought of needing to fill the shoes of a person so precious to someone was frightening, and I quickly dismissed the idea. Rowana, embarrassed by my embarrassment, hastily stood and left the room.

Chapter Fourteen

It was after ten. The lack of light stung my tired eyes as we were forced to move closer into the fading flame of an oil lamp, squinting to see the page. I could only imagine Bennett's disguised frustration as he tried to explain the school day's lesson to me in simpler words. He sat beside me, his arm loosely wrapped around a bent leg, using the end of a pen as a pointer when he spoke. I lay flat on my stomach, several feet away from him, listening, but absorbing little. He knew it just as well as I did, and we eventually came to the mutual, wordless agreement to try again the next day. As I closed the moleskin journal for the night, thinking Bennett was also preparing to leave, he asked how I'd gotten in trouble with my teacher after only the first half of the first day. I excluded the specific details. Bennett must have sensed how much it bothered me that I had all but forgotten how to write, and reopened the journal, placing his pen in the crease and turning it toward me.

"Write the alphabet."

"I'm not that bad," I answered, though it was probably a lie. I couldn't help but take his attempt to help as a deeply personal insult.

"I didn't say you were. Writing it out will help you, and we need to get the teacher off your case before she starts thinking about this for more than a couple seconds."

I reluctantly picked up the pen, and wrote the alphabet in large letters across both pages. When I thought it was done, I looked up at Bennett as if waiting for him to correct it.

"That's very good, if you're a Stoleh."

I frowned, immediately beginning to search for what was wrong even though I saw nothing. I recognized the markings on the paper, but as for order, I had little more than a guess.

"I don't mean that in a bad way, Amaryllis. I'm just saying that you're not a Stoleh here. We can't afford anybody investigating why a Haritite our age struggles to write out the alphabet."

Bennett took the pen from my hand, and pointed out four or five instances where I had switched two letters around, where my lines needed to be rounder, and where my round shapes needed to be straighter. Only on my third try did he say it was good enough.

"What's wrong with it?" I asked. He sounded like he was giving up, and I wanted at least my alphabet to be perfect for tomorrow.

"Nothing, really," he answered. I didn't believe him, and persisted. "Similar letters look the same when you write them. And your 'G' is a six."

"It is not."

"Yeah, it is. Look at it."

I didn't respond, knowing he was right. It was just one letter, but after two failed attempts to do something so simple, I felt ready to break the pen in two and throw it across the room.

"I always wrote them like that," was my only defense. Bennett laid his hand on top of mine, guiding it to form what I guessed was his idea of a real 'G.'

"Start writing them like this," he said. I looked from the paper to him, debating whether or not to scoot away. Bennett seemed to realize, and he hastily took back his hand, quiet for a long time afterwards.

"If I ask you something, will you get upset?"

"I guess it depends on what it is."

He paused again as if still unsure if he should say it or not.

"You told Rowana that the Guard came into your borough during a Cleansing. What is that?"

I impulsively looked away, shuddering once at the name. In addition to the brimming, nauseating feeling in my stomach, it was equally sickening to know that Nemirens knew so little about what went on only miles from their own homes.

"I'm sorry," he said shortly, trying to dismiss the topic. "I shouldn't've asked."

"No, it's alright," I answered, staring blankly through the floor as I sat up. Hunched over, I wrapped my arms loosely around my knees, pulling the irritating dress over my legs again. "I don't understand the strategy behind it, but every so often the Guard picks a random borough for a Cleansing. They march into it in lines, hell breaks loose for an hour, and they're gone. They take a bunch of people with them, and if we put up too much of a fight, that's when they'll open fire. They say it's... population control, but only for Stoleh."

91

Bennett stared at me, ashen, his mouth almost hanging open. "Will they take kids?"

"They'll take anybody. Once they hit a certain number, I guess, then they leave. It all depends on who comes. Some Guard just treat it like business. But others hate us with a fiery passion and go out of their way to cause as much destruction as they can. We haven't been in a Cleansing since I was five. But they took both of my parents last time. I don't want to think about who they'll take if it happens again."

Following a tense silence, I felt Bennett's hand rest slowly on my arm in an obligatory gesture of support. If anything, it only made me regret telling him something so personal to me and my people, something a Nemiren would only shake their head at, and forget about it by the next morning.

"I'm sorry," he repeated. I was surprised by how genuine his reaction seemed. "You don't have to talk about it."

Bennett shakily moved his hand, gathering his journal and pen Serah and Vince had given him, and waited for a moment as if waiting for me to say something, or at least come back to reality. But I felt I couldn't look him in the eye after that, and forced myself to believe he wasn't there as he stood up.

"Good night," Bennett said, closing the door. By the time I brought myself to answer, he was already gone.

Chapter Fifteen

The next morning, Fendrel wasn't at her desk. Either that, or she'd had sixty birthdays last night. When I passed her on the way to my chair, Mrs. Cromwell didn't acknowledge she had seen or heard me. Only a few girls arrived earlier, including this demonized Melodie person. Her group stood talking and giggling near my seat, though I couldn't force myself to engage in their conversation. Minutes later, a fist tapped lightly on my section of the table. Riley had angled her chair directly in front of mine, staring with a surprised, fascinated expression.

"Did she say something to you?"

I shook my head, concealing my face with a hand like the entire room was watching me.

"Don't look now, but Melodie was glaring at you like prey," Riley turned her eyes, but not her head, toward her. I briefly glanced up in Melodie's direction, and saw her preoccupied talking to another girl.

"I told you not to look!" Riley hissed. I quickly faced her again. "What did you do?"

"I've never even spoken to that girl. She was probably looking at someone else."

"Maybe, but she might just think you're an easy target after yesterday. She wasn't here in the morning, but one of her underlings must have told her an overly exaggerated version of what happened by now."

"I'm not afraid of her."

"It's not her to be afraid of. It's her family. Melodie's father is high up in the Guard, and her uncle's high up in banking. Most of the teachers have known her since she was a baby because of all her older siblings. And she's a total brownnoser. Everyone falls for it except me, Emeline, Mrs. Cromwell, and now you. She's a natural at getting kids in trouble around here, so just avoid confrontation, and eye contact, and you should be okay. Trust me, she can literally ruin your life with a bat of her eyes and a *please, Daddy?*"

Riley seemed to speak from experience, and taking her advice to heart, I concluded that anything to do with that girl meant attention, and attention I didn't need. With her being related to someone in the Guard, I definitely needed to keep my distance.

The classroom didn't settle as quickly in the morning with Fendrel absent. Mrs. Cromwell eventually induced silence with a threat of making everyone stay an hour after school. After announcing Miss Fendrel had taken ill the night before, she jumped right back in to the short timeline from yesterday. I removed the crumpled notes from my bag, and flattened them on the table, still ashamed of what I had mindlessly written down. A total economic collapse in the 1300's, conveniently followed by an outbreak of famine and disease that nearly halved the land's population. Internal fighting supposedly gripped the entire society, which was little more than scattered, unorganized, impoverish communities until the Lebon arrived. They squashed our puny rebellions and resistances, and established the four classes two hundred years later. No story seemed so contrived to me, and it was only made worse by the way Mrs. Cromwell spoke of it so unenthusiastically. The class's reception of this so-called lesson was disbelief, and judging by the whispering sneers and comments, Mrs. Cromwell simply must have thought she stood before a class of eight-year-olds, she was simply that old. I couldn't help but sympathize with her. She seemed more like a grandmother than an old, grouchy wench, as I heard someone say, and especially in comparison to Fendrel.

As Mrs. Cromwell, pacing to and fro before her class, turned toward my side of the room. I panicked, thinking she was looking at me again, and shrank a few inches into my chair.

"Riley," she said, and I almost sighed in relief. "You seem exasperated. Would you like to guess why I am revisiting this? Don't be shy."

"We never talked about it in depth that much," she said in an uncertain, embarrassed voice.

"That's right. Years ago you only memorized a list of events and were made able to regurgitate it. Now, we're going to look beneath the surface."

She sat down at the desk, breathing heavily from walking without her cane. Mrs. Cromwell quickly came back to her senses, and looked around at us intently.

"Who wrote this?"

She was met by quiet.

"You never told us who wrote it, Mrs. Cromwell," one girl shyly answered.

"I know that. I want you to tell me. Any volunteers or shall I victimize?"

The moment she said that, I was positive said victim was me. Sure enough, the next thing that left her mouth was,

"Delilah, why don't you tell us what you think?"

I froze, despite knowing it was coming. It seemed now that the entire class stared at me, waiting with bated breath for an idiotic response. As I scanned the six contrived events, I realized I had no idea what year it actually was. I only knew at least three centuries had passed since 1502, the last date. This was a short recap of the brainwashing lessons taught to much younger children, probably pulled from some sort of 'history' book.

"A Lebon had to write it," I spit out my first thought, speaking with more confidence than I had. It would have made me look all the more stupid if I was wrong.

"Explain," Mrs. Cromwell prompted me after a few seconds of silence.

"It had to be from someone high up in society who wasn't affected in a bad way by the invasion. This timeline just sounds like propaganda. It makes sense that the Lebon would try to make themselves look good."

"Could it be argued that an Etairan person wrote it? They have strong connections with the Lebon."

I considered it, and asked when the timeline was written as innocently as I could. I wasn't surprised to hear it was recent.

"I guess it could be argued if this wasn't written within the past several decades. This isn't Etairan," I said, the rest of the room seemingly marveling at what I said and the way I said it. I harshly reminded myself I was addressing a group of Haritites, but struggled to change my tone. "They have no reason to make the Lebon look like saviors

95

in front of the rest of us because there's no conflict in between them right now. The Etaira have to be careful not to pass the line where they are exceeding the Lebon. That's what starts the fighting."

"What about the Haritites, Nemirens, and Stoleh? How would you say we affect each other?"

The question seemed unconnected in the other two, and the genuine fascination in Mrs. Cromwell's face unnerved me. It didn't appear to be interest in my answer, but rather interest in me.

"Well, my neighborhood was close enough to Nemirena, but we were still sure to separate ourselves from the Nemirens. Everybody depends on them, though, even the Lebon. They make everything. If they were to stop, the mainland would come crashing down. I think Stoleh have a purpose for being created in a separate class, too. Every society needs a group to exploit as wrong and blame all their problems on. A lot of people think Stoleh aren't fit to live. But if they all went away, then everyone would go after a different group of people. Basically all the Lebon had to do was conquer an almost totally unarmed land, make up the four classes, and relax. They had us destroying ourselves from the beginning."

I stopped, strangely happy with my answer. The weight lifted from my chest only crashed back down when I realized I might as well have shouted from the window that I wasn't a Haritite. I had been careful to speak of Stoleh in the third person: 'them', instead of 'us'. But no normal kid would call something a Lebon wrote propaganda. These people probably believed their word was divine.

You idiot! I screamed in my mind as I lay my head down on the hard, cold table. Mrs. Cromwell took that to mean I was finished slowly revealing my identity to everyone in the room.

"Good. Very, very good, Delilah. Does anyone have anything to add?"

There was nothing. I kept my burning face concealed, like I could force the class to forget my presence, for the rest of the morning. When the same whispering spread throughout the room, I finally dared to sit up again. Midday must have been approaching, and I needed to find Bennett. For some reason, I thought he'd have some magical solution. Mrs. Cromwell sounded like she was getting into her last few sentences when a familiar man passed by. All he did was poke his head in, and I felt my body go stiff. After he stepped inside the room, I was dead afraid. He was a Guard, and not some random one. I had seen and spoken with him while wearing my fake Haritite patch in the streets near home. That, and another little problem.

I told him Ada, Arnold, and Delilah were doing a project for school.

There were many reasons why he could have been down there that one day, but the idea of running into him here had never occurred to me. I tried to position myself behind Riley's head, and think that he couldn't possibly remember me. It took Mrs. Cromwell a little while to realize he was standing there awaiting an introduction.

"Oh, hello, Hal."

He frowned, visibly annoyed. His giant presence almost entirely blocked the doorway, and everything down to the way he stood made me want to vanish into thin air.

"Mrs. Cromwell."

"You don't usually come on this side of the building until long after classes have ended. Can I help you with something?"

"No, we are just coming through as always." He turned and looked at Melodie. It was clear before either of them spoke.

"Hi, Daddy," she waved, sounding too perky for the monster Riley had made her out to be. The Guard acknowledged her existence, and that was as far as it went. He had been scanning the room, and though I refused to look at him, my gut told me I'd been found.

"Delilah, is it?" he asked. I forced a smile and a nod. *This is a normal thing for this man. You have to pretend it's a normal thing for you, too.* "How did that project end for you, Ada, and Arnold?"

"Fine, thank you," I choked.

"Did... your family move into the State? I hardly believe you walked from here to nearly the Stoleh Wall."

A shock befell the classroom as I quickly explained that my brother and I had moved to live with our aunt to have more opportunity in the State than what was offered in our neighborhood. It seemed easy enough to agree when the man reasoned that the assignment was from my previous school.

"You said your mother taught you at home," Melodie's voice said from the opposite side of the room. The girls to the right of me leaned back so I could see her. I met her gaze, and immediately felt defeated, and caught in a story. All I could do was nod again in the Guard's direction. I stammered for a few seconds, confusing myself with the array of lies swirling around in my head, until Mrs. Cromwell intervened.

"I gave the project, Hal," she said, and I began to breathe again now that the limelight was away from me.

"No, you didn't," Melodie injected herself again. "And she just started yesterday."

"For your information, Miss Vern," she frowned, the lines in her face deepening. "I contacted Miss Owen's mother before she came to our school. I thought it would be interesting to have someone who lived so close to the Nemiren markets and Stoleh Wall to come and share with us, who have never left the State, what life is like there. I would never send a young girl unsafely close to the Wall, however. You kept your distance, didn't you, Delilah?"

I continued to stumble over a couple words before I managed to stop myself.

"Yes, ma'am. I would never get closer than where I was when my friends from my old subdivision and I ran into Sir... Hal."

"Sir Vern," he corrected me. *Of course, stupid.* I told myself. *You could've figured that out.*

There was a short lived silence before he made up some reason to leave, and did so. Mrs. Cromwell dismissed us not long after he was gone. I nearly ran from the classroom, forcing myself into the middle of the crowd.

"A Guard came into your room?" Bennett already seemed to dread my story. He had found me in the rear yard just as Riley disappeared with a small group of girls. He and I stood away from the massive crowd in an effort to pretend we had any privacy. I didn't answer him, still anxiously mulling over my lacking excuse for suddenly appearing miles and miles away from the last conversation I had with Hal Vern. "Did somebody get in trouble?"

"Not that I know of."

Bennett frowned deeply, like he thought we should be barreling toward the edges of the State right about now, and lowered his voice.

"Do they have a reason to...?"

"Of course not," I all but snapped. Out of fear on the subject, I needed to change it. My hesitant admittance that I had given a too in-depth answer to a question only scared him more. Bennett didn't look like he even wanted to know, but still sighed in exasperation and asked what I said. Upon my ending of the story with the departure of Hal Vern, he stopped staring at me like someone had died.

"You lucked out with the teacher. What you said isn't that bad, anyway. At least you answered like you're one of them."

"But I said stuff a normal kid would never say," I pointed out. Bennett forced his hands into his pockets, and shrugged indifferently, leaning in a bit and speaking just above a whisper.

"You're giving them too much credit. People in your class might think you're a freak, but they're not going to suspect anything. Don't worry about it."

I half-smiled, and agreed, mostly because I couldn't bear to think otherwise.

Then I felt warm breath almost on my neck. I spun around ready to tackle someone, but looked up at an imposing girl, one of the four who had confronted Emeline, Riley, Bennett, and me about talking about the teachers. She was dark skinned, and stood much taller than I remembered from the day before. Aside from her height, posture, clothes, and snarky grimace, she could've been Stella. Behind and slightly to her left stood one of the boys. Bennett seemed to recognize him, and scowled.

"Well, your dumb class may not suspect anything," the girl told me, her lashing voice forcing the hairs on the back of my neck erect. "But now we certainly do."

I expected some sort of speech about how she knew I didn't belong there all along, and how she was going to report me to Madame Guise or some other threat. But she and the boy just walked away. They faded into the crowd, and I looked back at Bennett.

"Did you see them coming over here?"

He emptily shook his head, and we chose not to linger in case more of the eavesdropping vultures passed by. Within a few minutes, Emeline found us, flagging us down like she thought we were going to climb the walls and escape.

"How's the second day compared to the first?" she tried to smile, sensing the nervousness between us. I realized this kind of mediocre small talk made up a good part of normal peoples' lives, but I still couldn't help but lose almost all interest at the onset of conversations. I remembered how most greetings between Stella, Barney, and I went. It was less of a talk, and more of a conspiracy.

"Fendrel's not there," I compressed my answer into the simplest form. It was enough to tell her it could've only improved. It would have been alright, actually, if I hadn't opened my big mouth and that Guard hadn't shown up. But I couldn't mention either of these things to her, and I left it at that. She asked Bennett the same, and he didn't give her any more details. But as he spoke, I formulated how I could ask a question without hinting at anything. My completely unrelated thought rode on the heels of Bennett's last word.

"Why do the Guard come through this school?"

"They've been doing that as long as I've gone here. Probably before, too," she explained, uninterested. "This school wasn't always a school. Harold Drierie wasn't the first headmaster like most people think. He was the highest ranked in the Guard around here decades ago, and this building was the Rochonnell Garrison. But then it was moved somewhere else on the totally opposite side of the State some forty miles away. They say the Guard still comes through here to check up on the place, but we all know there's still something here they can't move and need to keep track of. There's all kinds of rumors about it. One says it's all behind some door in a shadowy corner that goes down into a basement, and that door is bolted on the inside and hasn't been opened in seventy years."

"You aren't at all curious about it?" Bennett continued.

"I don't believe that rumor," she said, dismissing it as a child's tale. "But I guess it would be nice to know why they come and sneak around until five o'clock so many times a month. Now that they've left, they're not coming back for a few weeks. They've let up on that a little. They used to come every other day."

Emeline looked over her shoulders as if routinely checking for any unwanted listeners.

"But my Granddad says they're just hiding it here so Idris can't find it," Emeline grinned slyly, and left for the door.

"Who's Idris?" I asked Bennett as we followed far behind her. He hushed me severely, glaring with wide eyes as if I'd said something truly awful. When we reached the door, he pulled me aside.

"You've never heard of him?"

I watched the rest of the active yard from the corner of my eye as if expecting to find an answer, and looked back to Bennett expectantly.

"You can get in massive, massive trouble for talking about him in Nemirena. I can't imagine what they'll do to you if you breathe the name in the Haritite State. All I know about Idris is he's the leader of a group who's been trying to dethrone the Lebon for some time. But they're so quiet, and no one ever hears about anything they do. It's not important. Forget you ever heard that, okay? Don't go around saying it."

"Alright, alright," I frowned. If I possessed no other skill, I could usually dance wide circles around the Guard. "You sound like my uncle. I'm not going to repeat everything I hear, y'know. I'm not five."

"I didn't mean it like that. It's just dangerous. You can't attract any more attention than you already have."

I let it go, agreed, and Bennett and I left in our separate directions inside the building. But that afternoon is when I realized what my 'very, very good' response cost me. Riley left the room, and I expected her to be waiting at the end of the hall like the previous day. This time, she made sure I couldn't ignore her. She waited directly beside the door, silently nodding her goodbyes to the rest of the room. When I was within a few feet of passing her, she said,

"Delilah, I want to talk to you."

I froze, and concluded that I could barrel past an old woman if I absolutely had to.

"Don't look at me like that. You're not in trouble. I just want to talk."

She put a gentle hand on my back and led me to the student's tables, motioning me down into a different seat. Mrs. Cromwell wasn't too overly round, but still had to turn her chair parallel to the table to get comfortable.

"You did well during this morning's class."

"Thank you, Mrs. Cromwell," I answered shortly.

"Why didn't you speak this afternoon? I was looking forward to your contribution."

"I'm sorry, Mrs. Cromwell. I didn't think there was a good time to speak."

"Is everything okay?" she asked. It sounded abrupt, though it was obvious it was coming. I forced an innocent smile on my face, saying everything was fine, and she only snapped, "Don't you start that with me. I'm a big people person, Delilah, and I know something is wrong. It doesn't take much to see it. Are you alright?"

"I don't want to talk about it," I changed my tune, knowing if I persisted with the Everything-Is-Perfectly-Wonderful act, she'd only grow more suspicious. I felt my face turning red as she stared, and finally sighed.

"I won't force you. But just know that I am here. If you change your mind, what is said in this room stays in this room."

I nodded in thanks, clutching the handle of my bag in a sweaty palm as I made my way to the door.

"Delilah," she stopped me again. I reluctantly turned around to face her. "Come over here, sweetheart. I don't want to shout at you."

I returned to the opposite side of the table. It must've looked like I thought she was going to pull out a knife and stab me. Instead, Mrs. Cromwell whispered in a warm, friendly voice.

"Try to make your face less of an open book."

Chapter Sixteen

As it turned out, Riley wasn't waiting there. Instead, Emeline stood at the last corner before the front door, smiling for no apparent reason.

"You guys got me thinking about this," she said as Bennett and I reached her. "I want you to meet somebody."

She began to walk away, and we didn't follow.

"Come on," she beckoned us with her hand and an overly wide smile. "He's not going to hurt you or anything."

The three of us weaved our way into the incoming sea of bright red: kids from the nearest school, I assumed. We eventually reached a one story building. But its height was not shamed by the surrounding homes, as most of them were the same way. And this particular one was longer, mostly brick, and had one huge, arch window. If anything, it appeared someone of more importance lived on this street. Bennett and I slowed to a hesitant walk as Emeline took three steps to the front door, and opened it without knocking.

"In here," she motioned for us to follow her again, disappearing inside the house.

"Ladies first," Bennett held open the door for me. I knew it was a common gesture, but still grumbled "you don't want to go in any more than I do" as I passed him. Emeline waited for us in a simple, dark kitchen, waiting for the door to close behind us. She threw her schoolbag in the corner, told us to do the same, and entered the open living space.

"Granddad?"

"I'm here, Emeline," an old man's feeble voice called. We heard his heavy footsteps enter the room, and our curiosity consumed our better judgment as we stepped around the corner. The man who had unintentionally given us directions to Rowana's was just as unrecognizable as his wife when we first saw her as the headmistress. He looked weak, sick, and was thinner than most old men. His walking seemed just as laborious as Mrs. Cromwell's, though he had to be twenty years younger. He waved Emeline off as she tried to help him down onto the sofa.

"I'm fine, Em. Fine, fine, fine."

"Don't push yourself too hard or-"

"I don't want you worrying about it. These things just come in short spells...."

"And they scare me, Granddad."

He momentarily ignored her, and eased himself onto the sofa without assistance.

"You have little to fear except the culture. You children best keep your distance, as it is nothing but the passing generations at the root of old age and sickness...." The pitiful-looking man regarded the room as if viewing it threw another eye, invisible to the rest of us. When he returned to his senses, he took notice of Bennett and me. "You know those two?" he asked Emeline in a more sane voice and tone. I was again surprised by his memory of us. "You are new to the area, aren't you?"

"I met them at school. Their aunt asked for me and Brice to show them around the first day," Emeline answered for us. "Delilah, Nicholas, this is my Granddad."

He smiled broadly, and waved us inside his home.

"Gregory," he told us. "Don't stand there. Take a seat, all of you.

Emeline came around and sat beside her granddad as Bennett and I shuffled to opposite sides of the room. I took a chair close to her side; he took one close to Gregory's.

"Did you do anything today?" Emeline asked him quietly.

"Ah, just waited for death. Nothing out of the ordinary."

"Granddad!"

"Don't Granddad me, that's all anyone in this world is capable of doing. And you're being rude to our guests, Emeline. Why did you bring them? They aren't interested in hearing a documentary of an old man's daily life."

She seemed flustered, but groaned and changed the topic.

"They're interested in what the school was before it was a school."

"*SO YOU TWO CAME HERE AFTER THE SECRET, DID YOU?!*" He shouted at Bennett, no less than a foot from his face. He flushed white, and nearly jumped out of the chair. Meanwhile, I stared wide-eyed at Emeline, though she wasn't facing me. But Gregory only laughed a broken laugh and leaned back again.

"Relax, boy. I was joking with you."

He slapped Bennett on the back, and he made a face unlike anything I'd ever seen.

"You two are not the first newcomers to wonder about that building. But you are the first Emeline has brought to me about it, so I trust her judgment." He stopped as if trying to remember something from the distant past. "It is twice the size of any other school in the area. It took me a year to learn my way around it, and my wife is now the headmistress. It used to be the center of activity for the Guard, I recall that much."

He chuckled at what he'd just said. I couldn't understand it.

"But then the Garrison was moved out of Rochonnell and into Sturwaller. They needed a new school, had no money or space to build one, and thus the Dreary... Druh-ear-re... School was established. The Guard returns just to check up on the old building."

Bennett and Emeline looked disappointed, and I knew I did, too. The old man strenuously stood, moving toward a mounted shelf, and fiddled around with a few things. When he rejoined us, it didn't appear he had anything new with him.

"Only to check up on the old building," he took something from behind him, and dropped it on the table. A key ring, though only one was on it: a plain, brass key, with intricate grooves and edges.

"The doctor would not be happy if he discovered I was out of bed during my spells. But I seem to have misplaced my old key to an unopened door in that school. I forget things these days. It would be absolutely terrible if the key fell into the wrong hands."

He stood again, and took Emeline's hand in between his, smiling at her.

"I'll talk to you later, Em. And it was nice to see you both."

We watched as he struggled toward an adjacent hallway. Before he vanished around the bend, he placed his hand on the wall, and called back into the main room. His voice definitely was meant to make something very clear to us.

"Prove to me you all are not the wrong hands."

Seconds later, a door softly closed, only leaving behind the uncertainty. Once we all stood on the steps and out of her grandparents' house, Emeline dangled the key in front of us. I thought she should've been a bit more discrete about this thing we obviously weren't supposed to have. Emeline was so eager to return to the school immediately, I felt bad to insist Bennett and I had to return to Rowana's immediately.

"Can you just tell her and then we can go?"

"I doubt it. But thanks, anyway."

"Actually, I don't think she would mind," Bennett contradicted me. I didn't intend to, but I glared at him much, much more harshly than I did Emeline. He caught my gaze, and shifted uncomfortably.

"Really?" the interest in her colorless eyes rekindled.

"I don't see why not."

"What about you, Delilah?"

"Fine," I said through my teeth. She sensed I was angry, but was too excited to mention it. Once she had gone, I held my hands in front of Bennett, choking the air.

"What the heck are you thinking?"

This statement was a lot nicer than what I originally thought was going to leave my mouth.

"I'll tell you later," he dismissed me, conscious of the bustling street.

"Nope, I think you better tell me now."

Bennett took my arm, dragging me along by the elbow, and stopped once we stood in a narrow alley in between Emeline's grandparents' home and the one beside it. Before he let me go, I shook my arm free, almost snarling at him.

"Look, we don't know why we were sent here, right?"

"Well, I don't know why I'm here. I'm not so sure about you!"

A random couple in the road heard me, and stared for a few seconds before moving on.

"My father didn't tell me anything about it, either. I promise you that much, but I don't really have a way to prove it. You'll just have to take my word for it, though I know how hard that is for you. Obviously Rowana is involved in something, so was that Allyson Hanchoré lady, and so is my dad. If our job is to find out our purpose for being here, then, yes we need to stay low. But we also need to take an opportunity. And Emeline doesn't have a reason to suspect anything. Even if she did, I don't think she would be someone we need to worry about."

"Everyone is somebody we need to worry about. I like Emeline and all, but she thinks we're... one of them. If she found out otherwise, she could turn on us overnight."

"Why can't you trust anyone?" Bennett rubbed his fingers in circles near the top of his head, acting like I had given him a headache of some kind, only infuriating me further as I spat,

"Because at no point in my life have people given me a reason to."

His exasperation gone, he now looked sad, sympathetic. I thought for years that if someone in another class could show that sympathy, then my situation could only get better. But I didn't want any of his. I started out of the alley, into the street, having no idea where I was going.

"You don't know the way back to Rowana's...." he came after me.

"I'll figure it out!" I shouted. Most people within a mile radius must have heard. I struggled to ignore the long, cutting stares as I blindly left that side of town. Bennett kept a good distance from me for several minutes of walking, which was a good choice on his part. But after I'd thoughtlessly stormed at least half a mile, I heard him again.

"Hey, Delilah," he called. I turned around ready to punch him as hard as possible should he come within my reach. Bennett had stopped, and was pointing up at seventy-three, seventy-three. It was almost impossible to backtrack and move past him with any dignity. I only maintained a shred by avoiding his eyes.

"Did you two come straight here today?" Rowana said from the table the moment the door closed.

"Yes, the streets were really congested," Bennett answered.

"No, he was agreeing to go back to the school tonight to snoop around," I threw my bag down on the floor and sat sideways in a chair with my back to them. I almost felt Rowana's glare.

"We're not snooping around. We're trying to find a door," Bennett explained with a harsh edge to his voice.

"I wouldn't care if you were going to look for the Fountain of Youth. If the Guard catches you, then they'll be keeping tabs on you from here on out. They'll eventually realize you aren't supposed to be here and neither am I."

"Emeline says there's no one there after six."

"Emeline is doing this with you?" Rowana seemed to relax in one way, and tense in another. "Is Brice going?"

"Not that we know of... how do you know them?"

"When I asked for another student to show you around, I specifically asked for Brice and Emeline. Let's just say I know her grandfather and his parents. But I still don't think it is a good idea...." She paused. "If you are convinced to go, then you cannot go wandering off without Emeline. She will not be suspicious to any Guard because her grandmother is the headmistress, but they will be curious about you two. Stick by her and whatever story she conceives in the event that someone sees you."

"Alright, we will."

"You will," I spoke from over my shoulder, twisting around in the chair. "I don't know if I'm going."

"Emeline's expecting both of us. If you don't come, you're going to have to come up with an excuse."

I opened my mouth to say something else, but I already doubted my ability to formulate anything worth lying about. It was a horrible idea, that much I was sure of, but I couldn't ignore how much I wanted to know what was behind this door of legend. Reluctantly, I grumbled, "I'll go."

Rowana insisted we could not wear our school uniforms. "Children simply do not wear them unless they are going to, are in, or coming from the building," she said. Taking the stairs two at a time, light on her feet for a middle aged woman, she went to dig out what she said were some clothes that belonged to her children. I found myself somewhat relieved before she returned. I would just be happy to get out of this patronizing little dress. However, when she returned, Rowana handed me a medium length skirt and button-down, high collar blouse.

"I'm sorry, my dear," she said, noticing my disappointed frown. "It is not acceptable for Haritite girls to wear anything but dresses or skirts in the State. It's just the way things are around here."

In a huff, I climbed the stairs to my room. Rowana's daughter was much taller and broad-shouldered than me, so the outfit was nearly falling off. She had to resize the skirt so I could wear it comfortably.

"What's your daughter's name?" I asked as she stuck the pointed part of a pin through the fabric. I was only trying to fill the silence.

"Audrey Maria," she smiled slightly when she said it.

"Where is she now? Is she married?"

"Somewhere in Sturwaller, and I have no way of knowing. She moved away after her brother's arrest and never spoke to me again."

Her beyond sad voice was my cue to drop the subject.

Chapter Seventeen

Emeline seemed like a different person outside of school, when she wasn't wearing that uniform. Her naturally streaked hair was only half up as she ran out to greet us in a checkered, light green dress with angled sleeves and a brown belt.

"My mother and grandmother bought me this years ago," she said, speaking to me. It seemed to take Bennett a while to even realize what she was talking about. "I thought I'd butter her up so she wouldn't ask where I was going. And just in case we run into the headmistress."

I nodded, and tried to smile. I guessed Haritite girls who were constantly in uniform were excited about ordinary clothing.

"Well, what are you waiting for?" she laughed. "There are no trapdoors or arrows that'll hit you."

"Why are you so excited about this?" I asked. Here was a nineteen-year-old young woman nearly jumping up and down in excitement over what was little more than a door in a ghost story. The longer I spent with her, the more painful my memories of Ellamae, who also rarely acted her age. She was either a thirteen-year-old, or aged, wise, and philosophic.

"I don't get out much. Besides, I know every nook and cranny in this building. It'll be so sweet to know what the Guard is hiding. I'm surprised they let Granddad keep his keys after his forced retirement. Maybe because he was so highly ranked."

I hadn't given a thought as to why Gregory Guise even possessed this key. If he was a retired Guard, it made sense. Then again he seemed like such a harmless old man, how could he at any point in his life been associated with those cold-blooded executioners?

"Why did they make him retire?" Bennett asked, also surprised.

"They gave him the letter when his spells started. After forty some years of service, too. That says something about the people who run the organization."

Emeline continued onto the front yard of the Dreary School. I followed behind her, and Bennett followed behind me. We approached the looming building in a single file line. The inside was dim, and the evening sky did a poor job of providing natural light. Emeline vanished down the middle hallway, and was carrying something when she returned. I realized it was an old step stool only after she set it on the floor, and grew three feet taller. A tiny *click* lit a mounted bulb above our heads. Emeline turned what appeared to be a small knob on the side, and the light shined much brighter. Moving the stool with her, she lit three others in the rectangular room.

"Can you believe someone gets paid to do this every morning?" she stepped down and picked up the stool again. "And they only have to light the rooms with no windows, too, unless the sun's not out. Only large buildings have these lights in Rochonnell; lanterns just aren't enough. But I hear Sturwaller has them in everyone's homes by now."

Emeline took a simple necklace from under the collar of her dress, and on it, was the key. She threw the chain at Bennett. Startled, he braced himself as if preparing to catch something with much more weight.

"I'm going to light the way as we go. You two try the doors."

"Won't somebody nearby notice if the whole place is lit up?" I asked.

"I'm not going to light the entire building. Just enough so we can see."

We did as she told us, not paying attention to each other, only the repetitive task at hand. Emeline lit the way, Bennett fiddled with the locks on all the doors, and I followed them around like a lost puppy. I wasn't sure why I had come to begin with, and filled an hour panicking at every noise that wasn't made by us.

"Relax, would you?" Bennett spoke quietly in my direction. Emeline stood above us, violently twisting the knob on a stubborn light bulb. "No one's here."

"We don't know that."

He paused. "I'll put it this way, then. If somebody was going to come shoot us all, they would've by now."

If he had said 'killed us all', it wouldn't have bothered me. But 'shoot us all' deteriorated an already frayed wire somewhere in my head. He seemed to realize the magnitude of what he had said too late, and lowered his head to avoid my wide eyes.

"I'm sorry. I didn't mean anything about the, um, Cleansings."

"I know that," I said shortly. We stood out of the last light, so probably out of Emeline's earshot, but I still didn't want to take any chances, and I really didn't want to revisit that conversation.

"I've never been great at talking to people," he tried to make up something for it. "I didn't have any friends at the farm. Now stuff doesn't come out right."

I knew I was supposed to be mad at him after what happened beside Emeline's grandparents' house that day. But I tried to make a joke of the situation just to lighten the dismal atmosphere. "I know that, too."

My attempt was lost on him, though, and another hour passed. It was dark outside, and Emeline's selective lighting of the bulbs strained my eyes. After all this time, we had still only gone through half of the middle hallway and small sections of the first floor on both sides. Emeline eventually sighed, dropped the stool on its side, and rubbed her forehead in both hands.

"We should go. Much longer, and we'll run into problems with the Guard in the streets."

Bennett moved to give the key back to her, but she only shook her head.

"You guys hold onto it. We'll come back tomorrow. Go on ahead. I have to put the lights out."

Bennett started down the hall without me, though I was nervous to leave Emeline there by herself.

"What if the Guard finds you in the streets alone? You said they'll be out soon."

"I'm the headmistress's granddaughter. I can come up with some favor I was doing for her. But you two don't have an excuse, so go now. I'll see you tomorrow."

I was slightly concerned for Emeline. But after she said that, I was more worried about us. Without any further goodbyes, I broke into a trot to find Bennett. I was sure he would be down the stairs by then. When I rounded the corner and set foot on the first step, I made out another head in the darkness. I jumped, almost falling down the remainder of the stairs, and nearly screamed.

"What?" he quickly forced himself away from the wall as if preparing to grab me if I fell, looking at me like I had finally lost my mind. "I was waiting for you, Amaryllis."

"And you scared me to death, Bennett."

The same one-note laugh came from the back of his throat, and we continued out of the building. Even though Emeline said the Guard shouldn't be too questioning yet, we stuck to the shadows. There were still a good number of people out, but

110

practically no noise filled the streets like it had in the afternoon. They were all just trying to get home. Bennett's photographic memory was the way home, so I didn't bother him during the walk.

I already expected Rowana to be waiting for us with a boatload of questions. That would've been correct, if only it was her. The headmistress of our favorite hellhole sat in a chair across from Rowana, who kept shifting her weight and anxiously surveying the room. Madam Guise was speaking to her quietly, intently, and she did not look happy. Rowana's wandering eyes soon saw us.

"Yes, see, here they are," she pushed herself up. Rowana faced Bennett and me, quickly glanced at the chair her company sat in, and then looked back at us. Her voice turned stern, "I told you to be back before dark."

"Uh, sorry, Aunt Rowana," Bennett quickly picked up the ball.

"And just what were you doing until this hour?" Madam Guise injected herself into the conversation.

"Good evening, Madam Guise. We were only walking around trying to get used to the State. It is much bigger, and the routes are still new and confusing."

I smiled slightly to agree with him. It was a polite, girlish, stupid kind of grin, and that time is one of the few I ever really, wholeheartedly tried to kiss up to someone. My effort was met with an even deeper frown, and I stopped trying.

"We will talk about this later," Rowana folded her arms. "Go upstairs and, um, do some schoolwork."

"There is no need to have your niece and nephew do all that on my account. Let them come join us. I would enjoy getting to know them better," Madam Guise continued with an edge of shrewdness. Based on the glare Rowana shot at space, I thought a certain unwelcome houseguest was about to get hit by the door on the way out. But Rowana allowed herself to be ordered around in her own home, and now gestured us to come with her. She reclaimed her chair, and the two of them left Bennett and me to sit together on the old, thinning sofa. I had a hunch Rowana didn't entertain much company, because none of the seats were angled to face each other.

"So, which neighborhood are you two from?" Madam Guise leaned forward, eager to expose us as frauds. My mind immediately went into double speed. *You know a couple subdivisions within the State. You should know at least one Haritite neighborhood closer to home. They're right there....*

"Thaltimer," I answered. Madam Guise looked like she'd taken a hit. She had expected me not to know. It was then I knew we had our first real, suspicious enemy. For the next ten minutes, she questioned Bennett and me about every facet of our fabricated lives, from the names of my birth parents to how his had adopted me into their family. Madam Guise couldn't have done a better job at showing us all she didn't care. She just needed us to slip up. This woman wasn't with the Guard, but she was just as dangerous. She was riding on intuition, and looking for hard evidence. Watching what we said couldn't have convinced her we were ordinary Haritite teenagers, but it could keep her from convincing real Guard of the fact we weren't. Frustrated at our ability to perform under pressure, she finally abandoned our pasts and turned to her next weapon of choice.

"Delilah, I was talking with Miss Fendrel earlier. When my teachers are out, I always visit them to ensure they are alright, you understand."

I nodded, and asked just for the show, "Is she okay?"

"Just a mild cold. She will be back tomorrow. But while we were talking, she had a lot to say about you."

I knew she thought she'd just caught me as a thin, challenging smile spread across her face. "She said you were having trouble catching up with the rest of the class...."

"We never attended a school in Thaltimer," Bennett intervened. "Our mother insisted we be taught at home so we could help her with our grandparents while they were ill. Now both of us are behind in a real class."

"Actually, I spoke with your teacher as well, Nicholas. He doesn't seem to have nearly as large a problem with you as Miss Fendrel has with Delilah. Now he did say you were slow, but that is to be expected of a new student. Miss Fendrel complained that Delilah could barely write. I know she must be exaggerating. Julia tends to go to extremes," Madam Guise took a folded slip of paper from the pocket sewn onto her skirt. She opened it in front of all our eyes, sweeping it back and forth as if to reinforce it in our minds. It was the notes Fendrel had made me rewrite ten times, the writing barely any better than my first attempt and the words so small and run together that I couldn't tell where my sentences began and ended.

"But if you prove to me that this," Madam Guise curled her fingers into a fist, crumpling the paper in its center, "was a practical joke, then we will let your difficult first day be water under the bridge."

"This is ridiculous," Rowana finally objected from her chair as Madam Guise held the paper out for me to take. "You cannot make her rewrite that. It is inexcusable she was forced to the first time."

"I am not making her rewrite the entire thing. Only that last sentence. If she fails, then my job would require I say something so their mother can be investigated for neglecting to teach her sixteen-year-old daughter how to write."

The thought played in my head like a continuation of her sentence. *And once they find out our mother is nonexistent, the Guard will be the next ones looking into us.*

"Now, Madam Laurie, would you happen to have a pen?" she gestured for her to give me one.

In a nervous huff, Rowana stood and took a slender, black one from somewhere in the bookshelf. She handed it to Bennett, who passed it to me. He doubted my ability to correct a sentence that I couldn't even read, that much was obvious, but he still attempted to smile reassuringly at me.

"You cannot help your sister, Nicholas."

"I'm not planning on it. I'd say the reason her paper looks like this to begin with is because she was angry at the teacher who made her do it for no reason. This doesn't mean she can't write, Madam Guise. That's a little insulting," Bennett crossed his arms, and leaned back to appear indifferent and relaxed about the circumstances. "Show her," he said to me, though I was looking at the paper, hopeless.

I bore down on the arm of the sofa, facing away from the three of them. Drawing thin lines to separate the words of my last sentence, I touched each with the pen. I didn't realize until then how closely related Fendrel's lesson was with Mrs. Cromwell's. It sounded as if the sickening sentence belonged at the end of the timeline. I couldn't imagine rewriting it, and momentarily considered refusing. The first time was wrong, and a second would be nothing short of treachery. It sounded too similar to what Hal Vern had told Ada, Arnold, and Delilah the week before.

The Wol was bilt in the yer 1552 as a safty precauson.

Despite every fiber in my body wanting to rip the pointless, indoctrinating notes in two, I rewrote the sentence in same way beneath the original, squeezing it onto the very last line of the page. I sounded out every word in my head, which only confused me more since they were all spelt the way they sounded. Something buried deep in my brain came to mind as a remembered my daily rounds in the marketplace: a posted sign, a Guard's proclamation, something that had infuriated me enough to remember over the years. It was, more or less, the exact same sentence I stared blankly at now. The last two words stuck in my mind over everything else.

The Wall was bilt in the yer 1552 as a safety precaution.

Without moving the paper, I looked up. Madam Guise strained her neck to see my writing, and she was still frowning.

That means there's still something wrong. I cursed in my mind, and moved my pen nervously back and forth between 'bilt' and 'yer': the only two words I knew were missing at least one letter. And after two minutes, Madam Guise grew jittery, looking ready to jump up and tear the paper to shreds. I had run through every letter of the alphabet, as I remembered them. The process of elimination had brought me down to what I believed to be the only options.

The Wall was built in the year 1552 as a safety precaution.

I held out my paper to Madam Guise, flinching when she snatched it from my hand. She squinted at the words, and I began to panic. Bennett lightly tapped my hand. I felt only slightly reassured as he mouthed *you're right,* though we waited for the headmistress's ruling for another minute.

"Yes, well," she coughed. "We will still be keeping an eye out. That took her much too long."

"Do as you must," Rowana advanced toward her, still standing by the bookcase. "Now if you will allow me to show you out."

Defeated, Madam Guise balled up the paper and dropped it in a pail by the door. Rowana wished her a lovely evening, and slammed the door after she had gone off the steps. As she bolted it shut, Bennett removed his hand.

"You had me scared for a while."

"I got it right," I spoke as if in shock.

"I told you writing out the alphabet would help."

"Amaryllis," Rowana cut in as she walked across the room, signaling for me to follow. I stood beside her in silence as she lit the oven and took a cast iron pot from the cabinet. "Do you want to tell me why you were writing those notes so many times?"

I told her about how I had gotten on Fendrel's permanent bad side. At the end, she laughed.

"Julia Fendrel is married, but she cannot have children. I suppose that is why she is the way she is. She treats her students as if they are all her own daughters, and disciplines in the same way."

"How do you know?"

"Audrey had that woman as a teacher for three years. Nearly every day she would bring a paper like yours home."

Chapter Eighteen

  The days in the Haritite State turned into a week, which lazily led into another, and then another. Bennett, Emeline, and I started out going to the school every evening. By the time we became aware of all the skeptical people watching us pass by just before the curfew, we had almost gotten halfway around the building. Still, that key refused to turn in any door. To avoid any confrontation, we lessened our night visits to three times a week. During school, Fendrel had given up trying to place my stupidity on a pedestal for the rest of the class to laugh at. But nevertheless my greeting and goodbye was always a disapproving stare. Mrs. Cromwell, after realizing that I truly did not want to be called on again, left me alone. After almost every class, she would ask me the same, concerned question. I only passed Madam Guise once in the hallways. The abrupt, angry spring in her step told me I had also earned a place in her bad books.

Meanwhile, Riley became like a best friend to me, almost equal to Stella after only three weeks. She, Emeline, and I always spent midday meandering through the rear yard of the school. Bennett hovered close by for a while, as if he felt obligated to keep an eye on me, though he seemed to have made a few friends of his own. We barely saw each other during the day, though he still worked with me on my writing every night. If Riley was slowly replacing Stella, then he was easily replacing Barney. I knew once I left here and returned to my reality, both of them would fade into a memory. I never gave a thought as to what I would say to Uncle Graham and Aunt Clarissa, and the only person I found myself badly missing was Rose.

As I began the slow process of getting situated amongst the Haritites, shadows still loomed over our small group of three in the backyard of the school. Namely, these shadows were Melodie's 'underlings,' as Riley called them, and clearly they had nothing better to do than to spy on me after that one incident. Under constant watch, we were careful about what we said. Emeline and Riley put forth their effort to not speak about teachers or anything else which could be contorted to land them in trouble. I did the same, but was also all the more careful to not drop any obvious hints. Rumors circulated within that crowd quickly, and now it appeared as if a third of the building was weary of Delilah Owen and Nicholas Layne. Teachers, of course, took no part in the students' private lives, and only came to do what they were paid to.

My sixteenth birthday came and went, though I never said anything about it. If I were home, my birthday would have meant Uncle Graham working longer days to bring home a bit more money. With that small raise, Aunt Clarissa could prepare a larger dinner than usual. Niles and Oakley would have given me something they'd made or found themselves. In years past, it had been a piece of tree bark where water had left interlocking lines and patterns on it. Although it was useless and rotted in less than a week, I knew they would spend forever looking for something they thought was interesting enough to give to me. Last year, long before she left, Ellamae carved a doll about six inches long. Rose sewed some tiny clothes, and that was their present to me. Ellamae said she knew I was too old for toys, but she wanted it to mean something. At night, she told me she wanted it to mean protection: that she was always looking after me. I knew nothing of her plans to abandon us, and thought she was talking about while I was out with Stella and Barney. Whenever I began to think of any of them, I couldn't help homesickness, no matter how uninviting home was at times. I told myself we only had two more weeks until, according to Mr. Johansson's letter, we dropped our lives here for no one else to claim.

Toward the beginning of our fifth week in the State, the transition between the seasons began. I always struggled during that time with headaches and almost daily nose bleeds. But it had never gotten as bad as it was then. I barely stayed awake during class, coughing so loudly and often that girls began to give me an evil eye, and I lost all appetite. It got progressively worse over two or three days, and on the way to Rowana's, I was so detached that I forgot several streets. I resorted again to following Bennett.

"Amaryllis," he stopped me in front of the house. No one was within earshot, but we still lowered our voices whenever we said each other's real names. "Are you alright?"

I nodded absently, rubbing my forehead in both hands. He persisted, refusing to let us inside until I admitted, "My head hurts...."

"Are you alright?"

"You said that already," I smiled a little, though it hurt to move anything on my face. It took Bennett a while to understand the humor. That night in the jail felt like a lifetime ago. As much as I missed Rose, Stella, and Barney, there was always a nagging dread that in two weeks, I would never see Bennett again. I made the thought bearable by stupidly thinking we could still be friends, but he and I seen together in public could never turn out well. I wouldn't put it past the general population to go tell the Guard I was pestering a Nemiren. Even if Bennett told them I wasn't, they could arrest me anyway for disrupting the peace. If you were to examine all the Stoleh in prison, a third of them would've been rounded up during Cleansings, and a small fraction of them would've missed the Wall, stolen, begged, or committed some other 'petty crime'. The rest were arrested for disrupting the peace: the degrees of which varied. Most any interaction with someone from another class was a high offense in the category.

Bennett's worry seemed to overshadow any reaction he could have had, and I felt his eyes on me as we entered the concrete hall in the back of Rowana's home. Inside, I wordlessly passed her, dropped my bag on one side of the sofa, and nearly collapsed onto the other. I laid my head on the arm of the chair, untying my hair from its usual school-uniform tail to block more light from my face.

"Did you get in trouble at school today?" Rowana's voice along with her tapping footsteps followed us into the room. She asked this question every afternoon, never 'how was school'?

"No, Rowana," Bennett and I said at the same time. He spoke, I sounded like I was grumbling.

"What's the matter?" I heard her come beside the sofa, hovering over me. I gave her the same answer as Bennett, and struggled to push myself up. The light pounded behind my eyes, but I still saw her frown. "It's nothing."

Rowana tenderly moved my hair out of the way, and felt my head with her hand. I scooted away from her touch just as she removed it, scrutinizing her hand as if I had just burned her. She asked me if I felt sick, and I lied, telling her it wasn't overpowering.

"Then we will just wait and see what happens. But I don't want you going anywhere tonight."

I opened my mouth to protest. Bennett and I had already agreed to meet Emeline at the school in a few hours.

"I think Bennett can take care of himself. I don't know what you three hope to find behind this door you keep talking about. But if you are so set on it, then that is your choice. If they find it, I am sure they won't keep it from you. Stay here tonight. Your headache should blow over by morning."

Overwhelming pain in my head bound me to the sofa until Bennett left for the school. After he said goodbye and the door had closed behind him, I covered my eyes with my arms and fell asleep.

I woke in the exact same position. My neck was stiff from lying on the arm of the sofa, and my headache still nulled and crushed my senses. Its intensity had gone down, but not enough to make a difference. I mistook the woman in the chair for Aunt Clarissa. She was sewing what appeared to be a long, tri-color blanket: a deep brown, a maroon, and one thinner line of piercing green. In the haziness, I almost asked my aunt when she needed me to go to the center of town. A sharp twinge of reality saddened me when the form morphed into Rowana. We wordlessly stared at each other for a couple seconds, and she set aside her materials, walking past me. I heard her attempting to revive the fire.

"Don't make anything in the middle of the day for me. It's a waste," I mumbled, and heard a slight laugh. Within ten minutes, Rowana came back with steaming copper bowl. She balanced it on the arm of the sofa, and returned to her own chair. Without touching it, I looked at the contents of the bowl: a thick, misshapen piece of meat atop a mound of brown rice. I knew that five weeks in the Haritite State would degrade my past ability to function without a stable supply of food. In preparation to return home, I began skipping a meal every few days so not eating every night wouldn't come as a shock to my body. Rowana figured out what I was trying to do within a matter of days, and sternly told me I was being ridiculous. She also insisted that while I was under her roof, I was going to eat every evening whether I liked it or not. When that didn't work on me, Rowana played the guilt card and said it was so lonely in her home most of the year. We were leaving her life forever in just a short amount of time, and having dinner with her every night was a wonderful chance for her to get to know us better. I thought I had done a pretty decent job at making my life transparent to her weeks ago with my tirade about Cleansings. Nevertheless, the guilt card was something I couldn't stand. I gave in most of the way, though I still made a conscious effort to eat less.

"Where's Bennett?" I asked blearily, still adjusting to the sudden light.

"At school. It's eleven o'clock in the morning."

I scrambled into a sitting position and shielded my eyes from the window. It should have occurred to me that the sun was out and in full glare.

"Calm down," Rowana continued her sewing without looking at me. "You are not the first to stay home from school for a day. We'll see how you feel this afternoon. Take the time to relax. I doubt you ever have the chance."

She was right. I failed to remember one time in the past ten years that I had laid on a sofa all day. It wasn't nearly as liberating as I envisioned it to be. Without the excitement of running around in the shadows with Stella and Barney, or even the lesser stimulation of going to school, I didn't know what I was supposed to do with myself. I tapped my fingers in the palm of my hand and watched Rowana sew for what felt like hours. She was perfectly comfortable under my stare, and didn't speak to me. The one time I tried to push myself up, I was sharply told to stop moving. As the day progressed, I began to feel weaker, though I hadn't so much as gotten a drink of water on my own. Rowana apparently sensed this, and started to ask every five minutes if I felt any better. I didn't trust myself to open my mouth, I would've groaned, and I only shook my head. By the time I knew school had let out, I was certain I was going to be sick. As I slowly drifted off again, I felt her hand on my forehead, and opened my eyes. Fear must have flushed my face, and her blurry, shapeless form gently shushed me. When she left my limited field of vision, it hurt too much to follow her with my eyes.

I fell into a gray state of limbo for a short time, never feeling so alone on Rowana's sofa in the Haritite State. I didn't want to lie there in a quiet, insulated home with plenty to eat and no one to bother you. I wanted to hear Aunt Clarissa's soft voice as she brought us anything in the house that could be used as blankets, and hear everyone's late night conversations when the five kids were forced into Niles and Oakley's room to stay warm in the winter. Those days felt long over now more than ever, like I had ultimately abandoned my family and there was no more going home. After a surreal yet vivid daydream of watching myself try to explain my six week absence to them, my pounding headache startled me. I still hadn't moved, but Rowana had placed a pillow behind my head. It took me several seconds to realize she wasn't around. Bennett sat on the opposite side of the room, leaning against a bare spot of wall, seemingly reading. When he noticed I was awake, he closed the book, his finger marking the page.

"You have to see this."

I began to force myself into a sitting position only to realize I was trembling. The reason I even attempted to move to begin with was so he could sit down. Bennett saw this, and instead sat on the floor close to my head. I managed to reposition myself as he flipped through a couple pages, eventually turning the book around for me to see. The print was large, but wouldn't draw my attention away from a creepily detailed drawing on the left page. I counted thirteen people. There were few elderly and fewer young people: most were middle aged adults. They stood in three single file lines set in front of each other, shortest in the front and tallest in the back. These people all stared out from the page, and if a look could cut, theirs easily did.

"Who are they?" I asked Bennett. The caption beneath the picture wasn't clear to me.

"Idrisans," he answered barely above a whisper as if afraid someone outside might hear the condemned name. "This is what I was talking about earlier. Idris is their leader, and the resistance themselves are called Idrisans."

"You said mentioning their name is illegal. Why would there be a book if the Lebon are trying to keep them nonexistent?"

"It makes sense now," he turned the page, not paying any attention to me anymore. I repeated myself, and he looked up again. He sat on his legs, holding the book

119

diagonally in front of us. I felt uncomfortably close and tried to retreat into the sofa as he continued.

"The Lebon do try to make them nonexistent, until they capture a few. Then it's a public execution in Imperiam, which is apparently a huge deal. They all have a hearing with the Imperial... after the Lebon equivalent of Guard finishes torturing enough information out of them. This is a record of the last big execution seven years ago. It's not in detail, though. It sounds like it was mostly written to make the Lebon feel good about themselves and squash any thought in the general population's head. But here's the thing," he flipped back to the picture. "This was never supposed to get anywhere near the general population. This book is supposed to be in Imperiam."

"How do you know?" I asked dubiously. Nothing from Imperiam ever made it past the Etairan Mountains.

"They would never, ever put this out for people to read. The executions are in Imperiam because they don't want anybody else to know. It sounds like most people don't. This entire book is schematics of where in the Wilds the camp might be, past failed missions to find them, and a few logs of their action."

"This is the same camp Serah was talking about?" I tried to envision such a place. The Wilds was a general term for any heavily forested area. They were scattered around in random splotches all over the land and met in one, expansive woods in the east. All roads that led near the Wilds were guarded. It now seemed pretty clear why.

"Looks like it," Bennett sighed, suddenly traumatized like he had been hit by a ton of bricks. "The Lebon apparently know something about correspondents, like what Rowana called herself and Allyson Hanchoré. It talks about them being in the State, in Nemirena, and a few all over the place. That's not all, either, look at the names of the people here."

I squinted to form letters in the names of these people who had died in Imperiam seven years ago. None of them stood out to me until I reached one that lined up with a young, sickly woman, Ellamae's age or slightly older, standing in the front row.

Ruth Backenstose.

Now that I focused on her, her glare seemed the harshest of all the people so carefully drawn. Her black hair was cropped short, framing her hard, bitter face, and one of her hands sat discretely on a young boy's shoulder in front of her. The moment I saw them both, it was too easy to substitute me and Rose.

"That's the last Stoleh who came to the Haritite State before us. Serah said she was executed in Imperiam."

"You know what this means, right?"

"She was an Idrisan. Rowana is, Serah and Vince are-"

120

"My father is," Bennett stared hopelessly at the drawing directly on the page. I craned my neck to see his expression, and knew he was picturing his dad amongst these people who awaited their execution in the most painful way possible. "The Idrisans probably went through a lot to get a hold of this."

"We're here doing work for them. We aren't going home after this. We signed ourselves up for their camp," I finished my first thought. I was in a total panic by then, and that fear easily gave me the strength to sit up. Bennett began to deny what I thought was a blaring truth when the door flew open without warning. He almost slammed his own fingers in the book as he closed it. Rowana entered first, saw what we were looking at, and seemed to recognize the cover. Her eyes widened, and she shot Bennett a harsh glare as she nearly ran into the house, and grabbed the book from him. Rowana hid it behind her back as a man followed inside. It might have just been because I was lying down, but he seemed tall and imposing. Two things that couldn't be mistaken, however, were how lanky and young he was. As he causally observed the room, Rowana dropped the book out of sight on the kitchen table.

"This is her?" he gestured at me, closing the door behind him. I shifted and looked away.

"Yes," Rowana answered with a hint of spite or even sarcasm in her voice. She approached us, and Bennett was practically pushed away by the two. I watched him melt into the background and sit on the staircase out of the corner of my eye. The momentary uncomfortable closeness I felt with him was nothing compared to this total stranger looming over me.

"Delilah," Rowana began to speak in a strained voice. I couldn't tell whether it was related to her catching us with the book, or having that man in her home. Something told me it was a little of both. "This is Doctor Onwetend. He's going to tell us why you are feeling so ill."

I noticed the black leather bag only after he set it on the floor. My refusal was instinctive, though he wouldn't acknowledge it, asking Rowana about her relationship to me.

"She is my niece," I watched her clench and unclench her fists at her sides.

"Where are her parents?"

"She lives with *me*," Rowana snapped. He seemed to just pick up on her aggravation, and stared at her strangely. "I ran all over Ceaves looking for you only to be told you had gone home early for no just reason. I continued to wait for you for another half hour and I presume you are going to stand there for the remainder of the evening before you finally decide to do your job."

He clearly didn't know what to say. So he pretended he hadn't heard her. The man placed his index finger and thumb on either side of my neck below my chin. He pressed inward, and quickly turned my head to the side, which triggered a coughing fit. Doctor Onwetend quickly took his hand back, waiting for it to pass. Several more of the fits made him impatient, and he sharply pulled my arm out from under me. He picked up the skin on my wrist twice as if expecting a different result the second time. Aside from the fact that I had no idea what he was doing or looking for, his frown after five minutes started to scare me. The last thing he did was back away, and tell me to stand up. I shook, but managed to get my feet onto the floor. When I laboriously pushed myself up, my vision went black for several seconds, my brain throwing itself against my skull in an effort to break it. I was about to fall over, yet all he did was stand there and study me. Rowana, still glaring at him, helped me back onto the sofa. I remained sitting upright in hope I would look at least somewhat put together. That act ended when he spoke again.

"Well, she shows all the signs of mild pneumonia."

There was a sudden pressure on my chest which had nothing to do with being sick. My heart literally wrenched as I forced myself back down, laying my head on the pillow and staring off into space, my eyes open until they dried and burned. I knew the color had drained entirely from my face, and it didn't take long for them to notice. Before he said anything else, I choked out, "How much longer do I have?"

He suddenly seemed confused, and looked at Rowana as if expecting either an explanation or a punch line. "How much longer do you have to do what?"

"To live," I lifted my head slightly off the pillow, trying to maintain a straight face through my sweltering panic. There were many things worse than dying, but in my mind, few worse than dying in the Haritite State. However the man's expression first deepened, and then changed. He laughed loudly. I easily felt on the verge to tears, and my own expression only got deepened and shook. When Doctor Onwetend finally regained a little self-control, he felt my head again. Only this time, it was clearly part of some twisted joke.

"Perhaps a bit more severe than I thought," he shook his head, but still laughed under his breath. Pretending I was no longer there, he turned back to Rowana. "She can return to school in a few days, whenever she feels ready to. Just have her rest and drink a lot of water. A small amount of garlic can help as well."

He retrieved his bag, pushed it up onto his arm, and shoved his hands into the pockets of his long jacket. "Come get me if the condition worsens," he paused at the door Rowana held open for him, and tipped an invisible hat in my direction. "We might have to pencil out a will."

I was still trying to understand what had happened as he disappeared outside. After yelling into the street: "No, I am most certainly not paying you after I spent an hour tracking you down! Have a nice evening!," Rowana failed at gently closing the door. Without looking at me, she disappeared into the kitchen. I breathed quickly, but silently, and felt like I could throw up. How could he just leave after that? More importantly, how could he laugh in my face?

Bennett returned from the staircase. I knew my face was readable, and he sighed sympathetically, only unnerving me more as he knelt in his original spot.

"You're okay," he tried to smile, though it wasn't very convincing.

"I'm going to die?" I said as a question.

He shook his head, "Of course not."

I continued to argue with him as if I knew any better, explaining how outbreaks of pneumonia had devastated entire boroughs in years past. If the first didn't kill you, it weakened you enough for the next epidemic to finish its work. Bennett only insisted that pneumonia was little more than a common cold, and that I probably picked it up from someone at school and just needed to rest for a couple days. Nothing he said made any sense to me, and neither one of us were getting anywhere, until everything abruptly snapped into focus. The horror nestled in my chest remained, but the reason it was there changed. Bennett hesitantly picked up my hand, interlocking our fingers and trying to talk me back into reality. I didn't acknowledge him, but my breathing slowed to a normal pace as I stared blankly through the plain ceiling, frowning.

"What are you thinking about?" Bennett asked.

"Pneumonia kills people," I finally made myself look him in the eye. When our beloved storyteller went from the sniffles to his deathbed in a matter of weeks, Aunt Clarissa was one of many people on our street who went to help care for him during his last few days. She took Ellamae with her, and naturally I wanted to go because he had meant so much to Rose and I, and still meant a lot to our cousins. Ella told me several times that I didn't want to be there. I envisioned it wouldn't be pretty, but nothing could have prepared me for it. I never actually spoke to him. But I saw enough to know what pneumonia did to people, and he died four days later. Pneumonia was as good of a death sentence as being caught outside of the Wall after eight. But I had never considered what it might mean to a Nemiren or Haritite. I suddenly felt beyond stupid for asking that man what I did.

"I'm telling you, you'll be fine. He even said you can come back to school when you feel up to it. If it was that bad, then my father would've been gone and so would I."

"It's nothing to you," I said bitterly, all the sudden anger targeted at Bennett. "But in my borough, when someone gets pneumonia, the epitaph is underway the next morning. No one except family is allowed around them and that's a risk they choose to take. The next people they see after that are the gravediggers. Your people don't die of pneumonia, but mine do."

I sat up again, trying to steady myself. My back was to him, but I twisted my body around and continued loudly.

"Because we don't have real doctors, and everyone lives so on top of each other in such terrible conditions that the smallest thing turns into a plague within a week! Pneumonia to the rest of the population is just some annoyance. But to my people, they seriously do have to think of their last wishes!"

Bennett moved closer to me, balancing himself on the very edge of the sofa, and tried to take my hand again. I moved out of the way.

"You're not going to die," he said intently, and I felt the same unease of being too close to him. But if I moved, it would look like I was shying away. "You know that, right?"

123

"I'm so sick of pretending!" I shouted at him like everything from the jail to the Haritite State was his fault. My voice cracked at the end, and a saturated cough overtook me. In a way, I guessed I was subconsciously blaming him. The only reason I was there was because his father had decided to send me with him. But I couldn't deny the fact that it all went back to getting caught stealing that squash, which only made me angrier. "These people that they have no idea how good they have it! These five weeks have been the first time in my life I haven't had some sort of bounty on my head just because I was born!"

Rowana returned to the room. She slowly lowered herself on the other side of the sofa with a copper cup of water in her hands. I pushed it away when she tried to give it to me, and she somehow lost her grip on the curved handle. The water spilled all over the floor, splashing the three of us. Rowana didn't even flinch, the harsh way she stared making me less aware of what shying away would look like.

"If you had this life then I doubt you would be half the person you are today. Think about how you would change if you hadn't always had to struggle. You've been here long enough to see the way children your age operate around here. You would have been raised to schmooze up to adults with a hidden agenda. People in power justify it by their parents' power. Why do you think the same families and their friends have held most positions for generations? You have more freedom than you realize, and are fortunate in a few ways that these people are not. I don't mean to say your life has not been hard. It most certainly has not been fair to you. But without it, you would not be Amaryllis."

Truthfully, I wasn't sure whether being Amaryllis was a good or bad thing. It always seemed as if I skipped the stage of childhood innocence, and now fell short in one way if not another as a dirty thief. Yet Haritites undeniably lived in a haze, having no concept of life outside their State. They could have access to the information, but they chose to be ignorant. We had no access. But at least we had some insight as to the way power worked, and what it did to people.

Rowana let the water soak between the floorboards, and brought me another cupful. She placed it in my hands, making sure I was holding it this time. After she left, Bennett took her place next to me. I hadn't expected to see him smiling.

"I meant to tell you yesterday. Emeline was doing a favor for Mrs. Cromwell, and she says she's found the right door."

Chapter Nineteen

I had convinced myself if I was never caught by Mr. Johansson, then I would have died. Though Rowana seemed convinced I would've never gotten sick to begin with. She said I had caught whatever Fendrel had, and it turned into pneumonia over the course of several weeks. I swore she was going to file some sort of complaint against the school by how livid she was. It seemed like that woman was always fuming over something. But, to me, she was definitely justified.

Rowana had me stay with her for five days, though the symptoms were almost totally gone in four. My warm welcome from Fendrel was being told to stand up and recite the beginning some kind of document that, by its long winded and big-worded title, was probably important to Haritites. After so many weeks in school and so many nights practicing, my writing was better than it had been months before, and actually legible. I picked up the bare minimum of each lesson, only getting by with Bennett's help. I received the second lowest passing mark as my first grade, and couldn't help a temporary sense of pride, almost disappointed that it would all be left meaningless the following week.

After I returned to school, Emeline and Riley hovered over me, asking if I was alright every time I coughed. I told them I was fine, though Emeline would only lecture that I should've stayed home for at least a week. Two days passed with no change, and the other girls finally stopped making a conscious effort to stay ten feet away from me at all times. Perhaps the only difference I noticed was an increase in what Melodie's cronies. Their seemingly constant presence placed even further restrictions on my conversation, and I found myself not speaking at all while on school grounds. Cromwell attempted to be discrete, but she began trying to wring answers out of me at every opportunity. As ironic as it might seem, I began to play stupid to avoid more attention. But even if I was silent from the time we came in to the time we walked out, every time I accidently looked in her general direction, Melodie had a suspicious and accusing glare plastered on her perfectly proportioned face. But nothing truly erupted until I had started to really worry about my upcoming journey home.

Five of us stood there in a deformed circle. Riley, Emeline, Bennett, and some other boy I didn't know who had followed him over. He seemed halfway decent, and didn't have the same imposing aura as what the four of us jokingly called 'the enemy.' All I really remember about him now is how awkwardly tall he was, and his name started with an A. Let's call him Arden, and how he stood awkwardly, looked down at the ground, and tried to speak to Riley about something no one understood. It was so apparent that he was even a little sweet on her, though she was totally oblivious. Just as the rest of us were to the three approaching from the side.

"Delilah," a harsh, commanding voice called from a distance. Not counting our conversation from across the room, I had never spoken to her before. I still knew who it was before I even looked up. What shocked me wasn't her or her two backups, but a large ring of kids that had already stopped to observe. They looked on with major curiosity as if expecting a giant fight. When someone has so much influence over an entire building, you can't help but wonder what sort of lies everyone is fed about how important they are. I only drew more attention to myself by pretending I hadn't heard her. Bennett tried to cover for me by saying aloud and openly that we had to be somewhere. The three moved in the direction we were about to follow and stood there with their hands on their hips. This gesture stirred something within the crowd, and it now seemed like time had frozen. Even the tiny children were watching with a kind of fear. Melodie could see I was unnerved by all the people watching us.

"Cromwell told us you had pneumonia. Why did you come back so soon? Are you trying to infect us all?" she crossed her arms. I bit my lip, more in disbelief and annoyance than anger, and moved in her direction. I was not going to stand twenty feet away and yell a banter battle with her. Once we were within a comfortable distance, I spoke in a normal voice so not to engage the onlookers.

"Can I help you or something?"

"Actually," she put her arm around my shoulders and tried to lead me to walk with her. It seemed innocent enough, but my feet automatically took root in the ground. The more she urged me forward, the more I was determined to stay there. My interrupting whatever plan she had didn't faze her, though. Melodie removed her arm with nothing less than a tiny smirk on her face, and a remark to her two underlings about my paranoia.

"Fine," she continued loudly, pulling the crowd back into what I already sensed would become a one-sided fight. As I picked out even more harsh faces among the students, I couldn't help but feel it was the entire school versus me. "Have it your way. What I was going to say is I'm more concerned with how I can help you."

That sounded painful beyond measurement. Trying to avoid her gaze without instinctively studying the ground, I looked above the ocean of blue-uniformed kids, and stared at the looming wall surrounding the Drierie School. Amaryllis Carter the Stoleh, or Delilah Owen the Haritite, I was always bound by some form of the Wall. I frowned slightly to myself when I considered it, and Melodie took that as my response to her thoughtful gesture.

"As in help you reach the same level as a ten year old in arithmetic, or history, or anything else, for that matter. Quick, what's nine multiplied by three?"

A deep, low sound echoed from the audience, and barely contained laughter from Melodie's cronies. I couldn't quite wrap my mind around why this seemed so awfully important to them all. Melodie was only another kid; one who clearly needed something else to do besides pick insignificant skirmishes in the yard.

"Not until you reach the same level as a ten year old in maturity," Emeline glowered at her with much more ferocity than she seemed capable of as she, Bennett, Riley, and Arden enveloped me from the sides. The same sound emitted deep within the crowd, and their heads all seemed to turn in unison, waiting for Melodie's comeback. I guessed this was their form of excitement in their otherwise dull, uniform lives. Melodie pulled her very blonde ponytail over her shoulder and studied the five of us with nothing but a condescending frown.

"At least we," she moved her hand around to indicate herself, the girls behind her, and the gathered crowd, dropping her hand back by her side just in time to avoid pointing at the five of us, "Have been in the State long enough to have some common sense. But I would think even some girl from a disgusting place like Thaltimer would know the alphabet. I was embarrassed for you in class. I almost felt bad for you. Miss Fendrel is right. You're like a Stoleh."

The kids gaped at her as if she'd just cursed. She took careful measures to pronounce every letter of the word mockingly, and at length. I tried to give her a dubious stare, but couldn't hide my sudden, overwhelming desire to punch her. I kept my mouth shut, itching to retaliate with another comment, but telling myself I couldn't stoop to that level. It was exactly what she wanted.

"What's your issue?" Riley filled in the space, repeating my thoughts in words. "Don't you have anything else better to do than pick fights with people?"

"I already said the only thing I wanted to do was help her," Melodie momentarily lowered her voice, but not enough for the closest people to miss it. Whispers of '*what did she say?*' echoed among them for a moment.

"Just like you only wanted to help me and my family," I watched Riley shift her weight and bite her tongue. She left me to wonder what exactly had happened, though I could envision a rather ugly picture just by the burning hatred behind her eyes.

"He deserved it," Melodie spoke in a normal, if not sheepish voice, running her words together.

"You know he didn't do it!" Riley shouted at her. Emeline put a restraining hand on her arm.

"Look," I attempted to end the conversation. As I spoke, the crowd reluctantly began to dissipate and file toward the door to return to class. The two behind Melodie paused only a few seconds before following them. Without an entire building to support her, she seemed much smaller and isolated. "I don't need or want your help. Thanks anyway."

"I think you do. If you don't want Madam Guise to find out who you are."

I felt my face conform to total shock, and couldn't catch myself in time.

"You know what, never mind. I don't know what I was thinking. If that was true, your head would've rolled by now. See you in class, Delilah," she began to walk away. I knew she was expecting me to follow her and demand how she knew, because she was heading in the opposite direction of the building. The only thing that kept me from going after her was, again, the fact that that's what she wanted. But I couldn't help myself. This girl, who had no idea how pathetic her life truly was even in comparison to mine, wasn't going to have the last word with me. I had no idea what I was going to say until I stood directly behind her, and Melodie turned around with a smug gleam in her eye. Bennett, Emeline, Riley, and Arden stayed behind. They were all waiting, but I knew Bennett must have been telling me in his mind not to risk everything when we only had one more week left here. I took the thought into account, and what left my mouth was much smoother than I previously thought.

"Trade your polished, black sandals for the undersized, scuffed, sheepskin boots of a Stoleh. It might surprise you, maybe even change the way you look at life. Perhaps it might change you so much that you stop and consider next time you're about to step on someone to get ahead," I paused, and knew my voice was changing before I spoke again. The Guard always told us we had disgusting little accents that blared our intellect to the rest of the population. After many years with a fake badge, I had reduced what little of mine down to nothing. I purposely contorted my voice for the emphasis. "Then

128

again, maybe you oughta just stay away and hide in your perfect world. 'Cause you'd get lynched, sweetie. You'd get yourself lynched in five seconds."

That stupid, infuriating smile that'd curved her lips the entire time went completely away. Her jaw might as well have dropped open because that's the new way she looked at me. I knew now that she hadn't expected her insult to actually be correct. And that shock, that fear, turned slowly into disgust. She took one step away from me, her readable expression morphing into hatred.

"You have something to say to me, say it," I snarled. I felt like we weren't even in the State anymore. This was back home, within just miles of the Wall, where Haritites, Nemirens, and Stoleh segregated themselves in the streets to not come close to each other. I had just said a sugarcoated version of what I'd always wanted to tell Haritites after their firing squad of remarks, and I saw no immediate deadly side effects.

"I have nothing to say to you or any of your little disgusting, criminal kind except-"

"What the heck are you talking about?" I cut in. Her pained expression tipped back into confusion, though she quickly caught herself. "Did you seriously think I was...?" I laughed, sinfully enjoying every moment of holding the upper hand. "You're crazier than I thought. I told you I moved here from Thaltimer. But I've met Stoleh before. A couple little boys used to sit on the same street corner every evening until Guard chased them away. Who knows if they were ever caught? It's easy for people in the State to despise Stoleh because none of you have ever seen one, much less tried to understand one."

"There's one standing in front of me now," her lowered voice shook, her baseless anger leaving what felt like a tangible barrier between us. I would never understand why Haritites thought my existence somehow infringed on their quality of life, and suddenly I needed to die in order to make the world a better place. I guessed it was something that truly didn't have a foundation outside of the fact that it was simply the way things had been for hundreds of years. "And I'm going to make sure she's not standing here this time tomorrow. You are so busted, girl. That was the worst possible move you could've made."

'Girl' was a drawn out, sharp insult, and was most often my title at the Wall even though they had my name written down in front of them. I clenched my fists as Melodie composed herself, and started to walk around me back in the direction of the imposing school. Before she had even passed me, I turned on my heels, coiled my fingers into her ponytail, and yanked as hard as I could. I wasn't thinking about consequences, only showing that girl that she wasn't as divine as she believed herself to be. Despite how hard I pulled back, I didn't expect her to actually fall, and casually took a few steps away so she wouldn't land on top of me. Her coughing was only distorted by the sound of shock as the wind left her. Melodie refused to look me in the eye to preserve what remained of her dignity. When I knelt calmly beside her, she froze in a half-sitting, half-standing position, and her animal-like gaze locked furiously on me.

"I am not afraid of you," I duplicated her look. "Or your so called connections. You and I both know that the Guard would need some damn good proof before they laid their hands on a Haritite child. You have nothing except your word, and even if your father was the Imperial, he would not and could not incriminate me. What are you going to do? Go home tonight and tell Daddy there's a Stoleh in your class? Even if I was one, you'd never get him to question, much less arrest me."

There was nothing for her to say. She knew I was right.

"By the way, nine multiplied by three, the answer is twenty seven," I stood and looked down at her. "Now get up."

I turned around only to stop short. Instead of Bennett, Emeline, Riley, and Arden standing a good distance away, Madam Guise was directly behind me. I immediately felt less concerned about what this situation looked like and more worried about how much the headmistress had heard.

"Either one of you care to explain?" she folded her arms, looking behind me at Melodie in the same, intense way. I relaxed slightly. If she had heard the thick of it, her response would have been much different. Melodie, still in an awkward position below us, was silent, and so was I. As if expecting me to run away, Madam Guise instructed me to stay put as she reached her hand out to Melodie, unaffectionately forcing her to her feet. She took her left arm in one hand, and my right arm in the other. We were marched to a different door than usual, where Madam Guise forced Melodie and me to walk in front of her and into a hallway I didn't recognize. Though her face remained bright red, Melodie knew where we were, and went slightly ahead of me. She hugged herself in preparation to throw up all the way down the hall. Madam Guise stopped at a door just after we turned a corner and could see the front entrance of the school. She pushed and held it open with one hand, using her other one to lovingly invite us inside. Melodie passed me, and I now noticed how pale she had become.

More captives waited for us. *She must have brought them here first and then came back for us,* I thought. *That's why she doesn't know exactly what happened.* I squeezed myself in between Bennett and Riley, leaving Melodie exposed in the middle of the room. The lack of windows led the school to over-illuminate the area, and I looked down at my shoes until my eyes could adjust to the brightness. What I originally pictured a headmistress's office to look like was not what was laid out before us. There was no desk, no books, nothing except several cheaply made chairs arranged in a semicircle. Immediately after entering the room, Madam Guise whipped around and locked the door like someone had been pursuing us. Before she spoke, we knew where we would end up. We saved her the breath and took our places in the chairs. There were just enough for the six of us. Emeline and Riley angled their chairs to face each other slightly, and Bennett scooted his a bit closer to mine. Arden anxiously wrung his hands in front of him on one end, and I somehow ended up beside, yet further away from, Melodie. This was clearly not a multipurpose room. The fact that they actually had an area dedicated to these kinds of things told me this school had more problems than it let on. Madam Guise moved to stand not quite in the center of all the chairs, and we slowly looked up at her.

"Someone start talking... Emeline?" She jerked her head around to look at her. Emeline sucked in her breath under the glare of her grandmother. "Well?"

"It really isn't that big of a deal, Madam Guise. It certainly isn't worth missing class for," a tasteless, edgy laugh left her for all of two seconds.

"I come outside and one of my students is on the ground. That is a big deal," she snipped. "You," she pointed at me with a shaking finger. "What do you think you are accomplishing? If there is one thing I do not tolerate here, it is harassment."

I met her steel gaze with a doubtful one. She clearly took it as an insult.

"I didn't go looking for any trouble, madam," I grumbled. Madam Guise declared that the only thing she cared about was who laid their hands on someone else first. Her eyes momentarily shifted to Melodie, but then came right back to me. A mute cloud had befallen that girl, and she stared off into the distance with her eyes wide, retreating within herself like a terrified puppy.

"This isn't fair," Riley boldly intervened. "Melodie provoked it, and got what she deserved."

Madam Guise moved over to her like a serpent. "Nothing excuses pushing another student onto the ground."

Arden mumbled something, and Madam Guise promptly told him to repeat it.

"She didn't push her."

"Then what happened, hm?"

"I pulled her hair," I halfheartedly admitted. I just wanted the meeting to end, whether or not I ended up in her scary detention hall for my final week as a student. Within the next few seconds, Madam Guise had gripped both side of my chair, leaning in my face.

"I do not know or care what you could get away with in Thaltimer but here you will not ever-"

Loud knocking cut off her threat, and she quickly stepped away from us.

"You wanted me down here, Madam Guise?" I heard Mrs. Cromwell and her breathing at the door. "Or should I say you wanted me down all of those stairs?"

"Your student," she continued with an edge. "Was caught fighting in the middle of the yard."

"Which one?" Mrs. Cromwell turned her head toward Melodie, and stared at her without any response.

"Miss Owen."

"Now I doubt that," She brushed it off, looking at Madam Guise with a dubious expression.

"I saw her myself!" The headmistress asserted quite loudly, dictating her final ruling. "And considering she has been here for over a month, I would say she should know better anyway, this is entirely unacceptable. She is to stay after school for the next two weeks...."

"You are most welcome to stay here with her in a huge empty building until eight o'clock at night," Mrs. Cromwell crossed her arms. "But I am not."

Shock shone through in that woman's typically expressionless face.

"Madam Guise," Mrs. Cromwell continued, sighing. "I am with children all morning, and teenagers during the afternoon. I am seventy-one years old and you know for a fact I have been trying to retire for several years. The only thing preventing me from doing so is the school's wishes. I have also already promised to watch my toddler age grandson tonight and tomorrow night. I simply do not have the time or energy to stay here with Delilah for four hours. I truly do not think she would have started something unless she was deeply provoked, anyway, so two would have to be at fault. And would you like to tell Hal Vern that his daughter is in this room right now?"

She was quiet. I could have sworn I saw Melodie cringe.

"In that case, let us try it this way," Mrs. Cromwell looked past Madam Guise and at Bennett and Arden. She asked if the two of them were involved, and I watched Arden shake his head vigorously out of the corner of my eye. Mrs. Cromwell promptly dismissed them. Arden jumped to his feet and was gone in seconds, though Bennett hesitated, looking at me, until Mrs. Cromwell repeated herself. Once he had reluctantly gone, she moved on to Emeline and Riley, asking them the same question. Still under the stare of her grandmother, Emeline gave a polite 'no ma'am,' as Riley argued,

"Well, no, not directly, but how can Melodie get away with going around calling people Stoleh?"

I picked up the anxiousness in Mrs. Cromwell's expression, however Madam Guise made her opinion known.

"You do not ever say that again," she pointed harshly at Melodie. She appeared afraid to even attempt intimidation with her the way she did me, so she resorted to pointing and wagging her finger around in the air space between them. "You do not even realize what you say. You cannot go around saying that to people, especially with your father's position in the Guard. Do you understand that what you intend to be an insult could be taken as a threat because of it? And even not, even if he was the lowest ranked officer in the State, that race and our civilization possess no comparison, which is why the Wall and many, many miles separate us from them. Think about what you are saying next time something comes out of your mouth."

Melodie appeared to take an invisible blow of some kind with each word the headmistress said. It seemed as if I should be the one receiving those, but after my weeks here, I had become used to the way these people viewed the rest of us. It also didn't register until her fourth sentence that she was speaking of me, of my family, of everyone I grew up with and knew. Of course I hadn't forgotten who, or what, I was. Stoleh was no foreign word, but five weeks had still rendered it strange to me. I figured that would all end quickly at the first nasty comment, the first time getting roughly spit out of a moving crowd, or even the first glare.

"As far as you two go," Mrs. Cromwell continued, not making a second attempt at forcing Riley and Emeline to leave. "Stay out of each other's way. Because regardless of any hard feelings you must coexist. Let this be water under the bridge, and do not speak of it. Do we understand each other?"

She didn't seem to be speaking of Melodie and me understanding each other, but us understanding her. Neither of us responded, and they sent the four of us out ahead of them. Emeline slipped upstairs in the same stiff silence as what we were met with inside the class. Mrs. Cromwell rejoined us after a long ten minutes, once again out of breath from the stairs.

"Now," she said. I watched her intently. This was the second time she'd taken up for me, yet the first I'd really considered the fact that she had to have known something since day one. "Where were we?"

Chapter Twenty

As we followed behind Emeline into the left wing, I recognized the doors as immobile barriers we had already tried. And after spending weeks looking for our nonexistent prize, I believed we'd covered every square inch of the building. I spent the afternoon detached, wondering in which lonely, overlooked corner the secret waited. I asked Bennett why he and Emeline hadn't already gone inside, and he said they wanted to wait until I was with them.

Two staircases later, we stood in another hall, the walls barely outlined in half-lit gloom. By the time Emeline slowed in front of a door, I knew we had checked the area weeks ago.

"We've been here...." My voice trailed off when she turned the knob. No key needed. It was unlocked. Every hall in the building appeared the same to me, especially at night, yet I momentarily considered that I should've recognized the room I had spent seven hours of every day in. Emeline quickly disappeared inside, and Bennett followed, propping the door open for me with his back. We weaved our ways around six individual tables sitting there in total darkness. These inanimate, organized objects only seemed to threaten us just as every other shadow in the building. When we reached the back of the room, I began to wonder why Bennett and Emeline were acting in awe of a completely blank, stone wall in front of us. I knew there was no door. I wasn't that unobservant. Entering any hole in this wall would result in walking out onto air and plummeting from three stories up.

"Help me move this," Emeline began uselessly shoving against what I thought to be a bookshelf. It was by memory, not my eyes adjusting. I felt my way to the other side, and pathetically exhibited my lack of arm strength as the bookshelf stubbornly remained in the same spot. We didn't make any progress until Bennett took over my side. Inch by inch, the books and materials on the shelf fell to the floor along with a screeching sound as they dragged the case across the floorboards. Once they had succeeded in scooting it to my right enough to expose the wall behind it, I heard the rough thumping noise of Emeline dragging along one of the chairs to stand on. I knew what the sound was, but its suddenness in the otherwise silent area still scared me half to death. Once the small bulb above us had momentarily blinded me, brightly illuminating just that corner of the room, I finally got a look at the door. Despite being behind a dusty, metal bookcase, the hinges and knob looked as if they had been recently spit shined. The feeling of apprehension nestled in my stomach left, its sheer normalcy disappointing.

Emeline yanked the key off her neck and roughly forced it into the lock, yielding a soft, innocent click. Something solid barred the door from the inside, leaving only a foot of space. The three of us pressed against each other as we all fought for a glimpse into the plain darkness that lay on the other side.

"What is it?" Emeline withdrew. She tried to open the door the other way, but some sort of inner mechanism would not allow it. "I can't tell if there's anything there."

"It's a staircase," I answered, feeling around the entrance of the claustrophobic room with my foot. "That's what's blocking the door. It's going up."

We backed away from the opening and one another in unison. Our long pause was interrupted by a conversation moving down the hallway. A tight panic overtook me as the gibberish of distant chatter drifted into the room. After five weeks of coming and going with no problems, I knew it was only a matter of time before someone figured out what we were doing.

"Someone's here?" Bennett reasoned aloud, speaking as if it was a question, not reality. I quickly followed with my first thought.

"Where are we supposed to hide?"

Emeline tried to force the door open wider to no avail, and finally gave up, frantic.

"Here, you're small. You can squeeze through."

I wasn't anxious to be forced into a tiny space with no escape except into the unknown upstairs, which was, in all likelihood, another small, box room. For all we knew, someone else could've been up there. The scenario somehow reminded me of the shed back in Nemirena.

"You can fit too," she told Bennett, pushing us both in the direction of the cracked door. "Both of you go. I need to fix the bookshelf."

"You think when they come by here they aren't going to notice you or the fact that the door's exposed?" I asked, halfway inside.

"I'll tell you a secret. If you act like you're supposed to be somewhere and nothing's wrong, you can make anybody believe you. Just don't hang around up there for twenty minutes."

The voices turned down a different hall, away from us for the moment. Bennett forced me into the room as he began to squeeze himself through the door behind me. The moment he was an inch out of the way, the door was slammed shut from the outside. I jumped, and whipped my head around as if to ensure he was still there. I was met with an uncertain stare, and I didn't move for several seconds.

"Go on," he eventually spoke up, trying and failing to reassure me with some form of a smile. "I'm right behind you."

I turned my attention back to the staircase in front of us. Clutching both sides of splintered rails, I began to ease my way up the steps. Despite having more space, Bennett remained almost on top of me as we surfaced into more darkness. I stood there tensed in a battle-like position as Bennett walked around me and into the area.

"Bennett?" I spoke just above a whisper in the direction of the blind shuffling noises coming from the center of the room. I began feeling around for the wall, hoping at some point I'd bump into him. Before I'd moved two feet from my original position, a larger version of the lights Emeline tended to in the halls shined from the middle of the area. Its full glare was only blocked by a large, completely empty display shelf in front of me. "Bennett?" I called again, a little louder.

"It's empty," was his answer. "They must have moved everything to the other Garrison. But there has to still be something here they're protecting if they covered this place. And why would they still come through the building all the time?"

The question wasn't intended to be answered. Bennett returned to the other side of the room, and I walked in aimless circles for only a few, tense minutes, scanning the vacant room for any interesting sign. Bennett continued around the corner as I paused, and then dropped to my knees in front of a dark-stained table. The underside seemed oddly shaped, and from where I sat, it appeared to have another, separate compartment attached to it. This didn't stand out as anything important to me at first. I was distracted by the looped, red thread dangling down from its center.

"I found something," I said aloud, jumping to the conclusion. For all I knew it was nothing at all, but the pressure of our ticking clock was more than enough to escalate my desire to get in and get out. Bennett knelt beside me as I rubbed the string with three fingers, pulling it out from under the table to show him. I didn't expect another key attached to the end of the thread would fall onto the floor. We stared at it as if not sure what it was until Bennett took the string from my hand. Using the edge, he turned himself around and lay half under the table, looking up at the seemingly tacked on compartment. He first frowned, and then looked back at me without moving.

"Look at this."

I hesitated, but developed a crawling motion as I tried to adjust myself under the table. An indistinguishable noise echoed up from the bottom of the stairs, the shock causing my limbs to turn to jelly, and I fell on my back almost on top of Bennett's arm.

His half questioning, half concerned stare told me the sound had been generated by my own paranoia.

"You don't need to panic," he tried to tell me.

"If there was ever a time," I answered, trying to direct my attention back to the task at hand. I couldn't help but struggle to peer around the imposing shelf blocking my view of the staircase.

"Who leaves the key to something like this in the lock?" I thought aloud as Bennett eased the key into a lock mechanism plainly located in the center of the compartment.

"Someone who wants us to find it," he said, concentrating on turning the unwilling key to our right.

My mind immediately went to Gregory Guise, imagining the sick, old man we had seen weeks ago sneaking in here and leaving the key for us to find. Once Bennett had forced it around three quarters of the circle, something barely audible clicked from within the lock. The compartment unhinged in the front, loudly flapping its new jaw, and a large book casually slid from the inside. It landed on Bennett's stomach, and he gave a short, low sound of pain as he removed it, holding it above our heads. There wasn't much to it, although its sheer size was enough to make me wonder who in the world had this kind of time.

We wordlessly backed out from under the table. Bennett sat the book down own its surface, where we continued to stare at it as if expecting a change in the past five seconds. I moved to open the front cover, but stopped dead when I could've sworn I heard another voice. As it heightened, I wondered how any sort of panicked figment of my imagination could get louder. It took the slamming of the door below for me to realize it was actually happening. Bennett gathered the book, and before the horror had completely ballooned inside me, I abruptly seized his free arm and led us to the opposite side of the room. We quickly and quietly positioned ourselves about two feet from the exit, only the largest shelf in the room separating us from the presence. I became more aware of my breathing, thinking it might as well be shouting, the closer they drew near us. By the time they surfaced into the room, I had sucked in my breath, and stood pressed against Bennett. He shook his arm loose of my sweaty grip, and wrapped it tightly around me, forcing us closer to the barrier as if we might melt into it and disappear.

It sounded like only two people, laughing together on the opposite side of the shelf. I impulsively squeezed my eyes shut, and accidently let out a little breath. I knew it was a matter of ten footsteps before our little operation, starting as arguably innocent curiosity and ending in a heist from the Guard, was destroyed. However, when the two men entered the room, the one closest to us blocked his companion's view of our corner, distracted him with the reminiscent conversation, and picked up their pace as if eager to get to the other side. A draft from the open door blew the smell of liquor into my face. It was clear it came from the bumbling man experiencing problems putting one foot in front of the other. Bennett and I both recognized his usher, and watched, stunned, as Gregory Guise closed the table's open compartment, twisted the key, and stuffed it

137

into his pocket all in two seconds as they walked by. The other man was already ahead of him, out of view. He said something that I couldn't understand, and the old man laughed with gusto before moving to follow him. He wasn't halfway around the second shelf when he looked straight at us with a harsh, urgent stare. No one had to tell us again, and as he disappeared to the opposite side, boasting to the other man about something that had happened many years prior, we silently slipped to the stairs. We pressed ourselves against the wall on the way down, taking the steps one at a time with long pauses in between, until Emeline starkly waved us down. Once within the classroom, we spared precaution and took off running, refusing to stop until we had left the school's front yard behind. Emeline struggled to ask what we had found as she choked on her gasps for air, bracing her hands against her thighs for support within the protection of a short, cramped space in between two homes. Less than a foot separated us from her. Bennett held up the book, and she looked at it without much interest.

"Why was your granddad there?" I asked, also wheezing, just beginning to calm down from the rush of panic.

"I don't know. I told him today we found the right door and were coming tonight. Maybe he got worried and came to check on us. The man he was with is another retired Guard, a drunkard. He probably ran into him and followed him to the school. They were just talking about the olden days or something like that when the other guy saw me trying to organize everything back on the bookcase. I told him I was just doing a favor for my grandmother, and he didn't think anything was wrong with it. But he did see the exposed door."

"He knew we were there and what we had done," Bennett spoke next, looking down at the book.

"Of course Granddad knew you were there. Did the other guy see you?"

We shook our heads.

"Then we're safe. You two hang onto the book and look through it. I can't go home with that thing. Take the side roads back to your aunt's, and do not get caught with it."

With that, she wished us good luck, and jumped back into the street, pacing in the opposite direction. We watched her until she was no longer visible. Having absolutely no idea what side roads meant, we took the normal route behind the houses at a much faster, silent pace. But no matter how deathly quiet we were, it'd be a terrible joke to think we could get past Rowana. Bennett held the book behind him as we entered through the back into an empty, dark room. I thought maybe she had already gone to bed, and we shuffled across the area toward the winding stairs. Halfway up, her voice almost gave me a heart attack, and I nearly fell down the steps.

"You two," she said in the darkness, pushing past us and into the kitchen area. A lantern on the counter was lit, and we walked behind her without being told. When she turned around, she shook her head at us. "Are going to worry me sick. Why must you keep going to that school? I saw a group of Guard coming down this road on patrol, and I thought they were going to stop there and find you!"

Gregory Guise and the other man were obviously not there on business, so this patrol must have passed. But we were lucky we weren't caught on the streets if the Guard was flooding Rochonnell tonight. Without any response, Rowana's next question shifted to our only proof we had finally found the door.

"What is that?"

"Oh, uh," Bennett stammered, looking like he was going to attempt lying about it. The fact that I could already see it, and so could Rowana, only confirmed that we were sunk. "It's a, um, book..."

"Thank you, Bennett," Rowana frowned, rubbing her forehead with one head as she took it from him. "I'm not that old."

Rowana flattened the book on the table, and began to flip through it. At first her expression seemed dubious, but as one minute turned into two, she turned the pages slowly, taking in everything on the page. Her eyes were soon wide with a disbelief we couldn't understand.

"Where did you two find this?"

"The door was hidden behind a bookcase in the back of my class. That book we found in some sort of secret compartment underneath a table," I told her, knowing there was no point or reason to make something up. After another long silence, she gently lifted the book from the table. Rowana took a chair for herself, and sat down, dazed, with both her hands pressed firmly on top of the cover in her lap.

"Rowana?" I asked after a while. She still didn't move.

"We've sent spies into that building, knowing they might be hiding it there all these years. They failed numerous times, and then two children stumble across it without even trying."

"What is it?" Bennett and I asked in unison. She looked up, smiled, and held it out for one of us to take.

"I want you to skim through it. See if you can figure it out for yourselves."

Bennett did nothing, so I hesitantly retrieved the book. The two of us silently went upstairs, and paused in the narrow hallway. Before he said anything, I was already leafing through the pages. For every one filled with words, were two with intricately drawn diagrams, maps, and other pictures. Bennett and I stood side by side against the wall, trying to find anything obviously monumental. After a few still minutes, Rowana passed us on the way back to her room, brushing by us like we weren't even there.

"What do you think?" Bennett asked long after her door had closed.

"Looks like a much more detailed version of what you found on Rowana's shelf."

"But that was of the Idrisan camp," he took the corner closest to him and opened the book wider. He pointed to the small title, though I had already seen it. Unlike the rest of the steadily, carefully drawn illustrations, this was written almost in chicken scratch.

Kieriana

Before I asked, he clarified, already knowing I had no idea what that was.

"I know it's in Imperiam. If I remember right, it's the Imperial's manor."

"Have... they ever gotten their hands on something like this before?" I asked as if afraid to say the real term. He frowned, and then shook his head.

"Not a chance. They would've gone after Imperiam already."

"How would we know if they have or not?"

"Because then the Lebon would've shipped out, or every last Idrisan tracked down and killed after they lost. They would get squashed, anyway. It's not like some quiet resistance has any advantage over those people."

We agreed to take the book to Emeline tomorrow. All night, I thought about Bennett's grim, but still accurate description of how any resistance's attack on Imperiam would be dealt with, or disposed of. Needlessly stated, it seemed rather depressing. But not as much as the fact that was who we had unknowingly chosen to side with.

Chapter Twenty One

  The last thing I felt comfortable doing was taking that book, apparently a treasured breakthrough for the Idrisans, back to the school. However Rowana insisted it could not be kept in her home. It was simply that precious. In the worst scenario, the Guard would never think to scrutinize Emeline or her grandfather if, when, someone realized what was missing from the upstairs room. I secretly hoped Nicholas and Delilah would have mysteriously and tragically vanished by then.

With the book inconspicuously tucked in my schoolbag, I took the stairs two at a time up to my floor, already worried we were late for the fifth or sixth time. There seemed to be a lack of other kids in the halls. A small panic attack struck me when I realized the door to my class was closed. I braced myself for Fendrel's usual speech, knowing the morning would be spent exhaustingly writing out another selection of her choice. To my surprise, I stepped into an empty classroom. The door slammed behind me as I took a couple steps away from it, and Fendrel jumped a foot out of her chair. When she realized it was me, she regained her uninterested frown, only mumbling a short 'you're early' as I passed her. After some time, others began to trickle in, and I convinced myself the delay was a miscalculation on my part. I relaxed only in time to unintentionally eavesdrop on a regular gossip circle's conversation.

"The front yard is crawling with Guard. The little kids are still trying to get in the building."

"They were just here. Why are they coming back so soon?"

"By the looks of them, something's definitely wrong."

Horror-stricken beneath the steel mask on my face, I roughly kicked my bag under the table as if that provided camouflage. The next noteworthy person to enter the room was Melodie, and I only say noteworthy because of how different she still seemed. I thought whatever spell possessed her yesterday had carried over, and watched as she slunk through the middle of the gossip circle, breaking it up, and fell into her seat. For once not in its tight, uniform braid, her hair blocked her face for a while. However, when she moved her head to the side, I couldn't help but stare at the swollen, black eye consuming nearly half her face. I believed that, along with the bruise on her lower arm that she failed to cover up, told the story. For the first time, I felt an overwhelming sense of empathy for her. I momentarily considered that I could approach her in the afternoon, but told myself such as conversation wouldn't end in the heartwarming way I envisioned it. Her eyes locked on me for only a few seconds, and that was the only exchange necessary for both of us to get our points across.

The last one to shuffle silently through the door was Riley. For the first time in weeks, she sat down with her back to me and said nothing. From over her shoulder, I watched her nervously biting her nails, nearly shaking. I gently poked her, and she shuddered like it had badly hurt. Riley seemed to want to turn around, but she was preventing herself. When I spoke, any restraint present evaporated.

"Are you okay?" I asked her. She whipped around so that her hair licked my face as she turned. Fendrel promptly stood up, unaware or just uncaring of Riley's episode, and the only thing I understood her say through the tears was, "I'm so, so sorry, Delilah."

She eased herself back around and faced the front of the room again. Only seconds ticked by until she laid her head on the table and wrapped her arms around it, looking like she was trying to constrict herself. Inattentive of Miss Fendrel's opening into the lesson, I whispered again to Riley to talk to me. She became stone in that position, refusing. It didn't take much longer for me to figure out why.

Less than an hour later, the door was flung open. Unannounced and without hesitance, Hal Vern paraded alone into the room, his eyes scanning our faces, also undeterred by the teacher.

"Can I help you with something, sir?" she offered politely. He paid her no attention. I diverted my eyes from his iron stare, my slowly building fear spiraling out of control as he leisurely walked down the aisle between the windows and the end of the three tables nearest them. His heavy footsteps halted in the rear of the room, his presence looming over me. He waited for me to look at him with his hands clasped behind his back. I eventually did so to kill that one moment of horrible apprehension. I felt myself shaking to the core, and unable to actually look him in the eye. I faked it by looking at the crown of the proboscis cutting into the air away from the rest of his skull.

"Good morning, Delilah," his aura changed, but his horrible, bloodthirsty stare only intensified. If it had gotten much worse, he might have convinced me to shout my identity from the rooftop.

"Good morning, Sir Vern," I ran together and stumbled over my words, trying to disguise developing hyperventilation.

"Would you mind if I looked in your bag for a moment, sweetheart?"

I became engrossed by Riley's stone-like position, and barely watched as he stooped over to pick up the bag. He was nearly bent in half, and with his head almost beneath the table I thought I was safe from his wrenching glare for a few seconds. The top of his head quickly turned back into those eyes as he sharply looked up, purposely trying to absorb more of my radiating terror. I could no longer will myself to look away as he unlatched the bag with care, though already knowing of its contents. His expression didn't change as he pulled the heavy book free, and placed the bag flat in front of the girl beside me. She shrieked as he slammed the book on top of it, and then turned back to me with a new fire, instilling a new panic. Everyone in the seats around me and the seats around them jumped to their feet, screaming, pushing each other in a frantic effort to get to the safety of the front wall. Hal Vern wrapped his hand around my wrist, and twisted it in a way it shouldn't move. The immediate pain meant nothing to me. I joined in the other girls' shouting as he forced my bent arm inwards, nearly throwing me onto the floor by the legs of the tables. I began to turn the arrest into a pig wrangling affair as I kicked furiously, unmindful of the dress I wore, trying to land one blow in his gut. However, he seemed immune to me, and before I could, he had dragged me up onto my feet, and straddled me over the table. He continued to twist my arm almost to the point of it breaking, and leaned over to speak next to my ear. Before the first word had left his mouth, I burst into racking tears. The only weight they held to him was a formal admittance of my guilt. So he instead held his tongue, and started our short journey to the front of the room. Hal Vern roughly kicked my heels to force me in the direction, each blow filled with a passionate hatred. My knees had long since buckled by the time we reached Fendrel's desk. In the second he paused to recollect himself from wrestling with me, she only asked, "What is the meaning of this, sir?"

He abruptly turned me to face most of the gathered, horrified girls in the room, all of them nothing but disfigured outlines to my vision. I still knew Riley was not among

143

them. The only thought that rang loud above the sweltering panic was that somehow she had figured it out, or seen us, and turned us in. Caught here as a Stoleh spelled death with a thick, black, and clear pen. Caught here as an Idrisan was not fathomable, yet I inferred things worse than death were written in their agendas. Despite having known Rowana's affiliation, and ours as well, actually calling myself the name left a strange, all too real taste that was now bringing horrifying images of Ruth to my mind.

"I am sure you will be delighted to know that you have been instructing a Stoleh for the past six weeks," the man answered her almost nonchalantly, putting no emphasis at all upon these peoples' ultimate curse word. But his tone could draw no attention away from it, and a long, loud series of comments followed. "And not only a Stoleh, but one here doing work for the Idrisans."

Stoleh paled in comparison to the reaction that word yielded. Unaware, Hal Vern adjusted my arms to lock them behind me. The will to fight had fled my body in search of a more willing host, and only his constant upward pull kept me from falling to my knees. I was silent now, my fallen hair latching onto the tears streaming freely down my face. One of the thick, weighted manacles slapped around my right wrist, and was followed by a sharp, painful exhale from behind my head. It was tailed by a long, stiff pause ended when someone came to the side and pulled me away from him. She held me in a protective hug, but I still watched as Hal Vern crumpled to the ground, in the process hitting his head with near lethal force on a sharp corner of the teacher's desk. He struck the floor hard, one of his arms unnaturally forward as if his shoulder had in blown apart. Hal Vern was not getting up.

Mrs. Cromwell set the book and my bag down onto the table, and then held my head in between her hands. She wiped my face with her fingers, and I realized that some of the tears I felt were actually blood from my nose.

"Listen to me, Delilah. Take your brother, go out the back way, and run as fast as you both can go. Out of Ceaves, out of Rochonnell, out of the State. Do not stop and do not trust anyone to help you. Do you understand me?"

I did nothing, still breathing heavily and still recovering from that burst of terrifying adrenaline. I stared at Hal Vern, face down on the floor without any sign of life.

"He will not pursue you. His shoulder was permanently crippled from an accident many years ago, and now that entire fragile area is shattered. Your worry is all the Guard in the yard."

"How do you know this?" Fendrel spoke in almost a whimper as Mrs. Cromwell casually stepped over him, and to the back of the room. I stood unmoving, still waiting for Hal Vern to jump up at any moment as Mrs. Cromwell shoved the book back into my bag, and quickly made her way to me again.

"I told you many times, I am a people person," she responded sharply, breathing laboriously as she placed the parcel in my unwilling arms. Mrs. Cromwell urged me forward; all the way to the door until I faced the steady flow of other classes and teachers coming to see what had happened. "Remember everything I said to you. Go down the

144

front steps and straight into the foyer." The lurid sounds and voices of more Guard echoing from the other direction added forcefulness to her voice. "Now!"

Without any backward glance, I left a heaving Mrs. Cromwell in the door, and cut my way through the crowds as everyone kept their distance, too afraid to put a hand on me. They seemed preoccupied staring at the one shackle dangling from my wrist, wildly flying around by my side as I ran. I had forgotten ever venturing around the school that way before, but the loud noises of activity downstairs led me through the symmetrical building until the last staircase before the divided foyer. Halfway down, I saw two more Guard standing there, manning the area to prevent this kind of escape. They quickly turned around, not recognizing me by my appearance, but by the blood on my face. Before they seemed to process me, I took off back up the stairs as quickly as I had come. Another person waited for me at the top. Not a Guard, but Emeline telling me with more quiet gesticulations to follow her. After Riley's betrayal, I was even more hesitant to trust her. The gaining Guard convinced me I had no other option.

She led me up a narrow hall set off center in the building's structure, gripping my forearm as if I could not keep up with her otherwise. We cut around a sharp corner, walking sideways to regain some balance. Emeline directed us into a closet hidden in plain sight, the same color of the walls that surrounded it. She shut the door without as much as a vibration, and pulled me with her as she slid to the floor. We waited in tense silence as the two's footsteps grew nearer, then gradually softer until they disappeared altogether. Emeline let out a choked sigh, and reached across me. She picked up my wrist by the chain, and unlocked it with a small pick concealed in her fist. Without looking at me, she rolled the single cuff to the shadows of the opposite corner, its subtle clinking like a deafening explosion in the overbearing quiet.

"Riley spilled her guts to me this morning. She saw us going into the school at night, when she was out late with her mother. She told her dad, and then he went and reported suspicious activity to the Guard in exchange for his job back. Granddad told me they've been investigating you two for three weeks, more than enough time to brief everyone about you and gathering more than enough evidence against you and Rowana."

Emeline cracked the door, examining the outside hall before pushing it out. I stepped only inches behind her as we retraced our steps back to the stairs the Guard had caught me on a minute earlier. Before we reached them, she briefly glanced out a window that overlooked the yard.

"It's mostly clear. They have all come into the building. Bennett is with Brice. He should be long gone by now."

Equal amounts of shock and intensified fear froze me again. If he had gone, then I really was on my own. And aside from that, Emeline had called him Bennett, not Nicholas. If she knew our names, she knew everything.

"Amaryllis!" she more than snapped me out of it. Emeline pushed me forward to the stairs, and I gathered enough broken sense to walk.

To Emeline's greater surprise, they arrived from the adjacent hall as we descended into the now abandoned foyer. I jumped from the third step to the floor. He

145

picked up the pace, but under Brice and Emeline's stares and the stress of the moment, we did little more than look at each other, his gaze focused on the dried blood on the skin beneath my nose. I quickly scrubbed it off with my thumb.

"What are you still doing here?" Emeline hissed at Brice. He gestured in the general direction of the closed front door.

"That frenzy arrived only minutes after they got here. I couldn't get him out. We've been hiding out in the center hallway all morning."

"Rowana sent them to school early today so you could get him out first! If they go together, then they're more at risk."

"It's too late now. The yard's clear, but someone will see them running."

"Stay out of the back roads. If you're in a crowded place, they won't open fire," Emeline gave us a final piece of advice. I was still reeling from the idea that they had known the entire time, and worked this out with Rowana. She had to have caught wind of it, probably through Gregory, knowing the Guard would come for all of us at her home, and sent us to school early. In all grim likelihood, she had sacrificed herself for our safety. Rowana hadn't gotten us guides for the first day of school. She had gotten us guides for when this happened.

We couldn't stay in the foyer for much longer before all the Guard on the first floor made their way back to the foyer. The pounding noise and voices suggested they weren't much further away than the corner. Emeline and Brice stood side by side, in a nervous quiet, like they already thought we had a slim chance of making it out. After another unspoken goodbye or thank you, Bennett put his hand on my back and we forced open the door. A long, exposed sprint to free us from the walls of the school resulted in someone, positioned just outside, springing into the open. She was directly in front of me, and Bennett only skidded to a halt as she lunged and reached for my arm. She shocked us both, but avoiding an elderly woman wasn't as challenging as fighting with Hal Vern. I jumped back, and then made a beeline for the open gate past Madam Guise. She got a hand on me, but not a grip. Bennett stood there, shouting at me in panic as I watched multiple Guard burst out of the building in response to Madam Guise's screams.

I adjusted the bag on my shoulders as I caught up to Bennett, the headmistress moving to lead the pursuit. We took off down the street to enter the crowd, though I couldn't help but keep looking over my shoulder. The third time, just before we reached the already gaping people, I could've sworn I saw Gregory Guise holding her back, telling her *let them go.* I knew he meant us, yet the Guard could not incriminate him for anything. He could have just as easily been talking about them. I refocused my attention on the road ahead, and tried to forget about the dismissed Guard who had saved our lives as we left the Drierie School behind.

We dove headfirst into the crowd, struggling to stay together. I weaved in and out of random clusters of people, all the while trying to either keep up with or wait for Bennett. The more congested a street, the more protection we had, and so a market or bank was ideal. We still had no idea where we were going, or at least I didn't, but the crowds significantly slowed down the weighted, awkward Guard. Minutes into the confusing chase, my thighs burned, tightening and cramping as I tried to catch my breath. I could only tell myself to keep moving, even if at a hobble, putting one foot in front of the other. Bennett and I fought our ways through a line of people, and looked at each other to confirm we were both still alive. The shouting of the Guard had faded into a loud, ominous buzzing filling the air above our heads, and I had a hunch they weren't more than a minute behind us. And after so long, it seemed our luck had run out. We'd entered a part of town with only a couple odd people walking around. The Guard might've been gullible enough to believe my fake identity for years, but it was common knowledge, especially among Stoleh, that they were marksmen. Continuing straight through the nearly abandoned town circle would get a bullet in both our backs.

Bennett yanked on my arm and pulled me in between two buildings. I caught onto the idea quickly, and we started to move perpendicular to the Guard. With multiple streets in between us, I believed they had continued through the town circle, and were no longer a problem. We still didn't dare to slow down, running into people left and right trying to reach the next alley. But one person I barreled into left me lurching, and Bennett came back to drag me to my feet. He also didn't realize who had knocked me over until I gathered enough sense to run back into the mobbed street. Bennett caught up with me as the lone Guard pieced together who we were. Or if he didn't know the exact details, running from him must have implied we were up to no good.

It would seem that avoiding one Guard would be easier than losing the three. However the crowds on these streets heeded his shouts, and began receding to the sidelines. Horrified, we tried to follow. People wouldn't allow us within yards of them and continued to move away. They didn't know who we were, and were only reasoning that the Guard was after us. It still gave me the same overwhelming sense of paranoia I felt when back home: when one sideways look or false step could produce similar pursuits around the Nemiren markets. The most discouraging part was the fact that I had never, ever heard of a Stoleh getting away once the hunt started.

It didn't matter how skilled the Guard were. The man could not keep up with us while loading a gun, and for the first time the notion occurred to me that he wouldn't shoot regardless. Killing who the public believed to be two Haritite children had the potential to destroy their image, without which they had no power. Telling them our identities after the fact would always leave doubt and rumors they could not afford circulating. Of course if they caught us, we could easily be killed in secret without a care from any of these people. Putting as much distance as possible between us and this Guard helped our chances, yet it was only a matter of time before others caught onto the chase. The next person we ran into could easily be the last.

The quickly separating crowd forced us to move diagonally through the streets, spending less than half a minute in each one. I could no longer hear any signs of the man behind us, and soon recognized one particularly wide road from many weeks before. The first horse drawn cart riding in the distance validated it. Though we were nowhere near out of danger, the shortcuts we had taken led us to nearly the boundaries of the State, where Serah and Vince had first dropped us off. My relief was squashed by a harsh reality as I realized Guard combed the area whether a threat was expected or not.

No walls or watchtowers were present, but they covered every square inch of the borders of the State to prevent the entrance we won, and the escape we were now racing for. If Emeline had any idea what she was talking about, every Guard around here knew what we looked like, where we'd be going, and how we'd be getting there.

I stopped in my tracks against a building, my legs shaking, and something that tasted like blood in the back of my throat choking me. My breath came in sporadic wheezes, leaving me almost immobile after so long. Bennett stopped in front of me, trying to urge me forward, though he wasn't in much of a better condition. We hadn't drawn attention yet, but the moment we abandoned the shadow of the building would renew the pursuit. Simply waiting there was a plea for one of the other Guard to find us.

"Come on," Bennett spoke in a desperate voice. "We're almost there."

"We're dead," I choked, almost crying. "There's no way they are letting us out of here."

Less than two seconds after I'd said it, multiple people appeared from seemingly nowhere, approaching us from the left. In a panic, we tried to take off again, but I could find no more strength in my legs. They quickly enveloped us, and a man quickly took Bennett's arm to keep him from running. I hadn't yet forced myself away from the wall, and shrank when I heard him struggling, kicking at the man and trying to get back to me. I knew nothing either of us did could get us out of this, and couldn't look the horde in the eye until a stern voice told him,

"Bennett, stop fighting. We have to get you both away before they realize anything more."

I sank against the building, looking up in disbelief at Vince. The group gave us no time to process them, and herded both of us into the center. There were maybe six adults, and our conspicuous cluster walked for no more than a minute before I sensed we had raised suspicion. They picked up the pace, and the only way I kept up was a hand gently pushing me forward with every step. A sharp turn opened into the off road clearing we had been left in so long ago, and any act we were trying to feign evaporated. It was now a frenzy of getting us into one of the two carts parked there. Someone unaffectionately steered me in a different direction than Bennett, and barely waited until the last of the group had swung themselves over the side before giving the loud order to drive.

The cart pitched into the street, and everyone immediately hit the bottom, barking at me to follow. The only person still erect was the one frantically pushing the horses onward. From what I could tell, they weren't steering, people were running out of the way. It wasn't long before the firing began, and not much longer until I heard echoing, high-pitched screaming. The cart in front of us didn't slow down, and neither did we, so I figured the victim wasn't among us. What felt like an eternity later, everybody sat up again, and looked behind the cart. I forced myself up on one arm, still struggling to breathe, and peered over at what I could see of the Haritite State. As we left it behind, I could see many Guard gathered at its borders, watching us escape. There was no more shooting, no effort at all on their part to stop us. They acted as if an invisible wall prevented them from taking one step outside of the State.

The woman forced me back onto the cart, and who I originally thought was Serah revealed herself as a complete stranger.

"Relax," she said. She could tell my shaking anxiety wasn't left within the borders. She was right, and it was now mixed with the uncertainty of not knowing who had miraculously come to our rescue. Vince, driving the other cart, was out of sight, and I only looked around at people I had never met. "Guard stationed within that place cannot so much as take a step outside of its boundaries without permission. Another weakness of its system. We should be nearing the camp by tomorrow morning."

It took a long time for my breathing to return to normal. Half an hour later, I sat up and watched the four people near me. They returned my ambiguous stare until I shrugged my bag off of my aching shoulders and dropped it in front of the woman.

"We found it in the Drierie School," I couldn't think of any words to explain exactly where the book was located. The woman looked at her companions, and then offered me a fake, half smile without taking the bag.

"We'll worry about it later, dear. There will be plenty of time to discuss what happened."

Somewhat frustrated, I handed her the book myself. She politely took it, and flipped to a random page. Her expression and tone immediately changed, losing the tenderness. She passed it to the man in the corner.

"Scour that thing. I want to know every important detail by the morning."

"Done, Madam Hanchoré," was his answer. He immediately began from page one, and Madam Hanchoré, presumably the same Allyson, did not speak to me after that. People began to write down nearly everything the man said, and only after noon had passed did someone acknowledge my presence. The driver of the cart turned around, momentarily placing a hand on my shoulder and delicately rubbing my arm.

"Like I told you, Mr. Johansson would not have sent you if he thought you were incapable."

I said nothing. Serah turned her attention back to the long, undefined road ahead.

Part Two

Chapter Twenty Two

Hal Vern maintained a constant staring contest with my bowed head as we left the Haritite State. Our wagon had no tarp, no way to conceal my isolation. It rested on oversized, spoke wheels at a lowly five or six feet from the unpatched road. Each miscalculated turn and sudden movement made by the clearly inexperienced driver left me shaken, if not on the bed of the cart. With no useable hands to help myself, I became at the mercy of a young Guard who viewed me as nothing more than a piece of meat. Despite all his brutality, every time I was thrown off the raised bench, he harshly scolded the driver, demanding he stop cutting the corners. I almost would have preferred to keep my head down. I had no fear of these people. It was simply the shame of letting them get the best of me.

On the entrance road to the Etairan Mountains, multiple children leisurely wasted time, throwing what looked like tomatoes at the side of a tree trunk. The moment our rickety cart approached them, the boys' target became my head. It took multiple shouts from both the Guard and driver for them to laugh and disperse into the dark, surrounding woods. Only one had a good arm, and his rotten projectile remained latched onto the side of my face for a while as if sucking blood. I shook my head violently, and it slowly slid from its site, falling into my lap.

Less than half an hour following the children, Hal Vern had left me in the hands of two much more aggressive Guard. I felt their hatred for me in the bite of their push and step on my heels. No one bothered to unchain my uncomfortably bound arms that forced me into a slouching position. They left me in another darkened cell, not looking back. In deep contrast to the filthy, crowded Haritite jail, these people kept us separated and left no unturned stones where anything could be hidden. As I came to learn for myself in the few days that passed, this was a place for people on a long, long waiting list for execution, perhaps the only place on the island where Stoleh, Nemirens, and Haritites were treated as equal scum to the Etairan equivalent of Guard. Yet it was only a stop for Idrisans. As the Guard made well known, I was their only one. I existed almost entirely alone for the next two days, and only once did a female Guard, with no less harshness than her male counterparts, come in and pitilessly unlock my wrists. I welcomed the mobility and relieved pain, though the next moment I was pelted with two stale pieces of bread from the opposite side of the bars.

The cell block remained completely empty during the time I spent there. I was later assured on my way out that the wing was only for Idrisans. Here they would wait indefinitely until they had caught enough to send out to Imperiam. When I learned that twelve others preceded me in this fate, my heart sank deeper. I debated with myself if that treacherous bastard had a hand in their capture and eventual execution as well.

I was led through the prison halls, around cell after cell, forced to look at all the hopeless occupants. A bitter wind stung my skin the moment we stepped outside. It blew in from the sea, and swept up the side of the rugged mountain, dipping down into the corkscrew path leading from the prison to the dockside. The bodies of the Guard herding me further and further down shielded me from the worst of it. Though there were no more chains, almost every other step we took was trailed by another push forward, and into the Guard in front of me. I spent most of the long, silent journey being roughly tossed around amongst the four, until Hal Vern plucked me from the center, and dragged me by my shirt in front of them.

"Walk," he instructed, pointing in the direction. I looked at him as if I didn't understand. He forced me around, and gave me one final, halfhearted shove. "I said walk."

An impressive, swaying ship waited docked against the pier. I heard the activity aboard, however the rocky sand was bare, crunching under the heavy footsteps of the Guard. The other three stopped dead halfway to the pier, and Hal Vern took the leap from acting as if he had a shred of humanity, to going out of his way to make to paint a picture of malice for those awaiting us. As he shouted up to someone on the deck, I stared out into the churning sea, the smell of salt opening my eyes. Imperiam was an unclear, remote land off on the horizon, waiting with eager eyes and ears for our arrival. I had only heard and dreamed of the horror that awaited an Idrisan in Imperiam. Nothing could undo the damage now except agreeing to give them information. Jason, and who knows how many others, succumbed to that deal. I was already convinced nothing they said or did could turn me into the traitor he had become. Even if I was the only one killed.

A dockhand poked his head over the side of the ship in response to Hal Vern's shout.

"You were supposed to be here days ago," he yelled from his perch, frowning.

"I had to turn around and go back to the State. I have another one."

"There are only supposed to be twelve."

"She got here just in time, then," his voice left a chill traveling down my spine, though it truly didn't matter anymore. A minute later, locked beneath the deck in a humid cargo hold, I believed I and these other twelve people I recognized and loved would literally never again see the light of day.

Chapter Twenty Three

Traveling during the night enabled us to reach this illusive camp by the late morning. However, I had long since fallen asleep and didn't get the opportunity to see how Idrisans managed to enter the Wilds unnoticed. Instead, the familiar, low hum of a bustling crowd caused me to turn over and bury my face into the pillow. It was almost as if I'd just realized I was awake, and I sat bolt upright. The folded, wet cloth draped across my forehead fell into my lap. Wringing my hands nervously, I surveyed the room. If one thing was immediately apparent, it was that we were nowhere within my known world. The tent was made of a kind of rough canvas, deep, dark red in color. It was propped up by several wooden stakes, stabilizing it. I sat on a framed, metal cot, the mattress stuffed with a kind of straw similar to what we had behind the Wall. I kicked the woolen blanket off of me and moved to stand up.

"Do not rush yourself," someone placed a restraining hand on me. Startled, I pulled my arm loose, and faced the direction of the voice. In a chair directly beside the bed, sat a medium-height, medium-weight woman in her forties. Her eyes were set far apart from one another in her head, and seemed melancholy along with the other features of her stress lined face. Still, there wasn't one gray in her straight, dark hair. She pushed it behind her ears, and looked at the beaten down earth that served as a floor. It took that long moment of silence for me to remember she was Allyson Hanchoré. "How are you feeling?"

"Fine," I let my head fall into my hands, propping myself up against the uncomfortable, metal frame.

"Is your head hurting?"

"No," I lied, and another stiff pause wedged in between us.

"I expect you have many questions," she shook her head, and the sound of a choked laugh came from the back of her throat. I knew I was supposed to, but nothing would come to my mind. "As I am sure Gerald told you, I am the one who was originally going to receive you and Bennett in the Haritite State."

I only nodded, and after several seconds asked what had happened to fill the space.

"My father had me work in the State for years. He was very sickly, so I had to disappear from my forged life there and return to see him. He passed away around the time you and Bennett arrived at Rowana's doorstep."

I didn't know how to respond to that. I had been pulled into these conversations all the time in the streets of our borough, and had learned that sometimes it was best to say nothing.

"So as his only child, I had to take up the position. The others here with influence, those with Mr. Johansson's rank, did not like it at all, but they cannot change the fact that my father never had a son. In fact, Gerald was the only one who supported my return to the camp to inherit the title of Idris."

I couldn't help myself. "You're Idris?"

"I assume the name came up during your six weeks in the State. It is simply a designation created to pass through my family line so our real names are unknown. However within the camp, my father would simply laugh and demand people call him Theo," she smiled at this memory, but dropped the subject as if afraid of going off on an emotional tangent. "As you can imagine, it took a while for things to settle down after his death, and they still are. I was fighting with the others over being my father's

155

only living child when word came from Rowana that somebody had reported you both to the Guard, and we needed to come get you before things got out of hand. Unfortunately we could not find a clear path out and had many delays along the way. All that matters is we reached you before they did."

I wondered if she knew about the incident in the school, but another, more important thought occurred to me before I opened my mouth. "Where's Rowana?"

She frowned and looked away from me. I immediately assumed the worst.

"Rowana Laurie is a very resourceful and clever woman. I know she is capable of fending for herself. We will continue to communicate with our other correspondents to see if there is any news of her once we get ahold of things here. Now stand up," she instructed me, but still waited by as if expecting me to fall. "Hurry and get dressed. You have people practically in line to speak with you."

Only a minute after she left did I notice Delilah Owen's schoolbag waited on another stool in the opposite corner. Beneath it was a folded pile of normal, if not rustic, clothing. I was eager to hide any remnant of the Haritite State. Wearing a cream colored shirt with an open, deep red sweater buttoned halfway in the front, I shoved the wrinkled, unfolded uniform into the old schoolbag. Everything was still there except for the book, and I found myself staring at its contents as I struggled to fasten boots beneath the wide pant legs. One brighter object inside caught my eye, and I slowly took it from the satchel, turning it over to the front.

I was so enthralled by the image, I wasn't able to figure out what I actually held for several minutes. The colors appeared like those of a stained glass window, arrayed from the pinks and yellows on the left and transitioning into the teals and purples on the right. Small, oval shapes which looked like individual eyes appeared on every feather-like object attached to a green chested creature. I didn't know this animal. It seemed like an oversized, dressed up pheasant with small antennae for hair.

Inside, the journal was lined with darker blue pages, which opened to reveal over a hundred sheets of paper. A thin ribbon serving as a page marker led me to a tiny note pressed between the cover and the first page. I peeled it away, and immediately recognized the drawing, torn out of its original place. I could almost feel the Lebon equivalent of Guard standing in the background. They were probably laughing, joking, and making conversation with each other as their prisoners stood in front of a bare background, being painstakingly drawn. My eyes impulsively shifted to Ruth, though I couldn't maintain eye contact with her hostile image. Beneath the picture, a scribbled note caught my attention. I was almost surprised it wasn't in the easily decipherable code.

Amaryllis,

I found this sifting through a pile one day while you were at school. I planned on saving it until the day you and Bennett were picked up, and I'm sorry that did not go as smoothly as we all hoped. I pray for your safety and that you are receiving this at the camp.

During your time with me, I watched you two dutifully fill those moleskin journals Serah and Vince gave you. I thought you could use a new one. If nothing else, I want it to remind you of your stay here. Do not worry too much about me. I'll see you soon.

The lack of a signature led me to believe she had scribbled this in a hurry, and slipped the journal in my bag the day before. In a pointless effort to deny my own panic, I told myself she had probably not signed it because it wasn't necessary. Hesitant to leave behind my only remnant of Rowana, I carefully placed the journal in the bottom of the bag. I began to carry it outside with me, only to uncaringly throw it to the side seconds later. A colorful journal meant nothing to me now. The flap of the tent had been reopened without warning by my little sister.

We wound up on the floor right in front of the entrance. I buried my face into her hair, ruining her perfect braid, crying and thanking the otherwise empty tent many times.

"Who are you talking to?" she looked up at me, her face free of any tears. Though once she saw the state I was in, she quickly abandoned her long standing strong act. She tried to pull away several times, I could tell she wanted to talk, but I simply refused to let go of her. Eventually, she moved her arms up to take down her single plait, forcing me off.

"I'm fine, Arlie, stop," Rose said with a bothered, crooked smile as she re-tied her brushed hair half up, just enough to draw it away from her face. She wiped the skin beneath her eyes with a certain degree of harshness that made it seem as if she was reprimanding herself. I knew she couldn't stand to see me that way, and tried to do the same.

"How did you get here?" I asked her, the thought just coming to mind.

"It's a long story."

"The long stories are the ones that define us," I tried to form a similar half smile. I was quoting our older sister: the one thing she had said before she left that had struck us both. "And meaningful stories are the only ones we should ever be interested in hearing."

"Amaryllis," her tone, and just the fact she had used my real name, wiped the already weak happiness from our expressions. "I don't know what happened to Uncle Graham and Aunt Clarissa, or the boys, or Stella and Barney, or anyone at all."

She hid her face in her hands as if trying to gather the composure to continue. I had already reached out to her, and we sat huddled away from the tent's entrance. I hugged her beside me again, and she almost instinctively formed a freakishly long legged person with her index and middle fingers. She had him pace in a never ending circle around my knee, occasionally switching directions or continuing backwards. It was a nervous twitch, something I had believed her to have outgrown many years before, which signified she was going to ask or speak of something serious. The last time I had seen her do it was three years prior, probing an unwilling Ellamae about our mother.

"It happened the evening after you left. Uncle Graham, Aunt Clarissa, and Niles hadn't come back yet... I didn't know why," her walking man became lifeless and limp, and she began speaking in a detached haze. "Oakley and I watched them march in from the window for a couple seconds. I took him and we hid in their room, behind the sheet. The Guard didn't come into the house this time, but we heard a few shots, they're so much louder right outside, and all the shouting and commotion. They must've stayed for half an hour, and then we thought it was safe to leave," she stopped in the middle of her explanation, nearly trembling at the memory. *A Cleansing*, I thought bitterly to myself. *The last time they came to our borough was eleven years ago, and they had to show up during the six weeks I wasn't there to protect them.* I reasoned in the following seconds that it had been dumb luck they didn't ransack the house, or they would've found and most likely taken either Oakley or Rose or both. My being there wouldn't have solved anything. And the idea of our aunt, uncle, and other cousin left to fend for themselves in the middle of the street all but painfully eliminated their chances.

"I told Oakley to stay there, but I know he didn't listen to me, and I went out to look for everybody," she worked herself up to continue. "I didn't find them anywhere near the town center, or Uncle Graham's work. Then a man and a woman with no patches approached me.... I guess they thought I was some lost kid. They introduced themselves as nothing except 'people here to help us find our families.' Both of them kind of freaked me out and I said I didn't want help. The man told me I looked like someone he knew and asked for my name. I don't know why I didn't lie, but then he spilled everything. His name's Gerald Johansson. He said he's the one who sent you to the State to begin with. I-I made him stop by the house before we left, but Oakley wasn't there."

Mr. Johansson's presence behind the Wall did not alarm me in the same way it would have before knowing the truth. His motive, I questioned. But the concern over that topic came nowhere near surpassing a rapidly building bleak scenario of what happened to our already broken family. The only definite was Oakley, and left alone, I doubted his ability to last. Our list of relations was short, and even they would not jeopardize their own direct family for his sake. The only thing that could keep the instinctive fear away was forcing myself to disregard our last experience in a Cleansing. The Guard never took their operations by a set of rules. Our survival depended solely upon their home life and mood swings the day of the brutal attack.

Rose seemed close to her breaking point, the anxiety boiling over into the room and leaving an overall miserable feeling behind. She brought the topic to an unsettled close by mumbling, "Mr. Johansson's waiting to talk to you. That boy is already with him."

"Bennett?" I asked, though it was obvious. His whereabouts hadn't occurred to me until then. Rose stood, and extended her arm to help me up. I ignored it, and once I barely passed her eye level again, she looked behind us at the entrance.

"Whatever. Almost everybody who wasn't born into the camp used to be a Nemiren or Haritite. Nothing's changed that."

Rose ducked through the flap and left. I trailed her, and was caught in my tracks by the blinding sunlight outside the tent. The word 'camp' had painted an image of organized tents surrounding a fire spit in my mind. This was no camp; the Idrisans lived in a civilization all their own. Pitched shelters scattered the area, though they were outnumbered by impressive log cabins and outdoor working areas. Children congregated to play with polished marbles and chase each other through the wide arteries of the settlement, while a diverse adult population moved along, conscious to avoid them. Out of the corner of my eye, I watched a man lead an imposing, dark colored horse with a long, matted mane and tail into what appeared to be a large stable, and then come back out and lightly kiss a woman rationing supplies to a line of people. Everywhere there was activity, though order amongst it all. I couldn't see any boundaries to the camp. It continued on in every direction, though from where I stood, it seemed the structures and crowds were more focused in its center. I remained there, stunned by the dynamic atmosphere. It was almost like a rural, but equally lively Haritite State.

Rose beckoned me toward her, walking away. Before I moved, a little ball made of hide bounced and hit my leg. I studied it, until a young boy ran up to me. He paused, and we briefly stared at each other. Anywhere near the Wall, he would have run away and told the Guard, meaning I needed to cover my face and get out of there within the next few minutes. Instead, the boy held out his hands, bracing himself to catch the ball. When I continued to stand motionless, he looked at me in confusion.

"C'mon, throw it."

Under his stare, I reached down, and tossed the ball back into the air. He smiled again, and took off with his toy and another cluster of kids. Rose walked back toward me with her hands in her deep pockets. She removed one, and tapped a blank spot on her shirt, indicating the absence of a class patch.

"No Stoleh, no Nemirens, no Haritites, plus, more importantly, no Guard," she said, and began to pull me along behind her. "You'll love this."

We weaved our way through a thickening crowd to the center of the camp. Buildings slowly adapted a more circular arrangement, unto what seemed like the very heart. The bustling crowds stopped just beyond the final ring of cabins and tents, all under the shadow of one of the rare two-story structures. Ten enormous tables, thin but long, rested low to the wet grass, with five or six people maneuvering their ways among them. An overwhelming aroma emanated from a stumpy, one-room building directly beside and angled toward the large one. It combined the scents of many foods, making all of them near indistinguishable. Rose walked ahead and up to a light-brown skinned woman with chestnut hair. Upon seeing her, the woman carefully positioned her short stack of plates on the lowly table and enveloped her in a hug with her long arms. I clumsily followed Rose's path around the tables, and stood behind her. The woman steered us out of the other peoples' ways before speaking.

"What brings you up here right now, Rosalie? Didn't I tell you not to worry about helping out today?"

"I wanted you to meet-"

"Oh, everyone already knows your famous sister," she winked from the side, and then turned her head to face me. "You two made the biggest breakthrough in our history. That's why we organized this whole thing."

My blank stare was my response, and she gestured behind us at the tables.

"Tonight's dinner is for you and Bennett. We haven't done anything like this since before Elena Hanchoré, bless her soul, died. That nervous wreck daughter of Theo's wanted the camp to know about you, so don't be surprised if she makes you speak."

The outwardly put together nervous-wreck-daughter promptly left the main building, noticing us almost immediately. She wordlessly moved to the side and propped open the door, signifying that I was to follow her. She allowed Rose to accompany me for only a few seconds, and then stopped her with a shake of her head. Knowing she was no longer beside me, I turned around, cautious, though all she did was give me a subtle, innocent thumbs up and walk off with the other woman. After they had gone into the building producing the smell, I followed Allyson Hanchoré inside.

She immediately veered to the right and stopped at one of the many closed doors. She motioned as if to knock, but appeared uncertain as to whether or not she should touch it. Madam Hanchoré resolved this by cracking the door open for me, and fleeing into the adjacent hall. No sign of change came from within, and so I slowly pushed it open as if expecting a battle to ensue from the other side.

It was the first time I had ever seen him cry. Mr. Johansson sat across from him at the small table, his hand on Bennett's arm, speaking just above a whisper. Bennett's entire body shook, and he refused to look at his father. Neither of them acknowledged my presence until what sounded like a forced end to the conversation.

"Mom didn't die because she was sick, did she?"

"No. She was caught during the two weeks you were with your grandparents. To protect you and me, she lied about where she was from. Under any other circumstances, she should have been taken to Imperiam as an Idrisan, but I think the group of Guard who found her were acting on gossip. Instead of sending her off and risk being wrong in front of their betters, they decided it would be easier to kill her in Nemirena. I heard all this through Olivia, though, and she couldn't have known the entire story, either."

"So is there a chance she's still alive?"

"I really don't think so, son. If the Guard sent her anywhere, then word would get out and someone would have told them about you and me."

Shaken and at a loss for words, Mr. Johansson motioned me into a chair between them. Bennett sat with his fingers interlocking and pale, beholding the floor until his could regain his composure. His face was scarlet, though when he looked up, there were no signs he had been in such a state except for his bloodshot eyes. Pretending as though the talk had never happened, Mr. Johansson brought the topic to a permanent close by leaning forward, just as his did back in Nemirena, and staring intently at as both.

"Which one of you actually found the book?"

"She did," Bennett's voice broke in the middle of his sentence, and he breathed deeply. During this, Mr. Johansson turned his head to me and demanded, "Where?"

I didn't know how to explain a hidden compartment attached to the underside of a table without it sounding like the whole thing was a lie. "There was a-"

"I don't care about the details. Was it in that school?"

I nodded. "The door to the room was behind a bookcase."

"If I were Allyson, I would think again before sending out the same scouts. Their training should allow them to locate something poorly concealed by a shelf. Nevertheless, parts of the book are in the process of decryption as we speak, though their code is much more complex than ours. Allyson will ensure the information is transposed in several other places, and then the original will be burned. You two were our last mission to the Haritite State. Only our remaining correspondents will stay."

"When will we know what happened to Rowana?" I cut in, hopeful that he would have a more pleasant outlook on her situation.

"Once the Guard knows an Idrisan is stationed there, they will stop at nothing to apprehend her," he crushed more than my faith, he blew my entire image of her to smithereens. It suddenly felt like my only connection to her was that journal, just as my last shred of confidence in my aunt, uncle, and cousins stayed firmly wound around Rose's account. "Unless she has already found a way out of the State, her chances are very, very slim...." his voice trailed. He exhaled slowly before continuing. "This is a threat we accept, and everyone here knows the stakes. It happens too often to many good people, whom we can never get back. I do not want to tell you Rowana is now at the lacking mercy of the Guard. However, it is news you must be prepared for when it arrives."

I failed to find any words that could uplift the circumstances. It sounded like this was a regular tragedy, watered down to the point where it seemed a normal fact of existence. I could relate with my childhood and recent past, though Bennett seemed stricken by the idea of the outspoken, nurturing woman we had known enduring torture we could only imagine from the safety of the Idrisan camp.

"There are a few people you need to meet. After some time here, the rest will fall into place. Allyson should be waiting for you across the hall. You will find her and the others."

He didn't officially dismiss us, though it was clear our cue to leave had come. Bennett hastily jumped up and paced into the hall. Mr. Johansson sat with his arms now folded, staring blankly out the window.

"Amaryllis," he spoke without looking at me. "It is very important you address Allyson as Idris, and Idris only. There are ignorant people here ready to cause an uprising because she is a woman. She only allows those she trusts to call her Madam Hanchoré, and fewer by her first name. Unless she tells you otherwise, just say Idris."

I agreed, though he seemed too detached to hear. A nagging question made my voice a bit stronger, and I asked, "Why were you in my borough?"

"The Wall is a rather easy place to get around if you know the blind spots. When we hear of a Cleansing, those of us in Nemirena always follow to do anything we can for the surviving victims."

"Thank you for bringing my sister here."

"Yes," was the answer, and I closed the door behind me.

"Bennett?" I broke into a trot to catch up with him. Before we reached the corner, I had placed myself in his path for the purpose of asking a question with a predictable answer. "Are you okay?"

"Fine," he began to rub the side of his head like it hurt, but I knew it was an excuse to look away. Something inside my chest tightened with a familiar pain, and I hugged him. Bennett seemed to be in some state of shock. Eventually, I felt his arms come around my back, and one hand momentarily clutch the ends of my hair.

"I'm so sorry, Bennett. I know how much it aches."

"It hurts more to know he's lied my entire life. I couldn't not believe him when he said she died that quickly, all while I wasn't there. I knew she would never leave, so I just accepted it," he said without much emotion. The remark bled with an undeniable resentment, and I reasoned that no response could change what happened. Voices within a nearby room forced us apart. The head of a strange man emerged from the doorframe, and, seeing us only standing there, he impatiently snapped his fingers at us as a signal to hurry up.

162

Allyson Hanchoré, Idris, was seated at a table entirely cloaked by an ornate, crinkled map of some kind. Several other motionless statues of people stood around her. She appeared perfectly comfortable under their stares, and gave no sign she had heard us enter. The man with the unkempt, graying moustache slammed the door, and the entire room jolted.

"Emmitt," she said, unmoved. His bushy eyebrows rose as a reply. "Be patient with them. They just came from the Haritite State yesterday, after a rather terrifying chase."

"I'm aware," his husky voice responded. "A terrifying chase, without a doubt, and as consequence to the mistakes made, a life has probably been lost."

He directed this at us as if we were responsible. The way he stood over a foot taller than Bennett and glowered convinced me of it. Allyson was quick to rebuke him, though it didn't seem to matter in his eyes. This man wore a faded, long sleeve and high collar shirt, navy in color and adorned with unpolished copper buttons running along each side of it. The jacket alone gave me the impression that he was someone of importance, and seemed sardonic of everyone else's ordinary clothing. It took Allyson's small, deliberate cough to refocus everyone, particularly me, back on her.

"Bennett, Amaryllis, this is Emmitt Detate," she separated herself from her intense study of the map, and pointed a careless finger in his direction. His posture and expression remained steel. "He is our ocean general, meaning he oversees every mission we must take out at sea."

Ocean? I thought to myself. Spending my life surrounded by buildings, trees, and the Wall made it difficult to envision any sea within miles of civilization. Idris presented the other three men and two women as generals of something or posts, the heads of correspondent and Idrisan activity in a particular area. It was implied, but she still felt it necessary to explain that Mr. Johansson was one of the main posts on the pastoral side of Nemirena. Approaching the end of her introductions, few of which I retained, Allyson forced the light onto Bennett and I.

"We are nearly done transposing the contents of the book you found. With that information, I am going to launch another mission. I want you two to be involved. Whether or not you actually go is entirely dependent on what you can show us you are capable of," she paused for several seconds, her attention drawn back to the map. She dragged her hands across the paper in a futile effort to smooth it, and then unrolled another one previously concealed in the coiled ends of the first overtop.

"Come here and look at this," she said, and all of her generals and posts moved to allow space for us. An almost ovular shape drawn with an unstable hand rested in the center of the map. Within it, a series of scribbled names, dates, places, and various indications of landscape were positioned according to an elaborate scale on the bottom left corner. A much bigger mass seemed to be in the process of engulfing this isolated land, and was sketched with several coves and drop offs around its borders. This angry-looking place possessed much more detailed scenery and indecipherable labels over practically every inch. The added routes and figures placed out in the surrounding nothingness only added to the confusion, connecting nearly every location on the larger land. "Do you recognize this?" Allyson asked as I absorbed the drawing. Bennett gave a slight nod, while I could only stand there and pretend I had any idea what this map illustrated.

"Amaryllis?" she waited for my answer. Under the gazes of all those people, I felt beyond stupid as I forced myself into shaking my head. Allyson didn't seem exasperated by it, and sensing my discomfort, she began to temporarily speak in a more sensitive tone of voice.

"Let me see if I can help you, then," she let her hand drop to the table, outlining a general area touching the eastern border. "We are somewhere around here right now. The Haritite State is," she drew an imaginary, diagonal line with her finger four or five inches. "This area here. Nemirena, the scattered Haritite neighborhoods, and markets are about thirty miles east and take this entire region. The Stoleh Wall is just to the north of that. And the Etairan Mountains take up this whole peninsula way over here," she picked up her finger, and severed the area from the rest of the island. "Do you understand?" she verified, and I mimicked Bennett's original answer. Apparently not convinced, her next statement was directed at Emmitt Detate. "Let her go see the coast."

The idea of going anywhere alone with him already scared me, after the way he had accused us upon walking in the door. Idris had to repeat herself before I listened.

He marched down another hall and through a back door with his hands clasped behind his back. I broke into a near run to keep up, though still mindful to keep my distance. It didn't take long for me to realize we were approaching one of the stables. Though comfortably warm outside, the ramshackle building's humidity almost outshined its odor. Each compact stall held its antsy occupant so tightly that the horse barely had room to turn around. The only human presence besides our own came from two familiar people attending to two familiar animals. Serah noticed me first as I caught the closing, oversized door Emmitt Detate had surprisingly neglected to hold open. She did little more than secretly wave. Vince gave me a small, encouraging smile, and the two went about their business with the horses.

I trailed the pacing general to the stall in the farthest corner, which was twice the size of any preceding it. The reason appeared to lie in the fact that its tenant seemed much larger than the others. Its freshly brushed coat was mostly white, tinted somewhat brown by the surrounding, kicked up dirt. Only down by its hooves, two large spots on its back, and one small area above its lip were naturally dark. As I looked at her, she seemed to be staring right back at me, silent and still. Emmitt Detate positioned himself at the animal's eye, and swung himself over the gate. Making his way to the saddle mounted on the back wall, he never took his hand off of the horse. The first thing he said came long after he had saddled her, and stood bent over cleaning her hooves.

"She did not want you to leave because she thinks you are incapable of understanding. Her intention is to allow you and Bennett to develop separate skills so you can complement each other better if you are chosen for this suicidal mission she has in her head. Of course you both must learn to ride. I trust you have never mounted a horse before?"

The meaning of every word after suicidal ran together. I backed away excessively as he opened the gate with one hand, and led the massive animal with the other. I followed by the horse's rear and through the back door, which was propped open in an ineffective attempt to air out the stable. We emerged into a manmade, though horse-trodden, path veering sharply to the left into the surrounding forest. Emmitt led the horse into the open, just outside the entrance to the trail leading deeper into the Wilds. He held her reins firmly, one hand on the back of her neck, and watched me. He seemed to be waiting for something, and only after he patted her again did I realize what he wanted me to do.

"I can just walk," I stepped back from the horse as she ducked her head forward, snorting loudly as if impatient.

"Abiona is a big girl, but she's calm and experienced with the inexperienced. I must teach you how to ride, and she's a good starting point. I will lead her," He turned Abiona's side toward me, and held out the reins. "Hold these in your left hand. Place your left foot in the stirrup, bounce up, grip the saddle, then swing your other leg over."

I slowly, almost shakily, touched a bare spot on her back.

"You will unnerve her like that," He pushed my arm away from Abiona. No words of reassurance followed, and I dug my nails into my palm before reaching out to her a second time. Emmitt said nothing as I carefully followed the instructions he gave, struggling to gather the momentum to propel myself over Abiona.

"Was that so difficult?" he said before I could get situated in the saddle, still sensing my tension. I now looked down at him from the back of this large horse, having no idea how to handle her. "I will lead her," he repeated, quickly taking the reins from me and moving in front of her neck, mostly out of my sight. A few steps later, the last thing he spoke from over his shoulder was, "If you feel unbalanced, hold onto her mane."

Afterwards, I lunged for and held onto Abiona for dear life, unable to observe, much less appreciate our surroundings until the distinct sound of crashing waves reached us. Emmitt abruptly turned to the left, and stopped on a small, protruding peninsula no more than twenty feet across. The dizzying, rocky drop felt as if it were directly below Abiona's hooves as he walked much too close to the cliff for comfort. He turned us in a wide circle as if giving me the opportunity to see the vast, violent ocean for myself. The closest thing I could even compare it to was a small creek within a wooded area close to the Wall, where Niles and Oakley went to skip stones when their parents turned a blind eye. The overbearing smell of salt awakened my numb senses, gluing my eyes wide to absorb more of the sheer expansiveness. I had never given a thought to what was beyond our twisted society, or even how many miles the closest refuge might be. As we circled back around to face the way we had just come, I couldn't help but wonder why all these people didn't just get in a couple boats and sail away.

Emmitt brought Abiona to a halt, and gave me further instructions as to dismounting her. Regardless, I almost fell for fear of the nearby drop off. Leaving Abiona unattended, he walked dangerously close to the edge, bearing the ocean with a modest scrutiny. He clasped his hands behind his back again.

"She knows better than to walk off," he said without looking at us. "You cannot see it from here, but to the left is a secluded cove where we dock our ships. It is curved inland, a long, twisted channel hiding it from any Lebon ships. They do not view us as any threat, anyway, so they do not set out looking for us with the same vigor as before."

I hesitantly left the uninterested horse and walked to the other side of him, conscious to keep a reasonable distance from the plummet of at least two hundred feet.

"Why did we come here if you can't see the dock?" I asked, trying to speak over the waves.

"The idea wasn't to show you the dock. The ocean is humbling."

I didn't give much thought to that, though I sheepishly felt as if he had somehow infiltrated my mind with his next sentence.

"And hopefully it gives you some idea of why we do not all abandon ship, if you will, and leave the island. This place means more than a forsaken splotch of land in the middle of nowhere. Running away solves nothing. As long as the Lebon retain control, our people will be endangered for generations to come. The one thing you must know above all else is that we are all here for a common purpose, regardless of our differences. Everyone, whether they be here or stationed hundreds of miles away, continues to risk their lives in hope to one day reclaim Capria Rodalia."

"What is that?" I asked without thinking. There was no response. His eyes stayed locked on the ocean, accompanied by a deep frown. Without warning, his gaze switched to me. I couldn't help but shudder slightly as I tried to avoid that seemingly harsh, and too familiar, stare.

"How much do you know about the history of the island?" he asked. I suddenly feared the truthfulness of everything I believed I knew. His following tone led me to believe it was a lengthy, complicated, and unhappy story.

"The invasion of the Lebon can hardly be called an invasion. I would bet money that anything you have ever heard was overdressed and distorted by the ages and by the version they have spun. Of course they were aided by our own people. The web of connections is sickening. The truth is quite simple, though. The Lebon never came prepared for war. It was almost an overnight takeover, the majority of the population not even aware of their presence, much less assumed rule, until months after the fact. It was no difficult feat considering at this point the land was little more than a few unorganized villages and assemblies. That occurred centuries ago. During all this time, progress has been nearly nonexistent, as the Lebon did everything in their self-given power to ensure any connections we may have had were severed, so that we literally vanished from the face of the world. All resources that had the potential to be turned against them were exhausted. Years passed where the only social contract present came in the form of the extensive gap between the privileged and the poor," He stopped to draw a breath, a large one, and then let it go. "Calling the first several Imperials benevolent is an overstatement. However, they were so deeply sunk in greed and ensuring continued reign of themselves, their families, and the rest of the Lebon that they basically let the Guard and what would now be considered the Etaira govern. Five

166

or six rulers of the same bloodline passed until one, his name both unimportant and a disgrace, lured his adult son into a heated, violent argument."

"Why would he do that?" I couldn't fathom any reason why somebody would purposefully draw their own child into a fight. Emmitt shook his head.

"Some say he was simply insane. No one here will ever be able to understand why he did such a thing. It is no different than why his successors have done the same and worse to those they call their people. That man ended up slaughtering his son. He later addressed the other Lebon, claiming it to be a horrible accident, and shifting the blame onto a random servant. That servant was executed, and the son buried in secret. Aside from the pain he immediately caused, this was a time when Imperials did not have many children. Now his only heir was his second son. He was a spineless and brutal person: an already deadly combination intensified by bitterness toward his father for killing his brother. This Imperial was the first mistake in a long, continuing line of them. A weak, cruel ruler is always followed by a weaker, crueler one. His heir introduced the idea of the classes, though the details and organization the way they are today were not present until his grandson. The Wall took fifty years to build, consuming most of his reign. His death created a rolling, accumulating ball of bloody snow, as then a real revolt erupted from seemingly nowhere when the rest of the peasant population learned of exactly what these illusive conquerors planned to do. Its intensity was short lived, as we had few weapons, and fewer ways to sustain a militia. Nothing really resulted of that rebellion, except the Lebon's final and permanent assertion. As the years passed, more than Cleansings and the death hour were created. The Nemirens must now give more than half of what they earn in tithe, and bad seasons can leave them in terrible situations. The Haritites who enter the State are confined to the State and any step outside its boundaries is considered a crime. I do not mean to say that the Stoleh have not been made targets of most of their senseless wrath. I truly feel as if they believe we are all guilty of hurting them in some way, blindness instilled in the Imperial by his predecessor. Each and every one is literally born into folly. Its system is on the path to complete destruction, which will then undoubtedly result in a massacre. It's the only way Acwel Aloysius knows how to handle a situation."

He once again shook his head with rigor, as if his formal disapproval reached the Imperial himself. Emmitt ended the history lesson by taking hold of Abiona's reins. She appeared just as eager to get off of the seemingly shrinking peninsula as I.

Chapter Twenty Four

Ten long, low tables scarcely seemed enough to accommodate every last person. Yet somehow, they managed to cram the entire population into the heart of the camp, though more than half of who attended were left to stand. I sat on my legs to separate myself from the wet grass and dirt beneath. As the area's claustrophobia grew, I noticed everyone else seemed to have brought a blanket of some kind to sit on. I immediately felt even more out of place at the first table, situated between Rose and Bennett, which was clearly reserved for people of more importance. Across from us were Gerald Johansson and Emmitt Detate, in what appeared to be a disgruntled silence, among many of the less than enthusiastic others who were introduced earlier. Idris herself was the only one who remained a strict recluse, refusing to associate with the incoming people. Just a strawberry-blonde, tall, indifferent girl beside her seemed to have or desire that honor. As the smells and sounds of the abundance of food seeped into the area, I struggled to pry my clenched, sweaty hands away from my knees. I felt much too close to these strangers, and they were not at all subtle in their disapproval of my presence, of Bennett's presence, and particularly of Rose's. Only juggling two completely different conversations with my sister and Bennett could keep me from giving my seat to someone else.

To my surprise, the meat had no layer of crusty salt to scrape off, and the vegetables had not one rotten spot to eat around. No rationing appeared present as people passed the bowls down, scooped what they wanted, and continued the process.

When one became empty, it was quickly replaced by the efficient, large group of servers. People also didn't bother to wait for anyone around them, and commenced eating immediately after their plate was full. Despite our location and the other occupants' statuses, our table was one of the last to receive a heaping platter of brown rice, glazed with some kind of sweet-smelling sauce. The side plates of pork and assorted beans and peppers followed in from the previous table almost instantly. I took little of everything, and only to please those across us. Rose, on the other hand, seemed completely uncaring of their unattainable sanction. She took nothing except a smaller piece of meat, and two rolls of bread when they came around. I couldn't tell if she was just unused to the bounty, or if being among these people unnerved her that much. After I noticed her pattern, I scooped more rice than I knew I could stomach, and pushed more than half of it onto the corner of her plate.

The only thing that seemed under close watch was the distribution of wine everyone, including Bennett, Rose, and I, was allowed. I didn't know how to explain to someone clearly so accustomed to this why a sixteen and a thirteen year old did not drink. The same woman Rose had introduced me to earlier discretely made her way behind the two of us. I realized her presence only after she placed one hand on each of our shoulders. My head snapped back, and I impulsively moved away from her as she spoke to Rose.

"You don't have to drink it. Not many young people like the taste. You will see what it's for."

A few minutes later, someone else brought the three of us a different glass filled with water.

About halfway through the dinner, they lit a large, contained bonfire off to the right side, illuminating the area before us. Its heat was tiring, and its light blinding. In response to it, Idris pushed herself up from the ground. The crackling fire drowned out the crickets, and cast an eerie shadow of her as far as the third table. Her eyes momentarily scanned the rows of people. Most of them had their backs to her until she began a short, unfeeling greeting, and quickly turned the speech over to Mr. Johansson.

"For those of you who don't know him, Gerald has been stationed in Nemirena for more than fifteen years," she clarified before returning to her seat. Mr. Johansson earned a warmer reception, given in the form of their attention and brief, scattered applause.

"It has been a long time since I have seen most of you. The reason for our gathering here tonight has gotten around by now, or at least part of it. My son, Bennett, and his partner in the journey, Amaryllis Carter, spent six weeks in the Haritite State, and made a discovery many have pursued for years. With this information, we are now able to continue with a greater, more productive, mission very soon. Bennett?"

He little more than looked up at the imposing height of his father. He watched Bennett with a patient expression for a few seconds, and frowned down at us once he realized we were not joining him. Mr. Johansson instructed him to stand up. That was all it took for Bennett to hesitantly obey, and he turned around to halfway face Mr. Johansson, and halfway face the crowd. I remained glued to the ground, and it wasn't long before Idris stepped in, adopting the same tone in which she first spoke to me outside of the Haritite State. "Don't be shy, my dear."

I stood slightly in front of Bennett. No matter which form it took, this kind of exposure felt like a particularly cruel method of public humiliation. The gathering gave no response, their gazes dissecting us for more than thirty seconds before Mr. Johansson spoke again.

"Tell them exactly what you two found."

We stared at each other, clueless. This yielded the first reaction we received from the camp as a whole: laughter. Our demeanors were apparently readable, and everyone as far as I could tell chuckled dryly at our failure to identify what we had found. Even the first table, behind us, couldn't resist. I almost felt myself turning red, and developed an acute interest in my shoes. Bennett eventually mumbled something, unheard by the rest of the gathering. Mr. Johansson silenced them with a large sweep of his hand, and proceeded to scold them like children.

"I know they are young. However, you must listen to what they say. Bennett, speak louder."

"You said it was an atlas of some kind."

"An atlas of what?"

"Imperiam?" he answered back as a question.

"Where in Imperiam?"

"The Imperial's manor."

Any trace of amusement in the air left at those words. Based on the new impression they gave, I figured they were told the camp made some kind of huge breakthrough, but no specifics.

"Kieriana," Mr. Johansson gave them a more recognizable term, initiating the widespread murmuring. "This book is more than scattered maps. It is a collection of everything ever learned from our missions, dating back to the early days of the Idrisans, and information long overlooked. It contains copies of entire Lebon documents, and specific cultural ways, though those are in all likelihood dated. We cannot find any indication of an author, leading us to believe it is simply an accumulation, seized around two hundred years ago. Another century and a half passed before we even realized its existence, and during that time, much damage was done. Entire chunks of the last section are missing, and perhaps the most crucial map gone as well. There is only one reason why the Guard might not have burned it entirely. They hoped to find something within its pages that would lead them to us," a continuous, variable sound of resentment echoed back to him. He continued over the crowds' voices. "Once they realized nothing could benefit them, it was locked away for later examination, and its worth forgotten. Forgotten, until the day the Guard began investigating two children reported for suspicious activity at the Drierie School."

I forced myself to look over my shoulder at Mr. Johansson upon what seemed like the conclusion of his speech. Bennett and I eagerly followed as he began to return to the table. Emmitt Detate moved to take our place, and to his blatant irritation, Idris stopped him. I froze in a position halfway to the ground as she said, "I want you to tell them a little about your story, Amaryllis. They need to hear it."

She had not spoken loudly, yet I couldn't help but feel as if the entire camp heard.

"My story?"

"Of the four thousand people involved with us, only about a hundred are Stoleh-born. Of the five hundred people here right now, less than sixteen are, and none of them are open about their pasts."

I immediately turned to Rose. She also seemed at a loss, though one thing was clear. Idris had planned this. The only reason Rose and I were tolerated at her table had to do with our troubled roots, and her wish to use our story as motivation for her currently unwilling followers. I feared the possible consequence of refusing, though it still couldn't have been worse than being "open" about my childhood to five hundred outsiders. I shook my head, wearing a strained frown, though she seemed determined to make me talk.

"Please, they need to hear what goes on behind that Wall firsthand."

Still standing, I knew those closest to us now expected something from me. Nearly shaking and already flushed red, I stood straight and took in the many blank, waiting stares. I received no laughter, though I stammered gibberish for a long time before I could formulate a truthful, but not too revealing, account. I began with the simplest fact, speaking quickly to just get it into the stale air.

"I-I'm Stoleh-born." My entire explanation abandoned me the moment I realized I had grasped both attention and genuine interest. I now had no idea where I was taking this, and looked back at Rose as if her nervous expression contained the answer. Long, painful seconds of silence passed before I could bring myself to continue. "Most people are aware of the restrictions the Wall sets upon us... and the consequences of being late. But few know the hell that breaks loose in every borough behind the Wall at some point or another. The Guard call it a..." The word wouldn't leave my mouth. "A Cleansing because they consider it an easy method of population control. I was orphaned at the age of five along with my two sisters during one of them. They took our mother from us, and we received word much later that she had been killed. My father is being held in an Etairan prison, awaiting his execution for saving me and my sisters from meeting her fate. We were taken in by my mother's sister and her husband. They have two sons of their own, and my uncle is a clerk for the marketplace. He makes more money than most of our kind, but not enough for all seven of us. I have watched so many families break apart simply because they couldn't afford to stay together. Convinced this would not happen to us, I grew into the habit of stealing from various markets and areas in Nemirena. It became my second nature for six, seven years, until it finally caught up with me in Mr. Johansson's fields six weeks ago."

I stopped myself short. An urge to continue nagged me, though I knew I had gotten much more personal than I originally intended. So I remained there, standing, isolated, until a gangly man with brown, slightly wrinkled skin and long hair tied behind his head stood without announcement from the next table.

"My name is Claude Baki, and I am Stoleh-born," he clasped his hands anxiously in front of him, and spoke loudly to the ground as if trying to recall an agonizing memory. "My wife and our unborn child fell victim to a rabid fever that spread across our borough due to the horrible conditions in which we lived."

Another person, a young, pale woman with fiery hair, spoke shyly from a crowd of those who were standing.

"My name is Alanie Fay, and I am also Stoleh-born. I left the Wall permanently and found an Idrisan post shortly after my teenage brother was beaten to death by a group of drunken Guard for no other reason than the patch he wore."

"My name is Diane Fidan," an older woman spoke from almost directly beside her. "I am from the borough that was burned to the ground fourteen years ago."

Two more Stoleh seconded her. Five different people then covered every aspect of our society, ranging from our decrepit living, to the lack of any medicine, to shootings at the Wall after eight, to the terror that befalls a borough during and after a Cleansing. I watched in amazement as each one of them shared only a few sentences, and inspired the next one to follow. That one man had come to my rescue when I could find nothing else to say, and initiated it. Rosalie soon stood beside me. She said nothing, but absorbed the stories of our people as they spoke. Us twelve Stoleh held the attention of the entire camp. Despite the horror each individual detailed, I couldn't help but feel a sense of reassurance that Rose and I were not alone there.

However, the last person to speak grabbed my attention, and we stood there in a still shock. I quickly, impulsively, wrapped both my arms around my little sister as a young woman with straight black hair and piercing green eyes stood from one of the farthest tables. Despite the distance, her appearance was clear, and her voice crisp.

"My name is Ellamae Carter, and I am Stoleh-born."

I comprehended nothing she actually said. All I knew was she continued with a similar, more detailed, account of that morning eleven years ago condensed into only a few sentences. Riding on her last word, Gerald Johansson stood to regain control of the gathering. All Stoleh slowly receded back into the surrounding crowds, including Ellamae, without as much as a glance in our direction. Rose seemed ready to jump over the table to run toward her, and only my protective, restraining hug kept her beside me. I sat with her on the ground, both of us continuously looking over our shoulders in the general direction of our older sister, unmindful of Mr. Johansson's speaking. I remembered Bennett's presence after I felt part of his leg against me. In my concern about Ellamae and Rose, I had sat down closer to him than I thought. His knew something was wrong, though I didn't know if he could put the pieces together based solely from our conversation back in the jail. "My sister," I mouthed. He looked past me at Rose, and responded,

"I know she is."

"No, the girl who just spoke," I whispered, staring back to the sea of people that blocked my view of her. "That's my other sister. The one I told you left us two months ago: Ella."

He followed my intense gaze at those behind us. "How did she get here?"

I wanted to know the same. More importantly, I wanted her to explain why she got up and left with no word, no anything. Who had she met that dragged her into this?

"You have heard it before, and now you have heard of the cruelty from those who endured it firsthand," Mr. Johansson's voice momentarily divided my attention. "The Lebon and their puppets in the Guard have tried to convince the public for centuries that they, and they alone, provide the framework our society so desperately needs. They say they caught us as we fell, and restored order and union to an alienated land." His heavy fist cut through the air as he brought it down, looking like he would pound the table into the dirt if it were high enough to receive its impact. By now, his face was red, and he shouted over the crackle of the fire, "Show me, where is the union?! Where in the Haritite State have we heard of neighbors being neighbors, as opposed to always looking for a way to step onto one another? Where in Nemirena have we seen a successful worker able to show his achievement before the Guard take more than their portion to send off to Imperiam? And where have we not seen Stoleh treated and often killed like animals unfit to live? Show me, where is the order? The system of the Guard is so hopelessly corrupt and weighted by a person's status, a Stoleh caught conversing with a Nemiren is imprisoned for fifty years the same moment an influential Haritite pays a fine for slitting a man's throat. Is this the kind of framework our land deserves?"

An extensive silence echoed back to him, his only response the wildly churning, happily crackling flames.

"Centuries they have kept us within their rule, centuries we have allowed it, and centuries they have convinced us that we are not all one people. Etaira, Haritite, Nemiren, and Stoleh, what defining power are these titles unless we succumb to their authority? The Lebon have stolen what cannot be stolen from us. We are all traitors to what our ancestors founded our home to be! This land is not merely an island they can take from us. It is our children's birthright!" He paused momentarily, recollecting himself. "A sense of duty calls everyone here tonight to take it back for those unborn, those deceased, and those alive. Bennett and Amaryllis were our last mission to the Haritite State. Only our posts will remain. Yes, because the Guard have finally started to wise up and become a threat, but it goes much deeper than that. We have not been unhinging Imperiam the way we would like to hope by these intelligence missions. With the information we have gained today, we may stop nipping at its heels. Now, we go for the throat!"

A much more zealous crowd cheered as one at the mention of this. Amongst the frenzy, Emmitt Detate finally got his turn. He rose with his wine cup in hand, and then held it up as everyone else mirrored him. Not as much of a passionate speaker, his calm, serious voice resonated off the surrounding buildings and left a strong seal on Gerald Johansson's statement.

"To Capria Rodalia,"

"Capria Rodalia!" the camp chorused, and everybody took one, long swig of their wine.

I shuddered when Bennett tapped me on the shoulder. He appeared just as lost as I was, though I figured our minds wandered in two different places. Under the pressure of Idris's watchful eyes, we reached for our water glasses at the same time, pausing as we held them. Bennett shrugged, and silently clinked his glass against mine. He then reached in front of me slightly to do the same with Rose. She stared first at the cup, then him. Ever since we had sat down, she remained in a stiff, unwilling quiet toward everything he tried to say to her. A small smile now spread across her face. Their toast marked a truce in an unspoken conflict.

Chapter Twenty Five

Following another painstaking hour, hordes of people stood at once, leaving the widespread mess of the dinner behind. Only Idris and Mr. Johansson remained at our table, and he was required to step in when the Stoleh who first spoke, Claude Baki, walked right up to where Allyson sat and began a new scene. He accused her several times of lacking empathy, '*to force a child to address the entire camp about an event as horrific as a Cleansing.*' She calmly responded to his anger, saying she wanted the rest of the camp to understand the suffering we endured behind closed doors.

"We are not a bunch of victims," he spat back at her from behind Gerald. He then shoved his hands in his pockets, shook his head at the ground, and vanished into the crowd. Shaken, Idris examined Rose and me as if we were suddenly interesting creatures to her. She waited for a rebuttal of his claim, one that would assure her she had done no harm. Both of us remained silent as our eyes desperately combed the population for a sign of Ella. The only reason we hesitated going to her immediately following the toast was a stare from Idris that forbade it. No glare alone could have kept me from leaving. Only Rose's point that we'd draw a lot of attention kept me at our unwelcoming table, anxiously glancing over my shoulder every ten seconds. By now, she had to have left her place. As the minutes ticked by, I couldn't help but wonder if she was even looking for us.

Before long, the area was clear except for the five of us and the workers, beginning to tend to the unveiled, hopeless tragedy left for them. The paths leading away from the area were vacant. A still, almost eerie silence enveloped us as the ghost of the lively dinner lingered. Ellamae had gone.

"Where does she live?" Rose demanded of Idris after she came to the same conclusion, and she only held up her hands.

"I just returned from my position in the State six weeks before Amaryllis. I do not know your sister. I have never seen her here before."

Rose turned her attention to Mr. Johansson next. Before she spoke, he gave her a similar, crushing answer.

"And I have been in Nemirena nearly ever since Bennett was a toddler. Last time I lived here, the camp was half this size.... It is strange, though, newcomers do not simply walk in and become accepted. If we allowed that, we would have Lebon spies consuming us from the inside out. I don't know how she got here. Somebody already in our ranks would have to bring her."

A not too subtle presence nosily picking their way through the wreckage echoed from behind us, calling out the names only a handful of people could know, "Arlie! Rose!"

Ellamae made no attempt to reach us at the first table. This did not matter to Rose. She was on her feet and running in a matter of seconds, with me close behind her. If Ella were strong enough, she would have picked her up and spun her around. Instead, she clutched the back of her head, and held her there tightly. Rose absorbed the moment, and squeezed her eyes closed in a useless effort to prevent tears. Meanwhile, I stood by, watching, until Ella finally looked up from our younger sister and held one arm out to me. I was nearly her height, and so her grip loosened on Rose as she stood a bit straighter. Ella's hair was unwashed, but brushed, and pulled back away from her face. She wore a mid-length skirt and an elbow sleeve sweater of knitted cotton, which smelled exactly like the garden it had come from.

"So, I've heard bits and pieces," she gently released us, and pushed some dangling bangs behind my ear. "You went to the Haritite State and found what's left of the Atlas?"

"What are you doing here?" Rose gave me no chance to answer.

"It's a long story," her voice trailed off. I thought it ironic to her philosophy. Ella was never one to leave it at something like that. A story, no matter its length, she would tell. She had never kept anything from us, or so we thought, until the morning she left. Not only that, Ella then tried to completely reverse the question. "When I told you to never let them keep you from living your life, I didn't mean go get involved with the Idrisans."

"You're here. You're involved with the Idrisans," Rosalie frowned and folded her arms across her chest.

"What else could pull me away from you?" She tried smiling. It quickly evaporated when she realized Rose was anything but amused. The three of us waited in an uninterrupted silence until the reason for her sudden departure made himself known.

He joined our triangle from the path behind Ella. He appeared in his twenties, and stood nearly a foot taller than her. Everything from his sharply cut hair to the way he walked gave the impression of menace, though he smiled slightly beneath the light stubble beard. He looked down at us, and we only watched him, silent.

"Rose, Arlie," she began the worst introduction of the day. "This is Jonathon."

He grinned at us again, though the only response he received was Rose's sneer. I struggled to inhibit my own when his hand slowly, slimily, reached around Ellamae and rested near the top of her hip.

"I've heard a lot about you two," he was forced to pick up the one sided conversation. I doubted the statement's truth. "You've been here for less than a day, and you're already well-known, Amaryllis."

"I guess so," I broke my gaze, and stared at the ground. It took no time for me to notice the tips of Bennett, Mr. Johansson, and Idris's shoes stopping beside us. Ellamae was quick to introduce herself to the twos' questioning stares. Jonathon followed, though neither of them seemed at all friendly. When Jonathon shook his hand, it appeared Mr. Johansson's grip tightened to iron, not letting him go.

"You look familiar," he observed, not at all in a good way. His stare studied everything about him, and I noticed now Jonathon tried to avert his eyes. "Have I met you before?"

"I don't think so, sir," he answered politely. This calmed none of the reserves Mr. Johansson clearly had about him. "I have lived in the camp for several years."

"Your face," he spoke almost in a growl. "It reminds me of a bastard I saw once many years ago."

He released Jonathon, who recoiled slightly. Ellamae, taken aback, felt the need to introduce him a second time, as if to clear up any case of mistaken identity.

"This is Jonathon, my fiancé."

"Your what?" Rose held back no trace of horrified shock. "You're nineteen!"

"I'm twenty now, Rosalie," her soft expression hardened at us both.

"No, you're not," I frustrated her further with my equally serious voice. "I know when your birthday is. You're not twenty until next winter."

Ellamae shifted her weight to her other foot, and shamefully moved her hair away from her face. Mr. Johansson quickly forced the unwanted focus onto Jonathon.

"So, boy, how old are you?"

"Twenty seven."

"You look young for your age then, excuse me. How did you become involved with our camp, Jonathon?"

"I lived on the industrial side of Nemirena for about twenty years. I got into some trouble with the Guard because I couldn't meet the tithe while my mother was sick. The man I worked for settled the debt. He eventually confided in me that he was a correspondent, and had to return to the camp. My mother had since passed away and there was nothing left for me there. I came with him."

"With Eric, then?"

"Yes, sir."

"The Eric I knew would never risk his position and identity like that. He's long since returned to Nemirena, though it should not be problematic to send him a letter to validate your story. Good night to you all."

Mr. Johansson turned on his heels, and sharply motioned for Bennett to follow him. We exchanged an uncertain glance as he followed, and they disappeared into the same, two story building. Idris in turn attempted to repair a bit of the damage.

"Gerald never took well to newcomers without someone here to affirm they are legitimate. I'm sure he meant nothing by it."

It sounded to me as if he meant everything by it. Every word he said already blared resentment toward Jonathon. This seemed obvious to Ellamae, who kept looking up at him as if to confirm he remained the same person during his thorough questioning.

"Nevertheless," Idris coughed once. She gestured in the direction Bennett and Mr. Johansson had gone. "Amaryllis, you are going to stay here. Your sisters can come as well."

"Actually, madam," Ella stammered as Allyson turned toward the building. Rose took a very personal dagger at her objection. I felt the only thing left in my power was to discretely reanimate her walking man, and run from her fingers to her wrist. "I will walk with them, but I have been-"

"Is it too big a sacrifice to come stay with your little sisters?" She asked sharply, placing emphasis on our broken relationship with her. "And I don't know how long you have been here, however only family and married couples are allowed to live in the same home. For spacing reasons."

Neither of them dared to give a response. As Idris quickly retreated from the scene, Rose, in a trance, followed. I couldn't bring myself to look Ella in the eye, and caught up with her. We didn't see their goodbye. Our hint was the long thirty seconds that passed before Ella's footsteps halfheartedly pursued us.

The room had one, high window, and only two bare mattresses raised above the floor by thick slabs of wood. One for a single person, and another that appeared made for a person and a half.

"There are blankets in the chests behind each bed," Idris spoke as she closed the door. It was clear she knew something of the war that would ensue the moment she left.

Ellamae forced a smile, and moved in an attempt to hug us together again. She paused, nearly in shock, when Rose spat back at her, "You left us for him?!"

"Before you get too upset-"

"In case you haven't noticed, I already am! *Married,* Ella? He's eight years older than you! He's got a stubble beard like Uncle Graham!"

"It was a sudden thing, okay?" she retaliated, cornered, looking down at us both with a condescending stare. We were no more than a few inches shorter than her, and our unforgiving silence did not bode well. "I met him outside of Nemirena last year, and then he was called back to the camp."

A realization rapidly soured one of the more pleasant memories I had of Ellamae. Last year, when she abruptly became concerned with my dealings in the markets and fields of Nemirena, Ella had walked with me every day with her own homemade Haritite patch. I didn't know Stella or Barney yet, and her excuse for following me was an older sister's worry. She would only leave after I discreetly slipped into the woods, and find me shortly after I made my way back. I had never given a thought as to what she did during my absence. The timeline she now spoke of perfectly lined up with a secret meeting between the two of them, all while I literally risked my life for our family.

"And so that justifies you dropping everything, including us, and just vanishing one night?" Rose angrily addressed the ceiling, and then covered her face with her hands to hide the expression upon it. "And who called him here? Nobody's ever heard of him!"

"This Idris just got here after being stationed in the Haritite State for years. She doesn't know anyone."

"That's not the point," I mumbled, Rose shouted. "You just," she continued, almost in furious tears, "got up, and left. You gave us no reason in your letter. Were you content to just run off with this guy and never see us again?"

"It's more than that.... You-you wouldn't understand...." her voice became quieter.

"A forbidden romance between a Stoleh and a Nemiren," I shook my head, in disbelief. "Then the Nemiren turns out to be an Idrisan and the Stoleh just abandons her miserable life to follow him with no consequences. No one could write a better fantasy! And that's why it's a fantasy, not reality. You don't do that to your family. You at least have the guts to tell us to our faces!"

179

At that, the door quietly creaked open. The absolute last person either of us could bear to see at the moment stood there, waiting to be invited inside.

"I just came to say good night," Jonathon half smiled, though he quickly felt the tension in the room spiking at his presence. I could no longer bear it with fake composure, and silently pushed my way past him into the dim hallway.

In the absence of the fire, the air developed a harsh bite the farther I walked from the building. I burrowed my hands under my arms, taking out frustration by digging my nails into my flesh. The liveliness of the camp was drained by darkness, only senseless conversation emitting from within individual homes. Light was provided by these log and stone, cramped houses until, one by one, each were extinguished. Soon it seemed as though the lights went dark due to my presence, and I shuddered as I walked by. With every step, I tried to find a thought to replace Ellamae. The only one with the magnitude was a wavering image of Uncle Graham, Aunt Clarissa, Niles, and Oakley, all of whom I could barely hope slept behind the Wall right now.

The next sound to reach me seemed like that of a struggle. Barely audible, it was nothing but a few, aggravated grunts with long pauses separating them. The owner of the voice was female, and it didn't take long for me to pinpoint exactly where it came from: the only lit building in sight. One window was left wide open, and the temptation too great.

Her back was to me, though I immediately thought she was the same girl Idris had spoken to throughout the dinner. She stood alone in the center of an almost entirely empty room, engaged in combat with an imaginary opponent. Her blade stretched longer than her arm, the hilt natural in her hand. She wielded it in slow motion, skillfully measuring each of her movements with that of her adversary. Unaware of my presence, she continued this for a while before abruptly jerking back and lunging, another short, angry sound leaving her. In the process, her long, strawberry blonde braid flew from around her shoulder and brushed against her face. The girl, irritated, forced it behind her again. She gripped the sword, reached for her hair, and blindly chiseled away at it until more than eight inches fell to the floor, and her now shoulder length braid unraveled and fell in front of her face. I hadn't seen any change in her stature, but apparently she became mindful of my company as she hacked off more than half her hair. I nearly had a panic attack in the seconds that followed.

"What the hell are you doing? Are you asking to get minced?" she stormed from the center of the room, slicing the air once with her weapon, to the opposite side of the glassless window. Though a wall still separated us, I backed far away, stammering.

"No, I'm sorry, I-"

"Get out of here and go back to the Hall," she nearly snarled at me. "No one's allowed out after this time. They'll think you're some Lebon spy. Not that a Stoleh thief is all that better."

I remained glued to the ground, almost afraid she would walk outside swinging that sword around.

"I said scram!" The girl lowered her voice to an urgent whisper. She slammed the internal shutters closed, and no further sound came from within the stone cabin.

It was then I became conscious of my own surroundings. In a heated state of mind, I walked much farther from the building, the Hall, than I planned. I truly had no idea where I was, and retracing steps I had taken blindly seemed impossible. I now felt consumed by the camp, continuing on in a random direction in hopes of finding a landmark. After several minutes, I came upon a carefully constructed fence wrapped around an empty, weathered field and dark shack. On the opposite side, it met the Wilds that isolated us from the rest of society. I found myself drawn to its expansiveness, and leaned against the fence, propping my head up in my hands. The deafening silence echoing back to me from the Wilds made it difficult to fume over Ellamae and panic about Uncle Graham, Aunt Clarissa, and the boys for that one short moment.

"I didn't think I would find you here," a voice jolted me back to reality, and I almost fell forward over the fence. The darkness rendered him only a moving shape until he joined me. He wore the same navy jacket as before, blocking out the cold that seeped into me with every breeze. Emmitt Detate stood by me, examining the same field, but remaining a considerable distance away. I immediately slipped into an apologetic state, concerned I was outside when I shouldn't be.

"You couldn't convince me you were some kind of spy if you tried," was his answer. "And as you can infer, I go out for walks during the night as well." He paused for a brief second. "I see you've met Joana."

Surprised, it took me some time to realize he was referring to the aggressive girl with a love for deadly blades.

"How did you know?"

"You look like you've seen a ghost. I can't imagine another person who might be outside of their home this time of night... one who's capable of frightening someone to that extent, at least. She is an interesting one. Brilliant mind, and no ability to interact with anyone except Lukas. He's nearly a brother to her, and he mellows her out a bit when he can. Otherwise that girl is a neurotic disaster waiting to happen. In many ways she is like Idris. Allyson raised her to the best of her knowledge. Joana is not hers. The only thing we have ever known about the family she came from is her birth father's last name, Armin, because she was rescued as an abandoned toddler. Allyson was only twenty three. She had no business trying to care for a baby. Joana bound Allyson to the camp until the child was old enough to be self-sufficient, which she learned quickly. Growing up, Allyson insisted she be trained in combat. She devoted herself wholly to it because it is a release. Joana has much bitterness centered around her birthplace. It did not help at all when Allyson was sent to the Haritite State when she was thirteen. It was Joana, not Allyson, here to watch the man she called her grandfather slowly degrade into his deathbed. Six weeks ago when Allyson returned was the first time she had seen her in four years."

If I took away the sword, I could faintly see Rose left to fend for herself the way Joana was at thirteen. The image seemed almost as scary as it was cruel.

"The past several weeks have drawn themselves out much too long," he held his hands behind his back again. "We have all been on edge since Theo passed away. Gerald and I haven't been on speaking terms since he arrived back from Nemirena, but tonight he asked if I would also watch that Jonathon man. He acts like this with every newcomer he comes across here until he can confirm they are who they say. From the sound of it, you share his hesitance."

"You could hear us?" I grimaced at the ground.

"The entire upstairs could hear you. Mostly your little sister. I understand Ellamae disappeared and left you two a note explaining her absence."

"That note shockingly lacked information about Jonathon," I whispered spitefully to myself. Emmitt overheard.

"Well, she is nineteen. Therefore, justly ignorant. I highly doubt she will go through with it. You have every right to be angry, but try to show her some patience. You must ask yourself if you are willing to sacrifice your relationship with her over one bad mistake."

I gave no sign I had heard him. It was a thought I couldn't bear at the time.

"Do you know your way back to the Hall?" he dropped the subject. I shook my head. "Then you best follow unless you wish to spend the night in the horse's stable."

Emmitt started purposefully down the path he had come. I once again broke into a trot to keep up with him.

Inside, I opened the door to near blackness. I felt my way around the area until I found Rose. She appeared to be asleep, and as my eyes adjusted, I made out Ellamae's steadily breathing body across the room in the other bed. As I silently slipped off my boots and sweater, Rose turned over and looked up at me.

"He tried to say something to me," she dared to whisper only after I pulled the blanket back over both of us, and adjusted my pillow closer to her. "I left and walked around the building for five minutes until he came out."

I breathed deeply and shrugged my exposed shoulder.

"We can't do anything about it, Rose."

"I know," she looked over her back without moving as if she could see Ellamae. Rose shortly gave up and closed her eyes. "I'm glad you're okay. After the commotion around here, I worried they wouldn't even get to you in time. When are you going to tell me about it?"

"Tomorrow," I smiled weakly, and picked up her hand beneath the blanket. "Now go to sleep, you little felon."

Chapter Twenty Six

Unwelcome sun filtered into the room through the tinted glass window, the sudden light creating dancing, red circles across my closed eyelids. I laboriously sat up and rubbed them away. As my senses returned, I realized Ellamae had already gone, leaving a neatly made bed behind. Rose, clutching the end of her pillow, was still asleep. I began to slowly move out from under the blanket, and adjusted it around her. She turned her back to the light as I laced my boots and covered my exposed arms with the unbuttoned, red sweater. I sat on the edge of the bed, huddled in the middle of the warming sunlight, continuously looking over my shoulder at Rose. A light knock on the door interrupted the silence.

Before he spoke, I impulsively held a finger over my mouth. Bennett backed up to the opposite wall, and waited as I closed the door.

"They're waiting to talk to us."

"Who is?"

"I think it's just Allyson and that ocean general. They sent Dad out this morning with a couple others to see if the regular path out of the Wilds is safe. He won't be back until tomorrow, but he told me to tell you to watch out for your sister."

I glanced over my shoulder at the closed door, though I knew he meant Ellamae. The thought gave me a momentary chill, and I nervously dug my fingers into a section of hair near the back of my head. For the first time in years, I considered how matted and straw-like it looked. "What does he mean?" was the only response I could manage.

"I don't know. He's suspicious of her fiancé, but he wouldn't tell me why. Some of the other people said he always acts like this, so I wouldn't worry too much about it."

The word fiancé seemed to drive iron nails into my skin. I walked beside Bennett down the stairs, and to the same room as the day before, where Emmitt and Idris waited in an uncomfortable silence. I immediately assumed something was wrong, and wondered if one person living in this camp got along well with everyone.

"We were hoping to take you two around the camp today," Emmitt took several steps away from Idris, in some state of exasperation.

"You are going with Joana and Lukas," she was quick to follow.

"I have to respectfully disagree. They don't know their ways around the area yet."

"It isn't up for argument," Allyson feigned an interest in the map clothing her table. "They will be alright with them. We have much more pressing things to worry about, anyway."

Emmitt, his jaw clenched, refused to answer, or even acknowledge it when the two causally entered the room. Joana's gaze immediately shifted to me. She did not appear overly hostile, and examined Bennett without much interest. Slowly, however, she developed a steel stance and subtle frown in the presence of Idris.

"Are we taking Darius and Adney or not?"

"Your horse should be alright by now. Amaryllis is to take the big one, and Bennett that other black, white hooved animal."

Behind her, Emmitt mumbled in crippling frustration.

"Enough with the muttering, Emmitt."

"Their names are Abiona and Evana," he raised his voice much louder than necessary. Idris made no attempt to shroud her long, annoyed exhale, and grumbled a spiteful thanks. Joana, either unaware or uncaring of their discrepancies, attempted to force her shorter hair into a loose, disorganized bun with a thin leather tie on her wrist. She addressed the floor from where she stood.

"The training horse is too awkwardly large to be of any use, and they don't know how to ride. Why can't we just take Darius and Adney? Me and Lukas can lead them."

"Bennett and Amaryllis must learn at some point," Idris pointed out as matter of fact.

"It's not our job to mentor the Stoleh thief and the Nemiren cow milker." Her voice radiated off the walls and back to my ears almost as an echoing heartbeat. In a lukewarm, but progressively heating, anger, I mustered the courage to give a mechanical response.

"I'm not a thief."

"What do you call it, then?" her head whipped around, her lack of a blade more than compensated for by her sharp glare. "Selective pocketing? And I'm not interested in the sob story about providing for your little sister, either."

"Joana," Lukas, a strongly built boy of about eighteen with coarse, black, wavy hair cut just above his ears told her in a calm tone. She immediately sang a less condescending, but equally disdainful tune.

"Nobody got to this point because they lived a perfectly honest life without run-ins with the Guard and other classes. But don't think you can waltz in here as anything more than an honorary peon just because you found the Atlas." Joana spun around sharply, and left the room in silence. Lukas quickly picked up the sinking ball. He spoke normally in words, but with a thick, strange accent.

"Don't worry about riding as much. Abiona and Evana are older and mellow. They aren't going to take off and throw you to the ground or anything. We'll go slowly."

"Where are we going?" Bennett equally distributed the question between Lukas and Idris. Since he seemed to have no idea, Idris vaguely answered,

"The drop off."

Lukas looked at her strangely, but agreed, and moved to follow Joana. He had already disappeared around the corner of the hall when Bennett and I reached the doorframe.

"Amaryllis," Idris's preoccupied voice pulled me back into the room. She forced a small drawer in the desk open. To my surprise, Allyson then tossed a small projectile in my direction. I reacted, and barely managed to catch Rowana's journal in both my arms. "You left that Haritite bag in the tent. Nothing else looked important, so that was the only thing we kept."

I couldn't help but feel somewhat violated. Without much of a thought, she had rummaged through the only belongings I brought to the camp, and made her own judgments about what would be saved. I impulsively opened to the page marker, and frowned, distraught, at the missing image of Ruth with Rowana's parting words scribbled upon it. I breathed shallowly as we left the room, cradling the small book close to my chest.

We took the back hallway so I could leave the journal with Rose. Bennett asked what was wrong to break the lingering quiet.

"Rowana gave this to me," I stared distantly into the eyes of the green chested creature on the cover. "There was a note in it, and the picture of Ruth, but that's gone, too."

"She had no business doing that," Bennett said, at a loss.

"I guess it doesn't matter now," I paused with my hand on the doorknob. "Do you know what this is?" I asked, indicating the creature. He studied it thoroughly, but gave no answer.

185

Rose sat with her legs hung over the side of the bed, awake, but still in a state of limbo. My entrance brought her back down to reality.

"They're making Bennett and me go somewhere with two other kids," I told her. She frowned at my ambiguous description. "I don't know when we'll be back."

"What is that?" she took notice of the journal. I paced around the bed to the trunk, and carefully placed Rowana's treasure on top of a folded sheet. Rose adjusted herself to face me, and crawled to the headboard to look down into the chest.

"The woman I stayed with in the Haritite State gave it to me."

As I made my way back toward the closed door, Rose followed me with her eyes.

"Are you okay? Have you seen Ella?"

"She was gone this morning," I answered. Rose's only reaction was a somewhat bitter stare at the floor, and she remained silent as I left.

Several minutes later, we found them where we thought we would. As Lukas heaved a large saddle onto the back of a broad chested, gray horse with an uncut mane, Joana knelt below the gate that barely divided the stalls. She slowly unwrapped half-torn, grimy gauze from a midsize, chestnut colored animal that seemed scarcely capable of keeping still. Its pointed, white splotch of hair leading from its short mane to nearly its muzzle disappeared below the divider, and it made a sound at Joana, as if telling her to hurry up. Before I had located Abiona in the humid dimness, Vince approached us bearing tired, leather reins. In turn, Bennett and I took one step away from them.

"Someone used Evana with the younger children yesterday, and put her back in a stable on the other side of camp," he unmindfully forced the detached reins into my hands, and began to lead Bennett back in the direction we had come. His reaction prompted Vince to chuckle. "You'll meet up with them before they leave the camp. I'm sure Amaryllis can take care of herself until then."

Embarrassment more than anything else allowed me to quickly find Abiona. Serah's hidden presence in the back of the stall at first startled me. I dropped the reins on the packed dirt below us, and scrambled to gather them again as she opened the gate to the stall. Serah spoke in a low, almost cooing voice up to Abiona. She offered little interest in her as she skillfully turned her large body at an angle, taking up most of the path. I felt under intense examination by Abiona's one eye that faced me, like this animal could see through a person and judge them accordingly. It gave me some sense of reassurance that she didn't appear bothered by me.

"Take the clasp," Serah reached in front of Abiona's chest and lightly stroked a tarnished, metal clamp. I followed her hand with my eyes to a small hook nearly concealed in the thick, black noseband. "And place it here. Then do the same for the other side."

I felt Abiona's warm breath on my hands as I stretched them over her muzzle, and rubbed the metal hook. She lowered her head in response to my touch. If horses could smile, she laughed at the sight of me still standing on my toes to keep a grip on her noseband. Now more than ever, it seemed like she studied my every movement. I considered what Emmitt had said about unnerving her, and attempted to regain control of my shaking hand. Afterwards, I expected Serah to take the reins and lead Abiona to the rear door. Instead, she pointed me in the general vicinity, and gave me a gentle shove once she noticed Joana and Lukas were waiting for Abiona to move. With her long reins wound tightly around one hand, anxiety slowed my pace to a crawl. For every three or four steps closer I brought us to the door, she took a single, impatient one. Darius and Adney's protesting sounds and echoing snorts were soon joined by Abiona's, and I broke into a trot to get her out into the open. Following Lukas, Joana thrust herself over her horse's back, and pulled the reins sharply, causing him to mechanically turn.

"Joana," Serah somewhat timidly peeked from around the door. The way Joana impulsively buried her fingers deep into the horse's mane, and then disguised it by briefly stroking the hair between his ears and then the side of his head, was an ill-tempered remark in itself. "Be gentle with Darius. His leg is still sore."

"Yeah, okay," she answered in a stifled groan. She still continued ahead of us at a brisk pace, keeping just behind the organized structures that separated us from the crowds within the camp. The hairline path, adjacent from the one Emmitt had taken me through the day before, uncomfortably hugged them as they passed. Long after they had vanished around the corner, Lukas still waited patiently for me to find any sense of balance on Abiona. Adney, on the other hand, grew antsier with the passing seconds. Lukas gave me very specific, detailed instructions in a dead serious tone before proceeding to dismiss all of it with a shrug.

"You'll figure it out the longer you spend with her."

The dramatic landscape unveiled itself just beyond the densest area of the camp, somewhere between several enclosed, downtrodden fields and the mindful, task-driven crowds. Relatively stable land took a sharp, vast dip, and then gradually rose again somewhere off in the middle distance. Pine trees enveloped the area, blurring the lines where the camp ended and the extensive woods began. The area's rugged elegance made it all the more perfect, and its isolation was a long breath of air. For the first time in weeks, no looming cloud of fake names and histories followed me. The setting of the Idrisans' camp brought something solid to its previous translucent feeling, and now society itself felt like a nightmarish figure of the past. But despite all of the land's distracting beauty, I still could not separate my focus from each and every subtle movement and gesture I made to Abiona. In constant fear of falling off or instructing her incorrectly, only a low, steady hum convinced me to stop staring so intently at the reins choked in my hands. The barren area where Emmitt had found me last night was now bustling with an uncountable number of people, who seemed organized into odd groups without any clear assignment lain before them.

"It's crowded," Lukas spoke to either himself or to his horse as we walked by. "I can't believe they found enough people to keep those lessons going. They should be training with firearms, not swords."

We found Joana twenty minutes later, approaching Vince, Bennett, and another, impressively sized horse with a rusty brown hide. She and Darius circled around them in a wide arc like starving vultures before coming around to their other side. Vince did not lead Evana. He walked beside them, and spoke up to Bennett. Before we were within comfortable speaking distance, I could tell how much calmer he seemed about this than me, and before long, I saw he held his horse's reins in only one hand. Joana, just as eager to enter the wide, cleared forest path as Darius, walked steadily faster than the rest of us, though never stopped glancing over her shoulder as if to make sure we were still there. Lukas crawled along slightly behind Bennett and me. He was more absorbed in our surroundings than controlling Adney, who now seemed content to walk slowly in the woods. As we left the camp behind, the path began to turn less uniform, and morph back into the untouched forest. Lukas only broke his silent streak by telling me to walk ahead of Bennett and Evana to form a single file line. I struggled to keep pace with Darius as Joana skillfully weaved him in and out of the trees and over their protruding roots. Though it was harsh, I could see why she had said Abiona was too big to be of any use. But, as if annoyed with my lack of proficiency, it seemed like the training horse had adapted to me and took over, only using me as reference for which direction to turn.

Minutes grew into more than two hours, and I began to anticipate the end of the woods. Joana made several rounded turns, leading us through crevices in rock formations as we followed a path weathered into nothingness. After a long journey of walking almost entirely straight, her sudden veering to the left surprised me. Thankfully Abiona didn't turn as much as I indicated, and we followed Joana to a wide, happily foaming creek with scattered rocks forming a less than ideal path across. It wrapped around the base of a sharp incline, covered in all kinds of wild, green shrubbery in the middle, and with several dead trees along its sides. Ivy had taken possession of most of them. At the top, the steep hill seemed to level out into more live wilderness. Joana gradually brought Darius to a stop at the base of the creek, dismounted him, and unfastened from the noseband. Lukas and Bennett did the same, though Abiona refused to stop when I pulled back on her reins. If anything, she picked up her speed. As if she could understand me, I frantically told her to stop, panicking as we approached the river and impassible incline. She hadn't so much as brushed against a tree during the two hour trip, and now could she really walk into the water?

But Abiona stopped at the mouth of the river. She bowed her head and began drinking from it. I heard Joana's unsubtle laughter from behind us, and watched as she brought Darius to the bank, and looked up at me from the ground.

"If you want to make a horse stop, you have to sit back into the saddle and lightly pull on the reins. If you yank, it's going to rear up. Abiona won't, but any of the others would've tossed you off and you would've broken something in the best scenario."

I all but scrambled off of Abiona's back, and left her reins submerged in the water below as she nosily drank. Bennett and Lukas led Evana and Adney beside us. I could scarcely move as we gathered behind them.

"Are we just stopping here?" Bennett studied the obstacle before us.

"This is the drop off," Lukas gestured at the unimpressive landmark with a wave of his hand, sounding like he was cutting a long explanation short. "We're still miles away from society, but this is considered the boundary line between us and them. Theo used to make every newcomer ride here, back when he was well enough to escort them. I don't remember the exact words of his speech, but it was something to the effect of...." Lukas coughed as if in an effort to clear his accent. "Over this hill is the world you just left. Regardless of your standing in it, this is your one and only opportunity to return. Once we turn around, you will never see this place again. There will be no going back. If there are parents among you, brothers, sisters, or neighbors, you will either let your loved ones go now, or climb that hill and find your way home. The Guard mans nearly every known exit from the Wilds, but if you go straight up and do not turn, you will come to a residential area in a Haritite neighborhood, and you will reach it by nightfall tomorrow," he paused as if awaiting a reaction from us. Bennett and I only looked at them, and then each other. *My sisters are here*, I said to myself. *But I'm a daughter, a niece, and a cousin to some people out there, who may or may not still be alive.* And then there were Stella and Barney. The thought was somewhat hurtful, but I knew they could continue on with our daily heists in the markets and Nemirena without me. I could not imagine that my crossed out name in the Guard's book at the Wall had the potential to alter anyone else's world.

Absorbing our silence, Lukas then took what I'd never think to see again from a pocket on the inside of his fur-lined vest. He nearly threw the pieces of cloth onto the ground between him and us, Joana staring at them from the sidelines as if in contemplative disgust. There were three of each color: blue, red, and gold crumpled patches shaped like ancient shields scattered on the ground. A single, lilac one on the far right caught my attention. Etairan markings were strange, though simplistic compared to the design on a Stoleh's haunting identification.

"The last time you have worn an authentic class patch has passed if you return to the camp," Lukas continued, gesturing at the widest range of lives possible as represented by these pieces of fabric. "If you are not completely committed, choose one, and leave now."

He waited almost an entire minute, though it was obvious neither Bennett nor I had much to live for on the opposite side of what Lukas described as the dividing line between society and the Idrisan camp. At our given answer, Lukas collected the patches, and stuffed them carelessly back into his pocket.

"I didn't think so. Of all the times Theo did this, I never saw one person actually go back."

Following the previous Idris's cryptic discourse as told by Lukas, the two seemed to already be preparing for the agonizing journey back. As I knelt and pushed my sweater's sleeve up to fish for Abiona's reins, Bennett stood over me, waiting for Evana to raise her snout out of the water.

"How do you think they got an Etairan patch?" I spoke as if afraid of Lukas and Joana overhearing, holding the dripping reins between my hands in my lap and looking up at Bennett from the ground.

"It has to mean one person in the camp used to be Etairan."

189

"What Etairan in their right mind would leave their life to come to the Idrisan camp? They have what they have because of the Lebon."

"We don't know what really goes on between them. They aren't lacking anything materialistic, but something must keep them kissing the Lebons' feet."

I agreed with a slight nod, and several minutes later, he and I waited with Abiona and Evana by the indiscernible path back to the camp. Lukas sat above Joana on Adney, looking down at her as she inspected Darius's previously wrapped leg.

"He's fine, Joana. Dusk falls sooner in the woods."

"You and, erm... Bennett go ahead. I want to wash it again."

"It's not even an open bite anymore. The snake wasn't venomous."

"We'll be right behind you," she waved them off with a limp hand gesture. "Just go."

Why would she want me to stay with her? I shot Bennett another, probably more nervous look. He didn't seem nearly as concerned as I did, and he and Evana followed behind a reluctant Lukas and an eager Adney.

Joana began to scoop water with her hands, allowing it to drip down Darius's front leg. She seemed to be listening intently for the sound of their fading steps. After a while I realized she was washing the wrong leg, but I couldn't bring myself to say anything as I watched from Abiona's back. Joana waited until Lukas and Bennett were out of earshot. Darius didn't appear at all startled as she quickly stood, and brushed nonexistent dirt from her legs. Instead of placing her foot in the stirrup, she turned toward the river, and began to pick her way across the rocks and roots to the other side.

"Joana?" I called after her, pushing myself off of the saddle.

"Are you coming or not?" was her response.

She's not. She's not trying to go back to society. She doesn't have anything out there for her. I scrambled off of Abiona, constantly looking back at her as if afraid she would sense something was horribly wrong and take off.

"What are you doing?" I raised my voice to reach her on the opposite side of the deterring barrier. She gracefully made her way across and reached the other side. It seemed she had plenty of practice, though I could see that my foot was bigger than most of the rocks that separated us.

"Would you relax?" I could almost feel her exasperated sigh as she faced the sharp cliff before her. As she stared up at it, she appeared to be mustering the courage to actually reach out and touch the end of her world. "We're not going anywhere."

As she began to trudge upward by grabbing onto running vines of ivy, I couldn't make myself stand there and watch. The nerve wracking passage across the river was not as simple as the decision to follow at my safe distance. Though the current was all but at a standstill, tilting rocks appeared as if they would sink under my weight if I spent more than a few seconds attempting to find some sense of balance. By the time I stumbled onto the other side, my leg selectively landing in thorn-adorned undergrowth, Joana had silently and stubbornly forced herself halfway up the incline. Walking on this overhang seemed virtually impossible, the loose dirt sifting and eroding to the bottom with every step. I followed her example of using the dead tree trunks and ivy as climbing equipment, though I ended up with blood running down my hands and staining the sleeves of my near white shirt as a result.

The terrain leveled out as I carefully made my way over to her through the carnage of lifeless plants. I nearly wiped my stinging hands on my legs, only stopping myself at the last second. We had to avoid discussing something so strictly forbidden at the camp, and having blood streaks running up and down my clothes as if I had been attacked by a wild animal was guaranteed to draw attention. I reached Joana unnoticed. She was preoccupied staring off into the thick of the continuing woods, searching for some sign of human life. The first time she acknowledged my presence came as she pointed toward a remote area visible between the naked branches.

"There's a house way over there, one that's somewhere along the path to the Haritite State. Do you see the smoke?"

I hadn't until she pointed out the high rising, barely visible gray smog miles away from where we stood. I only looked at her, wondering why she was so interested. Though it appeared distant, a physical reminder that society had not vanished overnight made it seem as if we were within that person's backyard, and I only wanted to retreat back to the safe isolation of the camp.

"I know every corner of the camp and these woods. They've never let me go anywhere else. They send people out all the time, but I've been here my entire life and never set foot on one of the boats." She paused for a moment, studying the smoke. "I know they've said how hellish the island is. But when all you've heard is stories, certain things get difficult to believe."

"You're lucky if you've never experienced what goes on out there," I spoke in an almost irritated tone, surprising myself and her. For many people there, the camp was refuge. But to someone who had never left, its borders might as well be walled. Still, it was an easy slap across the face to basically be told my life and the many others similar to it was an improvement in comparison to the lives led here.

"If you had been forced to stay here your entire life because of an overprotective godmother, you'd feel differently."

"If you saw the people on the street, the inside of a jail, or a Cleansing, you would be happy you're so far away."

"That's what everyone says when they first come in here, you know. You're not special; ask anybody who came from outside, and most of them have lost just as much as you. They seem to think that this is some kind of safe net here to catch people who fall out of society, and everybody here is protected by the woods and doesn't have to worry about what goes on outside. If you wanted a safe and peaceful environment, this is probably the worst place you could possibly go. Look, the hard truth is everyone here is at high risk. We could move underground, but that doesn't change the fact that every time somebody gets caught, they could give the Lebon information and put a bullet in our heads from the comfort of Imperiam."

Joana stopped whimsically looking through the smoke, and her face developed a more natural, stone expression, as if the fantasy the distant house represented had gravely disappointed her.

"It wouldn't matter. There's no place better or worse than this. That's the reason why we're here, I guess."

"What?" I asked as she inattentively began to pick her way over and around the surrounding brush. Something about the question seemed to strike her, and she spun around with her legs spread apart on opposite sides of a tall patch of vegetation.

"There's no place better or worse than this," she repeated, continuing on. "My grandfather used to say that we might stand a chance of rebuilding with the ashes of Kieriana, but too many people here will only talk about burning it."

Joana spoke nothing of that house or civilization during the ride back. I followed almost beside her for more than two thirds of the painstaking hours, walking at a brisk pace as if trying to outrun the approaching twilight.

Chapter Twenty Seven

The following two weeks seemed to blend together into only a few days. Slowly, the fame Bennett and I had accidentally acquired leeched away, and people became equally uncaring about our discovery. The Atlas quickly fell out of the limelight and was replaced by an accumulating rumor about what the leaders of the camp were planning to do with its information. Living in the Hall, I could easily hear the senseless shouting at night. The only proof the arguments actually happened the next morning were the cold shoulders each one of them turned to one another. Gerald Johansson made every conceivable effort to keep Bennett and me out of the politics of the situation, though I didn't have much interest anyway. I believed the same was safe to say about him. To Joana's frustration, Idris was not any more open, and continued to pretend as if everyone collaborated on the future of the camp swimmingly. The four of us were always ejected from the Hall before half the camp had stirred, and sent to either accomplish some mediocre task or, as Idris called it, to 'training.' For Joana and Lukas, it meant going to instruct younger, uninterested kids in the field of weaponry. For Bennett, it meant spending the afternoon shut in a room studying a series of maps and documents, or down on the dock. Both activities were further ruined by the excessively bland and regimented post he was assigned to. And for me, it meant all day with Abiona and Emmitt in the fields and surrounding woods.

Though I was far from skilled at riding, I had at least spent enough time with Abiona to become comfortable with her: enough to grow accustomed to gently controlling her direction, and sometimes speed. Anything beyond, Emmitt could always whistle loudly from the sidelines and regain her attention. He told me I could now renounce Abiona for a younger, more nimble horse, but never forced the issue. After the first week, he gave up on the idea of getting me onto any other animal, especially one as restless as Darius or Adney.

"I've never seen her take a liking to anyone the way she has to you, but you must remember what I've been telling you," Emmitt borderline jumped backwards as we slowed to a walk in front of him. I surprisingly managed to keep steady after bringing Abiona to a slightly abrupt stop from cantering in a normal, endless circle. No different than the rest of the week, we had spent the better part of the morning in one of the several, fenced in areas, any wild grass long since pounded into the dirt by hooves. Emmitt would observe, always close enough that one nudge to the right on my part would trample him, and occasionally offer advice and correction. Easily more than half of what left his mouth during those long morning hours was the word *again.* His way of teaching left us little freedom, and he insisted that, at this point, I would sooner ride blindfolded than unsupervised. "If something happened, or she was frightened and threw you off, she could potentially crush you," he finished the typical speech, signaling we were nearing the end of the monotonous drills. Though he was unmoved by my constant requests to go someplace else, he seemed almost apologetic in his daily explanation. "Unintentionally, of course, but it is not unheard of. The absolute best thing you could do for yourself if it happened is to roll away from her so if she riles up, she won't accidentally step on you."

I couldn't help but wonder why he felt the need to talk more about what to do in case of a crisis over how to actually avoid one, as if it was inevitable. I figured it was always the first concern with new people as we returned Abiona to the adjacent stable. I always felt horrible leaving her in such a humid and dismal place, and asked Emmitt why we couldn't leave the horses in the fenced enclosures so they could at least walk around and breathe fresher air. He never seemed to have a straight answer, simply a recording of "That's Just the Way Things Are."

He didn't have to tell me where our next stop was. If we followed the regular schedule, we would now be joining Bennett and the post, whose name I never learned, in a cramped building located near the Hall. The work was much more tedious than riding, though Bennett and I usually passed the time making side comments when they turned their backs. The two would scold us for never absorbing the information they believed so crucial, but had already given up on actually forcing us to pay them more than half of our combined attention. As Emmitt and I left the stable, a congregation of children no taller than the middle strip of buttons on his admiral's jacket flooded in from the side. They narrowly separated themselves down the middle to avoid running into us. Emmitt raised his arms and held them close to his body above their heads, as if they possessed some kind of infectious disease. The children's herders followed a good ten feet behind them, having already forfeited the idea of controlling their harmless rampage through the center of the camp. Since everything ranging from the camp's simple operation to future planning rested on everyone else's shoulders, the overseers were kids themselves, barely a few years older. Rose only volunteered to partner with their original fourteen-year-old babysitter because she would finish her day's contribution much earlier than when she worked alongside the other woman. It was still a painful separation for her. Betty, she fondly called her, seemed to mean as much to her as Rowana had meant to me. And now, Rose described her new work partner as overly curious, with no shortage of questions about the 'outside world,' and ours in particular. *Her question filter obviously does not work very well*, she told me. The girl finally picked up on Rose's heavy hints when she snapped at her in front of all the kids, "I was two. I don't really remember what happened. Go find one of my sisters. I'm sure they would be happy to discuss the day the Guard shattered our family."

As if sensing my knowledge of the incident, the girl suddenly became interested in pursuing the children, and Rose watched her go.

"She said anything else to you?" I asked. A small smile spread across her face as she viciously stuffed her hands into her pockets. Ellamae had only recently begun to frown upon her habit, telling her almost on a daily basis that she still acted like a boy sometimes. Just out of passive backlash, Rose had begun to shove her fists deep into her knee-length pants more often.

"Nothing at all," she answered, removing one hand to shield her eyes from the sun as she stared up at Emmitt. They exchanged a wordless greeting, and Emmitt immediately appeared to access the situation.

"You are welcome to come, however I don't think you'll find what Amaryllis and Bennett are doing very interesting."

"No less interesting than what I find it to be," I said to myself. He heard, and shot me a glare comfortably situated somewhere between annoyance and thinly veiled agreement. Idris passed us, heading in the opposite direction. Emmitt called after her as if to ask permission and avoid another argument, though she continued walking, not reacting to us in any way. She appeared in some kind of trance as she kept down the etched out road, running into people left and right, and then proceeding without as much as a mumbled apology. Emmitt seemed somewhat bothered, or perhaps just irritated that she had ignored him, and turned his attention back to us, "I'm sure the little dark-haired girl can manage on her own."

The Hall was always abnormally quiet during the day in the absence of bickering leaders. The way the light reflected and cast shadows in the corners and very center of the empty foyer seemed almost unnatural as the sounds of our footsteps reverberated along the walls. When we filed in the open door, both Bennett and the post looked up from the same tired map, kept from coiling by heavy paper weights. In response, Bennett leaned back in the chair, distancing himself from the painstaking study of something we both thought so worthless. The man immediately rapped the table with his fingers as if to refocus his attention.

"We're not done."

Emmitt pulled two chairs sitting beside an open bureau to the table alongside Bennett, and then moved to stand off to the side. I knew Rose must have already regretted leaving the wild children and her new friend. The man opened his mouth to continue with what appeared to be another geography lesson, only to stop himself at a loud, echoing sound, filling the room with a stressful quiet. As if to ensure she was still between Bennett and me, I turned my head to Rose, who mirrored an intensified version of my bothered expression. Both of us believed we knew what the sound was. It was no different than what used to constantly startle us awake at one and two and three o'clock in the morning at home. Searching for some kind of reaction other than the confused but barely perturbed look on the man's face, I adjusted myself in my chair, hugged my arms tightly around its back, and watched Emmitt. He seemed to be listening to the still echo the sound had left, though it was quickly replaced by the renewed, muffled meandering of the outside crowds.

"What was that?" the man spoke first, speaking past us at Emmitt.

"I don't like it," was his answer. Emmitt released his hands from his normal iron grip behind his back, and wrung them anxiously in front of him. For me, that alone signaled that something much, much deeper was wrong.

"It sounded like a shot," Rose finally choked out, staring horrified at the wall like she could see the image of the smoking gun itself.

The man was quick to follow, "We don't shoot anywhere around here, sweetie. We take them out to the oceanfront so the bullets cannot find unwanted targets."

In response, two more of the paralyzing bangs followed in quick succession. The unnerving silence was short lived as Emmitt nearly leaped from his steeled position. To my surprise, he placed his large hands on the back of my seat, and yanked it away from the table. Startled, I jumped out of the chair and stumbled away toward Rose and Bennett. They looked from me to Emmitt with an indistinguishable amount of concern and uncertainty as he began to yank at a previously camouflaged drawer built into the table. It refused to budge, and Emmitt turned his attention to the shocked man, nearly shouting,

"Give me the key!"

"I don't carry one."

A momentary slew of curse language left him and spilled over into the already tense room as Emmitt pressed one hand against the table, one on the belly of the drawer, and braced his legs firmly on the floor. One excessively powerful, one-handed heave later, and he was hunched over on the floor skillfully loading a handheld pistol over the detached drawer.

"Emmitt, what do you think you are going to do with that?" the man finally came around the table. Emmitt stood, and held the loaded gun out to him.

"Go find Allyson."

The man continued to stand there, and had to be barked at again before he took the weapon, stuck it in his belt, and paced out the door, leaving us watching him. As Emmitt knelt down to take more ammunition, he told the three of us in a similar tone,

"Get behind the bureau."

"What are you doing?" Bennett wouldn't take his eyes off the individual bullets Emmitt continued to stuff into his pocket. Once we realized he was not going to answer, Rose asked with a nervous highness,

"Was that a gunshot?"

"I said get behind the bureau, now!" he pointed in its direction while taking an identical pistol from his belt and turning it over regretfully in his hands. Bennett stood up beside me, staring at my half-mortified face, and Rose's fully terrified one.

"Why?" he asked, and Emmitt seemed to lose all patience.

"If there's a gunman here, he is going to come for the Hall. We are the only ones here. I'm going to go stand behind the front door, and you three are going to sit behind that bureau because I've told you to three times!"

As Emmitt loaded a single bullet, wincing at the clicking sound his weapon barely uttered, I gently guided Rose to the tall, ornate chest sitting angled in the corner adjacent to the escape into the hallway. Bennett closed the bureau's doors, and struggled to move it out a foot so we could all access the safe corner it concealed. Before leaving, Emmitt came over to help him, and then harshly motioned us to move. As he forced the painfully loud armoire back into position, the splintered wood came closer to our faces, and we were forced into stillness.

Rose and I were almost in tears, though Bennett couldn't understand the scope as to why. She was just a baby when it happened, but from Ella's accounts, Rose had to have painfully painted an image to fill the void. I, on the other hand, remembered the final moments where Mom kissed each of our foreheads, and Dad said he loved us more than anything as he scarcely hid us with the old sofa clearer than anything else from my childhood. This was far from the chaos and terror a Cleansing evoked. But its repetition escalated the circumstances in my mind from the possibility of a lone gunman to a full Lebon invasion. I could only try to calm myself down enough to speak to Rose as we watched Emmitt's shadow skirt across the floor, quickly disappearing from our limited sight.

"It's alright, Rose," I struggled to maintain a steady whisper as I shakily parted her oily orange hair. I couldn't tell if she was listening to me or not. "This isn't like at home. They've got enough people and resources to take down one person if there's somebody here."

Her response was little more than blinking twice, and we all went back to the struggle to control the low sound of our breathing. Much louder voices from almost right outside the door startled me, and the end content of the conversation stopped my heart.

"We need you, now," a man's gruff voice echoed down the emptiness of the outside halls. I watched something change in Bennett's expression.

What is it? I mouthed. I could feel a couple tears gathered in the dark bags under my eyes, and hastily wiped them away in hope he hadn't seen them.

"It's my dad," he answered. I felt as if I should have gathered that from his reaction.

"I am going to stand by the door until we find whoever fired those shots in case they come here looking for Allyson," Emmitt's voice answered, and I relaxed slightly for only those few seconds. "We are not going to bury two Idrises within eight weeks of each other."

"There's no need. We've found the man."

"Is anyone-"

"It's Allyson."

The two's running footsteps left the building, and the sound of the slamming door awakened something within Rose. She forced her small framed body upright, and began looking for a way out.

"Rose, what are you doing?" I asked from the floor, cold and shaken by the idea that Allyson Hanchoré could already be dead.

"I want to go find Ellamae."

"I'm sure she's fine."

"It's not her I'm concerned about," she looked down at me with a degree of both fear and sadness. "I saw him walking behind Idris when she passed us."

We never had to clarify who 'him' was. It was the only name we ever used. I probably should have hurriedly denied it and tried to calm her down, though I admit I couldn't help my own suspicions. He'd barely spoken to either of us since the night he walked in on the fight, only acknowledging our presence if he ever dared to approach Ellamae while we were around. She told us on a daily basis we needed to give him 'a chance,' but any time the opportunity arose, I always felt as if something was off. I rationalized my anxiety by telling myself that I had taken too much away from Mr. Johansson's less than formal introduction two weeks prior. Despite how much we already decided we hated Jonathon, it seemed a far cry to accuse him of shooting Allyson while we sat there closed in by the bureau.

Rose, frustrated, stepped over Bennett and me. Emmitt had not quite placed the chest in its original position, and she seemed determined she was going to fit through the hairline crack between it and the wall.

"Rose," I frowned, inching my way upwards, bracing myself against the bureau. She paid no attention, and Bennett was forced toward me to make room for her.

"They've found the guy. I'm not waiting for someone to come get us out of here," she said over her shoulder. With all of our combined weight, we managed to force the bureau forward just under a foot. It was enough to barely free Rose and I, and Bennett squeezed through in a few seconds. Outside, the crowds seemed partially aware of a crisis, and seemed to be flocking to the left. Without speaking, Rose turned in the opposite direction in search of the area where Ellamae generally spent her days carting water from the river back and forth, or sewing stores of cotton into clothing.

"Come on," Bennett motioned for me to follow as I watched her go, strangely nervous as I saw her swinging braid disappear around the corner. And if what we heard had actually happened, then I wasn't sure I wanted to see the scene.

People appeared loosely gathered around a single, inconspicuous building far away from the Hall in some kind of residential area. A heavy cloud of strained silence and urgent murmuring hovered over us, making the area as a whole appear darker. There seemed to be no one barring the door, just an invisible barrier keeping everybody from drifting inside. Bennett and I made no attempt to struggle through the crowd, only looking around those surrounding us. By the expressions and tone of the congregation, I assumed they had been told something similar to what we overheard.

"Do you think Allyson is really dead?" I asked Bennett. I knew he would have no answer, I just couldn't fathom it on my own. My response came from a strange, short man standing in front of us.

"She's not. She's just inside."

A huge weight lifted off of me, and I wondered why the area was so deathly quiet if Idris was alright. When we asked the man what had happened, he only turned his back to us again.

"They haven't told us anything. They just said she's alive and went back inside. But there was definitely gunfire."

I jumped when a window beside us suddenly opened inward, though no one else seemed to notice. The unearthly strong smell of blood fled quickly from the room, and I impulsively covered my nose and mouth with my hands. As the horrible stench filtered through the air, other people began to stare at the conspicuously open window. I didn't even try to resist the urge to search for a sign of an unharmed Allyson inside, though what drifted out from the window should have been telling enough. Within the limited view, Emmitt stood, speaking urgently to Mr. Johansson. It appeared as if no one else was standing, though I could barely hear a weak, high-pitched voice from the other side of the room that definitely didn't belong to either of them. After the window was violently slammed shut again, that voice, presumably Allyson's, was the only connection to the narrow list of what could be happening. It wasn't until a different person began speaking that I realized who else was behind this closed door.

"How did you know something was wrong, Jonathon?"

"Anyone could see it in her demeanor."

I wordlessly left Bennett behind, uncaringly pushing my way through the crowd. No one made an attempt to stop me, only watching in surprise as I forced the door open.

"What are you doing involved in this?" I demanded, infuriated by her presence. Ellamae only stared me up and down, like she had no idea who I was. I looked to the floor, and saw the gruesome scene that resulted in the intense smell. The head had been carefully covered by a white cloth, stained red along the edges as a gathering puddle of blood seeped beneath the floorboards. The rest of the body lay exposed, dressed in normal clothing, unmoving. As my face contorted to the horror of the display, Ella stepped over the body, and came around me, covering my eyes with her hand, and trying to guide me back to the door. I stiffened my body, unwilling, and pushed her hand away.

"Who is that?" my voice sounded uncharacteristically small as I forced my gaze back down to the body of an unidentifiable man. Huddled on her knees in the corner, Allyson stared horrified at those standing around her. She was deathly pale, and near shaking, refusing to look at the corpse strewn on the floor.

"He was a spy, Amaryllis," Ella stood behind me, with one of her arms firmly across my collarbone and the other gently on my shoulder. Her presence, after spending weeks trying to resent her, was bittersweet, though I didn't have the will to break away. Bennett shortly appeared in the door, and froze in his steps as it closed quietly behind him.

"Block the door before all the children in the camp walk in to see this, would you?" Mr. Johansson told a man standing off to the side, and then explained to Bennett, "He was a Lebon spy. We don't know how long he's been here or where he came from." He sighed, and then turned his attention to Emmitt. "If there's one, there's probably more. We need to check into the history of everyone here before this happens again and all our lives become dependent on the same thread of coincidence."

Paying no mind to him, Emmitt squatted down on his legs in front of Allyson. Her senses came back to her quickly as he dangled his pistol from one finger in front of her face.

"I've told you since you arrived that you need to carry one of these. This is why. Do not ever let me see you without one."

She only stared at it.

"I am so sorry, I didn't-"

"Don't apologize to me. Just carry the damn gun before something like this happens again."

Idris obediently forced the pistol uncomfortably in between her belt and the fabric of her clothes.

"Our main priority now is to get everyone out quickly," Emmitt stood and refocused on Mr. Johansson. He spoke in a firmer voice as if trying to exert his authority over him. "If this man is from a stationed fleet, we're going to need to break up the camp and move."

"Moving with spies still among us will not solve the problem," Mr. Johansson was quick to follow.

"I will not jeopardize all of these peoples' lives in favor of frantically purging the population. We will burn this place to the ground and rebuild elsewhere before we are invaded and wiped out during the course of one night."

Listening to two of her father's followers argue over the future and livelihood of the entire Idrisan camp, the horrified look on Allyson's face intensified. Her voice shook to mirror her physical state as she made an attempt to interrupt them.

"Both of you are too eager to act. We will sail out and locate where this man came from. If there's a Lebon fleet hidden in the shadows of the island, then yes, we will have to move discreetly. If we cause commotion, they will realize that we know something. We also need to keep in mind that this man must have had connections outside of the camp somewhere, and if they do not hear from him within a decent amount of time, they will connect the pieces."

"What happens when they see our boats?" the two men finally agreed on one thing, and spoke at the same time.

"We will complete the project my father started and never finished many years ago, only for a different purpose."

Everyone stared at her with absolutely no idea what she was referring to. Allyson sighed, disappointed, and forced herself upright against the wall. She stared down at the body as if afraid of it, like it would jump up at any moment.

"We can discuss it later. Right now, we owe the people outside an explanation."

She, Mr. Johansson, Emmitt, Jonathon, Ellamae, Bennett, and I were met by a brief reaction, expressing a lukewarm relief that Allyson was unharmed. Still, by the way she carried herself and seemed scarcely able to stand, they knew that something traumatic had happened. Mr. Johansson guided Bennett and me toward the front of the crowd to show that we were not involved. Ellamae was obligated to follow, and Rose quickly found us there.

"What happened?" she asked me, cupping her hands around her nose. "What is that smell?"

I did the same thing to her that Ella had done to me inside. Rose seemed weary of everyone's demeanor, but didn't move. Gerald Johansson returned to the small group, and stood beside Allyson, who appeared hopelessly isolated. The series of questions began. Emmitt slowly got the silence his upheld hand called for as the senseless noise fell down to expectant murmuring.

"The camp has been infiltrated," he cut right to the chase. His bluntness seemed to stifle any kind of panicked response, though the shock was universally visible on peoples' faces. We seemed so untouchable here, and most people knew everyone. The idea that someone could live among us without drawing any kind of attention to themselves was just as unfathomable as it was stomach-turning.

"Who was it?" a woman in the middle of the group asked almost as if she truly didn't want to know. Emmitt joined his hands behind his back, stood straighter, and tried to speak in a more even tone to minimalize the eye-opening situation in front of the people.

"We know very little. All that we can confirm is that he was a kind of spy for the Lebon, which probably means somebody out there knows our location. However, if

201

he came from a fleet stationed nearby, then it's unlikely that the Imperial himself is aware they have found us," he paused, and looked around at Gerald, Allyson, and Jonathon like they had answers attached to their foreheads. "And none of us have seen him here for more than two days. The best scenario is that he had not yet contacted his fleet and they do not know he located us."

"And what is the worst?" another person in the crowd immediately followed his sentence. Emmitt refused to look anyone in the eye as he told them,

"The worst is he already communicated our location to them, and they will return to Imperiam after a few days of not hearing from him."

"Is he dead?"

"Two bullet holes to the head and one to the neck. I believe so."

Someone who appeared actually disturbed by Allyson's condition eventually asked a normal, but still seemingly out of place question.

"What happened? How did you find him?"

"Do you want to address that, Idris?" Emmitt stepped out of the limelight, looking at her hesitantly. "Or shall one of us?"

"No. I will handle it," Allyson stepped up, smoothing down her thick, straggly hair and wiping her fingers across her face. It didn't create the illusion that she was composed enough to talk about the past ten or fifteen minutes.

"That man came into one of the upstairs rooms in the Hall.... I was alone, and it was my fault I did not have anything with which to defend myself. He drew a gun and ordered that I was to walk into an empty building near the outskirts of the camp... and if I said anything to anyone, then he would open fire. So I came to this house, and I assume he had the intention of shooting me. But then, erm," she waved her quivering hand around in the air, trying to recall his name. "Jonathon followed behind him, and shot the man three times before he heard the door opening."

"How did you know what was happening?" the same person turned their attention to him. Jonathon stared at the ground for a while, looking like he felt very out of place, and only wanted to remove himself from the stressful attention.

"She ran into me on the road. She was white as a sheet and stumbling around. I knew something was wrong, and that man walked only about ten feet behind her and had his hand hidden in his jacket. When they entered the house, I just followed to see if she was alright. I heard him making threats from outside the door, and loaded my pistol so I could force him out of there. But when I went inside and saw he had one as well, I knew I had to shoot him before he killed one or both of us."

Jonathon was thanked by few, and scarcely applauded, though not given any kind of hero's coronation. He seemed thankful for it though, and moved away from them to stand beside Ellamae. For once, I didn't feel thoroughly disgusted by his presence. Allyson still appeared on the verge of a late panic attack, and a sympathetic woman much shorter than her placed a hand on her arm, and started to lead her back to the

Hall. Gerald Johansson followed, and Ella, Jonathon, Rose, Bennett, and I watched them leave. The crowd also began to disband, but then stopped and turned around to listen as someone asked Emmitt, "What are we going to do about this? Are we safe here anymore?"

"No one is completely safe here, and all of you knew that coming in," Emmitt responded philosophically, both annoying and unnerving everyone. "I believe we are going to take out a few of the boats and skirt around the general vicinity to see if we can find his fleet, if one exists. If I know what Idris was referring to when she spoke of finishing Theodore's last project, she intends to have our boats painted with a Lebon insignia so that we will not be obvious. If that is the case, then we will have to divide the mission into two separate days. It would have to appear to anyone lurking in the distance that we were on some kind of fishing venture or day trip. However, that is for us to worry about right now. As soon as we know more, so will you. Until we have any information, my advice to you is to remain calm, and at least be prepared to leave if we must."

"Where will we go if we have to move again?" Another timid voice spoke from the opposite side of the crowd. Emmitt immediately held up one of his hands as if that would pacify the people he had already made fear the absolute worse.

"I do not know if we will have to leave or not. I won't know until we sail out. If everyone begins to panic, then it will throw the camp into chaos and be difficult if not impossible to keep everyone informed."

"That wasn't the question. She asked where we will go," a man he seemed to have particularly irritated quickly pointed out his evasiveness. At a loss, Emmitt frowned deeply at the ground.

"To be honest, if it comes to that, we will probably have to split up the camp for a while. At least until we know that we are not being followed and have no more spies among us."

The idea of dividing the camp and fleeing from such a perfect spot of land seemed horrific to these people, and to me. No one had the courage to speak again, though Emmitt remained there, somewhat disheveled by the suddenly colder manner in which he was being received.

"Moving at the end of summer is a death sentence in itself. It is too late to plant. What will everyone do in the winter?"

"This is why we keep stores. And if the rest of us have to leave, then you are always welcome to stay and greet the Lebon when they arrive," Emmitt's voice hung in the air for a long time. After a drawn out, silent minute, he began to force his way out of the crowd and followed after Idris.

The five of us entered the Hall to be greeted first by silence, then by Mr. Johansson.

"Where's Allyson?" Bennett spoke too loudly, his voice resonating off the thick walls of the impermeable fortress the Hall used to be.

"Idris, Bennett. You need to stop calling her that," was his answer. He leaned against the wall, and breathed deeply, looking at all of us. "She is in her room with Joana."

"If the camp has to be divided, then they can't split us up, can they?" Rose continued with an edge of fear. I knew she meant her, Ella, and I, though I couldn't imagine passing the days without Bennett, either. And I guessed if Ella truly loved him, then I could learn to deal with Jonathon. Mr. Johansson continued to stand there, unresponsive, like he hadn't heard her.

"Mr. Johansson?" I asked, and shortly afterwards, Bennett finally pulled an answer out of him.

"Dad, will they separate us or not?"

"I cannot promise anything. But don't begin to worry about it until we know more. It's useless to build a future you cannot see yet. Hopefully, we will not leave at all. But if we do, I will do everything in my power to ensure you five stay together."

Mr. Johansson pushed himself away from the wall with his foot, approaching our small, uncertain group. His eyes were locked on Jonathon, that much was clear, and the rest of us took small steps away. He extended his arm toward him as if it was especially painful.

"I owe you an apology. You never did anything to deserve it, and I have been treating you like a spy ever since the dinner. Idris owes you her life, and since I know she will not say anything, consider this her thanks."

Jonathon accepted the truce with a nervous politeness, and Mr. Johansson turned around, leaving us alone in the foyer.

The rest of the day Bennett and I spent trying to forget about the situation. The humidity of the stable showed no mercy as it choked us more and more with each passing hour. Vince and Serah seemed immune, were happy to have our company, and put us to work brushing the horses' coats and cleaning out their hooves. Bennett stood in an uncomfortable, bent-over position with a variety of picks, while I gently stroked the horse's neck on the other side to keep it calm. Though we didn't say much, I probably would have just locked myself in the room if I didn't have the ease of his company.

Later in the evening, Rose had emerged from the Hall, probably having gone for one of her typical walks with the kindly woman she used to work alongside. I thought I was alone until I sat heavily on the bed and saw Ella against the wall. She sat in front of the open chest that contained our sheets, holding her knees up to her body in one arm, and covering her mouth with her other hand.

"What's wrong?" I lay on my stomach, forcing myself up on my arms to talk to her. When she looked at me, I easily saw the shock and dismay in her eyes. A sense of reality struck, and I stood up again.

"Ella?" I sat beside her. She moved her hand away from her mouth, and picked up something she had sitting on the floor beside her.

"What about it?" I asked. Rowana's journal with the strange creature on the cover had sat uselessly in the chest for the past two weeks.

"I didn't know Rosalie could...." her voice trailed off.

"Rosalie could what?"

"Look at what she's written in here." Ellamae flipped to the page marked with the thin ribbon. Two pages side by side had been filled entirely with delicately written words, large, dark, detailed drawings lining the outside edges. I knew Rose used to write poetry in her old journals, and didn't care that she had taken mine. It was her outlet. But Ella seemed ready to cry, and I took the journal out of her hands, squinting to read the words.

The shattered glass lies on the floor.

As the blood outside begins to dry,

The shots and sounds of marching boots have gone.

But their shadow still hovers in the sky.

The shattered glass lies in the streets.

As the fires are doused before they spread,

The sounds of shrill screaming and breaking doors have gone.

But the people who tried to fight are no less dying or dead.

The shattered glass lies behind the gate.

As few are buried, and everyone mourned.

It will always pass.

The blood of hundreds makes rivers out of streets.

But it will never wash away my shattered glass.

My breathing became shallow as I mechanically closed the journal, and held it tightly in my lap.

"There's no way she remembers that. She was only a baby," Ella finally worked herself up to speaking.

"She's heard a lot over the years, though. She can fit the pieces together and paint a picture."

I paused, and suddenly felt horrible for just remembering the ordeal that had brought her to the Idrisan camp to begin with. "And there was another Cleansing not too long ago."

A new kind of horror seeped into the room from Ella's reaction. She looked at me in a different way: like I was a figment of her imagination, like I shouldn't even be alive.

"After I left?"

"I wasn't there, either. I was in the Haritite State."

"Why didn't you guys tell me about this?" She seemed suddenly angry. I wanted to ask how in the world she believed our little sister had gotten here, but snapped back,

"You haven't exactly been around for us over the past two weeks, you know."

Ella was quiet, in neither denial nor agreement.

"Are the boys, Uncle Graham, and Aunt Clarissa okay?"

"I don't know. They and Niles were out in the streets when it happened. Rose said she and Oakley hid in the boys' room. The Guard never came into the house."

Choosing the perfect time, Rose inattentively opened and closed the door, not paying us much mind until she noticed our expressions.

"Are you okay?" she asked. Her gaze quickly shifted to the journal in my hands, and her face flushed red. Rose scrambled onto the floor in front of us, took it from me, and held in securely against her chest.

"You weren't supposed to see that," she muttered, ashamed.

"Rose...." I began, searching for the words. She frowned, and pushed one side of her fallen braid behind her ear.

"What do you think I did all day?" she asked us bluntly. "I was alone pretty much all the time while you were who knows where and you were out with Barney and Stella. I would just sit there and silently panic upstairs when you were late. I needed to do something besides talk to Niles and Oakley and walk around the borough. Why do you look so surprised? Did you think I wrote little limericks about white clouds and pretty rainbows?"

Rose swallowed, and looked away from us as she gently returned the book to its proper place in the chest. Roughly milking her hair over her shoulder as if trying to pull it out of her scalp, she nervously began to braid it again just so she could avoid our concerned gazes.

"I've never even seen a rainbow. I saw a Cleansing, and I write what I see and hear. Writing about what I think the world ought to be like is pointless. No one cares."

I moved away from Ella, and put both my hands on Rose's shoulders. She froze mid-braid, and stared up at me expectantly.

"I liked it," I told her, trying to smile.

206

"You know what I used to do every day while you were gone?" her pathetic attempt at smiling mirrored my own. "I used to make up entire fantastical lands and a bunch of people to put in them. They were always such good and real people too, and they'd always save the world. But one day, I realized I was just trying to get out of real life and... I couldn't get the same warmth from my characters anymore. So I stopped writing stories and started doing poetry."

"I think you're a really good writer," I spoke earnestly. I knew Ella must have been staring at the back of my head as if I'd lost my mind. "I'm not just saying that because you're my sister. I think you should keep doing it."

"That poem isn't finished yet," she said.

"Then you should finish it. And I think maybe you should give your stories another chance. I want to read one."

"I don't remember the day when Momma and Dad were taken," Rose's voice jumped octaves as she apologetically changed the subject, finally dropping her hair so she could cover her face with her hands. "But when I asked Aunt Clarissa and Uncle Graham, they both talked a lot about the windows of our house. They said they were busted in and there was shattered glass all over the floor. That's where I got the idea."

Her body stiffened as I wrapped my arms around her shoulders, holding her beside me.

"You don't have to explain yourself to us, Rose."

Gradually, she relaxed, and I heard her say in a breath, "Why didn't I take Oakley with me... then he would be safe here, and not wandering the streets. He's probably alone... he's just seven... nobody's going to help him...."

"I'm sure he's fine, Rosalie," Ellamae crawled behind us, placing one arm around her, and one hand on my back. I hadn't expected her to make any effort to comfort Rose after her month of absence, and weeks of avoiding us. To see Ella exactly the way she was before she left, when the two of us meant the world to her, something inside me wanted to be hesitant, and something else wanted to fall apart. "And think about all the places where Uncle Graham, Aunt Clarissa, and Niles could have hidden. The four of them are at home right now missing you and Arlie."

"They miss you, too," Rose craned her neck around to face Ellamae.

"I've been gone too long, Rose," I felt her sad sigh, and I heard something I had wanted to hear since we found each other here: a hint of regret for what she had done. "They've probably forgotten about me."

"You have no idea how much Aunt Clarissa cried when she found out you had left."

Something in the realization seemed to strike Ella hard. The three of us sat in silence, curled up against the bed, just breathing in the familiarity of each other, and wondering how we had even found our individual ways from our crowded bedroom and Mom's quilts into this convoluted mess.

"It felt like something was eating me alive when I left the Wall knowing I wasn't going back," Ella's voice sounded like she was admitting something deeply personal. "I couldn't figure it out until after we got to the camp. I would have never lasted here forever, not without you."

What she said next brought tears to my eyes, and all the bitterness I had toward her seemed to melt.

"I'm so sorry I abandoned you that way. I was too scared to tell you myself. I couldn't have made myself go through with it. It just seemed like I had to do it, like I was proving some kind of point by refusing to be a Stoleh forever...." her voice trailed off, and Rose covered her hand.

"Nobody wants to be a Stoleh forever. If I'd seen everything you had seen, I would've taken the first opportunity to get away, too."

"You don't have to say that," was her answer, and as if in response, a light knock on the door startled us. Without any answer, it opened, and Emmitt immediately paused, looking down at us. He didn't seem to know what to make of the situation, and so he withdrew back into the hall.

"I'll um," he coughed. "Wait out here."

He quickly replaced the door, and marked the end of our moment. Ella, Rose, and I still refused to move for several minutes. It felt like something heavy had been lifted from my chest. If I closed my eyes, I could pretend we were at home. Even miles and miles away, and even with all the heartache involved, there was a comfort in knowing I hadn't entirely lost my sister to Jonathon.

Chapter Twenty Eight

The man's body was disposed of quickly and without rites, overnight, off a cliff and into the wildly eager ocean. The manner suggested it was some kind of huge secret, despite the fact that the entire camp had heard a version of what happened. Idris took little more than a day to compose herself, and no sign of the ordeal was visible on her face as she addressed the camp with a silent Joana by her side.

"We've organized two separate scouting trips. We are sending two boats out, to be captained by Gerald Johansson and Emmitt Detate, to survey the area. We're looking for a stationed fleet that the spy may have come from."

Immediately following her to-the-point speech, the atmosphere within the camp drastically changed. When you passed through the residential areas, packing could easily be distinguished amongst the clamor. The Idrisans entirely skipped the transition stage of panic, jumping right into preparation for the worst result the scouting missions could yield. Even the horses seemed to possess a sixth sense, knowing something was about to change.

Emmitt was less than thrilled to be working with, and not over, Mr. Johansson, visible by the way he glared at the small, ragtag crews and stared disappointedly at one of the two boats. They were midsize, though the largest ones there, with two decks, solid wooden hulls, and perfectly triangular, blank sails. As I reached the end of the pier, I watched three people reaching their steady hands out to one of the boats. The three appeared to be meticulously painting a large insignia in bright colors, their faces creased in concentration.

"The Lebon insignia," Emmitt clarified to Bennett and me, pausing to watch the progress. "Much simpler and defined than their class symbols, isn't it?"

We nodded our agreement. The insignia's complexity paled in comparison to those of the classes, with only a few solid black lines encroached by thinner, wavy ones. To me, it appeared like wild ivy slowly creeping up a couple toppled beams. One of the painters raised his legs back onto the pier, turning around and looking up at us.

"The symbol was mostly completed years ago, when Theo was still with us, and it was washed away. I don't see the point in replacing it if you are taking the boats out tomorrow."

"It will dry overnight," Emmitt answered plainly, dismissing the topic.

"It does not matter. The waves will wipe it clean off in only a few trips."

Emmitt held his hands palm up and moved them up and down in time with his voice, speaking as if this was an all too obvious explanation.

"It will appear more authentic if the symbol is faded, as if the boat is taken out by the Lebon on a regular basis. That is for those of us who are going out to worry about anyway, not you."

Disgruntled, the man went back to pretending we were not there and continued his work.

Idris held little weight when it came to debating who actually went on these missions. The first one seemed to only be for the purposes of getting a feel for the water and casually drifting out, so Emmitt and Mr. Johansson didn't offer much of an argument when Lukas, Joana, Bennett, Rose, and I appeared on the docks at the last second before they raised the sails.

"Did Allyson say it was alright for you to be here?" Mr. Johansson asked Joana hesitantly. She momentarily stared at him as if she had been caught, though quickly regained her steely expression and answered,

"Why do you care?"

"If you are going to come," Emmitt intervened, knowing there was no point in arguing with her. "Then Lukas and Joana must go with Gerald, and you three will have to come with me."

"Why?" Mr. Johansson looked at him strangely before any of us could.

"We don't want to play our luck and squeeze five more people onto the same boat," Emmitt answered in a strained voice, shaking his head.

After we had separated ourselves into his groups and were out of earshot, he turned back to Rose, Bennett, and me. The three of us were barely on the deck, and his abrupt stop almost forced us into the lapping water.

"Gerald Johansson is a farmer. He does not know the first thing about sailing. I am not trying to be rude to him, but he will not listen to anything I say. I am only trying to make sure he will not get himself and everyone on his boat beached."

As if Emmitt had just realized Mr. Johansson's son was standing right there, he tensed, mumbled again that he *wasn't trying to insult him*, and sped off toward the crew to help with the sails. Bennett was clearly bothered by the comment, but didn't seem to have anything contradictory to say at the moment.

A blanket of still humidity had covered the camp for days, and it was no different in the concealed alcove. It seemed like hours before we began to feel the rocking that signified we had finally begun to move. Two people skillfully maneuvered the tiller back and forth through the narrow twists and turns of the alcove. Emmitt stood on the deck raised slightly above the main one, watching nervously over his shoulder to ensure the other boat continued to follow us. Over an hour later, as we left the area behind, the boat dramatically picked up speed, and it took a moment of scrambling to regain control. The sudden, intense wind blew all the sweat from my forehead, and I shielded my eyes with my arm as the sun's full glare began to beat down on us. The wind itself almost felt solid, plowing into and forcing me in every direction except the one I wanted to go. I wouldn't let Rose anywhere near the edge of the boat unless I was holding onto her in some way, in fear that she could lean over the rope railing and be blown into the bluish green depths below.

Something in my mind seemed to keep track of how far away from the camp we sailed. As the minutes grew into an hour, I couldn't help but feel the same hopeless exposure as when Stella, Barney, and I hopped the fence in Nemirena. We sailed a comfortable distance from land, and the landscape did not change very much as we continued left from the alcove. Tips of pine trees were barely visible over the sheer drop into the water beneath them, which made its presence known as it violently thrust itself against the jagged rocks, pointing skyward close under the cliff. The ferocity of the water near the island seemed unreal from where we were, as its peacefulness was only disturbed as we cut through. It took me much longer to become used to the swaying motion than Bennett and Rose. Once I had finally found my balance, an older woman nimbly skirted down the stairs, and ushered me toward the bow of the ship.

"Use your young eyes, Amaryllis," she said. I only watched her, still unused to most every stranger knowing my name. "Don't forget why we are here."

The moment she was no longer paying attention to me, I found Rose in the position I feared, bracing herself against the wooden rails. It was a better alternative to the rope that outlined the lower deck, but still seemed unstable to me.

"My young eyes don't see anything," Rose teased as I pulled her away from the railing by her arm. She cocked her head to the side, laughing. "You act like I'm going to dive off the boat."

"I'm just worried about the wind."

"Being here has made you a lot more paranoid than you used to be," was her answer, and I had nothing else to say about it.

With everyone else occupied either controlling the sails or steering the boat, the actual scouting part of the scouting trip seemed to rest with Bennett, Rose, and me. Evening settled with no signs, and Emmitt gave the order to turn back, shooting a single casing into the air to notify the other, still following and intact boat.

"He was wrong about my dad having no idea what he's doing," Bennett spoke under his breath though Emmitt was on the opposite side of the ship.

"He knows how to sail?" I asked, rubbing my eyes clear of the glaze that had coated them after hours of staring at empty water.

"Nemirena is surrounded by woods, markets, and Haritite neighborhoods," he answered. Though he didn't use a tone that suggested it, I couldn't help but feel stupid I had asked. "But he told me the other day that people forget that he used to live here long before a lot of the other posts and leaders came, and he's pretty familiar with the way things work."

At least ten people waited to help guide the boats into a position to once again be tied to the pier. Only a long, uphill hike separated us from the camp. The news, or lack thereof, seemed to ease a bit of the worry, though no one was ready to start unpacking until we sailed around the other side. Early the next morning, our severely shrunken crew gathered in front of the dock. Though we'd lost at least fifteen people, among the gained were Ellamae, who asserted that she was concerned about Rose and me and not at all interested in the voyage itself. Also Jonathon and maybe two or three odd people, bringing the number to about thirty total. Despite the reduction, Emmitt still insisted upon carefully dividing the crew.

"I'm not sure it is a good idea for you to come this time," he tried to let Bennett, Lukas, Joana, Rose, and me down easily. "It is more dangerous. If we are going to find anything, then we will find it around this side of the island."

"Our presence doesn't make it any more or less dangerous," Joana said flatly. We were no longer questioned, only told, "Do what you want. But you cannot say no one warned you."

I didn't understand the math behind it, but everyone somehow ended up separated differently. Bennett remained with Emmitt along with Lukas, Ellamae, and Jonathon; leaving Rose, Joana, and me with Mr. Johansson. Joana loudly verbalized our objections, but he only said we could always stay at the camp.

It seemed to take much longer to free ourselves of the alcove while following behind Emmitt's boat. Since our young eyes were not yet needed, Rose immediately found a little nook where she could lean against something, and write in the journal Rowana had indirectly given her. Paying no mind to the other people, who were annoyed by her relaxed demeanor and age, she continued to scribble circles on a blank page.

"What are you doing?" I eventually had to ask.

"This is how I come up with ideas."

Joana wasn't much of a conversationalist since we returned from the woods two weeks ago. I already dreaded the coming hours without Bennett to talk to as we managed to break through the heat curtain and into the openness of the water. As I forced my tired eyes to continue scanning the coastline and the immediate area for a sign of Lebon ships, I couldn't help but let myself mindlessly think about what was in the other direction, beyond that horizon. I understood the ethics behind Emmitt's speech, why we didn't just leave the forsaken island behind. But I knew if the decision were mine, I would have trouble resisting the idea of throwing Rose in a rowboat, and never looking back.

Hours passed, and nothing any more exciting than the previous day turned up. Though I was glad to be away from the routine of the camp, the sun had left painful, scaly burns on my exposed arms and face, and I felt relieved as it set. An echoing shot from the other boat signaled we were to turn back, and we began to form a wide arc, putting us ahead of Emmitt's ship. By the time I could finally join Rose in the minimal shade without scrutiny, it appeared she had written pages.

"I guess the circle thing works, huh?" I smiled as she unburied her nose from the journal. I felt a hovering presence behind me, and craned my neck to see Joana standing over us. I thought it fairly uncharacteristic as she lowered herself onto her knees half in the shade, and half in the remaining sun. Though there was enough room for her to fit, it appeared as if she didn't feel comfortable getting any closer to us.

"What is that?" she eventually asked Rose, indicating the journal. Joana had never spoken to her before. Flustered, Rose slammed the book shut and held it up to her chest.

"It's just my-Amaryllis's journal."

"It's yours," I told her. Even though she'd already taken it, she seemed relieved that I had officially given her the permission. "I'm never going to use it."

Some kind of recognition crossed Joana's face, and Rose tensed into a ball as she leaned in and looked at the cover of the book. Rose finally sensed she was studying it, and moved her arms so she could see the image of the strange creature.

"Where did you get that?" Joana's voice took an almost accusing tone. Rose was struck silent, and I intervened.

"Rowana."

"Who's Rowana?"

"Rowana Laurie," I mumbled, feeling somewhat betrayed. I couldn't help but literally worry sick whenever I thought about her, and could only try to make myself believe she had escaped somewhere in the State. "Bennett and I stayed with her in the Haritite State."

"That explains this thing," Joana relaxed slightly, indicating the animal. Rose and I looked at each other, and she seemed to recognize something in our expressions.

"You don't know what it is, do you?"

"Some kind of bird, I guess," Rose turned the book around to look at the creature staring back at her.

"It's called a peacock. Grandfather used to say that it was a rare, magnificent creature that no one dared to touch. There's a story that says when the Lebon came, they hunted them into extinction."

"You mean it was actually real?" Rose asked, almost in awe that such a beautiful thing could exist on this island.

"Of course peacocks are real," Joana laughed, leaning backwards. It looked and sounded like she was making fun of us, and I frowned, impulsively on guard. "They say the Lebon have entire coats made of their feathers. It's basically their second symbol. That's why they were selling them in the State. It's just an underhanded way of reminding you that you can't have anything without the Imperial's seal plastered all over it."

I knew it deeply bothered Rose to know that the Lebon had some kind of indirect connection with something she held so dear and personal, almost as if they were somehow spying on her. By the new way she looked at the journal, I would've thought she was going to rip out all the pages and let the cover drift far away on the lighthearted waves of the ocean. Joana, sensing she had done more harm than good, bit her lip and turned her head in the direction of the upper deck where most everyone else on the boat seemed congregated. Her face conformed to minute interest, the direness of the situation not easily seen in the heated argument between Mr. Johansson and some other deckhand. I couldn't make sense of the words from where we were, and felt obligated to follow as Joana abandoned us to get a better view of the excitement.

"Don't do it. It is not worth it," a petite, but firm-voiced woman spoke, though he wasn't paying much attention to her. The woman's eyes were held wide as Gerald Johansson tried to stand taller. He watched something invisible to the rest of us located off in the distance the way we had just come from.

"There's something out there."

"It is just a reflection, Mr. Johansson. The light can begin to play tricks after a long time on the water."

He barely paused, and then told the gathered, nervous crew in an even voice,

"Pull in the sails and turn around."

"Don't touch the sails!" the woman hissed at them, and everyone stopped, frozen. The crews' own thoughts on the matter didn't apply. They were only there to receive and carry out orders given by whoever was put in charge. Unfortunately for the woman, Mr. Johansson had Idris's implied approval.

"I know I saw something just beyond where the island curves inward."

"Even if you did, then there is still no need for us to go chasing after it!" the woman raised her voice as if that could give her any more influence. "If you go beyond that point where we first turned around, then we'll end up beached somewhere on the shores of the Etairan Mountains!"

Mr. Johansson motioned at the crew, instructing them to do as he said. In a last effort to make him change his mind, the woman pointed harshly at the three of us, not actually knowing we were standing at the bottom of the shallow steps.

"There are three children aboard! If you want to foolishly risk your life, then that is perfectly fine, but you cannot risk theirs!"

"We are out here looking for where that spy came from," he continued to humor the woman as the crew quickly filed past us down the stairs and to their positions. "If we return and say there is no ship when we are not absolutely sure, then everyone in the camps' lives are at risk."

As the ship veered sharply to the right, Joana, Rose, and I fell against the steps. Mr. Johansson's head appeared over us in seconds.

"Amaryllis, go to the bow and look out for anything different."

"What about Emmitt's boat?"

"They'll follow or not. All three of you go."

Rose and I waited until the ship was somewhat level again to move. Joana stayed behind, talking urgently to both of them from the lower deck, though I couldn't hear who she was seconding as we left. When we passed the quiet, but somehow deafening presence of the other boat, a sudden, faint but easily heard shout echoed across the water.

"What do you think you're doing?!" I could envision Emmitt's hands cupped around his mouth as he paced nervously back and forth on the upper deck. Mr. Johansson didn't respond, and in forced abidance, Emmitt's ship began to turn and speed up in a pointless attempt to catch up with us.

Despite the heating argument between Mr. Johansson and the woman, the crew did as they were supposed to do. I continued to divide my attention between them and the island, searching for any sign of this object Mr. Johansson claimed to have seen. Though after an exhausting hour, morale nosedived, and the crew began to purposely slow their efficiency in order to put more distance in between us and the nearing, as they called it, border: the drop off on the water. The second end of the world sat nearly upon the infamous Etairan Mountains. As Mr. Johansson responded to the crew's resistance by urging them further, paying no mind to them or the tense silence of the following ship, darkness fell quickly. We could no longer see if Emmitt was behind us. Finding an already elusive boat with only Mr. Johansson's whim as guidance seemed impossible in the blackness of an unlit night. And as the hazy peaks of the Etairan Mountains became visible, and not just nervously referenced, the danger of what we were doing only became more real. Our deafeningly silent, but steady progress abruptly halted at a sudden change in wind direction.

"This is suicide!" A man threw his hands up. Several others mirrored him, while everyone else scrambled to regain control of the boat. Their clamor and voices were

215

easily drowned out by the many mid-size waterfalls as rivers in the mountains fed into the ocean. "You cannot take us so far out. This was supposed to be a scouting mission around the camp!"

Rose pushed herself away from the railing, and walked past me on her way to the main deck. She disappeared into the confusing activity, and I watched from the bow, genuinely starting to panic that Mr. Johansson had a mutiny on his hands. I had a sense of debt to Bennett's father and couldn't imagine seeing any harm come to him all because of a stubborn decision to pursue a mirage on the ocean. But the crew didn't see it that way. I still believe the only thing that prevented them from abandoning their posts and organizing an attack on Mr. Johansson was a sudden lurch as the boat dipped dangerously to port. As the water rose, licking the deck and leaving shallow puddles, I leaned heavily against a mast. Before long, I held onto it as if it were life itself, my eyes transfixed on the blackness of the water, the ink.

"One of the shrouds snapped!" A man emerged from the chaos, shouting and holding one end of a frayed, soggy rope. "We've lost control of part of the main sail!"

"Compensate for it!" Mr. Johansson stepped down from his perch and moved into the crew to help. I couldn't make out Rose or Joana in the frantic scramble to level the boat, and felt as if I could only watch and hold onto the mast. The night sky was clear, though the ocean spray gave the illusion of a violent rain. It made the deck slick, causing several people to almost slip and fall from the boat. They eventually managed to stop it from capsizing, but couldn't bring it upright. Standing on the bow, I became more concerned with where the boat was going in the absence of steering. While everyone was preoccupied with the remaining sails, we seemed to be fast approaching and curving into a beach lined with wide, pointed rocks.

"Um, we're...." I said, though no one could hear my quiet voice. "The beach!"

I got most everyone's attention by shouting. However, the ones who mattered still wouldn't pay any attention to me or their surroundings. Mr. Johansson and two other men promptly yanked one of the attached ropes, overcorrecting the ship. They set us upright, but soaring to starboard, the bow heading straight toward one of the pointed rocks more than twice the size of the deck. I heard many people, including Rose, screaming at me to get away from the front of the boat. It took the deafening sound of crunching, breaking wood to persuade me to let go of the mast. As if in response, the boat shifted again, throwing me onto the deck and sliding to the edge of the boat. Gathered at the raised stern, the others chanted as one for me to grab the rail. I felt my body slide partially off the boat, my legs dangling above the churning water, and my sweaty, white palms clutching the rope railing. I could hear tentative footsteps making their ways toward me, though everything stopped as they braced themselves against the stairs, the boat continuing to tip until my toes submerged in the icy water. Only echoing shouts of *stay put, don't move!* reached me as the makeshift rope railing came undone in my hands. I tried to turn myself around and scramble back onto the ship, but only succeeded in sending myself faster, headfirst, and backwards into the void below.

The immediate impact snapped my head forward, and I felt a small spurt of blood in my mouth. The rest of me seemed paralyzed, my mind flickering between fear and stillness. I sank only feet more before lightly finding the dense, pebble floor, coming a bit more to my senses, and to terms with the fact that I was taking in entire breaths of water. It enveloped me, feeling like cold, thick jam, making it difficult to hold my hands over my nose and open my eyes to see the remains of the ship above me. The salt stung I struggled to gather the strength to kick upwards.

It seemed much longer, but only about eight feet separated me from air. I became aware of the burning sensation in my lungs only after I had begun to breathe again. I tried to move my arms steadily, control my painful hacking, and just keep my head above water to disguise that I couldn't swim. Light sloshing sounds came from the nearby shore, and I turned my head to see Mr. Johansson anxiously wading into the water.

"Amaryllis," he held his arms out to me once he was chest deep, struggling to remain standing as the waves beat against him. I hovered only a few feet out of his reach, and clumsily forced myself over to him, aided by the motion of the breakers. I sank below the surface again as I felt his hands coil around my arms. Mr. Johansson pulled me through the water, and held me like a bag of potatoes as he let us drift part of the way to land. I sat on his arms, my head a dead weight on his shoulder, my entire body racking from coughing up what felt like gallons of seawater. The crunching of rocks beneath shoes cut through the silence as Rose walked closely behind Mr. Johansson, looking up at me with tears on her cheeks. I tenderly shook my sopping hair out of my face so she could see I was conscious. Rose smiled in relief, and then held up the unrecognizable, dripping remains of her peacock journal.

"I saved it."

"I'm so sorry, Rose," I coughed, and my chest burned and tightened. I lowered my voice so the pain wouldn't be audible in it. "It's ruined."

"No, it's not. It just has to dry."

Mr. Johansson passed the ship, and I blearily watched as the last of the people managed to scoot and jump off the exposed side of the ship. After the last woman had landed on her feet in a foot of water, her scream echoed up the steep mountain face as the boat noisily fell on its side, the water pounding relentlessly around it and spraying us all with a heavy mist. I barely remained upright as Mr. Johansson set me down against another rock on the opposite side of the short beach. The whitecaps of the waves only touched me, but I still tried to move as far away from them as possible, as if in fear. Both he and Rose knelt in front of me. By the look on his face, it appeared my fall had made Mr. Johansson realize exactly what he had done to his crew, and the camp's ship.

"Are you alright?" he asked. When I didn't respond, he snapped his fingers three times in front of my face. "Amaryllis, answer me."

The crew and Joana approached us, and stood in a ring behind them. I felt hopelessly small and trapped, like a caged animal, and looked vacantly off into the distance. The same woman Mr. Johansson had argued with on the ship soon pushed him out of the way, and got onto her knees in front of me. It didn't make sense at first, why she ripped her scarf away from her neck and dabbed it along one side of my face. The sight of my own blood, probably from hitting my head and sliding on the splintered deck, rung a painful bell in my head, and I cupped my hand over part of her scarf. I tried to tell the woman I was fine, though she only pushed my hand away. So I remained still, listening to the rest of the crew as Rose curled into a ball beside me, her body heat comforting.

"What are we going to do now?" someone spoke, unsure exactly who to ask.

"The Imperial is going to get a message in the morning," a man answered bitterly, his voice directed at Mr. Johansson. "The Etaira have a big shipment of Idrisans to send over for execution."

"Don't say that," Mr. Johansson turned around to face everyone, though didn't stand. His voice offered no reassurance, only an order to not think the unthinkable.

"What can we possibly do, Gerald?" he nearly shouted back at him. Everyone tried to tell him to be quiet, though he only raised his voice. "We have no ship. We can only wait here until the Etairan Guard sees the wreckage and comes down here! You risked our lives and now everyone has to pay the price, including these three kids. They're the next Ruth Backenstose story because of you!"

"Enough!" a nerve snapped in Mr. Johansson at the mention of Ruth. He stood, walked up to the man, and was blocked by others before he could lay his hands on him. "No one is going to die," he looked away, shame in his voice as he nervously wiped his hands on his pants. "Let us figure this out."

"Who is 'us'?" the woman spoke flatly. "It's you, Gerald, a thirteen-year-old, a sixteen-year-old, Idris's daughter, and ten crew. No one is coming for us."

A large wave crashed over the ship, and everyone shielded their faces as the sharp spray reached us from the other side of the beach. Gerald walked off, saying he was going to look around, though we all knew he had nothing of the contrary to say. The woman wouldn't allow me to leave the rock, and the chilling wind made me shake violently beside Rose. She tried to get me to read something from her journal, though the words were blurred into almost nonexistence, the dark barely let us see the ghostly boat on the other side of the beach, and my neck felt too weak to support my pounding head. Focusing my eyes enough to read seemed impossible. The crew panned out around the beach, but we were surrounded by steep mountain paths leading into civilization, and dark rocks where ocean salt and barnacles had formed a thin, sticky layer. No one knew where Mr. Johansson had gone, and over an hour passed in cold, unmoved silence. These people didn't even appear panicked, or afraid of the death that seemed so imminent. There was no emotion, or at least it wasn't evident by their expressions. Joana found one sign of nearby life: a rotted stick. She began to delicately draw circles in the pebble sand to pass the time, deep in thought which no one dared disturb. The hour passed slowly, and my head seemed to throb more violently with the passing time. I felt cruelly left to contemplate our fates, and my little sister's presence only made it worse. Her calmness, almost satisfaction, as she squinted to make out her words was entirely set off by my anxiety.

"It's okay," she would tell me as she felt my sporadic breathing. "That other boat was following us. They'll come."

No one else was so sure, though the end of the first hour brought an identical ship safely near the shore. Everyone watched, whispering urgently, as a group rowed a narrow canoe toward us.

Emmitt stood up, almost turtling the unstable canoe, and stepped out. He began walking in two feet of water until he reached to the shore. He looked at me, and assumed what had happened. Frowning, he scanned our weary faces for a moment.

"Is anyone injured?"

"She was thrown into the water near the shore," someone told him, indicating me.

"Yes, I see that. She'll freeze to death overnight if we stay here."

Emmitt clenched his jaw as if he was struggling to hold his tongue, and then began to undo the buttons of his jacket. Though he wore another long sleeved shirt underneath, I still tried to shake my head as he came beside me and draped it around my shoulders. He ignored me, and I didn't argue any further once I felt the warmth of the jacket.

"You don't need to stay beside her," Emmitt told Rose. She tensed, unwilling to leave me. "We don't want you to get wet and cold."

"I'm fine here."

"Move, Rosalie," he told her starkly, frowning, and she hesitantly crawled away from the rock and found a place amongst the crew. As the canoe washed on shore, Jonathon, Lukas, and Bennett pulled it onto the rocky sand. Ellamae stopped short when she saw me, though Emmitt told her the same thing about staying away, like the cold I felt was contagious. She instead found Rose, and hugged her tightly. I only heard their whispering as the three joined us. I couldn't bring myself to look any of them in the eye, and buried my face into my shivering knees.

"Bennett, don't get near her."

"She's going to freeze," I heard him answer as he slowly lowered himself where Rose had just been. I was quiet, surprised as I felt both of his arms around me, forcing me to lean against him. It seemed some of the pain alleviated just by knowing he was there. Bennett didn't even say anything. He just sat there beside me and occasionally rubbed my arm when the penetrating wind screeched down the mountainside. Emmitt gave up on the idea of making him move in time for Mr. Johansson to appear from one of the paths. He stopped in his tracks upon seeing his son, though Emmitt quickly drew his attention, much less sympathetic over the fact that he was also halfway drenched.

"Are you satisfied now?"

"I do not want to start a fight with you," he held up his hands as if to show they were clean.

"We found what you so desperately needed to chase, so much so that you'd be willing to put all of our lives in jeopardy," Emmitt nearly growled. "It was a ship. Unfortunately, it was an Etairan skip. Not only that, but you sailed right past it in your blind effort to chase something that may or may not have been there."

"Why did you follow us then?"

Emmitt tightened his hands into fists, but didn't move. The way he looked at Mr. Johansson was telling enough of what he wanted to do to him for his little venture.

"Would you like to return to the camp and tell Allyson that an idiot farmer from Nemirena sailed off with Joana on board and now her daughter is forever lost at sea?"

'Idiot farmer' set something off inside Mr. Johansson, though he calmly answered,

"Well, I'm sure you've gotten rather homesick over the past twenty years. Why don't you go find your father's manor? I'm sure he would be happy to help us," he paused, and said the name as if it could stand alone in a sentence. "Wilfred."

"Never..." Emmitt started taking steps toward him, and was halfheartedly blocked by the crew. "...call me that."

"It is your name, isn't it?"

"Don't try to make this about me. You have put us all in this situation! Why must you act like you know everything, having been gone for sixteen years? Now look at where you are! It wasn't enough for you to recklessly endanger all of us. Now the entire camp is wondering where the hell we are, and is probably getting ready to uproot and move as we speak. They don't have enough supplies to last the winter! Do you think Allyson is equipped to handle an entire breakdown of everything we have ever known, and singlehandedly lead the camp into a new area? If the camp separates, then we have that many more chances to be found and caught! There are not that many habitable places in the Wilds, Gerald! If you don't see it by now, there is nothing I can tell you that could make you see the magnitude of what you have done!"

"Would you stop trying to doom the future?" Mr. Johansson stepped back, startled by Emmitt's, an unreadable wall's, lashing, echoing voice. Emmitt recoiled like a snake, and began to pace along the beach, shaking his head.

"Damn you!" he eventually shouted at him, the words striking us all. Once he realized his voice reverberated up the mountain pass, he lowered it again. "You are like a child! You acted on one impulse, and now the entire existence of Idrisans hangs in the balance. You cannot possibly understand how complex the system already is, and dividing the camp so many times only complicates it further, making it that much more fragile!"

Before Mr. Johansson responded, his face already red and fists clenched, a moving light walked slowly around the bend and down the path. We couldn't see the congregation over the rocks, but each step was a heavy boot on my chest, bringing us that much closer to being caught.

"You don't say anything, you hear?" Emmitt hissed at everyone, particularly at Mr. Johansson. "Let me handle this." He pointed at the ship. "Crew, look like you are attending to the boat. Go!"

The ten members of the crew scuttled away, and found something to do, wading hesitantly through the water as the approaching group discovered what they expected to be there.

"Who are you? You know you are on my land!" a booming voice shook my bones, and I wanted to disappear behind Bennett. The man, followed by an entire troop of what appeared to be Guard, walked to the center of the beach.

"Sir, you have my sincerest apologies," Emmitt went to shake his hand, though he was vehemently barred by the Guard. He recovered quickly, and gestured behind him at the capsized boat. "We came from Imperiam to deliver packages and messages from his Majesty Imperial Acwel Aloysius, and my partner lost control of his ship in the wind. They were forced to jettison the heavy parcels as the boat began to sink, and purposely steered the ship here onto the nearest beach so everyone could safely abandon it. As you can see, my ship is still intact and waiting, but unfortunately, all of the packages were aboard this poor vessel. We cannot support the weight of both crews on one ship, and have been stranded here for a while."

His story contained so much information the Guard didn't seem to know how to process it.

"Your ship is small to be from Imperiam," one of them eventually noted, unnerving us all. He ordered a smaller man, "Check the side."

He took the lantern, and casually approached the exposed part of the hull.

"It's faded, but correct," he raised the light to the symbol, squinting to make out what remained of it. The crew tried to pretend he wasn't there, though as he walked amongst them, they slowly retreated from the boat, standing in the water, watching nervously. I might have only imagined it, but I could have sworn I saw skeptical stares ripple through the Guard.

"What's wrong with her?" one asked. I stopped breathing, and stared into the dirt.

"How dare you!" Joana forced her way in front of us, her hands on her hips, and a dead serious expression on her face. The Guard took only seconds to size her up: her average height, stringy strawberry blond hair, baggy, light capris, and short sleeved shirt. Despite her demeanor, there wasn't much she could do to intimidate them, or protect us.

"There's no need to get upset, miss," the apparent leader of the Guard said with a short, terrifying smile. "If you all come with us, then we can discuss this inside. We will figure out a way to get you back to Imperiam and get some help for your friend."

It seemed all too obvious that they had the intention to shoot us before we even climbed the mountain pass. Perhaps it was the conspicuous symbol or the way we carried ourselves, but these people did not believe we could possibly be Lebon, and were more than willing to take the risk.

"Do you think I am stupid?" Joana straightened her back and spoke with an authoritative, vicious voice, surprising them. "You should hope that I return to Kieriana and do not tell my father that we were threatened by Etairan Guard after our ship ran upon land!"

Joana spat the words *Etairan Guard* in the same way Haritites spat *Stoleh* in the streets, as if these men were all hopelessly below her. The Guard were still not amused, and one said bluntly,

"You have ten seconds to explain who you are and why you are on a Lebon ship."

"With pleasure. I am Stephanie Aloysius."

I knew nothing of the Imperial or his family, however the last name hinted that Joana was trying to pass herself off as an Imperiess. The way she spoke probably could have convinced the Guard, if only she was made up and dressed with the same aura of status and power.

"When my siblings and I travel, his Majesty insists that we wear and carry nothing to indicate who we are in case something like this were to happen anywhere else on the island where we could be in danger," Joana scoffed, rolling her eyes like it was common knowledge. "I would think that you Etaira would know that by now considering how often his Majesty sends his advisers and officials across the channel."

Joana partially turned her body toward Lukas, Rose, Bennett, and me, shooting us a momentary, stern look. We were not to question or comment on anything she was about to tell the Guard.

"These are my brothers and sisters," she regally guided her hand to each one of us. We all shifted uncomfortably, but managed to maintain eye contact. "Silas, Alexander, Fiona, and Arena."

"You look nothing alike," the man who owned the land said, and a fake anger so realistic it actually appeared to frighten some of the Guard possessed Joana's face.

"It would do you well," she pointed harshly at him. "To watch your tone. We all have different mothers, you ignorant fool."

"And while you all stand there gawking and speaking out of your place," Lukas quickly picked up the ball, joining Joana so she wouldn't appear so isolated. He looked slightly more put together than her, in neater clothes, and we knew the Guard would be more inclined to believe him despite his different voice. "Arena was thrown into the sea when the boat ran upon land, and has since been unable to stand and hacking uncontrollably."

I immediately forced three whooping coughs, cutting through the quiet to continue building our legitimacy. My life had literally revolved around lying to the Guard since age nine, and the Etairan Guard shouldn't have made a difference to me. But there was something surreal about the lilac, gold-encrusted patch. The Etaira were so removed from the rest of the population, no one could really even prove they existed. They were hidden so far away in these mountains, and only a day's trip away from Imperiam. The only thing I felt I could do to both help our act and avoid looking directly at these people was continue to cough, but not unbelievably hard or long, to draw less attention to the gaping holes in our story.

"We understand, Imperien Silas...." the leader of the Guard shook his head, bowing it slightly. I breathed easier knowing that we might survive the walk up the mountain pass if everyone could keep their mouths shut. "However, we must see some sort of identification... you see, anyone could pretend that-"

"No, I do not see," Lukas developed a tone similar to Joana's, planting his feet firmly on the ground. "Where else could we possibly sail from? The rest of the island lives miles and miles away."

"If you are through treating his Majesty's children as Idrisans," Emmitt recovered from the initial shock of our story, and came to our defense. "Then I will give you your proof."

Emmitt gently picked the stick off the ground, turning it around in his hands multiple times as if trying to recall something buried deep inside his memory. He began to draw some sort of symbol in the pebbly sand of the beach, and the rotting stick finally broke in two upon its completion. Both the man and the Guard immediately accepted everything Joana said as true, and were all over the five of us, Ellamae, Jonathon, Gerald, and Emmitt in seconds, begging our forgiveness.

"Words are words," Lukas dismissed all of it, and discretely gestured at Bennett and me to stand behind his back. I felt sick and unsteady on my feet, leaning against the rock to remain upright. Bennett held his arm out to me so I could brace myself against it as we walked. "We do not blame you for doing your jobs. However, if you wish to keep them, you will allow the crew to return to Imperiam on the remaining ship, and lead us inside."

The Guard dutifully did as they were told, never giving a second thought to the Idrisans that had managed to infiltrate the impenetrable Etairan Mountains with nothing more than a poorly woven tale.

Chapter Twenty Nine

I tried to wipe the look of total awe from my face when we first set foot on the man's manor. Acres of land, peppered with extra buildings that were all more than three times the size of the house I grew up in, all sat in a still orbit around the main house. The house itself was of a size so unfathomable, it only seemed useless. The manor had its own plentiful food supply growing and grazing on one side, and the rest of the unused land was mostly covered in extravagant, trimmed gardens. The owner was apologetic for the 'state' of the land, saying he did not have much help in its recent upkeep. By the time he looked back at me, still hobbling alongside the boy who would once again have to pose as my brother, I had managed to gather my composure, and was looking around the area with a subtle interest.

I was separated from the others and taken to a different wing of the columned building, where I couldn't seem to remember to respond to Imperiess Arena. Thankfully, the three strangely garbed women I had been left with figured I was only unaware. Regardless, they were very conservative in what they said and did around me. As soon as they could politely leave, the women filed out the door, turning down the oil lamp in the front of the room. When their footsteps faded, I quickly sat up, lightheaded with a throbbing ache spread all over my body. There was something about the wide, four post bed, cotton sheets, and pillows that deeply sickened me. I forced myself up, leaning against the wooden frame as I walked around to the window. The view of a silent, man-made lake didn't help my feeling of isolation, and I sank against the wall, the silk-like curtains drifting lazily around me. An open window allowed a breeze to circulate throughout the large room. But the longer I sat there, the stuffier and more uncomfortable it felt. It seemed as if the area shrunk with the passing minutes, and soon, I needed to get into the plain corridor just to give myself a sense of normalcy.

Before I had struggled all the way to the door, it cracked open without warning. I froze, feeling hopelessly caught and exposed, like my identity would magically dawn upon one of the women when they saw I was trying to get out of the room.

"What are you doing?" Bennett's voice entered before he did. I relaxed as he took me by the arm, not even aware I had been falling to the side until he held me upright again.

"The walls were closing in," I answered in a small voice, tired and afraid to raise it. I was sure he would think I was insane, but Bennett seemed to understand, and frowned. Rose and Emmitt followed in behind him, and unnerved me again with their sad expressions.

"What's going on?" I asked Bennett as he hurriedly led me away from the draft of the open corridor. He wouldn't answer me until I had painfully lowered myself on the bed again. I held my head in one hand, trying to look up at all of them. I only became more anxious as Bennett sat beside me, keeping a small distance between us, and Emmitt knelt as if to break horrible news.

"They know?" I choked, my eyes darting to the window as if we could jump and run away.

"No, they don't. Not yet," Emmitt answered, shaken. He placed one hand on the corner of the bed, and began tapping his fingers nervously. "You two listen to me. Pretending to be a Lebon is not the same thing as pretending to be a Haritite. You have no one to blend in with. If these people begin to doubt you, they will send someone into your rooms at night with a hunting knife. You are not playing imaginary people anymore. Alexander and Arena Aloysius are an actual Imperien and Imperiess."

"What if-"

"Don't interrupt me, Amaryllis, this is more than a life or death situation," Emmitt whispered. Not as if angry, but panicked, like his time to speak was short. "Here is a basic outline of what you should know. You live in Kieriana on the Imperial's manor. Never call him your father, only his Majesty. The Imperial has forty-one children, one official wife, the Imperia, for the record, and nine others."

"Why?" Bennett's exasperated and disgusted expression probably mirrored my own. Emmitt didn't snap at him about interrupting, but answered shortly,

"It is considered acceptable for the Imperial to have as many mistresses as he wants because only the children by the Imperia are in line for the throne. Joana did not know which names she was saying when she gave the Guard a list. Unfortunately, Arena Aloysius is one of the three legitimate children the Imperial has, so she would have more influence and be closer to him than Alexander, Stephanie, or Silas."

A new sense of panic swelled within me. *That means they're going to expect you to be able to talk about him and the Imperia and who knows what else goes on there.*

225

"You will be alright," Emmitt moved his hand onto my knee. "Etaira do not know or care for the details of the lives of the Lebon. If you are asked, you can make something up. As long as it sounds reasonable, they will not know the difference."

"Emmitt, what did you draw in the sand?" I abruptly changed the subject, his ticket to getting us all onto the manor still bothering me.

"The Lebon symbol on the side of our boats is the modern one. A century ago, it was much more complex, and only a Lebon themself or maybe an Etairan person would know it today."

A realization so strange and frightening occurred to me, seeming so incredibly ridiculous I wondered for a moment if I should even ask about it. "Were you an Etaira?"

A pain unlike anything I had ever seen from Emmitt spread across his face.

"Another lifetime ago, yes, I was. I am the only one in the camp who came from the Etaira, which I know is the real reason why Gerald resents me so much. I never quite adjusted to the lifestyle lived here. My extended family and I only argued. The last straw was when I was forced to watch an Idrisan execution in Imperiam. It was more gut wrenching and shameful than anything I had ever seen in my life."

"Was it Ruth?"

"This was many years before Ruth came to us, Amaryllis," he said, sighing deeply. "I took one of my father's ships and left when I was twenty years old. I purposefully ran it aground on the opposite side of the island, and stumbled into Idrisans. They were ready and able to kill me right there because I hadn't bothered to get rid of my class patch, but took me back to the camp. I pleaded with Theo to spare me, tore that damn thing off of my shirt, and threw it on the ground. He caught hell for believing my story, that much was certain. But if he hadn't intervened, I know I would've died that day."

He stopped, and shook his head back and forth as if he could force the memories to fall out of his ears. The three of us couldn't help but stare. Emmitt never seemed to have much of a story. He was simply the man in the admiral's jacket at the camp.

"I am very worried," he continued. I thought that much was a given, though the way he spoke suggested he meant something different. "I cannot endanger any of you more than this. If someone were to recognize me or the ship I brought, then all of us and everyone at home would be at stake. That's why I have already spoken with the owner of the manor and the Guard. The crews and I are returning to Imperiam to inform everyone of what happened, alright?" Emmitt lowered his voice even more, to the point where he was barely speaking. "I will make sure Allyson does not complete the move, and knows all of you are here. These people are expecting you to stay for several days, at least until you are better, Amaryllis. Gerald, Joana, Lukas, Jonathon, and Ellamae are staying with you two. We've told everyone that Ellamae and Jonathon accompany you every time you leave Kieriana, and Gerald must stay to captain the boat back to Imperiam when they can get you one. Their names are Marten, Daniel, and Enola."

"Rose?" I looked up at her and saw she was crying. "Where is Rose going?"

A sound like a gasp left her, and she nearly knocked me over, burying her face into the ruffles of the collar on my nightgown.

"You have to be careful, Arlie," her words slurred together until I couldn't understand most of what she was saying. I gently combed her hair through my fingers, running her walking man around her arm. Neither of them had any effect. "You and Ella have got to just go with what they're saying and stay safe... so you can get on a boat and come back to the camp...."

I looked past her at Emmitt, but before I said anything, he strictly told me,

"Rosalie is thirteen. If they were to realize what is going on, I know you do not want her here anymore than we do. We are taking Fiona back to Imperiam with us because she is younger and restless to return home, as far as the Guard knows."

"Rose...." I whispered to her, having no idea what to say. My instinct was to keep her close to me, where I thought she was safest, but I knew the best place for her was at the camp with Emmitt and Allyson. Rose had no experience faking any identity, much less that of an Imperiess. If she was badgered, I didn't know if she could be careful enough to not let anything telling slip.

"I don't want to go back to the camp. Why does everyone think I'm going to sing like a canary at the first question?" she said angrily, her eyes quickly drying up. "I can handle it. I don't want to leave you and Ella here."

"They're expecting us to stay until we can get another boat," I pressed my forehead against hers as if I could block the two out of our personal conversation. "We're a week behind you."

"This isn't the same thing as the Haritite State. There are too many things that could happen, and you can't just talk big circles around the Guard like you did at home."

I couldn't think of anything to say that would make the situation better. We sat there for a long time before Emmitt gently took her arm and pulled her away from me.

"We are leaving very early in the morning. Go try to get some sleep."

"Let her stay in here," I said.

"Amaryllis, brothers and sisters by the Imperial have vastly different relationships than you and Rosalie. If they do not despise each other thoroughly, then they are not close. If she is here tomorrow morning, then the manor will know you two were talking tonight."

He spoke as if the manor was a living watchman itself, and just as dangerous as the people who lived in it.

"Rosalie," I said in a normal voice as they walked toward the door. Emmitt's glare butchered me as if I had shouted her name from the roof. "Keep thinking about Uncle Graham, Aunt Clarissa, and the boys, okay?"

It seemed unrelated, but there was some feeling inside me that said I had to tell her that, like their lives depended upon the two of us never forgetting about them. She nodded at me, and opened her mouth to answer from the hallway. Before she spoke, Emmitt lightly closed the door behind them. Just like that, Rose was gone.

I stared at the floor where her shadow remained until Bennett dared to say something.

"You know she's better off at the camp than here."

"I know," I forced myself to look away from the blank, laughing door. "But it doesn't change that I've done this to her twice now."

"You haven't done anything to her," Bennett shook his head, and adjusted himself to face me. I gathered my legs close to my chest as I listened to him. "We couldn't have done anything to prevent going to the State... and this is a result of my dad's ridiculous hardheadedness."

"Who do we think we are?" I dug my nails deep into my kneecaps. "Haritites are one thing, but the Imperial's children?"

"Lower your voice," was his response, though I didn't think I could possibly speak any softer. "What other choice did we have if we didn't want to end up shot on the beach?"

"We could've said we were just the people bringing packages."

"But then so many of us wouldn't be there, and neither would you, me, Rose, Lukas, or Joana," he said, looking reflectively out the window. "Joana was smart to figure something out to say to all of them. Now we've just got to make it look real."

I must have looked unconvinced, because Bennett quickly added, "I know we'll be fine. We may not have any idea how to play Lebon, but we'll be able to take most of our cues from the Etaira."

"I'm a Stoleh, Bennett. A Sto-leh. Not a Lebon. How can I just calmly walk among the people who openly spit on my family and think Cleansings are a reasonable and entertaining method of keeping control?"

"The same way you calmly walked among Madam Guise, Emeline, Riley, and everyone else. The only difference is the patch."

"Then there's the whole acting like royalty thing."

"Yeah, well," Bennett shrugged. "That too, I guess."

"Bennett...." I buried my face in my hands. He wasn't helping.

"And you're not a Stoleh anymore," he took one of my hands away from my face. I supported my head with my remaining one, watching him with my one open eye. "That changed at the camp."

"Because being an Idrisan is so much better around here," I laughed bitterly, and he only sounded in a defeated agreement. I took my hand back to prop my head up, resting the sides of my face in my hands so I could look at him. "And as long as I have family behind that Wall, I will always be a Stoleh. I could run as far away as possible, but nothing changes the fact that my people are huddled in boroughs, not riding horses in the Wilds or sailing around the island. That golden patch that makes our lives a living hell has been engrained too many times on the side of our minds to go away so easily. I would like to think that being at the bottom all my life gave me character and instinct, not just bitterness. It doesn't really matter whether I turned out to be a good person or not. That Wall made me who I am, and there's nothing I can really do about it."

Bennett halfway smiled, and braced his hands against his legs in preparation to stand up.

"Do you remember what Rowana told you in the State?" he eased back slightly.

"Which time?" I asked. Rowana had given us so many assorted nuggets of advice and kindness throughout our stay.

"When she said if you had been born a Haritite then you wouldn't be half the person you are today. I don't know if it means much to you, but your family, everyone at the camp, and I wouldn't want you any other way than you are. The Wall is and always will be part of you. And you're right, you could never run away from it. That doesn't mean it has to define you."

I blinked, unresponsive.

"Am I making any sense?" he asked.

"Yes," I smiled a little, something I now thought only he could make me do in the kinds of situations we had undergone together. A sudden burst of pain alarmed in my head, and I winced.

"You are an inwardly good person, Amaryllis," he continued. "I don't see how you could think you aren't. You just need to stop being afraid and trust a little. Then more of it would come out." Bennett paused a moment, and said with a sly grin, "But not right now. That would probably hurt your highbrow Imperiess visage."

"Get out," I laughed a bit too loudly. He stood up.

"Try to get some sleep unless you want those women to hold you hostage in here all day tomorrow. It sounded like it'll be at least a few days before they can get us another boat to go home."

With that, Bennett closed the door behind him. I crawled back up to the top of the bed, and tried to find a position that didn't hurt too badly. Everything seemed even more blurry than when I first fell off the boat, but I felt more aware than before. *Rose is safer where she is going*, I told myself over and over again, slowly beginning to believe the words. A relief washed over me knowing that she and Emmitt were going to tell Allyson everyone was still alive. No ship also meant the spy in the camp probably came by land, alone, meaning he couldn't possibly give precise directions even if he'd been given the time. We didn't need to move the camp. Though Rose and Emmitt were gone, I felt a strange sense of calm stay in the room throughout the night knowing that.

Chapter Thirty

I dreamt of my father, never so physically close yet still so unreal. His beard was inches longer, his clothes were tearing and filthy, and he sat unmoving in a cell. I could not hear what the Guard said, though by the look on his face, I could feel him enduring them on a daily basis. Not much else happened in the dream. He never looked up, and I never saw myself. For a moment, I wondered if he would remember Ella, Rose, or me if we were to walk right in front of him.

His image faded into morning. The sun seemed overly bright in the room, stinging my eyes, though my head didn't hurt as much. I felt two small, intersecting bandages on the side of my forehead, and couldn't help but feel violated. When one of the women finally returned, I tried to casually ask if Fiona and 'the man' were on their way to Kieriana. When I found out I had been asleep when Emmitt and Rose came again at six, I was infuriated with myself. I felt somewhat hurt they didn't rouse me as I was told I woke four hours too late to see them.

Bennett, Joana, Lukas, and I were left in an airy, decorated hall, at a long table with the place settings set as far from each other as possible. I felt uncomfortable in a tight, black dress, as if in mourning. The angled sleeves sat off my shoulders, and the only thing keeping the dress up was two thin straps. Though it was floor length and made of a thicker fabric, I couldn't help but feel as if I was missing the blue cover that displayed a Haritite patch. Before we took our chairs, not daring to move them closer to each other, I thought there was something moving in the deep pocket of my dress. I quickly turned my head, and saw Lukas withdraw his hand, not acknowledging me. He did the same thing to Joana. I realized he was slipping notes to us only after he discreetly walked faster to pass Bennett, shoving a folded piece of paper against his chest in the process. Bennett quickly slid it behind his proper, unwrinkled vest, and said nothing.

I didn't eat enough at the silent meal in anticipation of reading the note. We knew better than to open them while we may be under surveillance, so I waited until I could get back to the room, close the door, and sit against it before I began to fish for the pocket in rolls of the dress's drapery. The note was scrawled in average handwriting with numbered points:

1) The owner's name is Jabez Arundel. Do not give much information, but acknowledge him as if he is some kind of distant family friend.

2) They said the earliest they can get us a boat is two days from now. Until then, we will be expected to socialize and do whatever activities they might have planned, which may include touring the mountains. Act natural and as if these kind of things are normal.

3) Never let anyone see you acting like close friends. The Imperial's children are usually plotting to kill each other by adulthood, and rarely get along well.

4) Remember that you are Lebon. You are not connected with the island and know little about classes lower than the Etaira. Should these people try to explain something to you regarding them, listen and seem only minutely interested. Carry yourselves like royalty.

5) Tear this paper into unrecognizable pieces and let them blow out the window.

As I held the remnants of the note, allowing them to drift lazily on the cold wind whistling around the building, a knock made me jump, and drop the remainder straight down. The owner of the manor was waiting there, standing a safe, polite distance from the door. It was the first time I had truly gotten a decent look at him, and couldn't help initial shock from the size of his gut. No one else here seemed to be as round, or so revolting to me. It wasn't only his size. It was that combined with his pinched, two-chinned face, combined with his thinning, greased back hair, combined with the loose, starchy clothes that failed to disguise his weight. Such people were unheard of where I came from. They were only spitefully joked about by both Stoleh and Nemirens.

"A good morning to you, Imperiess Arena," he bowed low. I retreated slightly into the room, clutching the door as if preparing to slam it in his face. The man seemed harmless, if not all fingers and thumbs, but I only saw him as a threat. "I trust you are feeling well?"

I reached under my hair, lightly touching the bandages bridging the cut on my forehead.

"I am better, thank you," I answered shortly, trying to eliminate any contractions or other telling phrases from my speech.

"Excellent," was his answer. I couldn't help but feel a little scared, wishing I had answered differently. "Then you would like to accompany us?"

Though I had no information as to who 'us' was or where 'us' was going, the letter told me that anything these people had planned, we needed to go along with. I assumed whatever it was, Bennett, Joana, and Lukas would be there. The longer I spent formulating a response, the more imposing the presence of the man blocking my only possible escape route.

"Yes," I said, following far behind him down the wide hall and outside into one of the paved, white stone roads in the gardens.

All of the riding I had done with Abiona at the camp could not have prepared me for the horses stabled on the manor. Young, and used to maneuvering around the mountain passes, they seemed to take every cue from the rider. Lukas and Joana's performance impressed the Etaira, and mine and Bennett's at least passed. *Arena does not have the opportunity to ride as regularly as the rest of us,* Joana had slipped in casually, speaking to the man as if making fun of how awkwardly I steered the smaller, nimbler Abiona look-alike I had chosen. *She spends most of her time with or doing something for his Majesty.* It seemed to be an acceptable explanation. Because of it, people constantly gave me polite, intrusive advice, and acted as if the horse would jettison me at any moment. We rode the circumference of the mountain several times around the beaches. Jabez Arundel, awkwardly perched upon an equally beefy horse, scarcely knew where he was going. It took two or three hour-long rounds before someone else began to lead, and our party could go somewhere new. The Etairan Mountains were connected to each other by natural, rock bridges, with the nearest manor securely tucked miles away where the drastic landscape allowed. We never approached it, but could see the tip of a roof in the trough of smaller, twin peaks.

Partially hidden in the moving shadow of a few, more rounded mountains, was a two story building with a dome, metal roof. Constricting greenery crept up its walls, as several people hacked away at it with large hedge cutters. The entire place appeared to be crowded with people, all of them preparing for something.

"What's going on there?" Lukas spoke up, and the entire party halted.

"I am not sure," Jabez answered, roughly turning his horse.

"Girl!" He shouted at one of the workers scurrying around the building as we approached it. A ripple of apprehension was sent through the gathering as everyone froze, and stared at the imposing group of people on horseback towering over them. Finally, in response, a black haired girl no more than fourteen or fifteen years old scuttled toward us. She was dressed in plain, colorless clothes, with a faded yellow, open, sleeveless jacket over top. I frowned as I looked down at her, and she avoided our gazes. There was no possibility she was Etairan. If not, then I couldn't help but wonder where she had come from.

"Yessir?" she choked, afraid of speaking to us.

"What is happening here?"

"I think it's a play, sir. I know at least five families are comin'."

Jabez dismissed the girl. I watched her as she gratefully ran back to the others, who were all dressed similarly. At a safe distance from the building, I stopped paying attention to our eager tour guide, and stared absently over my shoulder, watching the small figures of the workers swarm in and out of the playhouse. There seemed to be an element of grace in their inner workings, and a mystery about them. They pulled my lacking interest away from anything else the Etairan Mountains could offer.

It wasn't much of a surprise when Jabez later found the four of us, silent and spaced out from each other, in one of the gardens, and announced that we were returning to the playhouse that night.

"Of course only if you are interested, your highnesses," he quickly added, the pride in his voice sheepishly leeching away. "However, we have already sent a boy to inform everyone that we have the honor of your presence...."

There wasn't much we could say to that.

Without Rose, I had almost entirely forgotten anyone else besides the four of us were stranded. It unnerved me to know I hadn't seen Ella all day. Apparently, she, Jonathon, and Mr. Johansson had arrived ahead of us at the playhouse, and were standing outside. I wasn't forced to dress like I was attending a funeral, but felt even less comfortable in another snug, sea green dress as I realized most everyone was staring at us. Still, it was all about maintaining an unreadable face, and I managed to carry myself with enough composure to appease people. The tin, dome ceiling was more egg-shaped, and covered in a wide, intricate mosaic. A blended hue of red and blue in its center sprouted long tendrils that dipped down the metal lined walls, and rose again into the lilac outline of the tainted glass. The floor stooped inward around to the stage: an unassuming, risen platform beneath the artful ceiling surrounded on all sides by chairs. An almost supernatural haze from so many cigars drifted in the air, obscuring the detail of the mosaic and carrying the loud conservation to the front door. I already thought I could choke in this atmosphere.

"This way," Jabez gestured Lukas, Joana, Bennett, and me toward a set of shallow stairs leading to a balcony. Instead of individual seats, there were three long, backed benches, each raised slightly higher than the one preceding it. The four of us barely fit on the first bench. Jabez and two other Etairan men who appeared to be longtime friends of his took the one in the back, the smoke from their cigars giving us a small coughing fit almost every time they exhaled. Minutes later, I think Joana must have accidentally shot them a dirty look, because we finally received our introductions.

"My apologizes, Imperiess," Jabez laboriously forced himself out of his seat. As revolting as he seemed to me, I guessed there was something to be said about how he did not smoke along with the other two. His friends seemed to take their cue from the word 'Imperiess', also stood, and bowed slightly. "Allow me to introduce Imperien Alexander, Imperiess Arena, Imperiess Stephanie, and Imperien Silas."

He pointed to us in the order we sat on the bench, giving a regal hand gesture with each name. It felt strange to sit beneath them, and I made a conscious effort to make my back straighter. As if she thought I was about to stand, Joana pressed her foot hard on top of mine in a powerful message to only smile and nod.

"To what do we owe the... honor?" one of the two finally seemed to notice the accumulating smoke in the balcony, and put out his cigar in a glass ashtray balancing on the arm of his bench. He burrowed the cigar's butt deep into the ash, and for a moment ground it into the bottom of the dish, sending small bits of ash and puffs of gray back into the air. Though he was nowhere near the same sight as Jabez, something in the way he put out a measly cigar just seemed intimidating to me. You never saw anyone smoking in the main part of the island: Stoleh, Nemiren, or Haritite. I figured it was considered a luxury that the Etaira could import from Imperiam.

"A crew ran our ship aground on a beach near Sir Arundel's home. We are here only until we can get another passage back to Kieriana," Joana answered shortly. Meanwhile, the other man reluctantly passed his cigar down to be disposed of. I didn't seem to get that as I watched him, he studied me, and appeared to be staring at my face.

"That couldn't be Imperiess Arena," he sat up and leaned forward. I quickly looked away. Bennett and Joana frowned deeply, already preparing to spit out and stumble over a story to whatever suspicion he had. But the man then leaned back again and laughed heartily. His voice brought back a vivid image of Gregory Guise, and a shiver ran down my spine as I envisioned him sitting there. "Even as a child, she would be too fretted about her appearance to wear bandages on her face."

The four of us forced out a choked laugh. I quickly turned my back to the man, and ripped the two white dressings from my forehead. I could still feel a faint throbbing behind the slightly swollen cut as I awkwardly turned myself around again to face the one-sided conversation.

"I wouldn't expect your highness to remember someone like me," he said. I sensed that the man's entire explanation was simply to flaunt in front of Jabez, as if to show he had some sort of personal connection with the Imperial's large, dysfunctional family. "You were but three feet tall when I saw you with your beautiful, noble mother last time his Majesty made the trip over to the island. For a moment, I thought your presence would mean he had come again for the first time in years," the man paused, continuing to stare thoughtfully. I tried not to shift under his stare. "You looked very much like her many years ago with your long hair: so blonde it was nearly white. But children do branch off as they grow older, I suppose. If you do not mind my asking, what happened to your forehead?"

"Imperiess Arena is unlucky, is all," Jabez answered for me. His voice suggested that he was trying to end the talk before the play began. "When the ship beached on shore, she was tossed overboard because she is too thin."

I tried to think of a response, but could find nothing to fill the space. Out of the corner of my eye, I could see, almost feel, Joana's deep, disapproving stare directed at the man. He quickly looked away, mumbled an apology for his intrusiveness and disrespect, and then scuttled toward the stairs to return to the growing audience. The girl had said there were five families, though it was hard to imagine all the people here somehow belonging to one of them. There would have to be between fifteen and twenty from each household. It took me a while to remember that family here didn't mean the same thing as family to the rest of the island. Judging by the size of Jabez's home he kept seemingly to himself, twenty-five or more people could easily live under one roof in the manors peppering the mountains.

The room mechanically quieted as a stout figure made their way onto the stage. From the balcony, we could only see one side of their face, but hear clearly as their voice echoed around the walls. He seemed to just be announcing the play, referencing many Lebon and Etairan places and people I wasn't familiar with. As he concluded his introduction with a long string of glorified comments about the Lebon, I couldn't help but think that he only went out on that limb because he believed Alexander, Stephanie, Silas, and Arena were there. He stepped down, and was given obligatory, light applause. As if in response, Ella, Jonathon, and Mr. Johansson filed in from the stairs, and took their seats on the bench behind us. They said nothing, though I felt Ella briefly, discreetly brush her fingers against my shoulder to let me know she was behind me. It seems silly now, but I felt reassured knowing there was some kind of barrier between the four of us and the Etaira.

"This story again?" the man's whispering voice still reached us.

"It's a true one."

"Yes, but the truth is uninteresting after the fifth time they tell it."

The amusement behind watching people pace around a stage and recite lines was lost on me, but I tried to pay attention as it started. I had nothing to compare such an experience to except real life. There was not one playhouse anywhere on the main part of the island. Truthfully, it was disappointing, as people only stood around and unemotionally spoke their parts. At least for the first half, then I thought I realized what was actually going on. The same five people who had been on stage the entire time separated, and froze in their positions as every oil lamp in the room dimmed, then turned completely off. A large murmur of excitement ran through the audience. We couldn't tell the reason from the balcony for a while until a bright, bobbing light was seen moving down the aisle. *Torches?* I frowned at the five moving beacons as they walked silently to the stage. I had seen them sparingly used around the borough when we ran out of oil in the winter, but that problem shouldn't have existed in the Etairan Mountains.

"It's all part of the play," Jabez's voice told us. We didn't respond, transfixed by the contrast of the dripping torches against the darkness. As they were carefully handed up to the actors, a mortifying thought occurred to me, though I hadn't understood enough of the play to be sure. *If this is supposed to be some kind of representation of a Cleansing...* I mouthed to myself. Bennett thought I was trying to say something to him, and leaned closer to me. In response, I only shook my head. What happened in our world couldn't interest the Etaira enough to discuss it, much less produce a play about it.

"Stephanie...." Lukas's distinctive voice said as the torches neared the stage. I looked beside me, and saw Joana already had one hand cupped over her mouth, her eyes wide and looking off into the middle distance. She was pale and near shaking, like she would spring up and storm out of the playhouse at any moment. Lukas kept his hand firmly on her knee, but seemed hesitant to do anything else for fear of those behind us. "It's fine. It'll be fine...." he continued, barely speaking.

"I can't watch this," Joana leaned forward, and Lukas reached his arm across her lap to press down on her other leg as if he could prevent her from standing. Joana had already made up her mind.

"Imperiess Stephanie, is something the matter?" Jabez watched as she passed them on her way to the stairs. She dismissed the question with a wave of her hand, covering her mouth and coughing several times. Her tapping footsteps echoed back up to the balcony, and finally, so did the opening and light closing of the door.

"It's the smoke, I tell you!" Jabez hissed at the remaining man. "What did I say about doing that up here?"

He didn't respond, only staring at the seething ashtray. I kept my body facing forward in hope it would look like I was watching the slow, unnervingly eerie progress, but my head turned the way Joana had gone. "Don't," Bennett mouthed to me. My eyes ran from the exit to the stage to him--unable to focus as the ritual continued. The air itself seemed to weigh more with the passing seconds. There was something about this play that instilled a sense of panic in me, like I were in some kind of immediate danger. I didn't realize I had been silently hyperventilating until I struggled to tell Bennett,

"I can't do it, either."

I thought I felt him try to take my hand as I skirted past him, though I was already out of his reach, anxiously squeezing a handful of my dress as I tried to avoid looking at the men, Ellamae, Jonathon, and Mr. Johansson.

"Imperiess Arena-" Jabez began again. I sensed he was going to try to talk me into staying, and mimicked Joana's excuse for abruptly leaving.

"I cannot bear the smoke," I covered my mouth, and quickly turned my back to all of them, taking the stairs two at a time.

I didn't expect there to be so many people standing by the door. They looked at me, and most stared as if I had caught them doing something criminal. I made a path for myself just by walking forward, taking the heavy door handle in my sweaty palm without a word. I could hear the play resume behind me as I almost frantically forced open the door, and nearly shrieked when the sound and light of fire exploded behind me. My panic was offset by a large round of applause for a man who had just blown onto one of the flames, stirring it wildly as its haunting sound resonated off the metal walls. I felt I could lose my mind if he did that again, and opened the door only enough to slip out. It closed heavily behind me, cutting through the silence. I took deep breaths of the untainted air, trying to gather my senses as well as my composure. Arriving here and assuming another, much more radical identity had frayed my nerves, and it felt like the simple presence of the torches had completely severed them. The idea of the Etaira including something about a Cleansing in a play was almost comical. But when Guard entered the Wall carrying those things, everyone would gather at the outskirts for tense minutes, waiting to see which borough they planned to light up the sky with if met with any form of resistance.

I braced myself against a column, staring distantly at the ground, and trying to get my breathing under control. The steps were in the corner of my field of vision. Sitting only a few feet from me was a boy my age or slightly younger, staring up at me without blinking, frozen. I stumbled away from him, almost tripping over my dress. A group of at least ten yellow-vested workers mirrored the shocked expression on my face, waiting in dread for me to react to their presence.

"I'm sorry," I eventually slurred, searching for the words. "I didn't see you."

They seemed afraid to answer, and continued to gawk at me expectantly. I averted my eyes, and lifted my dress to walk down the stairs and onto the path. They moved as far away from me as possible, and then quickly reformed what seemed to be a uniform line at the bottom of the steps.

"Don't do all that on my account," I said, yet the shocked, nervous expressions watching my every movement didn't change. I desperately examined the immediate area for any place I could possibly disappear into. The forest of pine trees spanning from the side of the playhouse to as far as the eye could see seemed to be my only option, and I allowed the dress to drag in the dirt as I walked away.

Chapter Thirty One

I made a conscious effort to walk only straight so I could find my way out, though the scattered pattern of trees seemed to work against me. The stillness of the dark pine needles and rocky dirt told me I was alone, but I couldn't bring myself to sit down anywhere. Every darkened area seemed to harbor a threat in my mind. No matter how many times I scolded myself, I couldn't just say that the torches were supposed to be an amusing light show and let it die.

I wasn't all that surprised to find Joana, but couldn't stop staring at what she was doing. She rested on her knees, pushing small rocks around with a stick, in such a state of focus that she didn't notice me. I couldn't make out exactly what she was drawing until I got closer. Joana shuddered, looked up at me, and seemed to calm down only slightly.

"Are you alone?" she asked me from the ground, returning to her drawing.

"Yes," I answered. Joana motioned me closer with her hand until I knelt on the other side of her work, careful to keep my distance as I looked at it. A partially filled 'S' connected to three downward humps. The first divided into two lines: the rightward one branching off again into simple, swirled designs, and the leftward one leading into a lone arrow.

"Is it right?" Joana stopped moving, though kept the stick firmly planted in the ground. Though the symbol possessed unspeakable power, I had never truly studied it the way I painstakingly learned every line and curve of the Haritite patch. It bothered me that Joana knew it well enough to duplicate it. When I heard of how she was abandoned as a child and taken in by Allyson, it only made sense that she was born with a yellow patch. But she was so tightly wound and withdrawn sometimes, I knew trying to build upon that as our common ground could only result in her angrily marching off back into the woods. And by her demeanor and the way she avoided my eyes, I could tell this was an even touchier topic surrounded by years of bitterness for her.

"Yes," I said again. "It's right. Why?"

"Are they looking for us yet?" she ignored the question as she violently scratched out the identification curse of a Stoleh. I shook my head.

"But they'll probably be out soon. They think we left because we couldn't stand the smoke."

"Well, that too. It was disgusting," the features of her face wrinkled as if she was still inhaling the overpowering stench. Her voice trailed off for only a moment. "They're all disgusting. How can you think something like that is entertaining? The worst part is that they actually believe it's all true."

"What were they doing with the torches?" I dared to ask, and Joana shot me a brief, petrifying glare. In a few seconds, though, her expression softened.

"You don't know much about how things work, do you?"

I didn't know how to continue, or if I even should. Joana laughed quietly at my silence.

"That thing's not even a play. It's just dramatized propaganda. I heard of it from my grandfather, so I know how it goes and how it ends. Do you realize who those five people on stage were supposed to be?"

"Stoleh?"

"Even worse: Idrisans. They depict us as some kind of terror rebels who want to topple the oh-so divine government and replace it with their own scary oligarchy. The Lebon wants to constantly primp up their image for the Etaira. They're so paranoid that because they're still natives to the island just like everybody else, they could turn against them. The torches are representation of something Idrisans supposedly did ten years ago."

"What is it?" I asked. Joana spat on the remnants of the symbol, and finally looked me in the eye.

"They say that Idrisans burned part of a neighborhood down and killed twenty or thirty odd Haritites."

An image of the busy peace present in the Idrisan camp came to my mind. Not by any stretch of the imagination could I see anyone doing anything even remotely close to setting a fire in a crowded area.

"There's no fire damage to any of the Haritite neighborhoods, and I've never heard anyone talk about it," I felt my face fall into a frown.

"That's because it didn't happen. We have no reason to attack the mainland; that doesn't even make any sense. But because the Etaira are so isolated from the rest of the people, they'll accept anything the Lebon says as true," Joana sighed. "Honestly, I think even if they saw it themselves, they'd still believe the Lebon over their own eyes."

We sat in silence as a strong, cold wind whistled around the trees, causing the pebbles to tumble quietly along the ground.

"How does that play end?" I asked. Joana looked away, standing up and brushing all the dirt from her red, silk dress.

"They follow those five Idrisans for the first hour of it, and show them planning another attack when they are caught. The remaining hour is spent showing everything leading up to their detailed execution in Imperiam. The ending is the only part of the entire, sickening production where the actors show any interest."

Joana shook her head, and dismissed the topic as she stormed off in the wrong direction.

"We came from over there."

"But if we go this way, then we can get out of the woods behind the playhouse and say we just walked around. It would be a lot less conspicuous than coming out the way we came in."

I followed alongside Joana as we weaved our ways around the protruding roots and low branches. We halfheartedly tried to come up with something to say to Jabez or the others as we walked, though after a while in the unchanging landscape, I pointed west toward the entrance of the woods. I suggested that we start to move inward instead of just circling the area, and ended any kind of conversation between us. I felt almost dazed by what she had just described as the play's ending, and tried to convince myself that the dark-haired woman on stage had no resemblance or connection to Ruth.

Our silence was sharply interrupted by a nearby moaning sound. We were close enough to the back of the playhouse that I momentarily thought we could hear what was happening inside from right there. Joana paused, and looked around us for a human source.

"Did you hear that?" she eventually asked me, sounding like she had already convinced herself that the sound was simply wind.

"Yes," I turned around. Immediately, I thought I could see two forms deeper in the woods. The same moan shook my bones again, and I began walking, leaving Joana standing there, wondering how to respond. They were further away than I first thought. I still couldn't tell exactly what was going on until I silently adjusted myself behind a tree ten feet away, poking my head around the trunk to watch. On the rocky, jagged earth beneath us, someone dressed in the yellow vest of the worker lay with an arm pressed hard over their stomach in pain. The same black-headed girl Jabez had called over earlier in the day sat on her knees beside him. She solemnly looked him over, and was inattentive as I took steps away from the tree. Only after I was near on top of them did I realize that the person on the ground appeared to be another boy our age. His blond hair was caked with dirt, and a steady trickle of blood ran down the side of his face from somewhere beneath it.

I watched the girl wordlessly and sharply take his hand and hold it in between hers, as if forcing herself to offer the gesture. It seemed like some sort of internal barrier prevented her from saying anything. The same mechanism also froze her on the ground as she looked up at me, squinted, and immediately turned her head away again. I couldn't stand to tower over them, and I dropped quickly to my knees beside her, alarming both her and the boy. Still, she would not speak.

"Are you okay?" I asked her. She took a short, choked breath, and answered,

"Yesmiss."

"What happened?"

"I dunno, miss. I found him."

I looked at the boy, and saw the distance in his sunken eyes. Frowning, I lightly placed my hand on his arm to let him know I was there. He winced in response.

"What happened to you?" I repeated, and the boy struggled to turn his head and look at me.

"She's not an Etaira, Charleigh," he told the girl, and she clammed up further. "She's not wearing a patch. That means she's a Lebon—probably one of the Imperial's forty some bastard children."

Surprised, I said nothing. Charleigh released his hand, and scooted back in the dirt as if afraid of what had just come out of his mouth.

"Save your breath. Go ahead and kill me, I dare you," The boy looked me straight in the eye. Just his cutting stare made it feel like he was inside my head. "You can't possibly take anything more away from me."

Something in the spiteful, lasting words seemed familiar. The boy flinched, and nearly snarled at me as I tried to wipe some of the mud away from his eyes. I sucked in my breath when I finally saw it, and I leaned over him with both my hands on his shoulders.

"Get off of me, you little primped up slave driver!"

"How'd you get here, Barney?" I lowered my voice, though his eyes widened at the mention of his lost name. Several seconds passed until he forced himself up on one arm, making me back off. He stared at my face for a long time, and didn't seem to quite put anything together until I pulled a pin out of my hair and let it fall loose.

"Arlie?" he touched my arm as if expecting me to disappear at any moment. I knew hugging or any other display of some kind of emotion used to make him uncomfortable, but I did it anyway. Though I had barely moved, I seemed to knock the wind out of him, and had to help him lie back on the ground again. Barney was never broad chested or bigger than average anywhere, but now he just looked like a beaten sack of yellowish skin and fragile bones. As I sat back, we only stared at each other.

"Some errand," Barney tried to laugh bitterly, though it seemed to hurt him too much. "How'd you wind up here?"

"I asked you first."

He frowned deeply, like the memory itself was worse than the state he was currently in.

"The Cleansing, Arlie. There was another Cleansing after you left. I'm so sorry, but I don't know what happened to Rose, Oakley, Niles, or your aunt and uncle. Me and Stella were on the far side of the borough, and we didn't have time to get home. Somebody who lived nearby took as many people in as he could. He locked us and two younger kids in a bedroom, and we thought we'd be okay for a while. But when we heard the Guard outside, Stella made the kids get under the bed. After a while, I got her to listen to me and she rolled under there with them. By then the Guard was breaking down the other side of the door. I went and sat in the opposite corner of the room so they wouldn't see me trying to get under the bed and find Stella and the kids there, too...."

Barney stopped, and looked away, distant.

"Barney?" I asked, and he continued the story like I had jolted him back into reality.

"There were about twenty of us. The Guard loaded everyone on a cart after we got far enough away from the borough, and walked alongside it. They said if anyone so much as stood up, they'd shoot them. They took the cart somewhere isolated and made us wait until after eight that night to leave the Wall. When we reached the jail, only sixteen of us were left. Another group of Guard were waiting there. They took half of us, gave us these clothes, and brought us here."

People taken in a Cleansing wound up working for the Etaira? I thought to myself. Another question immediately followed behind it. *Could Mom be here somewhere?*

"I haven't seen her, Arlie," Barney knew what I was thinking by the look on my face. "And I've met pretty much everyone."

It felt as if something inside me had shattered for a second time, and I forced myself to continue the conversation to dismiss the thoughts.

"Rose is safe," I told him. He smiled slightly just to show he was listening. "She was with me for a while."

"How did you wind up here after a Nemiren errand, anyway?"

242

"It's complicated. I'll have to tell you later."

"You aren't going to have a later," Joana's voice scared us all. I looked over at Charleigh, and felt a pang of guilt when I saw how genuinely confused and terrified she was. Joana frowned at us, and slowly lowered herself onto the ground in our circle. "A friend of yours, I presume?" she pointed a careless finger at Barney. I nodded.

"He was taken during a Cleansing and brought here."

"Where do you think the Etaira and Lebon get people to work on their manors and act as servants? More than half of all Stoleh kidnapped during those violent roundups are here or in Imperiam. You didn't know that?"

"They just tell us one day at the Wall that our friends and family are dead."

"They could be," she shrugged. Her demeanor seemed cruelly indifferent, though I could see something in her expression suggesting she was bothered. "Or they could be here. Most would probably tell you they'd rather be dead." Joana paused, and looked at Barney. "Why are you in the woods?"

"Who is she?" Barney asked me, only looking at the way Joana was dressed.

"To you, right now, I'm Imperiess Stephanie and she is Imperiess Arena."

"You're a what?!" Barney raised his voice to a normal volume. In the silence, it sounded like he was shouting. I tried to quiet him, only making him angrier. "You spend a few weeks in Nemirena and all of sudden you're an Imperiess now?!"

"Be quiet," Joana hissed at him. "You don't know what you're talking about."

Barney ignored her, and struggled into a sitting position. He took my arm in his hand, though his grip was loose and sweaty.

"You're here willingly? Did you forget about us and your family, or did you just disown us for this?!" He pulled his hand down as if trying to rip the sleeve of my dress. "Take it off. That's not who you are!"

"Barney, calm down," I shook myself free, and backed away. Joana unaffectionately forced him to the ground. I tried to make my voice gentler as I watched the blood running on his face and the hurt in his eyes. "You're tired, and you're not thinking straight or making any sense. How could I jump from Nemirena to here, anyway? I told you I was coming back. If nothing else, you know I would never leave Rose after what Ellamae did. Come on, I can't stand these people because of what they've done to my family. How could I live here?"

"Then if you care anything about us, tell me what happened."

Joana nodded as if granting her approval for me to give Barney a shortened version. I wanted to tell him, I knew he deserved to know, but I couldn't seem to form the words to describe how I had come to play dress up as the people we had cursed every day of our lives for years. I told him the man who had sent me on the errand is an Idrisan, summarizing the Haritite State and our escape from the Guard in a few sentences. I skipped most of the explanation about the camp, and said we had to come up with the story that we were some of the Imperial's children so they'd get us another boat away from here. Even though Barney only stared at me blankly, I was relieved to see the look of distrust and absolute betrayal leave his face.

"What the hell is an Idrisan? Who dragged you into this mess?"

"We don't have time for this," Joana nervously glanced back in the direction of the playhouse. "Look, the bottom line is if they find out we aren't who we're telling them we are, then they'll have a field day with the firing squad. You don't tell anyone, got it?"

"I won't be talking to any of them, anyway. I tried to run away twice already. I've gotten caught and beaten like a slab of meat both times. If I go back again, then I'm the one who will end up getting shot."

"I won't let them touch you. The Etaira have to do what the Lebon tell them to," I told him, but Barney still didn't seem to trust me all the way. At the time, though, the most important thing to me was getting us out of here and him help.

"What are you going to do after this, Arlie?" Barney asked. The doubtfulness in his voice hurt me. "Just sail back to wherever you were?"

"I'm going to come back for you as soon as I can," I said with as much certainty as I could. "Just don't try to run away anymore for me, okay?"

Barney eventually nodded, and then moved a hand up to his head, grimacing. As I started to help him up, Joana seemed to just notice Charleigh.

"You, too. You don't talk to anyone."

"Charleigh doesn't really talk at all," Barney answered, and she looked away as if ashamed. "She's partially mute. She won't communicate with any of us ever. She only responds to orders and questions the Etaira give her."

Joana licked her lips, embarrassed she had said anything to her, and then knelt on the other side of Barney to help me pull him to his feet. He could still walk, though he leaned sparingly on us as we took a few practice steps. Charleigh followed dutifully in our wake until Joana turned around and told her,

"Then that's an order. You didn't hear anything tonight, do you understand me?"

"Yesmiss," Charleigh mumbled, and was once again as quiet as ever. Even the footsteps she took seemed cautious, passive, and soft in comparison to the three of us. Despite the stone shield of silence that surrounded her, I knew we didn't have to worry about Charleigh revealing anything.

The workers stood in their uniform line as we walked back around the playhouse to the steep front steps. Their posture and stillness signified that someone of importance, who followed us outside and interrupted their circle, waited on the stairs. I couldn't help the way I looked at those ten people differently, envisioning their lives to be so alike what mine had been. I knew it was a figment of my imagination, but it seemed to me like some of those worn faces were creepily familiar. Bennett, Lukas, Mr. Johansson, Ellamae, and Jonathon stood in a separate circle in the middle of the steps, conscious of the workers, while Jabez and several other Etaira frantically spoke to one another at the bottom. Our entrance caused an entirely new scene to unfold, and as I absorbed the stunned faces of the kidnapped Stoleh watching two Lebon practically carrying one of theirs, I heard one of the Etairan men tell Jabez,

"It's the one that ran away two days ago. It's his third time."

Jabez came out to us as we tried to steady ourselves.

"You did not have to bring him here, Imperiesses... we could have gone and gotten him."

"Well, it is too late for that," Joana nearly spat. Jabez recoiled slightly from the remark, and she took the time to add, "Is this the way you treat these people?"

"He has tried to run away multiple times," he answered, surprised that the Imperial's children would look twice at any Stoleh worker. "Situations such as this must be nipped off before they... spread. Sometimes, they require to be dealt with severely for the greater good."

"Whose greater good, might I ask?" I found the words. If he was so incredibly shocked by the fact that we cared how they treated their workers, then he would've fainted at what could have left my mouth if I hadn't been trying so hard to contain myself. "This is inhumane. Here's a lesson for you: if you treat them with a sense of dignity, then they might learn to respect you instead of just running about out of fear."

I knew there was no truth to it. It didn't matter whether the Etaira treated them with respect or not; none of us could ever find it in our hearts to willingly abide by the rules of people who had taken you miles and miles away from your home and family. Still, I figured it was better than simply spewing off at these peoples' horrendous treatment of Barney. Jabez and the other Etaira gave us their so-called sincerest promise that they would treat the workers as fellow human beings. However, as two yellow-vested men approached us, bowing their heads, and helped Barney away from us, I distinctly heard one of them say to another,

"Get the Guard to pick him up later tonight."

"You," I turned around, and stood taller, speaking in the clearest, most authoritative voice I had, "will not lay one hand on him. He is not to be punished."

"With all due respect, Imperiess Arena, he has tried to run away three times."

"He is not to be punished," I repeated. "It is appalling enough that you treat these people like dispensable scum, but it is new territory to lie to me! I have said that you will not hurt him, and if I find out later that you so much as whipped this boy, then I can snatch your world out from under you like *that*," I snapped my fingers sharply, and received wide, believing eyes. "If you want to prove to me that you yet have some humanity, then you will start by pardoning him."

It felt as if I had everyone's attention, with the shockwave of my outburst spreading over both the Etaira and the others.

"Where does he live?" Lukas came to our side, with his arms folded and a scowl on his face.

"They all-"

"I'm not talking to you," he spoke flatly. "I'm asking them."

"We sleep in shanty houses on individual manors, sir," one of the men holding Barney upright answered quickly and quietly, trying to get it over with. Though Barney's head was hanging down and he seemed unresponsive, I knew he was listening to us, trying to decide whether or not I was still the same person as I was months before. "I think he lives on Sir Dempsey's land."

"When he is not trying to escape down the side of the mountain, he does," the man from the balcony stepped up, sulking at the ground. I couldn't tell if it had to do with Barney running away again, or the fact that the Imperial himself had just indirectly forbidden him to dispose of the problem.

"You will take this boy into your home," I told him, and he seemed genuinely disgusted. "And you will see that he gets cleaned up and given something to eat."

"Straight away," he grumbled in agreement.

Barney, the Etairan man, and the two Stoleh left shortly before the unknowing crowds began to file from the playhouse, discussing the repetitious plot. I gathered enough bits of information to put together a melancholy mental image of the ending I had missed, which more than confirmed Joana's description. In the busyness, the seven of us managed to unnoticeably separate ourselves, and stand by the side of the building, away from the prying ears and eyes of Jabez or any others.

"That was Barney," I frowned at Ellamae's questioning stare. Her mouth nearly dropped open.

"Who is Barney?" Mr. Johansson asked quietly. "And why are you willing to risk us all over him?"

"You know those two kids who were with me every time I came to your fields?"

"I see...." he nodded briefly. I only then realized the uneasiness of what I had said. "He must have wound up here after that Cleansing."

I looked away, shaken, in time to see Charleigh scuttling quietly along the ground with two other workers: one older man and one young woman. They stopped an uncomfortable speaking distance, awaiting permission to approach us. For long seconds, we only stared at each other.

"Yes?" Joana eventually asked.

"You have to give us consent to speak," the woman answered.

"Alright, go ahead."

"We only wished to say thank you for helping him. The third attempt at running away is always punishable by death."

"We've all tried it once, of course," the gray-haired man continued, and the woman glared harshly at him. "Gotten our backs split open for it, and then had enough common sense to never do it again. But poor boy, he tried to escape his first week here, was caught, and right after he was on his feet again, went for it a second and third time. That spirit would have gotten him killed had it not been for you, Imperiesses. You're a rare kind around here."

As if fearing backlash for what he had told us, the man turned on his heels, and walked away. He was followed quickly by Charleigh, who offered not even a smile or nod of recognition.

"Can I ask you something?" I said to the woman before she could also leave. For a moment, she didn't seem able to reply. It took a while, but she eventually answered with a small bow. "Why does that girl only respond when we or the Etaira ask her something?"

"Charleigh has been here since she was very young. She learned to adapt and curb the grief by only speaking when they speak to her, or give her an order. She has done this for so long that now her mind prevents her from ever saying anything to us. Even if the Etaira ask her something, but do not form the sentence as a question, she cannot answer, and they know that by now. They ridicule the poor girl for it all the time."

"How old is she?" Bennett asked from behind me. He had only seen her earlier that day and was clearly disturbed by it.

"Everyone assumes that she is somewhere between twelve and sixteen years old, but nobody truly knows. No one knows her real name either because she never said it. The Etaira gave her the name Charleigh eventually, though they do not use it much."

"Why Charleigh?" I looked past the woman, watching as the girl faded into the line of yellow vests with the old man. The woman almost cringed in response to my question.

"Sir Dempsey once had a dog named Charleigh who was rather stupid, but always came when called."

Chapter Thirty Two

After the scene at the playhouse, Jabez made no other attempts to orchestrate another outing, or speak to us at all. He would only bow if he happened to accidentally stumble into the same room, and scuttle away in a resentful silence all because of the way I had taken up for, as far as he knew, a random Stoleh worker. Despite all of the tension, two more nights passed, and the four of us were still alive. The conflict apparently made the Etaira more eager to get us on our way. At the same table on the third morning, Lukas walked quickly and with purpose into the room ten minutes behind the rest of us. He ran his fingers through his hair as he sat down, and told us all in a quiet voice,

"I heard them talking. There's a boat waiting for us."

Joana, Bennett, and I sighed in relief, and struggled to wait at least another ten minutes to leave. We couldn't afford to earn the Etaira's suspicion at the last second. Jabez and his friends weren't much for goodbyes, and didn't even stay to see the boat off. As insistent as they were that we take a crew to help with the sails on the modest skip, Mr. Johansson firmly stated that they did not want to bother sending them back to the mountains after they crossed the channel. *His Majesty will keep the boat to replace the one that was lost. Thank you for your generosity.*

With only the seven of us on board, Mr. Johansson was strict on assigning set tasks to ensure we could sail through the channel in one piece. Once safely out of sight and reach of the mountains, we could then veer to the right and ride a coastal wind all the way back to the camp. It seemed too simple to the rest of us, and we watched each other's movements carefully. With his pride depending on returning us safely, Mr. Johansson kept us focused on the task at hand, scolding us harshly whenever someone so much as opened their mouth to speak.

It wasn't long before we drew uncomfortably close to a legend. Imperiam looked no different from the rest of the shoreline in terms of the dramatic drop offs and pointed rocks surrounding it. It was almost perfectly circular: a hopelessly isolated, remote land sitting nearly in the mouth of the biggest bay of our island. It seemed ironic that such a place dictated life and limb for thousands of people from so far away, and when they are so outnumbered. Brainwash wasn't just their most influential tool. Their only method of keeping control relied on the self-directed animosity between the classes they created.

Bennett, Lukas, and Joana managed to keep the clothes they had worn on our first trip. Somehow, Ellamae got a hold of mine by dancing delicately around the Etairan women.

"You cannot return home dressed as you are," Mr. Johansson told us, beginning to ease up on his captaining once we could no longer see the pier. We changed separately in the musty, humid cabin beneath the deck. Though the baggy rags smelled like salt and sweat, I felt a sense of liberation as the four of us pitched the fancy, expensive clothes into the ocean to either sink, or wash up somewhere.

"What's wrong?" Bennett found me staring emptily at the island two hours later as the weight of the afternoon sun reached its peak. I jumped at the sound of a voice, though I was happy it was him. If his father had found me, I would've been in for a long, angry lecture for neglecting the simple tasks he had laid out for me.

"What if they were just waiting until we left to punish him?" I asked no one in particular. No matter how badly we wanted to put as much distance between us and that place as possible, I couldn't help but feel like a piece of my authentic past stayed behind with Barney. What disturbed me almost as much as what our departure could mean for him was the idea that that was what I considered both him and Stella to be now: the past. I would always care about them because of how long we knew each other, and remember how invincible and accepted I would feel because I knew they had my back, but something about Barney's reaction to me seemed to water down everything I thought I knew about our unspoken alliance. Bennett's silence told me he was considering the same thing, and that he wouldn't put it below them to take the evening's events out on Barney, or even Charleigh, now that we weren't there to intervene.

"Did you tell him you were going to come back?"

"Of course I told him I wasn't going to just leave him there. But he was so angry at me. I don't think he believed anything I said."

"How could he be angry? I'd think he'd be glad to know you're alive since the last time he saw you was before the Haritite State."

"He basically said I had turned into one of them."

"Who's 'them'?" Bennett leaned against the rails beside me. I began to pick off small fragments of the splintered wood, and flick them mindfully into the sea. "The Etaira?"

"Just outsiders. With me, him, and Stella, it was always us against the world. Anyone who wasn't in our circle we considered 'them'."

"Bennett!" Mr. Johansson's booming voice startled us. I knew in my mind he was going to chew us out for doing nothing. "Turn us hard port!"

He reacted, and all but dove toward the tiller. Though once Bennett actually held it in his hands, he stared as if mesmerized, having no idea what to do with it. I went to the other side, and asked, "What are we doing?"

"Bennett, port!" Mr. Johansson's voice now seemed panicked, though both the boat and the water were calm.

"I-I think it's this way," Bennett pushed the tiller toward me, and at the same time, I began to push it toward him. We stared at each other for a moment until he switched directions.

"The *other* port!"

Flustered, we sent us into an uncomfortably narrow turnabout. The boat steadied after a few seconds, though we were now sailing in the direction we had come from.

"Why are we going back?" Bennett called, and Mr. Johansson only pointed at the hazy outline of the horizon now behind us. Though the upper jaw of the bay's mouth partially blocked the view, I could see several ships sitting just beyond it, as if waiting for us. In a trance, Bennett and I left the tiller. Jonathon stepped up to take it before we could cause any real damage.

"What are they doing?" I looked around at Mr. Johansson, Joana, Lukas, and Ellamae's expressions, glancing over my shoulder as if to make sure the ships were real, and really forcing us to turn around.

"It's an armada," Lukas answered dismally. In response, a string of curse words left Mr. Johansson. "They're blocking that way because Lebon and Etairan ships wouldn't typically travel across the channel in the opposite direction. It's an easy way to catch people who aren't supposed to be here."

"Why can't we just go that way?" Ellamae pointed around the other side of the island, past the Etairan Mountains, as if we couldn't see.

"We cannot sail past the way we just came. They will recognize the boat. We haven't been gone for that long. If they send another one after us, then they would look for a way we could have escaped. If they found the alcove, we'd be done."

Mr. Johansson paced around the deck for several, agonizing minutes before he shouted toward the back of the boat,

"Jonathon, take us to Imperiam!"

250

Jonathon obediently turned the boat despite the uproar that followed by the rest of us: especially Joana.

"We can't dock in Imperiam! They know who is and isn't supposed to be in their waters!"

Mr. Johansson regained his confidence, and gestured at the farthest side of the isle where a steep depression took hold of the landscape.

"You see that?" he asked us, waiting for our scattered responses before he continued. "The west side of Imperiam is inhabitable until two or three miles inland where the land levels out. There are no docks, no manors, but there have to be several concealed places where we can hide the boat. We will wait until late at night before we sail back past the Etairan Mountains."

Our reaction wasn't the one he hoped for. Getting anywhere near that ominous, quiet landmass seemed to beg for something even worse to happen.

"I think we're making this a bit too simple for them, don't you think?" Lukas finally spoke, though the closer we drew to Imperiam, the clearer every crevice in its rock, the more irreversible Mr. Johansson's second valiant decision seemed. "They're going to catch a group of Idrisans and not even have to worry about shipping them over. They were already hiding out on the cliff face."

"We're not even staying the entire night. If you think up a better idea, please let us know."

Lukas barely paused. "Why don't we take the sail down and stay right here until nightfall?"

Mr. Johansson momentarily pretended as if he hadn't heard, and walked toward the mast. Not to take down the sail, but pull it in to make us go faster. He spoke in a cool, calm voice as he tied an unbreakable knot in the rope, and then allowed the slack to slowly feed through his hands.

"One, we will drift and have no way to control it. Two, if that armada moves an inch, we're right in their line of sight. Three, if another Lebon or Etairan ship comes through here, which they probably will as evening comes, we're caught in the middle and have nowhere to go. I know you all are eager to get home, but we have only one chance, and one, clear shot. We cannot waste it waiting here for someone to find us."

As we approached Imperiam, Mr. Johansson talked Jonathon through every minute adjustment in the ship's position, starting with a quick turn into the narrow shadow and safety of the cliff face. His theory seemed true enough to me as over an hour passed, and all we saw were untouched beaches, sitting overlooked under the cover of the pointed rocks. He slowed us down to almost a crawl, allowing the sail to luff, looking for any place hidden from the armada and openness of the channel that could house our boat for the coming hours. What he eventually found looked almost too perfect to be real. The dark, damp beach felt more like a cave as its mothering mountain cast a long shadow over it, forming an elongated triangle in the water. Jonathon was forced to make a wide arc to align the boat, and tack toward the tight opening between the beach and the shelter that separated us from the channel. This one-sided mountain seemed to feed straight into the ocean, its slope coming out just far enough to entirely conceal the boat.

Ellamae, Lukas, Joana, Bennett, and I sat on the edge of the deck and pushed ourselves into the foot of water, which in itself seemed an entirely different color. While Jonathon and Mr. Johansson tossed a crude anchor into the shallow water from the other side of the boat, we picked our way across the beach. I was the first to notice it.

"People come down here," I froze in my tracks, raising my voice up onto the boat. "There's a path. People come down here."

"Did you say something, Amaryllis?" Mr. Johansson asked inattentively as he and Jonathon joined us on the beach. Frustrated, I walked up to a seemingly cleared, thin trail that appeared much too steep to climb. The apparent traffic it had seen over the years said otherwise. I only pointed at it as if afraid the Lebon would be alerted of our presence if I so much as breathed on anything of their making. Everyone gathered around the foot of the rocky path, staring at it, and wondering where else we could feasibly hide.

"I don't think it's manmade," Mr. Johansson tried to put down everyone's worry. "There can't be anybody within miles of where we are. In order to get to the nearest home, you would have to climb up here, and walk over our heads partially up a mountain with no paths to reach the other side."

"But it looks like-"

"Erosion over decades, not people. If the path were dirt, footsteps would leave impressions, but not on rock."

Our choice was to either believe what he said, or assume this path would yield a Lebon at any moment. No one could bear to think of the latter, and so we did the only thing we could do: spread out as far away from it as possible. Ellamae and Jonathon separated themselves into the corner. She sat perpendicular to him, leaning against his arm with her legs delicately over his lap. He held her hand, saying something. I couldn't hear it from the opposite side of the beach. I tried not to stare, though it seemed sad to me. I liked to forget that she still referred to him as her fiancé, and go about things as normally as possible. They made it almost believable by the way they acted under constant scrutiny, like something about them would always be forbidden. I felt guilty for acting so selfish, like she somehow owed it to Rose and me to never speak to him again, and told myself that I needed to let it go. Under any other circumstances, he would've seemed perfectly kind, gentlemanly, and all the other things she, Rose, and I fantasized about as little girls. It was just the way he appeared from thin air and drove a wedge between us.

Mr. Johansson refused to stop pacing along the shore, allowing the water to lap around his ankles. The four of us stayed close to the boat, staring, and watching it bob up and down with the constricted motion of the breakers. Joana seemed content to draw shapes in the rocky sand with her finger, sitting against Lukas and telling a story about Theo. Bennett tried to ask about Stella and Barney, but he quickly saw that it bothered me to talk about them. He abandoned the subject, and instead tried to lighten the atmosphere with a retelling of an incident with the Guard on his father's farm years ago. He made me laugh once, though I wasn't really in the state of mind for it. There seemed to be something about our presence on a beach in Imperiam that was more than intimidating. It felt almost immoral that we had stopped here for refuge on our way back to the Idrisan camp.

"Arlie," Ellamae jumped at our first moment of quiet, and sat on her legs in front of me. I hadn't expected her to leave her little niche without Jonathon. "Come here. I want to show you something."

"What?" I asked, skeptically looking past her at the unchanging, dark scenery. She only grinned at me, and repeated herself. Ella claimed on a spot in the middle of the beach, and motioned for me to sit across from her. Under my watch, she swept all of the smaller pebbles away with her arms to reveal a square of colorless rock beneath it.

"What are you doing?" I eventually asked her.

"Do you remember this?" she ignored me, picking up a select number of large bits of gravel into her hand.

"I am supposed to?"

She smiled, and held her closed fist out over the square to me. I reached out my hand, and she let ten of the tiny stones fall into my palm.

"You were only three. I didn't think you would. Mom used to play this game with us, but you were too young to understand it. You would sit on her lap and, as you would say, help her," Ella smiled at me again, and laughed. "I used to get so mad at you because you would say you won every time, and Mom let you believe that you did. Once I accidentally yelled at you, and then Mom started fussing, and you started crying, and Dad came downstairs because he had no idea what was going on."

"What happened?" I asked.

"We never played the game again," Ella said, still laughing, and then shook the small rocks in her hand. "Mom called it Sowing Seeds. You take the rocks, scatter them around the square, and then you get to keep whatever is left in its boundaries. If the next person gets more than you, then they get to take two of your rocks, and the other way around. You can also bet if you think the next person can't get more than you and double the wager. You're done when you run out of pebbles. Got it?"

"I think so," I told her, unsure as to why Ellamae was trying to engage us in a sentimental child's game. Yet it took no time at all before we were playfully accusing each other of cheating at every turn, almost forgetting the others and where we were. With only two people, games passed quickly and controversially, the arguing over who won continuing into the next round. Jonathon was the first to hesitantly join, and only because Ella hounded him about it for five minutes. I felt somewhat uncomfortable and outnumbered until Bennett sat beside me, followed quickly by Lukas and Joana. They stood firm that they only wanted to watch, and that we were being too loud, for all of thirty seconds before they also picked up a random handful of rocks, barely eyeballing the amount, and entered in the middle of the match.

"Dad?" Bennett eventually turned and looked at Mr. Johansson, who continued to relentlessly walk up and down the beach. "Do you want to play?"

"No thank you," he answered quickly, continuing his endless journey to nowhere. "You all keep going. Just keep quiet."

"Then would you at least sit down or something?" Bennett asked in an almost stern voice. Surprised, Mr. Johansson paused, and stared at him. "It's stressful just to watch you."

Mr. Johansson stood still for a while, and the game paused as we all waited for some kind of response. Finally, he sighed and approached our circle. As he lowered himself beside Bennett, he jokingly pushed him to the side and said, "I hope you're better at this than you are at cards."

The rest of us chuckled, and Bennett eventually swallowed it with a grain of salt. Despite the simplicity and repetition of scattering stones in an etched out square, there was something about sitting around it which had the ability to drown out our surroundings. As the time passed, we had to keep adding new facets and more rocks to the game, to the point where it became endless. Even Mr. Johansson was remotely interested, though always keeping an eye on the path, and twisting around on occasion to watch the blank, dark shoreline. Still, Bennett seemed in awe and even excited that he was trying. Jonathon, on the other hand, played a few lighthearted rounds, and then paused as if a brick had crashed over his head. Ella asked him several times if something was wrong, but he would only shake his head, unresponsive, and passively continue his turn. We had almost forgotten our eagerness to leave until the sun's sinking light cast red caps on the distant waves.

"We must wait until one or two in the morning if we are to be certain it's safe," Mr. Johansson told us, standing up, and marking an end to the game. "Everyone needs to try to sleep for a few hours. It'll be a long night."

At his order, Joana, Lukas, Bennett, Ellamae, and I were to fit ourselves into the cabin, and he and Jonathon would remain on the deck. Though it was only one or two feet long, there was a metal ladder which allowed us to climb back onto the boat without violently rocking it. Beneath the deck, it felt twenty degrees warmer, and the dark, blank room didn't appeal, either. We savored the occasional wind that blew in from the open door, which at least circulated the rationed air. The five of us could comfortably stand in the cabin, but lying down, we were almost touching. The longer I stayed there with only the palms of my hands to separate my head from the musty, damp boards, the more I became convinced the room was shrinking.

As my eyes partially adjusted in the darkness, the outlines of those around me began to take shape. Lukas and Joana sat slouched against the wall. They leaned against each other, actually seeming to be falling asleep. Though their relationship looked complicated at times, as I looked at them, I considered that they had known each other for years. After her grandfather died, Joana only had Allyson, whom she didn't appear

254

close to. I'd seen Lukas associating with other people, a couple boys his age, but he never once mentioned any kind of parent. They didn't really have anyone they could trust as much as each other. I frowned, somehow reminded of Stella and Barney, and turned on my other side to face the wall. Staring at it, I realized that I was almost afraid of sleeping on this boat, like something drastic would happen during those few hours. My bones felt weighted and aching, and the steady motion sickened me after a while. What felt like hours later, I decided that I could live with one sleepless night if we could arrive at the camp by that time the following day. I tried to silently push myself against the wall, but paused halfway with my weight entirely on my arms. As the next sweet breeze filled the cabin, I turned my head toward the door and let it dry the sweaty pieces of hair stuck to my face. I saw Ella, laying sideways with her back to me. I debated whether or not I could talk to her, and chose to stay quiet.

"There's something almost eerie about this boat," a voice whispered from above and beside me. I could barely distinguish it from the sound of the water gently lapping around us outside. Alarmed, I tensed, and took a while to recognize it as Bennett's. He already sat against the wall, and I forced myself up the rest of the way.

"I'm more concerned about what's out there," I answered, my head turned toward him, but my eyes trained on the door.

"We'll be gone in a couple hours," he tried to find something reassuring to say, but couldn't convince himself or me of anything.

"At this point," I said, and was harshly shushed from across the cabin. "I'm a little amazed we're still alive."

Bennett agreed, and we said nothing else for fear of disturbing the others again. I listened to the sound of my own breathing, which seemed so loud in comparison to the lack of movement and noise around us. When I felt his hand on top of mine, I cringed, unused to the feeling and reminded of the miniature tantrum I'd thrown in the Haritite State. Bennett took back his hand in response to my reaction. I was embarrassed enough for the both of us, and adjusted myself away from the corner, close enough that I could have laid my head on his shoulder if I tilted it slightly to the left. Even though we couldn't speak to each other, and truly had nothing to say anyway, there was a comfort in knowing Bennett was going to wait out the long hours with me.

Chapter Thirty Three

Subtle, tentative footsteps shook me from my state of limbo. I assumed they belonged to Mr. Johansson, and watched blearily as a form hovered in the door, blocking the cool breeze from entering the cabin. It lightly stepped over my seemingly sleeping sister, moving around to her head. Crouching down, it appeared to simply look at her, move out of the way in time to not be hit as she stirred, and leave as quickly as it had come.

"Did you see that?" I asked Bennett. Regardless of whether I actually fell asleep or not, my head had somehow ended up on his shoulder in the twenty or thirty minutes that had passed. Bennett didn't say anything, but I felt him nod. "What was he doing down here?"

"I'd like to think he was just walking around," he whispered, bothered. Neither one of us moved as if it was crucial Jonathon, though he was gone, thought we were asleep. "Should we go up?"

I thought about it for a while, and then looked at Ellamae.

"She'll say we're treating him like he has something to hide again if we follow him," I spoke in an exhale. The undersides of my eyelids burned as I closed them. But before I allowed my mind to wander, I glanced briefly around the room to account for Lukas and Joana.

The only word that can describe it is bloodcurdling, and it woke all of us with a terrifying jolt. I couldn't help but feel like I'd heard a similar kind of shriek before. Bennett, Ella, and I only looked to each other for a source. Though it took several seconds, Lukas recognized it sooner than we did. He scrambled upright, leaning against the wall, staring down at the empty place beside him.

"Joana?" he asked the room as if genuinely expecting an answer, and then took off running, stumbling, onto the deck. "Joana!"

"What happened?" Ellamae stayed on the floor, rubbing one of her eyes as Bennett and I moved to follow Lukas. I paused, looking down at her almost in disgust by her lack of concern, and didn't trust myself to open my mouth. The ghastly smell of blood attacked my senses before I even reached the empty deck, as did yelling, senseless voices. I watched Bennett as he sat on the side of the boat and propelled himself forward, forgetting the ladder.

"Don't touch her!" Lukas's voice immediately followed. Despite the threatening air, I could tell even from the boat that he was crying. As Mr. Johansson's shouting became clearer, I was almost afraid to look over the side.

In the middle of the beach, he advanced upon a strange, short, young man, who was much more kempt than the workers in the Etairan Mountains but wore the same yellow vest. He appeared terrified, and I would have sympathized with him had it not been for the polished, bloody sword in his hand. As Mr. Johansson demanded where the man had come from, Jonathon stood close to the path, unnoticed but frozen. He watched as Mr. Johansson held his hand near the back of his belt to give the impression he had a gun, though I knew he didn't. Ella hesitantly came beside me and stopped. She stared open-mouthed not at the sword, blood, or shouting, but at Jonathon, who was safely hidden in the shadows for the moment. I followed Bennett off the boat before she asked me again what had happened.

Joana lay hunched over with her side buried into the gravel, pale and shaking violently. A spreading, wet blossom of blood stained the ground beneath her as she held the top of her right arm with her left. Lukas tried to move her, but whenever he so much as lifted her slightly from the dirt, she responded with an equally bone-chilling scream. Still, she looked straight at him as if pleading him to do something. Bennett stood close behind Lukas. Every time he moved, he was told again not to touch her. When Lukas saw me standing there, he snapped the same thing, though I didn't care. I knew next to nothing about wounds, but it seemed common sense that the more gravel

257

she got in it, the likelier she would get an infection. I barely tapped her shoulder to let her know I was there. Joana's eyes snapped from Lukas to me, empty, distant, and seemingly having no idea who I was.

"Get her on her back," I told Lukas. Flustered and in a panic, he only looked at me for several seconds, which all seemed too crucial to Joana's life to spend staring helplessly at each other. "I said get her on her back!"

He tried two or three times before he finally managed, struggling to continue while she screamed so loudly. The gash was much deeper and dirtier than I originally thought, almost cutting her arm to the bone. Without the hard press of the dirt, the blood seemed to pour. Gagging, I frantically attempted to think of anything we had on the boat that I could use to wrap it with, and suddenly felt beyond idiotic for throwing all of the dresses and outfits from the mountains overboard. Now we had literally nothing except the clothes on our backs.

"Drop the sword!" Mr. Johansson told the petrified worker, and he immediately did so. "What are you doing here?!"

"I-I was supposed to deliver the sword by the morning, but he found me up in the woods... said he could lead the Imperial to a group of Idrisans... she startled me and I turned around and...."

"Surprise, surprise, surprise!" Mr. Johansson marched almost through the young man, pushing him roughly to the ground, where he remained. Jonathon appeared shocked, like he hadn't expected Mr. Johansson to see him, or at least conclude anything from the worker's vague description. The closer he got to Jonathon, the more it looked like he was willing, able, and more than happy to strangle the life out of him. "You're nothing but a little conniving bastard after all!"

His confrontation with Jonathon finally moved Ella to get off the boat. I stood up as if I could physically bar her from getting involved.

"Help me wash out her arm," I tried to distract her.

"There's something wrong... he couldn't have gone anywhere... it's only been a couple hours...."

"Ellamae, she's going to die if we don't do anything," I said flatly, and she cringed as if I'd just hit her. Without asking, I took a thin, shawl-like cloth she had around her shoulders, balled it up, and threw it at Bennett. He quickly knelt on the other side of Joana, while Lukas talked to her and I went to the shoreline to scoop water with my hands.

"What did they offer you in return for this?" Mr. Johansson continued, his voice shaking, and Jonathon began to retreat backwards toward the path. "Was it worth knowingly handing over who knows how many people for execution?!"

"I-I don't know what-" he stammered, walking up and sliding down the steep path as Mr. Johansson advanced.

"I knew who you were the moment I saw you! I only tried to convince myself you were not because no one else would even consider that you'd have the nerve to show your face at our camp," he spat, and a strange calm came over his voice as he gestured behind them at Ellamae. "She resembles Ruth a bit too, wouldn't you think, Jason?"

To hear the demonized name again and put a familiar face to it seemed unreal. *Jason to Jonathon?* I thought. *That's not much of an alias.* I momentarily looked up from Joana, though continued to let the water run down her wound with just enough force to wash away the gravel layer by layer. Bennett had gone back onto the deck and found a small stash of buckets for controlling leaks in the boat. She returned with one so I wouldn't have to keep running back and forth, passing the man every time, with half a handful of water. Choked shrieks occasionally left Joana, though she was for the most part silent, perhaps also listening to Mr. Johansson and whoever Jonathon or Jason was supposed to be. Ella seemed to have a delayed reaction to it all, only standing there looking from the sword to who she thought was her fiancé, the person she'd left everything she'd known for. But between Joana, the man, and the confrontation, I didn't have any attention left to sympathize with her.

In response to hearing his actual name said aloud, Jason scrambled to escape using the path, struggling to pull himself up the incline in such a panic. He still managed to run out of reach before Mr. Johansson could get a grip on his leg. By his sudden, tempered fury, we knew Mr. Johansson wasn't letting him amble off so easily, and that Jonathon really had nowhere else to go except up the sheer mountainside. Mr. Johansson wordlessly chased after him, quickly forcing himself up the narrow trail. We heard little of his shouting voice from below them, and everyone except Ellamae became narrowly focused on Joana.

"Who is he?" she asked in a quiet, but steady voice that contradicted the painful vibrations that shook her entire body. Lukas picked up the hand on her good arm, and held it up to his mouth. "Who did he say he is?" she repeated.

"Don't worry about it," Lukas told her. His cooing voice only seemed to upset her more, and he answered, "He's a just a slimy turncoat who helped execute thirteen Idrisans eight years ago. He's the one who turned in that Ruth girl. He went and found that worker so they could get the Imperial's Guard down here. We're closer to civilization than we thought."

"Then we have to leave," she mumbled distantly, trying to sit up, causing the thickening wound to spurt. Lukas and Bennett forced her down. As the last of the visible gravel rolled off her arm, Bennett took the nearly dripping shawl, and pressed hard on the deepest area of the jagged gash. It wrapped from the front of her arm to nearly the back, and we couldn't clot it with what we had. Joana seemed unnervingly calm throughout it all. Only minutes later, Ellamae was over by the path, out of shock and into hysteria over what had just happened. It looked like she was trying to climb up and go after them--Mr. Johansson's echoing voice torture for her. When she finally did vanish up the trail, I decided that Joana was our main concern, and to let Ella do what she was going to anyway.

I tried to blame it on my imagination, but Joana seemed to grow paler with the passing minutes. We couldn't ignore the signs that what we were doing wasn't enough, nor that the man who had done this to her was still sitting there, like he was waiting for someone to take the sword and decapitate him. Bennett flipped the now red, drenched cloth and wrung it out on the beach, splattering all of us. I recoiled slightly, shivering, and had to separate myself under the auspice of refilling the bucket. Wading knee-deep into the water, I crouched slightly, trying to wash away the blood on my skin. Even from the shore, I could hear Lukas continuing to talk to Joana, trying to give her something to hold on to.

"Lukas?" she asked in a child-like voice, like it was only her and him. I turned around and hauled the swinging, spilling bucket back onto the beach. "Where's Darius?"

"He's at home, Joana," he answered in a low voice.

"Do you think his leg is healed yet? I feel bad that I let him get bitten by a snake. It scared him."

He only stared at her, stricken that she would ask about her horse after what had happened.

"Lukas?" she said again, her eyes wide as if expecting earthshattering news.

"Yes, I'm sure he's fine," he finally muttered, and she seemed to relax.

I placed the bucket beside her, momentarily searching the path for any sign of Ellamae. I didn't expect to see anything. As I lowered myself to the ground again, a loud, echoing splash cut through the air. Lukas, Bennett, and I all turned and watched the man, who was still in a state of guilty shock over what he had done. He sat in the same helpless, exposed position, only staring back at us. I wondered what kind of destructive internal mechanism kept him from high tailing it out of there as he finally, shamefully, hid his eyes. The silence of the one splash hovered over us as I struggled to redirect my focus back to Joana. But there was something about it that felt so unnatural, like we were suddenly being watched. A renewed sense of fear settled over us when we heard people stumbling down the path. The sounds were delayed in getting through to Joana, though when she realized someone was coming, she tried and failed to sit up again.

"Who is that?" she asked, unable to turn her head enough to see. "Who is it?"

Mr. Johansson ducked to fit through the awkwardly-shaped mouth in the rock. He led Ella, white-faced and quiet, behind him by her arm like she would try to run away. After glaring menacingly at the worker, he unaffectionately released Ellamae, and kicked the hilt of the sword until it was far away from the paralyzed man's reach. When he saw the state Joana had entered in his absence, he wordlessly forced Bennett and me away from her. He removed his straight, pressed vest, delicately lifted Joana's arm from the dirt, and placed it underneath, wrapping it tightly around the original, virtually useless scarf. Though a disfigured, red stain bloomed in only seconds, the extra gauze seemed to stabilize and lessen the flow. As Lukas and Mr. Johansson attended to her, I hesitantly approached Ella.

"Are you okay?" I asked lamely.

260

"He-he killed somebody?" she looked up at me, hoping I would disagree and offer some other explanation for what she'd just witnessed.

"Basically," I answered, and became aware of my unfeeling voice. I tried to smile weakly, though I doubt I looked very convincing. The idea that we had existed in the company of someone like Jason was chilling, and enough to make anyone question who they trusted. "I'm sorry he wasn't who you thought he was. But it's not like you had any way of knowing."

"He was just using me so he wouldn't look as suspicious as he would have if he went back to the camp alone," she spoke to herself. There was nothing I could say to make such a revelation any more acceptable.

"Did he get away?" Bennett said, still standing behind his father. Mr. Johansson looked up at him, but was careful to avoid Ellamae's gaze.

"In a sense, he did. He did not want to face what he'd done or what he'd become. Jason thought it would be easier to end his life."

The eerie splash was sickeningly put into context. Jason had thrown himself from the side of the mountain rather than get caught.

"He... jumped?" Bennett stepped back, shocked.

"I had backed him into a corner. He saw it as his only option. He went in headfirst, so the impact probably snapped his neck," Mr. Johansson spoke absentmindedly, turning his attention back to Joana. "I am only sorry that there is no real justice for Ruth or any of the other people he had his hand in executing."

"How did he become a spy or even get back into the camp?" I asked, though I sensed he was trying to end the discussion. Despite his steely, seemingly unaffected expression, Mr. Johansson was obviously somewhat taken aback.

"The accepted theory is that after he left the camp for the Haritite State without Ruth, he was caught. Instead of executing him, the Guard offered him a deal: his life for help in capturing more Idrisans and, eventually the camp. He spinelessly took it, and carried it farther than necessity ever called for. Unfortunately, he managed to slip in to the camp because very few there would recognize his face, only the name, which he obviously changed." Mr. Johansson paused, shook his head, and ended it with, "But I suppose now we will never know why. What matters most is that he will never do it again."

The scuttling sound seemed much louder than it was in the unnerving stillness. As the man nimbly fled up the passage, he came within feet of me, and I cringed. The moment he was gone, Mr. Johansson swore, conflicted between Joana and chasing him down.

"Bennett, Amaryllis, take that sword and find out where he's going," he told us. We immediately looked at each other, mortified.

"That thing costs four times as much as everything on the farm combined," Mr. Johansson explained in an exasperated tone, tearing his attention away from us. "The

Lebon exchange swords as gestures of peace toward each other, and if one disappears, then they'll send their Guard all over the place looking for it. Just go drop it somewhere it plain sight farther away from here, and walk around to see if you can see where that jackass came from."

Bennett knelt beside the sword as if in awe of the intricate, spiral, golden hilt and the Lebon insignia engraved at the top of the blade. He dipped it in the water to wash away the drying blood, and carried it awkwardly far away from himself.

"Do not," Mr. Johansson stopped us with a stern voice. Already in front of the trail, we turned around to face him only to see he wasn't looking at us at all. "Get lost up there. We must leave as soon as she's stable."

I only looked from Ellamae to Bennett, and finally, to the huge red blemish that now concealed Joana's entire arm. Mr. Johansson told us to keep each other safe as one, last effort to encourage us, and we were left to face the mountainside. Bennett went first up the incline, making it to more even ground. I took much longer. The rocky, almost vertical path had only small nooks where I could place my feet. I saw Bennett place the sword on the ground, and take a few cautious steps out to me. If I fell, I would've pulled him down with me, and was uncertain about taking his outstretched hand.

"Take it," he said, noticing I was beginning to slip. I half-dove and caught his hand before I fell, and he pulled me up onto the level ground. Figuring out where to leave the sword or where the man had vanished to was another story. Although the land was covered in a deep, thick forest, it was smooth enough to walk on in front of us. The gradual hill which eventually led to the mountain was on our left, and a dizzying, undivided drop into the ocean on our right. The strong wind blowing in from the coast was filtered only slightly by the trees, relentlessly directing us through the woods. We tried to keep track of where we were going, but the deeper we walked, the harder it became. I wandered beside Bennett for a while, staring at every seemingly isolated area that backed to the sheer drop into the sea, wondering if that had been the place where Jason ended his life. It was appalling to think about, and too easy for the antagonist in the story that had stayed with me since I first heard it. I felt as if somehow, eight years later, we had betrayed Ruth by letting her murderer simply kill himself. The more I thought about it, I began to consider that Mr. Johansson could have easily pushed him to his death. I tried to shake the thoughts, telling myself that he didn't have the capacity for that kind of anger, and reached for the sword. Bennett let me take it, and I moved to gently lay it on the ground like a baby, not a blade of deadly obsidian.

"Not here," he shook his head. I paused, looking up at him, wondering how deep in these woods and how far away from the beach he planned on taking us. "It's too close. A straight shot to the beach."

"But we'll be gone by the time they find it."

"We still have to find out where that guy came from. If he goes back and tells someone, then the Guard will be on their way in half an hour. We need to know how close they are."

The landscape soon forced us to turn toward the mountain. We trudged upwards for at least ten minutes, almost on all fours, weaving in and out of our original path until we agreed upon leaving the sword half exposed behind some wild shrubs.

"We should take some of these," I rubbed the dry, prickly spindles of leaves in between my fingers. "I remember how people used to build fires to heat up rocks, and then put them on an open cut to close it. It's really painful, but it keeps the wound from getting infected."

"Doesn't that only work if it's not bleeding?" He squatted on his legs beside me. I shrugged, ripping several thin branches from the bush.

"I don't know," I moved to stand up. "But it can't hurt to bring them so we have something to start a fire with."

Bennett gathered a couple broken sticks lying around the brush. The sound of him snapping them into smaller pieces seemed much too loud and recurrent.

"What are you doing?" I eventually asked, lowering my voice as if we were surrounded by people. He only stared at me strangely.

"You need to create friction with sticks if you want to light the leaves on fire."

"I know, but-"

The thought of cracking sticks actually resulting from footsteps didn't occur to me until I could feel the presence behind us. I slowly turned on my heels, and craned my neck to look up at an imposing, scowling man whose face and demeanor was too similar to Hal Vern's. I knew I shouldn't have been looking him in the eye, but something about him froze me there. The man's remote presence seemed to confirm my paranoia that the Guard must have known something about where we were.

He waited until Bennett worked up the courage, or stupidity, to also look at him before he bent over, reaching in between us. We quickly scuttled apart. I thought he meant to grab Bennett or me, but his hand instead found the uncovered hilt of the sword. The man painstakingly pulled it out from behind the shrub, and lifted it from the ground, examining it.

"We've been trying to find you all day," he spoke in an even voice, and I relaxed slightly, thinking he believed we were delivering it like the other worker. What he said next, however, crushed that excuse. "This thing is worth more than both your lives. You're not the smartest race, but I would think you would know better than to not only try to run away, but to steal one of the swords on the way out."

That man wasn't delivering any kind of gesture of peace, I suddenly felt worse for him. *He was trying to get the hell away from here. He probably knew of the beach and was on his way to it when Jason found him. We were on his escape spot.*

"We didn't steal the sword, sir," Bennett began playing our new mistaken identity, and was promptly told to shut up.

"You think getting rid of your vests makes you unrecognizable? We'll shoot both of you in front of the other workers," the man said, no emotion or change in his voice. "It'll make everyone else think twice about running away. I swear, every damn night we're chasing one of you down. Personally, I would just assume we let you run and starve to death once you realize you have nowhere to go. But of course then everyone would just follow you, and we can't have that now, can we?"

The man ran his fingers lightly down the blade as if checking for imperfections.

"Stand up," he ordered, still staring deeply into the sword.

Bennett and I looked at each other as we did what we were told--trying to think of some magical answer that could help us. Though nothing could make the man disappear. I stopped breathing as he roughly turned me around by my shoulders, keeping one hand coiled around my arm, and the other around the hilt of the sword. I faced Bennett now, my eyes wide and unblinking as I felt the man move. He took all my hair into his fist and pulled back with enough force to make me stumble. I thought for sure he was going to cut my throat, but he dragged the pointed tip through my hair. I could feel the coldness of the blade on my neck as he progressed slowly, daring me to make a sound as he cut six inches or more. When he was done, he pushed me forward and down. I fell nearly on top of Bennett, numbly feeling the ends of my hair now barely below my ears. The man nodded at the sword as if pleased with its work, and gently eased it into an empty sheath hanging diagonally from his belt.

"Sir, if you would allow me, I can explain," Bennett spoke quietly, shocked by what he'd just done. This time, the man kicked him in the stomach, and Bennett made a fist across his torso, grimacing but silent. I looked hopelessly at the ground, and then the sword. I wondered how many hours would pass until the others would be forced to leave us, and what Ellamae would tell Rose when they arrived at the camp.

The man had a standard handheld pistol attached to his belt, and felt no need to keep a hand on us. We trudged halfway around the mountainside, waiting until the ground was more accessible to climb before continuing up the mountain. When the landscape dramatically turned downhill, a layer of slippery mud from a recent rain caused us to nearly slide to the bottom. With mud caked in dry, cracking layers on my legs and the hem of my pants, we emerged into a lesser forested area an exhausting, terrifying hour later. The man seemed unbothered and only interested in marching us to an expansive, gated, light-colored stone wall off in the distance.

Several Lebon Guard manned the area. The only difference between them and the Haritites was a fancier, but still remarkably similar wardrobe. Their statures and expressions were so reminiscent of the Wall I knew that I couldn't help but blink twice as if expecting the past hour to evaporate before my eyes, and to wake up on the boat, having had one of the worst nightmares of my life. Bennett and I avoided their gazes, but I could still feel the interest that resulted of the sickening sound as the blade rubbed against its sheath, and the man pulled it halfway out to show them.

"Why did you even bring them back here?" one of them said, truly asking why the man had not killed us in the woods.

"Why waste an opportunity to set an example for the rest of them?" was his answer. He hesitantly relinquished the sword to another Guard, telling him to return it to its proper place. "Inform everyone we've found it. Our night's work is done. We will gather them in the morning."

"Not quite done," another person told him as he forced the unlocked, metal gate open himself. "We have to ensure these are the two. We've got a woman that saw the runaways taking the sword who can validate them."

The man unenthusiastically agreed, professing not to understand what other explanation there could possibly be. We were taken within the walls of another manor, though this one appeared to span miles. Its layout was much more organized and symmetrical compared to Jabez's, with several huge homes, fields, and smaller buildings. Anything else I could imagine was needed to sustain a small society was already there, in addition to what appeared to be gardens peeking from behind the largest structure. Building wasn't the right word for it. It was more of a multi-level castle built of different colored stones, with two imposing towers uniformly placed at its ends. If Jabez's home was awe-inspiring to me, being in the presence of such an active, majestic but corrupted place was enough to paralyze.

Inside one of the compact rooms of a smaller, L-shaped structure, waited a miserable-looking woman accompanied by two Guard. She was at least forty-five, but could've easily been much older by the lines on her face and graying, brownish hair. She was dressed similarly to the other runaway worker: only a step above colorless rags for clothing with a blaring yellow vest. The woman stood shifting from foot to foot, nervously twirling a section of her long, tattered skirt, waiting to be spoken to before even daring to glance at Bennett and me.

"Are these the ones?" one of the Guard demanded, and the woman took several seconds to face us. We were not who she expected, and she only stood there with a confused look on her face, looking expectantly at one of the Guard and awaiting permission to speak.

"Are these the ones?" he repeated vehemently.

"No," she said. They all seemed to think she must have been lying, and several threats echoed back to her. "The one who took the sword was a man of about twenty-two or twenty-three. These are children," she spoke like they wouldn't have known otherwise.

"They were found over a mile from here in the woods with the sword."

"They are not the ones I saw," she shook her head. A stiff silence lingered for a few seconds, until Bennett cautiously spoke, pausing after almost every word as if awaiting another punch in the gut.

"That was what I was trying to tell you in the woods, sir... we were only out walking and found the sword in the bush."

The man who originally found us grabbed both sides of Bennett's collar, and shook him once, nearly picking him up off the ground.

"Even if you did not steal the sword, you so much as taking one step outside these grounds is considered running away. There was certainly enough activity at the gate this afternoon for you to slip out, and no one can endorse your story."

"We don't have time for this," the only woman in the group of Guard crossed her arms, irritated that they were in fact not done for the day. "We still have a real thief and runaway to catch before the night is out. It's probably gotten around by now that he's still missing, and if we don't find him and put this down before tomorrow, then they'll all get ideas."

It didn't take very much to figure out 'put this down' meant execute the worker in front of his peers, just as they planned to do to us. As disturbing as it was, it honestly didn't surprise me to know that these people didn't really care who they killed, as long as they had someone who could carry the blame and stand as a sacrifice. The Guard began filing from the room, now uninterested in us. Soon only the one man, with his hands still clenched around Bennett's collar, remained. He roughly pushed Bennett back, and spat at both of us.

"You have no idea how lucky you are tonight. If either of you ever set foot outside these walls again without written permission, you're as good as dead."

The man slammed the door on his way out, leaving us alone with the silent woman, who watched his every movement until he was gone.

"You stupid, stupid children!" she raised her petite, strained voice at us. "You never leave these walls. Had they not had another runaway to catch, they would've beaten you within an inch of your life for it! Trust me, I would know."

The woman pushed her sleeve up to her elbow, revealing long, snake-like scars all over her arm.

"Even if you have nothing assigned to you a certain day, you walk around looking for something to do. You cannot just take a walk here. It does not work that way. Are you fresh from the ship or something?"

I nodded our response. Her expression softened, though was still overwrought with a permanent, natural frown molding her face.

"That wall," she lowered her voice again, "is not the one you are used to. There is no more eight o'clock rule. You are only allowed to leave with written permission and a task to accomplish, and you must return by the end of the day if you do not want to be treated as some kind of escapee. Do you understand?"

We absentmindedly agreed. As I stood there, I envisioned Mr. Johansson pacing along the beach, panicking over where we were, Ellamae slumped against the rock in a state of grief and betrayal as she replayed Jason's death in her head, and Lukas leaning over Joana, trying to keep her calm. I knew there was no immediate way out of this manor. If they decided to wait for us and Joana didn't make it, I would feel like she had died because of us.

"Come," the woman sighed, walking through us to the door. "Let's get out before they remember you or me later."

266

We followed in silence behind the woman, though I kept looking at Bennett for some kind of telling expression. He seemed in a state of watered-down shock, like he'd taken a kick to the teeth and was still trying to recover from it. I felt it was in my place to say something, because the people here once lived in the same homes and boroughs as I, but could only grasp at fragile straws. We soon entered a miniature shanty town crammed into a shadowy corner. A ten minute walk away and hidden from the rest of the manor's view, it seemed temporarily set up there, as if it had to be ready to take down in the morning. All I could see were fourteen or fifteen wide, canvas tents loosely circling a spit and cauldron, though the number of people seemed to overflow its circumscribed borders.

A low, flickering fire hissed below the cistern. Three people sat around it, each one in charge of a separate chore. Everyone coming into the settlement formed a line in front of them, and it took another five minutes before we reached the front.

"Good eve'nin, Angie," one of the men tipped a shabby hat balanced on his head. He reached into a wooden barrel, and took out a clay bowl. He dipped it and his hand into the soup, pulled it out, and let the bowl drip until half empty. At the same time, the man beside him pulled a piece of bread out of another uncovered box, and submerged it in the soup. She politely refused, and only accepted the rolled, thin blanket held out to her by the other woman, who had a large stack of them sitting beside her.

"Aren't hungry tonight?" the man wearing the hat smiled at her, revealing several missing teeth, and took a long, joking whiff of the sad meal. "The bread's not hard this time. That means they're happy."

"Or drunk," the woman distributing blankets added, and all of them laughed. A small smile even crept onto Angie's face.

"You know I don't like to be called that, Liam," she tucked the blanket neatly under her arm, and motioned Bennett and me to stand beside her.

"Who's them?" Liam asked, pushing his hat up higher on his now visibly bald head and squinting at us. He immediately began to hack deeply and uncontrollably, a distance developing in his eyes as he cupped his hands around his nose and mouth.

"What are your names?" Angie waited for him to finish, and then turned to us. I wasn't sure whether or not I wanted to give my real one this time.

"Bennett," Bennett answered, assuming that these people were harmless enough. I saw nothing wrong with giving my name after that, but something inside me poked at my nerves, strictly forbidding it.

"Um, Arlie," I mumbled several seconds later under all their stares. It was a pitiful excuse, and truly not even a real fake name, but it somehow seemed safer than Amaryllis.

"They just got here," Angie explained. The three of them frowned sympathetically. "And the Guard welcomed them with a threat of execution. Give them some dinner and a blanket so they can go find a place to lie down before the tents get too full."

Angie patted me once on the back, and walked away, disappearing into the confusing, yellow-vested crowd without another word. Bennett and I each thanked them for the bowls and blankets, eager to get out of line.

"You'll be alright," the frizzy-haired woman tried to smile up at us. "Just don't draw any attention to yourselves or cross the Guard."

I thought it was a bit late for that, but nodded anyway.

"And if you ever wind up in the same room as the Imperial, don't even look at 'im sideways," Liam shook his finger in the air, moving to serve the next person.

"The Imperial?" Bennett and I asked at the same time. I felt my mouth drop almost open for a moment.

"He don't come outside much, but that don't mean you won't ever see him or any of his kids when you work inside the castle."

"The Imperial lives here?" Bennett asked as if to be certain he didn't mishear.

"Welcome to Kieriana," the young, dark-haired man in the middle responded, dropping another piece of bread in a bowl of soup. "Where justice is spat upon, but law is worshipped."

"Angela will tell you," the woman shook her head. "The Guard locked her up for a couple days without food one time all because they caught her talking about her daughters."

"Did you say Angela?" I asked a bit too breathlessly. *Angie* hadn't registered with me, and that woman looked nothing like what I remembered about my mother. I tried to recall everything Ellamae had told me about her: her textured hair, straight nose, and overbite, and couldn't see it. Then again, I hadn't paid much attention.

"She's got one of the saddest stories here. She had three little girls, you know," the woman continued, and I felt my eyes widen, impulsively scanning the crowd for a sign of her, all the while trying to tell myself not to slip into an uncontrollable exhilaration. "But she still remembers all their birthdays; it's so sweet. Just last week she told me that her oldest daughter was going to be twenty in a couple months, and she hasn't seen her since she was eight."

Part Three

Chapter Thirty Four

All accounts of the Imperial's physical appearance were written with blatant exaggeration. He was a tall, but not imposing man, broad chested, but with lanky arms. They let his black hair grow long for the purpose of tying it back, revealing his sharp facial features and square chin. The largest figurehead in existence sat with his legs akimbo and his large hands clasped in between them, leaning back into the simple, but large presence of his throne, only remotely interested in us. Before they brought us into the hearing, as if it could truly be called that, the wide open corridor was lined with tables. Every official and figure waited to get a glimpse of their miserable prisoners, their doormats, their scapegoats. As I walked slowly in line with the others, conscious only of my rhythmic footsteps, I wondered what monsters we had been painted as, and if we truly lived up to that image.

After what felt like months in darkness, the light shocked and hurt my eyes. We were not in chains, but our procession was guarded at the front, middle, and back. They forced us into a line parallel to the front, off-center table, which was occupied by a kind of council consisting of the eldest man from every Lebon family. The Imperial's throne rested regally in the middle of the room, as if just there to observe. It emanated power, but the person seated there was irrelevant.

"This group of Idrisans is charged with treason," the man in the center of the table rose, placing his hand firmly on the surface for support. He continued to read off our names in succession, moving down the row. When the person on my left was announced followed by the person on my right, I looked up, and squinted at the feeble man as if unsure his voice and presence were real. My head spun painfully, overwhelmed by the number of people and all their blank, unaffected gazes. I came down to reality when I heard my mispronounced last name echoing down the long hall: the final victim on the man's list. In response, a hand wrapped itself entirely around my upper arm. It pulled me from the line. I felt the browbeating stares of the others as the Guard left me on the far right, remaining close behind my back so I could hear his breathing and not forget his looming company. I took several seconds to regain my balance and attention, lightheaded from the sudden movement. Though I could still feel fingers discreetly enveloping my hand, and looked down beside me at Bryn. His small, unmarked face shot me a supportive smile, and I tried to return it so he wouldn't worry any more about me than he already did.

Bryn was a clam when I first met him a year ago--when our boat first came to Imperiam. I pried him open day by day, trying to find something behind his resolute, eleven-year-old face, and he eventually told me what he remembered of his short life. He was born a

Haritite, but his family fled from the State when he was very young. He never told me why, only that they wound up in the same place later as Idrisan correspondents. *Baba wasn't careful,* he would say. *That's all there is to it.* Bryn had spent the past two years, fifteen weeks, and four days in a downstairs cell in Imperiam, which he now shared with me and two others. *I like having the companionship,* he said every day as if he'd never mentioned it before. *Things haven't been the same since they took Baba and Mama away.* It happened that they were executed last year, around the same time I was caught at the Wall, with the last shipment of Idrisans Bryn and his family had arrived with. He was spared death because of his age, but never heard of any alternative plan for him, and just faded entirely into nonexistence except at four in the afternoon, five times a week, when they brought him a meal.

"Let go," the Guard behind me told Bryn in a gruff voice. He obeyed, but squeezed my hand one more time before he dropped it. *My soldier,* I mouthed to him. I'd called Bryn that so many times, he didn't need to hear me to understand. Despite how his life had turned, Bryn once shamefully confided in me that he had wanted to be in the Guard when he grew up as a younger child. Of all the heartbreaking things he'd ever said, this was the only time I ever saw him cry. *You're something better than the Guard,* I told him. *You're Bryn the Soldier. Nobody can take that away from you.*

We all knew how this was supposed to go. Our unbroken, sacred bond came in the form of our unanimous answer to the one question we were about to be asked. The first of us in line was Declan, a strongly built man of about forty who was unflinching in his silence against the Guard, even when questioned. He was led in front of our line, standing exposed and under the stares of the council of men, though his demeanor did not change. His response, aside from being one of the only things that I'd ever heard leave his mouth, gave me a sense of courage.

"Do you wish to accept the covenant his Majesty already offered?"

"His Majesty can shove his covenant up his ass," he spoke subtly, politely tipping an imaginary hat at the Imperial. In a delayed repercussion to what he had said, the Guard roughly forced him back in line, where he stood quietly, satisfied. Each person afterwards was read the same, sickening concordat. I knew Jason must have accepted it two years ago when he stood here in our shoes, stating that he would aid the Lebon in capturing and executing more Idrisans stationed around the island, and give them information as to the whereabouts of the camp. If nothing else, I took pride in knowing such a deal existed. It meant we were a threat. So much so that these people would be willing to work with one of us: the frightening scum stuck to the soles of their shoes.

He'd told me not to worry, that he'd done it before, after all. But I felt a piece of me walk alongside Bryn, holding his hand and calling him my soldier, as he was led to the front of the council. They looked at him, pleased, thinking they now had someone they could manipulate.

"Hello, Bryn," the man smiled thinly, glancing down at the paper because the boy's name had fled his mind only seconds after reading it aloud. "You know, we can help you if you help us. Would you like to agree to a deal?" he paused, and felt the need to add, "Or die?"

"You're a whole lot older than the person who was here last time," Bryn cocked his head to the side, examining the man closely. "I ain't gonna help you do nothing. I couldn't anyway, so I don't know why you keep askin'."

"Are you an Idrisan, Bryn?"

"Baba was. So I guess I am too."

A strange, otherworldly fury clenched my feeble senses when the entire room snickered at his honest response. As the Guard turned to lead Bryn back to the line, I watched the Imperial hold his chin in his fingers and lean forward as if fascinated.

"Stop," his voice seemed to halt time for every Lebon in the room, though it was not in any way unusual-sounding. The Guard seemed to know what he would say next, and brought Bryn like a piece of meat before the throne.

"You were here last year with your parents, weren't you?" he asked. I clenched my hands into fists, watching Bryn nervously. It took his response to remind me that Bryn had a quiet, humble insight well beyond his years, which was so innocently unbeknownst to him.

"I been living in your basement the whole time. But they don't take me out with the dogs."

"You say you are an Idrisan?" the Imperial continued, not swallowing or seeming to understand what this little boy had just told him. "Do you even know what that means, son?"

"You say yer a Lebon?" Bryn asked, imitating the tone of that man's every syllable. The Imperial leaned back again, amused if not surprised.

"I am a Lebon."

"You don't even know what that means, but you sure do think you do."

At the throne's silence, the Guard practically tossed Bryn back in line beside me. I looked down at him with near foggy eyes, never so proud of anyone. He only smiled at me in that partial, but still enduring way that could make the past year blur, leaving a bright numbness in my mind.

"Get him out of here," the Imperial's voice barely made it through to me. Bryn's head snapped back toward him as if horrified, and then he looked up at me. I felt all the more guilty because I knew he was not fearing his fate, but mine, such was his way of thinking that he could and had to protect me. "The boy is barely older than Arena. He does not know what he's doing. I will not have him executed."

"What should we do with him, your Majesty?" one of the Guard asked as multiple crept from the wall and stood behind Bryn.

"Put him somewhere where work is needed," the Imperial told them, waving his hand around in the air to dismiss them. Any trace of mercy in his decision to spare Bryn's life again was nullified. Two Guard already had their hands on him, and despite the backlash I knew I'd receive, I wasn't going to let the last opportunity to say something to my soldier slip through my hands.

"Bryn, Bryn, everything's going to be alright," I stooped over, speaking in a cooing voice, feeling his sporadic breath on my face. Other Guard immediately reached to separate us. I had no strength, and stumbled over my last words to him, raising my voice enough for the room to hear as I helplessly watched them take him away. "Don't worry about me. I don't want you to cry over me, okay?"

The doors slammed, and something within me went dark. Because I told him not to, I knew my Bryn would buck up as he always did when the morning came and passed. But I also knew I would cry for him at night.

I was finally marched to the table in the footsteps of my predecessors when the room calmed. I felt under particular scrutiny partially due to my being the last one, though mostly as a result of what I had nearly shouted at Bryn. It seemed as if the Lebon suddenly knew something deeply personal about me, and I hid my face for a moment to regain my composure, preparing to say exactly what I rehearsed. When the man asked me about the covenant, I paused, trying to envision exactly what was running through Jason's mind when he gave the sole 'yes,' to the astonishment and disgust of any others who may have been captured with him. By then, I had gone two or three, I could no longer count, days without water. It had started when I retaliated to one of the Guard's taunting questions. Sensing the weakness surrounding my person, the man at the council's table also started what should have been a simple question with a momentary second glance at my name and a chilling, thin smile.

"How old are you, Ruth?"

"I think I'm twenty-one," I mumbled, and was harshly told to look at the man and repeat myself. He seemed hesitant by the way I stared through him like he wasn't there, opening and closing my mouth several times as if remembering how to speak.

"You think?" he asked with a fake interest after I'd said it again.

"I don't know if my birthday has passed once or twice since they found me," I said, my wandering eyes running distantly around the room, catching the Imperial's marginally bothered gaze. "But you might as well stop pretending like you care a damn thing what happens to me because I will tell you nothing."

I was roughly jostled, and the man believed that marked the end of our hearing. I heard people standing and moving in the background until Acwel Aloysius waved at the Guard, telling them to bring me to him.

"What's wrong with her?" he spoke over me. The person on my right answered.

"She has been too outspoken since the moment she got here, your Majesty. A few days without water quiets her down."

"I see," he leaned forward more, almost out of the throne. "You may stand back."

The Guard receded away from us, and I held my arms over my stomach as if to support myself. I mustered a deep glare, but still struggled to focus it on him.

"Can I ask you a question, Ruth?"

"I already said no," I said, and he shifted his weight again back into the throne.

"That's not it. Do you know that boy?"

"His name is Bryn, if it matters to you. And yes, of course I know him," I nearly spat. My tone of voice couldn't affect him.

"Why did you tell him not to cry over you?"

"Because I know I will die tomorrow, and I know you will make him be there to see it. I may have come from the Stoleh, but I am not stupid."

275

"You were not born an Idrisan?" he asked, visibly surprised. I looked behind me at the others, who watched me in the same way I had watched Bryn.

"I lived behind your Wall at the mercy of your Haritite Guard for the first seventeen years of my life. Only half of us were born without a patch of some kind," I paused, catching my breath, and continued speaking on my exhales. "You know, where I came from, Haritites can literally get away with murder. But if one of my people were to rub the Guard the wrong way at half past seven, then they would hold them down in front of the Wall for thirty minutes, and shoot them at the stroke of eight for being late. How does that sound to you? The fact that you think we're all born into what we do only shows that you have no idea what goes on all over the island."

"What do you do, Ruth? What do you think you're doing to help your peoples' situation by running off with the Idrisans to terrorize the well-to-do parts of the island?"

I gaped momentarily, having originally thought that the Imperial must have invented the lies surrounding us, not been fed the information. We called him a figurehead out of spite, but now with him sitting in front of me, the name actually seemed suiting.

"What do I do?" I repeated, turning the words over in my head. It didn't take long to convey exactly what I thought. "After this, I hope I get to haunt your dreams for the rest of your life."

At that, I felt the Guard returning to put me back in line. Before they reached me, Acwel Aloysius said as matter of fact,

"You do not have to die. You've been given a choice."

I felt my eyes open wide, like I was seeing through another, new pair. The features of my face tightened, and my jaw dropped in slow motion. A possession took hold of my legs, and shakily forced them to take steps toward the throne. Though I barely moved, I watched the Imperial sit up straighter, staring down at me, disturbed.

"I...." I told him, intentionally raising my voice this time to ensure the room heard. "I-I...."

Nothing else would leave my mouth, despite all the words swirling around in my mind. I could feel the sweat beading off my forehead, and a confused haze washing all the strength from my body, returning conscious control of my legs to me. I stopped advancing, staring at the Imperial as if I suddenly had no idea what was going on. When I tried to walk again, a shudder ran up my leg, and it gave out from beneath me, the rest of me following. Even from the floor, I continued to look through him.

"Stand her up," Acwel Aloysius nodded the Guard in my direction. "But give her some water, would you?"

I heard one of the two leaving, and barely saw her as she knelt beside me a minute later. The only resistance I could offer was stiffening my body and not even making an attempt to sit up. When she unaffectionately turned my head and started forcing water down my throat, I felt no relief. It might as well have been poison, and I coughed uncontrollably like she was drowning me until the Imperial told her to stop.

"I. Would. Rather. Die. Than help you," I gasped for air, still hacking painfully as the Guard stood me in between them. "Did you hear me that time, or am I still speaking another language?"

"It is your decision," he held one of his hands out passively, like he had nothing to do with what would happen to me tomorrow morning. "Have you anything else to say?"

"I'd like to applaud you for one thing, if you'll let me," I said, and he raised his eyebrows, awaiting a lashing comment. "You know exactly how to divide a people against itself, and how to dance delicately around what you're allowing to happen in order to make it seem justified. I guess you can sleep at night because you yourself do not persecute anyone, though being aware that it happens and doing nothing is just as bad. Congratulations, you caught us: thirteen scary, destructive Idrisans. On the contrary, the only thing we've done is refuse to live in your corrupted hierarchy. The fact of the matter, which you try so hard to pretend doesn't exist, is that I was Stoleh before I was an Idrisan. I left your caste structure for a reason. And guess what? The majority of our camp is actually Haritites, so it's not just bunch of poor people either."

"What is your point, Ruth?" he asked as if I was wasting his dearly valuable time.

"It was my stupidity that brought me here, so I'm not going to curse your name for what you've done to me," I held my shaking hands out in front of me. It must have appeared like I was strangling him in my imagination. "But people from every class in your society do every day. Still, they cannot truly complain if they sit there and do nothing. So, technically, I guess you're right. You are entirely innocent of all the murder and kidnapping, all the thievery and injustice, and all the poverty and exploitation. You may blame all your shortcomings on us, and act like it'll all be buried with us. So again, congratulations. Tell me, how does victory feel?"

In the dead quiet room, a deep noise could be heard reverberating up the walls and down the window panes. It was isolated and seemingly powerless, but still struck the poor, miserable man on the throne.

It was the drawn out, gaudy sound of my clapping. And I continued giving the Imperial his well-earned applause until the Guard put my hands in manacles, forced my head down, and returned me to the line.

Chapter Thirty Five

The following morning, I had to be shaken awake, my face icy to the touch. If I could see anything immediately, it was that the sun hadn't risen yet. Halfway through the night, I decided to fold my blanket and lay in between the two halves, in hope of blocking the chilling breeze that circulated throughout the tent by its wide open flap. Only the presence of so many bodies crowded together kept any warmth inside, and the blanket felt no better than air when the merciless wind drifted through.

Outside, the reason why the small settlement looked so temporary was revealed. Our first job of the day was to take down all the tents, ensuring nothing remained of our presence, before anyone else stirred. I helped the best my slow-moving, frozen hands would allow, constantly opening and closing them to regain feeling. Even as my senses returned I was distracted, almost in a panic, walking around everywhere looking for Angela. Despite the compelling evidence, I refused to let myself believe she was my mother for fear of being crushed a second time. I was too young to comprehend it eleven years ago. I couldn't imagine reliving it with any sense of understanding. As nearly everyone I spoke to pulled me aside to ask what was wrong and make a worthless attempt to calm me down, I felt strangely at home, not necessarily in a good or bad way. I left it at I had just arrived here and was lost.

By the time the sun had half-risen, the Guard made their first appearance. All the workers seemed to have a sixth sense, knowing exactly when they were to arrive. We'd just folded the last of the tents, and all that remained was a pile of canvas and the cauldron, sitting in the moving shadow of the manor's wall. Everything else had been run to the nearest storehouse, like someone would take it if it was left out. Without any introduction or greeting, they separated people and began verbally assigning tasks. When Bennett and I passed, we were given yellow vests, and vehemently warned not to lose them again. We were sent to a two or three acre field, which basked in an area of the manor where shade was limited, along with maybe fifteen others. Bennett seemed almost content to till the soil in one of the fallow fields in preparation for planting, or he was at least centrally focused. I figured this was the kind of work he used to do, and could imagine himself at home, where shifts ended. The Guard occasionally walked by to ensure we weren't so much as speaking to each other, and keeping our heads down was difficult. Each time one passed, they would roughly push me forward, ordering that I either move faster or do a better job. After only two hours in the sun, I felt weak, almost dizzy. I paused for a moment, leaning my weight against the rake.

"Come on, you've got to look like you're working," Bennett's voice urged, taking the rake out from under me to bring me down to earth. I momentarily glared at him, until I saw that the Guard, the same man who found us in the woods yesterday, was fast approaching with another at his side. They stopped walking behind us. We tried to pretend they weren't there until one of them said to the other as some kind of joke,

"She's worthless here; she's too scrawny. Go put her in the kitchen."

I let the rake fall quietly to the dirt the moment I felt a hand on me.

"Pick it up," the man spat. "Go put it away, and then come back here."

I watched Bennett out of the corner of my eye as I dragged the rake past him. He paused while stooped over, and tried to smile at me. The man kicked his leg hard enough to make him lose his balance, though Bennett managed to stay upright, and lowered his head again. During this entire journey we'd been forced through, it seemed exactly like what Olivia had told me in Nemirena. I was going with him. Now, in a place with a fate that only befell Stoleh, I felt my stomach sickeningly turning. He was suddenly going with me, and this was where we ended up.

The man took me through a long corridor, and down longer stairs, holding a door open for me at the end of the hall. He did not enter the room, but slammed the door barely after I was inside. I shuddered, still trying to wipe sweat off my face and catch my breath from the fields, now standing in the middle of a bustling room filled only with other Stoleh workers. It was much more aromatic than outside, I gave it as much, but it only seemed like an added torture considering we were preparing the food, and then returning to rebuild our settlement and be thrown the scraps.

I wasn't sure what to do, and stood there with my back pressed against the door. Its coldness was relief, and I looked at the ceiling with my eyes closed, trying to breathe deeply for a few minutes.

"They had no business putting a little thing like you in the fields," a familiar voice spoke from directly in front of me, and I jumped, staring mortified at an older face covered on one side with brown spots. If he hadn't started coughing hoarsely, I wouldn't have recognized him without his hat. Liam began to walk away, motioning me to follow him with his finger. The crowd mindfully parted for him, and I had to stay in his shadow to avoid being trampled as we moved to the other side of the kitchen. Under a flickering bulb, there was a narrow, tall table pressed against the wall, half hidden beneath a rack of various spices. Liam paused, bracing his elbow against the table, and patted the seat of a chair.

"Come up. Catch your breath."

I eased myself up into the chair, nearly folded in half with my arms in my lap, and my head down. I didn't notice Liam had left until he returned with a tin cup half full of water. He placed it up on the table, pushing it toward me.

"The Guard wouldn't be very happy if they found out about this little cup," he smiled slightly, though serious. "So it's our little secret, agreed?"

I nodded, snatching the cup in both my hands, spilling a little in my lap and down my neck as I drank the water in one swallow. I felt Liam's eyes watching me, and wiped my mouth, embarrassed. He moved the cup down the table, blending it in with the spice rack. Liam opened his mouth to speak, only to suddenly be overtaken by another coughing fit. He tried to control his hacking as I finally started breathing normally, waiting for him to continue.

"Sorry about that," he choked, rubbing the back of his near bald head. "They tell me I shouldn't be working in the kitchen, that I may infect the food. But no one's come for me yet, so I've stayed behind this door for the past five years."

I said nothing, trying not to stare at the large age spots forming a shape similar to half a heart on his lower, right cheek. Liam waited patiently for the next three or four minutes, giving me the chance to cool down.

"Where'd you come from, Arlie? Are you and Bennett related?" he asked, leaning back against the table.

"The borough closest to the Wall," I walked my fingers along the edge of the table. It brought back a sudden recollection of Rose, and I stopped, dropping my hand in my lap. It would've been easy to lie and tell him Bennett was my brother, but I couldn't make myself say it again. "And no, just good friends."

"I think Angela came from there to," he nodded in vague recognition. None of the many Stoleh boroughs had names. We assumed they were referred to by number just as we were. "But I suppose you were too young to know her when she was taken."

"Have you seen her since last night?" I asked too eagerly following the end of his sentence. Liam stared at me strangely, and I looked away.

281

"I'm sorry, I haven't. Why?"

"No reason," I mumbled, hearing footsteps beside us. I raised my head to see a firm, dark-faced woman with her hair pulled tightly behind her head. She was dressed much neater than the rest of us, but still wore a vest of a subtler shade of yellow. I thought for a moment she was some strangely clothed Guard or other overseer, and the way she snapped at Liam didn't help.

"Why are you just standing around? They'll be blaming me if we aren't ready on time!"

"Don't worry, Arlie," Liam ignored her. "Ida is one of us. She's just strict about keeping everyone working because she takes the worst part of the grief if something goes wrong."

"Yes, they dress us rather nicely when we're going to be in public sight. You're still a dog, just one in a fancy skirt," she shook her head, and then turned to me. "I've never seen you in here before."

"Arlie just came to us last night, the poor girl," Liam put his hand on my back and pushed me gently, indicating in was time to get out of the chair. I stood in between them as he continued. "The Guard had her in the fields, and finally decided she couldn't handle it and left her in here."

"We're not usually this frantic," Ida glanced at the busyness behind her in time to avoid an inattentive man carrying a large pot. "But the Imperial is hosting a small gathering with the Council of Patriarchs. They always seem to eat more at these things than what a month's ration was for my family at home."

"Patriarchs?" I asked.

"The eldest man from every Lebon family. There're about fifteen or sixteen of them, but each and every one of 'em brings a horde," Liam clarified, laughing at a joke he hadn't yet told. "They're all just a bunch of ill-tempered, ugly old men. They all look the same. I can never tell Sir Sordid from Sir Snob."

"Don't let any of 'em catch you talking like that," Ida snickered, loosening up and folding her tiny arms. "They almost had my hide when I called one mister instead of sir. I'd hate to think what they'd do to you."

"Nothing more than what they've already done, I can assure you that much," was his answer.

"We'll see. I need you to make sure everyone's doing what they're supposed to. You're my eyes in here while they have me running around upstairs."

"I'll do my best to keep the panic level up," Liam winked teasingly as he picked up a tin, holed can from the spice rack. He vanished into the organized chaos, and Ida smoothed down her skirt, beckoning me to go with her. She said she knew something I could do with a tender smile, like she thought the list was limited, and explained it was a treat in comparison to the fields as long as I didn't get any brave ideas. I didn't even ask where we were going, and only followed her out of the heat of the kitchen. Ida left me with some people I hadn't seen anywhere else amongst the population. They were other girls my age and size, who were apparently just as useless to the Guard. There were about seven of them: the two in the front carrying several large, empty pails.

"Mallory," Ida quickly walked me up to a girl walking alone in the back. I cringed. She looked like an older version of Rose. The only difference was her brown eyes. The girl paused, and the line slowed due to our presence. "She just got off the boat and was already kicked out of the fields. Let her go with you."

Mallory only nodded, and I found myself trotting to keep up with her and the rest of the girls as we neared the manor's wall, leaving Ida behind nervously watching us. Despite the two Guard following close behind, I could see why hiking a half mile from Kieriana was considered a bittersweet, pleasant experience. It was quiet and much cooler in a carved-out dip in the mountainside. I couldn't believe anything could grow there with a lack of soil and sun, though judging by the inch deep puddles of water, the area held the mountain's extra rain runoff.

The Guard only glanced occasionally at us as if to ensure no one was trying to escape. Unlike the fields, they didn't care that the girls all broke off into groups and talked while swarming around the low bushes, picking every edible berry and dropping it into one of the four tin pails. There seemed to be a running game in place where one out of every twenty or so berries picked was hurriedly and silently eaten when the Guard turned their backs. None of them were ever caught, but something about it scared me too much to try.

Mallory kept to herself on the far side of the ditch and so did I, ten feet or so away from her. Neither of us could find anything to say to each other, and breaking the silence didn't seem necessary. The only time we ever neared each other was to approach and drop handfuls of dark, bluish berries into the pail evenly spaced between us.

Eventually, picking and delivering berries became mind-numbing and mechanical. My concentration wandered to Joana and the others: either on the beach or on their way home. I kept staring at the rim of the shallow dip, wondering if I could get up and just run as fast as possible. I hadn't seen any guns on the Guard, and there really was no one around to stop me. Before I could convince myself to attempt a race to suicide, I anxiously said in a quiet exhale, *you have no idea where the beach is, and you'll starve before you find it. Bennett's still on the manor too, and so is Angela. You can't just start running and leave them.*

I nearly screamed when Mallory fervently pushed my hands away from the bucket, scattering the berries I had just gathered on the ground.

"Are you out of your mind? Pay attention to what you're doing lest you want to get both of us executed!" she hissed, and glanced at the Guard looming over us. She swallowed, nearly in tears over what had almost happened, and went back to her work. I dropped onto my hands and knees, picking up the berries and blowing on them to dust them off, wondering what was so bad about them.

"Get rid of those," Mallory said, shaken.

"What's wrong?" I asked from the ground. Her face creased, and she gently removed one of the berries from the bucket and took another from my hand. She held them side by side. Though they were both blue and approximately the same size, I could now see the difference.

"This is what we're picking," she raised the fruit in front of my face, and then let it fall back into the pail. Mallory then showed me the other one. I saw it was notably shiner and more circular. "A big handful of these can kill you in twenty-four hours. If we were to accidentally feed it to a Lebon and kill him, then the Guard would spare nothing in finding out who picked it. You and I would both be done for."

Mallory placed the berry back into my hand, and I stared as if transfixed, unsure what to do with them.

"Do something with those things," she repeated. "Quickly, before anyone else finds them. You have no idea how many of us would be tempted to swallow that whole plant."

"It's poisonous?" I said quietly as a question, surprised by the way she could say something like that in such a calm voice. Mallory nodded her head.

"We're worthless eaters to the Guard because we can't do the backbreaking work. If the Imperial ever got sick of berries and nuts, half of us would be gone. Trust me, they wouldn't be upset about it. Whoever was left would be turned into a full-time handmaid and never leave Kieriana again."

One of the Guard barked an order to get out of the ditch, and present the four buckets to her to ensure they were full enough. As the other girls struggled up to their ground, Mallory took the handle of our pail, only for it to come off in her hand a foot in the air. The bucket landed on its side, spilling half of its contents on the dirt. I dropped the poison berries a fair distance from the rest, and moved to help her. Mallory scooped big handfuls to refill the bucket as quickly as possible, only to turn to stone in the shadow of the Guard standing over us.

"Why they even send such clumsy, inept girls over here I will never understand," I felt his voice on the back of my neck, and shuddered.

"The handle on the pail broke," I turned my head and looked up at him. Once I saw his face, I knew speaking was a mistake. The man's hand lunged and grabbed my wrist. A choked shriek left me as his grip tightened, putting sharp pain on the joint.

"Did you hear me ask you a question, you little tramp?" he forced me up off the ground, and yanked my wrist forward, pulling me in front of his face. "Did you?"

"No," I whimpered, afraid to breathe. The Guard scowled and dropped me, moving all the berries into a pile with his foot, including the poisonous ones. I could see the difference when Mallory held them together, but they looked identical in a mixed pile. Pretending to be unaware, Mallory continued to scoop the last of the berries on her side, dead silent. I looked up at the man, opening my mouth to tell him some of what was left on the ground was poisonous, but his cutting stare silenced me. While I sat there, Mallory leaned over the bucket, gathered the all of berries in both her hands, and let them fall carelessly into the pail.

"You never, ever speak to one of them unless they ask you something," Mallory leaned close to my ear and whispered. Still scared stiff from the episode, 1 jumped at the sound of her voice.

"The poison berries are mixed in there somewhere," 1 told her as if she didn't already know. For fear of the Guard, 1 lowered my voice to the point where 1 was only moving my lips halfway through the sentence. Mallory stared anxiously at our handle-less pail, now in the hands of the man.

"If you try to tell him now, they'll say you were trying to poison someone and shoot you the second you set foot in Kieriana."

"What are we supposed to do, then?"

"Look," she snapped under her breath. Mallory meant to say my name afterwards, and only then seemed to realize she didn't know it. "Your options here are to forget about it and hope everyone either doesn't touch the berries, or a poison one ends up on every plate instead of the entire handful. Or, you can try to get into the kitchen and pick out all the ones you can see, if you can find the bucket at all."

The Guard, walking in front, told us to be quiet.

"My name is Arlie," 1 slipped in before the silence could settle.

"Not anymore. Now it's girl, wretch, tramp, or whatever else they want to call you."

We passed the fields on our way back to the kitchen, and 1 scanned the area for a sign of Bennett. It was difficult to distinguish him from all the others, working mechanically and silently under the harsh gazes of the Guard. When he looked up, he seemed to immediately recognize me amongst the rest of the girls, and paused for a moment, leaning against the rake just like 1 had done. His face was bright red, and 1 could see his legs wobbling slightly even from where 1 was. 1 didn't realize how intense the concern in my expression was until he made a discreet hand gesture. 1 could almost hear him saying *don't worry about it*, and felt a gut wrenching sense of guilt that he was still toiling out here and 1 was only picking berries. He stopped paying attention to me when a Guard passed behind him, and our group continued on toward the castle to drop off the pails. We were not allowed to stay in the kitchen. After the Guard had closed the door tightly, locking in its smells and sounds, they disbanded us. The rest of the girls vanished deeper into the hall, while 1 followed Mallory up the stairs and back outside.

"Where are we going?" 1 asked, shielding my eyes from the sun with my hand.

"The people in the fields only get water during the day if we go draw it and bring it to them. Sometimes, the Guard won't even let us do that if they're in a particularly bad mood," Mallory answered, veering off in a different direction. "But they'll probably just ignore us right now because of the gathering tonight. 1 need you to help me get to everybody so no one passes out of heat stroke before the end of the day."

285

I didn't get to see Bennett as we walked down different lines of the workers, giving them water from a bucket. There was only one cup, so we had to wipe off the rim before handing it to the next person. But they were already so exhausted and sunburned, they didn't even pay attention, downing the water in seconds, thanking us, and returning to their work before the Guard could say we were sidetracking them. I tried to be polite and engaged, though I couldn't take my mind off of the one handful of poisonous berries lost in four pails of nearly identical-looking ones. It was unlikely they would all get served to the same person, but even if someone only got sick and didn't die, I had an anxious feeling that the Guard would be looking for us tomorrow.

The sun began to sink and the activity around the gate had already started by the time Mallory and I finished running up and down the fields. We were hot and out of breath ourselves, but there was literally nothing left of the water.

"Where's the kitchen again?" I set my empty bucket on the ground, nervously looking from the gate of the manor to the castle.

"I'll bring you down another way so you won't have to worry about the Guard," she answered, taking both buckets, and returning them to the wells on our way around the building. Mallory led me through an unguarded side door, and paused in front of a narrow, winding staircase downward.

"Down here, and then you can follow the noise. The door opens in, so watch it and don't slam into somebody. The Guard is waiting on the other side of the main entrance, and could come in unannounced at any moment. Do not let them catch you."

I managed to blend into the busyness, which hadn't slowed down at all since the morning. If anything, the action had picked up a frantic momentum, and I could hear Liam's distinctive voice as I searched desperately for a sign of berries anywhere on the line of prepared dishes.

"Ten minutes!" Liam shouted at everyone. It took a while for him to realize I was walking around as if hopelessly lost.

"Who're you looking for, hon?" he walked up to me, slinging a dirty, wet rag over his shoulder. My behavior alone must have told him I was in a panic, because he already frowned, concerned.

"Where are the berries we brought in here?"

"Good question," he looked at all the plates, gathered together on large trays, barely balancing on individual tables. "Do they want them now?"

"No," I said quickly, moving away to find them myself. Liam's ten minute mark ticked by as I paced around the kitchen, which was much larger than it initially seemed. The berries had all been washed and organized into smaller portions on the corners of several dozen plates. I had no idea where to start or when someone would come to stop me from ruining their creations. Starting with the right side of the table, I tried to distinguish the poisonous berries just by looking at the piles, and could identify only three. No matter how careful I was to take them while no one was looking, I knew it was a matter of time before someone noticed me.

Workers dressed similarly to Ida began to file in from the main door, and take trays from the other side of the room. As my hope sank with only three of the original twelve or thirteen berries in hand, I saw a small mound nearly divided down the middle between life and death on the second to last plate. Without thinking, I dove for it and scooped half of them from the dish. Breathing a sigh of relief, I counted the berries in my hand, thinking I'd gotten most if not all of them. I turned around, holding my handful close to my body, and ran into someone who had been standing right behind me. The berries scattered over the floor: more than half of them rolling under the counter. I recoiled, gripping the edge of the tabletop, and looked up at a female Guard. Her glare was no less intimidating than the others.

"What are you doing?" she asked in a light, but mocking voice. I only gaped at the four remaining berries on the floor.

"I-I-"

"I haven't seen you in here before, so I am going to assume you are new and do not know better," her shrill tone sent needles up my spine. "It is common sense, but you all seem to lack it. If you steal food from here, then the punishment is sitting in the lockup for two or three days. And when I am in charge, I tend to forget to feed you too," I sucked in my breath when she harshly took my chin, forcing me to look at her, and stared right through me. I stopped breathing all together when she moved her hand, and stroked my cheek with her fingers. "But you have such a pretty little face, so I'll tell you what. You can save your tears, pick up the berries, go wash them off, and put them back. But I won't be so kind to you next time."

"You don't understand...." I began, though I quickly shut my mouth, remembering what Mallory had said about speaking out of turn. In response to those three words, the woman pushed me hard away from the table. I didn't fall, so she did it again, forcing me onto the floor. Several people watched as I gathered the few berries by the woman's feet, not even considering reaching under the table for the rest. She used her hand to tell me to stop before I stood again, and then held out that same hand to take the fruit. I let the pieces fall into her palm. The woman looked at them for a while, like she was expecting them to get up and walk away, and then suddenly kicked me hard in the stomach. As I gasped, she practically threw my head against the counter once, twice, and then pulled my face back by my hair.

"Don't let me see you in here again," she snarled, placing the four berries back onto the plate without washing them. I sat upright, though leaning my pounding head against the counter. I gripped my shoulders with my hands and stayed there as others stepped silently around me to retrieve the trays. Minutes later, the door slammed, and I dared to look around me, realizing I was alone in the kitchen. I felt so hopelessly isolated: like I was looking up from a pit and couldn't see anything beyond. I wondered if, despite her silence, this is what ran through Charleigh's mind every day, eventually turning her into a psychological mute.

In constant fear that the Guard was about to return, I reached under the counter, feeling around with my eyes closed to block the painful light. Returning to a sitting position, I examined the remaining poisonous berries. I tried to tell myself that

287

I'd hopefully saved someone, whether that in itself was something to be thankful for or not, from a lethal dose. The longer I stared at their threatening skin, the more I worried that there could be one too many still on that dish. If a man died tomorrow, I now had several Guard who knew my face.

The door opened and closed. I convinced myself to look up, the light still throbbing behind my eyes, only after I heard it click locked. Liam cumbersomely weaved his way around the counter, and supported his weight on one leg as he knelt in front of me.

"Are you okay, Arlie?" he asked. I nodded slightly, holding my wet fingertips up to my forehead. He grinned thinly at me. "You're going to have a nice-sized shiner from that."

Liam then noticed the berries sitting in my open hand.

"Did you try to take those?" he spoke as if stunned I wasn't disciplined much more severely. I sat up, and looked at him like he could do something about the plate which had already left, explaining away the situation while trying to control the speed and volume of my voice. Liam only bit his lower lip, quiet. After a few seconds, he sighed and held out his large, rough and scarred hand to take them. I dropped the berries one by one into his palm, and he stood up, keeping them closed in tightly. He held his other hand out to me.

"Don't worry about it, hon," he called me that again as I held onto his hand. He lifted me to my feet, and stood by to ensure I could walk. I felt sick and lightheaded, but still managed to put one foot in front of the other. "It's only four. The worst you'll give any of 'em is a well-deserved stomachache. Let 'em eat poison berries. It saves the lives of more birds, you know."

What he said made no sense at all, but it still made me smile. Despite his different appearance and interesting sense of humor, something about Liam reminded me of Emmitt.

When we approached the shanty town, tents were just beginning to be erected. This time, they were much farther away from the castle, tucked in the shadows out of the sight of important guests. Many of the faces I recognized from the fields. It didn't take long for Bennett, red faced with sweat stains all down the front of his shirt, to find us. He seemed scarcely able to stay upright as well, but still looked at me with a creased brow and nearly open mouth, standing as if to catch me if I collapsed.

"What happened?"

"Just the-the Guard thought I was trying to steal food," I explained, my voice sounding like I was confused about it myself.

As soon as one of the tents was standing, Liam found the pile of blankets, and brought one back to us. He stood by the flap of the tent as Bennett helped me down. His knees almost buckled halfway to the floor, and he had to sit beside me. Lying flat on the ground underneath the darkness of the tent helped make my eyes less sensitive, though my head continued to pound. Eventually, I slowly moved my hand up, and delicately felt the tender skin under my eye.

"Rough day?" Bennett tried to smile down at me. I painfully turned my head toward him, and mumbled,

"I thought I lived in hell before."

Bennett frowned, and glanced over at Liam as if to make sure he wasn't paying attention to us.

"Anything I can do?"

"If you hopped that wall and ran down to the beach to see whether or not your dad's left us, that would be a huge weight off my mind," I placed my fingers against the side of my head, pressing hard inward, searching for a sweet spot that could relieve the pain.

"Trust me, he's still there," Bennett slipped a hand beneath my head, just trying to support it up off the ground. In response, I turned again and then forced myself to sit up, hugging my knees with my forehead braced against them.

"How can you be so sure?" I asked.

"He wouldn't leave without us. If nothing else, Ellamae wouldn't leave without you."

"We've got to get out of here, Bennett... Joana could die soon."

He breathed deeply, and only answered,

"I know. Let me think about it."

Liam slowly returned to us, and sat on the other side of me.

"Can I ask you something, Arlie?"

I momentarily panicked that he had heard us, but nodded, lifting my head.

"Why did you want to find Angela this morning?"

"No reason," I hastily looked away.

"People don't get that kind of hope in their eye for no reason, especially around here," Liam said firmly. "You can tell me. I'm good at keeping secrets."

I paused for a long time. It wasn't that I didn't trust Liam. I just didn't want him to think I was out of my mind. Without an answer, I looked at Bennett. I already told him why I was so adamant on scouring the place for her earlier today, though he'd only stared at me with a sympathetic look on his face, unbelieving. I could've easily been wrong, but something about Liam's demeanor suggested I might get a different reaction.

"Both my parents were taken during a Cleansing when I was five. They told us my mother was dead, but I guess they would've told all the families that no matter where everybody ended up...." I stopped, searching for some form of the normal, saturated pity I always received whenever I told this story. Liam was only waiting

289

patiently for me to continue. "Angela was my mother's name. I heard someone say last night that she had three daughters, and I have two sisters. But I wanted to see her again before I got my hopes so high. She was dead for eleven years."

"Don't you think Angela would have recognized you when you told her your name?" Liam asked. I frowned, trying to remember whether or not Ella called me Arlie back then, or if she began to after the Cleansing.

"My real name isn't Arlie. It's just what my sisters call me."

Liam cocked his head slightly as if looking at me in a different light.

"You have her eyes and her tiny freckles," he smiled. "I can see it. Now we just have to find her for you. Give me a moment, hon," he stood up, and returned to the opening of the tent. If I knew what he was going to do next, I would have never told him anything.

"Deacon!" Liam shouted outside. An exhausted-looking man much taller than him came barely into my sight, standing half inside and half outside the tent. Even though he was right there, Liam barely lowered his voice. "We have to find Angela."

"No one's seen her since last night. We think they came and got her earlier this morning to go on some trek over the mountain to deliver something with a couple others."

"Then she should be back any minute now. Go wait for her an' erryone else by the gate."

"I'd rather not get shot tonight, thank you, Liam."

"This is important!" Liam declared loudly, slurring his words, frustrated. "Then don't stand in plain sight, fool. Just make sure she comes back here as soon as possible."

"What's the matter with you all of a sudden?"

"We may have one of her daughters here with us."

Over half an hour seemed to pass. The crowds could be heard outside as everyone formed their usual line, though no one was currently allowed inside our tent. Liam later brought two dinners and another blanket for Bennett, winking once at me, and leaving to remain just outside the flap.

"I guess the scraps get better when the Imperial has friends over," Bennett said, looking at the much thicker soup and one-and-a-half pieces of bread for each of us.

"No," I shook my head as I took one of the bowls and set it on the towel in front of me. I struggled to keep my head up, but lying on the ground was no more appealing than sitting up and eating. "I think Liam gave us his."

The longer we waited, the more nervous I became over Liam's statement that Angela should have arrived 'any minute now.' Bennett tried to tell me that the group still had some time before they would be treated as runaways upon return.

"I'm sure she's alright," he adjusted himself closer to me. I moved the bowls out of the way, and then suddenly swayed to the left, falling into his shoulder as if in too much pain to sit up.

"What if she's not my mother and it's just some coincidence?" I asked weakly, having no interest in pushing myself back up.

"Then you haven't lost anything, have you?" Bennett pointed out, gradually placing his hand on my opposite shoulder, and I was quiet. Just as it appeared things were winding down, the sickness leeched away, and my head only hurt when I turned it to the right. There was a feeling of ease and security in sitting there with Bennett, but also a nagging discomfort. An annoyed, tired gathering of people were camping outside the tent, and I could hear a woman's voice sharply telling them to get out of her way.

Liam accompanied Angela inside, though hovered a fair distance away from us. As I forced myself upright again, she dropped quickly to her knees in front of me. When she saw my eye and the way I still held my head up in one hand, she frowned, taking her own, folded blanket and placing it at the head of mine to function as a pillow. I refused to lie down, and we only watched each other for another minute.

"Are-are you Amaryllis?" she stroked the side of my face, mindful of my eye. After what that woman had done in the kitchen, I shuddered painfully and looked away. Angela pulled back, surprised. Neither one of us were willing to take the first, death-defying step.

I brought myself to nod after an agonizing minute. Quiet and acting like she was about to wake up from something, Mom put her hands on my shoulders, and then slowly hugged me so I leaned against her. It wasn't exactly the excited reunion I saw in my dreams, but it was certainly as tearful. I stayed there frozen, just crying as she reached around my back and brushed her fingers through what remained of my hair.

"I heard Arlie and thought...." she whispered. "That you looked like what I imagined my Amaryllis would grow up to be. But I couldn't make myself say anything." She swallowed. "And-and Ellamae and Rosalie?"

"They're fine," I answered. "They aren't here."

"I'm so sorry I wasn't there for you," Mom's voice jumped. I felt terrible that I wasn't experiencing an equally overwhelming reaction. "Where have you lived for the past eleven years?"

"With Aunt Clarissa and Uncle Graham," I told her. She appeared stunned that the five of us could have sustained ourselves, and even more so when I mentioned Niles and Oakley, realizing Mom knew nothing of them. She repeated their names to herself, turning them over in her mouth.

"I worried for many years that Clarissa and Graham wouldn't be able to help you and your sisters because of money. Graham was only a clerk when it happened. I don't know how he could've provided for seven."

"I stole," I choked out into her shirt, unsure why I was confessing right at that moment.

291

"You stole?" I felt Mom's gaze on top of me. There was a sound of hurt in her voice, and for the first time, I felt a penetrating remorse for what I'd done over so many years. "You stole what?"

I went off on a ten minute, feverish tangent, telling of my fake Haritite patch, of sneaking around the markets with Stella and Barney behind my aunt and uncles' backs, and of bringing home anything I could in a homemade, cut-out book. I couldn't help but apologize every other sentence, yet Mom continued to stroke my hair, shaking her head to dismiss the topic.

"I am so happy to see you, darling," she kissed the top of my head, burying her face in my hair. "But it breaks my heart to see you here."

I couldn't let my mother believe I'd gotten to the Imperial's manor under the same circumstances. Not even considering the fact that Liam was still standing by and listening, and Bennett sat practically right there watching me blubber out our entire story, I spilled literally everything starting from the day Mr. Johansson caught me in his fields. As I got closer to telling the present moment, I tried to slow down and catch my breath so I might maintain a shaving of dignity after I finished my long, rambling account. Marveling at how she understood a word I said, or at least pretended to, I was somehow already convinced that Mom was going to think I'd grown into a deceitful, precarious person.

"Ellamae is still here on the beach?" she lightened her voice until she was practically cooing at me. I sat back, hugging my knees, and shamed myself into getting at least a partial grip.

"We think they're all still there."

"And this Jonathon?"

"His real name's Jason. He killed himself."

She said nothing more on the subject, but touched the side of my face.

"You don't have to be ashamed, Amaryllis. Not many people would have the courage to do what you did from such a young age. If you had not tried to steal that squash, then selfish me, I wouldn't be able to see you now after so long. I'm not upset with you, darling. You've taught yourself some precious lessons over the years. And it sounds like Rosalie looks up to you very much."

I'd always thought Rose was so much purer and more sincere than me, and would do anything to protect her from the world so she could keep that innocence. I was the worst role model she could possibly have, and that's why I rarely allowed her to come with me outside the Wall. She wasn't going to take after me, ever, and to hear my mother say she had was demoralizing. It seemed just as great a blow as her poem about shattered glass. When Liam came back to us and sat beside Bennett, he looked from him to me with an unreadable expression on his face. I knew I needed to say something, but only watched him, waiting for a reaction.

"Um, please don't say anything to anybody," Bennett stumbled over his words, trying to find them. "We don't have any more than two days before-"

292

"Ah relax. If the Guard were to wise up to anything around here, it would only make our lives more difficult, anyhow," Liam shook his head and stood to leave, smiling down at the three of us. He seemed more imposing standing above us, though his kindly aura felt safe and trustworthy. "I better let some of these people inside. Don't worry about anything. We all have our skeletons in the cupboard, and yours is by no means the worst."

Liam paused for a moment, and then asked Bennett, "None of the Guard have asked you your name yet, have they?"

Bennett looked at him dubiously and shook his head.

"Then I'd suggest you think up a Stoleh name, son. They probably won't know the difference, but just in case, alright?"

Liam winked at him, gently placed a hand on my arm, and left the flap of the tent swishing behind him.

Chapter Thirty Six

No one seemed to have heard the name of Sir Terrance until word came late the following morning that he had fallen violently ill. The brother of a man in the Council of Patriarchs was the instigator in what the Guard's gossip circle made out to be a near civil war, with accusations flying between the bureaucrats over who had poisoned this man's drink. No one thought of toxic berries, or really gave more than a few sideways looks at any of their Stoleh workers. A few immediately placed the blame on us as a whole, saying every last one of us in Kieriana had something to do with it. Their voices were more than drowned in the resurfaced past scandals, the obvious, bitter tension amongst the other influential Lebon, and even a distrust in the Imperial himself. It appeared all was not well behind the manor's wall, and it really had little to do with any kind of outside threat. I breathed easier knowing the Guard now had more important conflicts to attend to.

There appeared to be someone new in Kieriana every hour on the hour--only there to spit off at another Patriarch. The Guard kept those of us not trained or dressed like Ida mostly out of the main hallways of the castle, sticking many people in places where they didn't usually work and had no idea what to do. But despite the fact that it was a flaw in their system, we took the beating for the widespread dysfunction, and many people were sent to the lockup and whipped.

I was embarrassed by the way I had carried on the night before, but something important occurred to me later as a large group of us were led downstairs into a room nearby the kitchen. In the midst of my reunion with my mother, I had pushed Bennett off, not paying any mind to him or the fact that his mom was still missing if not dead.

The thought ate away at me as we walked side by side into the tall-ceilinged room. But with Mom and Liam with us, I decided to wait until we were alone. It seemed like an address from the Guard wasn't a regular occurrence, and everyone whispered amongst themselves for a while. Still, the moment one of them stepped up to talk, a sudden weight of silence dropped on every conversation in the room. The man kept it brief, basically condensing a speech into a few threatening sentences.

"As it has gotten around by now, one of the Patriarch's brothers was poisoned somehow at the gathering last night. I am only here to tell you that if the filth responsible is among you, you will report it today. If you do not, then you will all be treated as conspirators," he stopped, though he received no response. "That means death for the poisoner and hard times for the rest of you."

"And if one of you did it, then you get fined, correct?" a voice spoke loudly from the center of the crowd. The Guard immediately began pushing their ways through us in search of the owner, but the source was too vague to locate. Before they could make an executive decision to randomly pick someone to hold responsible, everybody simply turned around to leave. The man in the front of the room yelled at us to get back to work to maintain some sense of control, though most of us were already gone.

I lost Mom in the congregation, though she had told me to expect that, and find her later. Liam quickly retreated into his adjacent safe haven, leaving Bennett and I together in the crowd. Just around the corner from the door to the kitchen, I took him by the hand, and pulled us aside. As I waited for the bulk of the crowd to pass, Bennett looked at me, probably expecting that I would start whispering about Joana and the others. He was in no way prepared for me to start profusely apologizing about the previous night.

"You don't have to say any of that. You have nothing to be sorry for," he interrupted me. I didn't realize how much I had worked myself up until I stopped talking.

"I just feel terrible that I brushed you off like that and I wasn't even considering that your mom is still missing."

Bennett looked away, uncomfortable, and I felt much worse for actually saying that out loud.

"I-I'm so sorry, I..." I started speaking with my hands, both of them moving in circles around each other as if trying to come up with something to say. Staring at the floor for an answer, I only mumbled until I felt Bennett take both of my hands to stop my nervous movement. He half smiled, and then pushed them down and back as if returning them to me.

"Amaryllis, you haven't seen either of your parents since you were five. I understand. I don't expect you to watch what you say around her on my account, okay? It's really fine."

I ducked my head, nodding, but still unconvinced. When we started walking again, Bennett chuckled slightly under his breath.

"What are you laughing about?" I asked.

"You basically said in the Etairan Mountains that you weren't a good person, but you're constantly worrying about other people. I've never heard one selfish thing come out of your mouth. I wish if you were going to worry, you'd worry about getting out of here, not about acting overemotional when you thought your mother was dead for eleven years."

I frowned for a while, but then smiled to myself, walking into him teasingly as we neared the stairs.

"Stop!" a voice called at us. We froze, and stared up at a Guard walking toward us from a different staircase at the end of a hall leading left. I couldn't help but jump to the conclusion that somehow they had figured out the poison berries, and my connection with them in the past five minutes.

"You," the woman told me. "Come with me."

I looked at her as if I didn't understand, and she shot me a harsh, annoyed stare.

"You aren't in any trouble, girl, not yet," she gestured for me to follow her, beginning to walk away.

"I'll meet you in front of the kitchen later," Bennett whispered next to my ear. I nodded silently, trotting after the woman. I was afraid to walk alongside her, so I maintained a following distance, quickly bowing my head whenever she turned around to ensure I was still there. She led me in silence through several halls and up a winding staircase. At the top, two more Guard gave me a dirty look as I passed behind the woman into a closed-off, wide, sunlit area. We stopped in front of an impressive door.

"Knock," she told me as she was leaving. I wanted to call after her to ask what I was doing, but stopped myself before I said anything, just watching her exit. Alone in the bright corridor, I took several minutes to work up the courage, with each passing second imagining a worse presence waiting in the room.

"Come in," a faint voice answered my knocking. Inside a small chamber with arch ceilings and a large, high window, a girl older than me sat on the corner of a bed. This girl looked like some kind of expensive doll, with long, white blonde hair half held by pins into a loose bun. The features of her face were small and pointed as if they had been carved that way, and she seemed very delicate in a smooth, dark purple dress. She looked up at me, and her porcelain face formed a confused expression.

"Who are you?"

I said nothing as she stood up, revealing her impressive height, though leaning against the post of the bed. Her dress was open in the back, and she held the front up with her hands as she walked closer to me.

"You may speak in here. There is no one around but me," she spoke lightly, and not like she was trying to talk down to my lower level of intelligence.

"My name is Arlie," I answered. Shortly afterwards, I realized she probably didn't care. "The-the Guard sent me up here."

"You aren't in any kind of trouble, Arlie," she parroted the woman, though the way she said it made it seem entirely different. I guessed the look of anxiety was still on my face. "I only wanted someone to help me with something."

I assumed she meant lace up the dress, and took an impulsive step back, knowing I couldn't. But the girl came closer to me, limping, and turned around. She lifted one of her arms up to reveal a widespread, swollen, purple bruise hugging her hip and seeming to stretch down to the top of her left leg. I stared at it for a long time, quiet until she asked me,

"Is there a mark?"

"It's very big," I told her, wondering how someone who looked so paper-like managed to do that to herself. The girl sighed, and faced me again, pulling the sleeves of her dress back onto her shoulders and starting to lace it herself.

"I fell off a horse yesterday," she explained. "I asked the Guard to go find a girl who could look at it because... to be honest, I do not trust them as much and was embarrassed. I apologize if that woman scared you."

"It's okay," I answered, watching as she skillfully tied her dress as high as her arms would allow, which was enough to let her release the front. As the girl tried to walk a few steps, she grimaced and reverted back to limping.

"My father would be furious if he knew," she looked up at the ceiling as if it was listening to us. "But he does not need to know. It will heal on its own."

"Are you sure you're okay?" I asked, surprised that I was even letting myself talk. I didn't know who she was, but 'father' suggested she was one of the Imperial's many children. "It looks bad."

"There have been worse," was her answer. "You don't need to be concerned about me."

The girl didn't officially dismiss me, and I stood there for another minute as she hobbled back over to the bed, and sat down again, wincing. Her eyes closed for a moment as if deep in thought, and I slowly made my way to the door, thinking that was my cue to leave.

"Do you hear it?" her voice startled me, and I turned around, looking at her as if caught. The girl smiled thinly at me, and then motioned toward the area below the window. "If you press your ear against the wall, it's louder."

I followed her direction just to appease her, and slowly pressed the side of my face against the cold stone as if expecting an explosion. Below us, I could hear the faint, cadenced sound of a powerful instrument. There were no breaks or falters in the rhythm, only a flowing sound that seemed so distant through the stone. Robust, handmade, six-string instruments were popular behind the Wall, though no one in my borough was skilled enough to reveal any beauty within them. This music simply sounded perfect, even excessively so.

"What is that?" I asked, staring off into the middle distance as I let the sound run through my mind, trying to comprehend it.

"It's music," she laughed at me, and I shrank away from the wall. "Have you ever heard anything so beautiful?"

"No," I shook my head, the melody still replaying itself in my head.

"He writes all of those songs himself," she leaned back on her arms, listening whimsically. I could no longer hear anything, but I nodded, assuming she was talking about the Lebon playing downstairs. "I feel so badly for him at times. He has such a lonely life."

The girl suddenly sucked in her breath, and forced herself upright again. What she said next caught me off guard.

"If you don't mind my asking, how long have you been here?"

"Only two days."

She frowned, gripping her bedpost for support, and staring at me as if expecting a story.

"Who did you leave behind?"

Leave behind? I thought. *Does she realize how all these people who've broken their backs here for years came to Kieriana?*

"My sister," I said, not realizing the bitterness in my voice until after I'd answered. The girl seemed taken aback by my tone. I stood there awaiting some kind of retribution.

"Were you close to her?"

"She means everything in the world to me," I accidentally snapped, stressing the present tense. Though I had just seen Rose a week ago, the reality of our situation also meant if Bennett and I couldn't get out of here soon, she was truly alone with Ellamae. I couldn't bear to hear any past language associated with her.

"I have many sisters," the girl sighed in disappointment. "But I cannot say all of their names, nor recognize them when we pass. I have a half-brother whom I speak to, but I've always wanted a real sister."

The girl stopped, and looked at me sideways once. I averted my eyes, though I could hear her painfully trying to stand again.

"Can you bring me that little chest sitting on the armoire there?" she pointed behind me, giving up. I picked up the polished, red oak chest with three fingers on each hand as if afraid of getting my fingerprints on its surface, and held it out to her from an uncomfortable distance. The girl leaned forward to take it, and set the box in her lap, lifting the cover and rummaging through its contents for a while. When she removed an indistinguishable piece of jewelry, dropping an attached, dangling necklace back into the box, I stepped away again.

"It's not going to hurt you," she held the palm-size piece of tinted brown metal upside down in her hand. "Take it."

"No, thank you," I stuttered, looking wide eyed at what I thought was a brooch of some kind. I had seen Haritite women wear them before, but there was something so foreign and menacing about the one in this girl's hand, it seemed alive. For a moment, I wondered what had possessed her to offer it to me.

"Please, I want you to have it," she extended her hand further. In response, I withdrew the same distance.

"I can't take that," I said a little more firmly, though I was still scared to reject something this girl was trying to give me.

"I like you. You're different from all the others," she momentarily took back her hand, though I knew she wasn't finished trying to force me to accept what she probably believed was an offering of truce. "You don't just keep your head down and scuttle about like a rodent."

I knew exactly how shocked and disgusted my face must have looked by the way she quickly went into an explanation for what she'd just said.

"I mean that you don't seem so afraid of me. The other workers have had the dignity beaten and threatened out of them. You haven't been here that long, but your eye is black, and you still had the nerve to basically tell me off. I think it's nice to see someone who hasn't lost themselves just trying to survive here."

That's all the people do here, try to survive under the orders of people like you, I watched her hand as she held the brooch out to me again. *If you call them rodents again, then I'll make you regret saying you appreciated being stood up to.*

Of course I knew I'd never have the courage to lay a hand on a Lebon, especially when I had something to lose besides my life. I stepped up, and took the brooch, turning it over in my hands. When I saw the intricately sculpted design, I nearly dropped it. At the top of the brooch, adorned with blue and green, light-reflecting jewels, was something like an eye. Its milky center drew attention away from the embellishments, and a wavy line sliced down its middle.

"Do you know what that is?" she asked. I shook my head slowly, in awe of the design. Its sophistication was only one more reason why I wanted to get rid of it as soon as possible. "It's a peacock feather."

Peacock was a strange word to me until I remembered what Joana had said about Rose's journal. It was like a second symbol of the Lebon, because it was beautiful and refined. Realizing that, I felt immoral simply touching this innocent piece of jewelry. The girl smiled kindly at me, though I knew the look on my face was still mixed between shock and severity.

"I'm sorry. I wasn't trying to insult you," She frowned, finally picking up that her comment still didn't sit well with me.

299

"I understand," I lied, quickly moving to leave, and to stuff the brooch deep into my pocket. When I realized I no longer had any, I closed it tightly in my fist, and hid it behind my back. The girl allowed me to nearly run back into the corridor without any form of thanks. The thought didn't cross my mind since I was planning to drop the brooch outside somewhere before I was caught with it.

I blindly made my way past the Guard and to the stairs, the cool feeling in my hand a reminder of the form of Lebon presence which followed me. As I took the steps two at a time, I watched the passing windows, but couldn't see the sky. At the bottom, I struggled to remember which way I had come from, and worried Bennett was already waiting for me. There were several other Stoleh workers around, but I couldn't make myself approach them with the brooch still hidden in my hand. Standing there, I looked around at the three available hallways, trying to determine which one led to the other staircase.

"In quite a hurry, weren't you?" I felt a voice practically breathe down my neck. I didn't have to turn around to know it was the Guard. The same two from upstairs moved around me like snakes, staring down at me like prey, and I shrank. "What's in your hand?"

Before I had a chance to move, the man on my left seized my hand. My fingers cracked as he forced them open, and let the brooch fall to the floor with a subtle, fatal tap. I stared at it for a long time, deathly silent as the man's hand wrapped itself around my lower arm, forcing it backwards behind me. I thought he was going to lock my hands into manacles, but he only held me in that vulnerable position so the other Guard could kick my legs out from under me.

"Thief!" I heard as I hit the floor hard on my stomach. Though my eyes were down, I could hear the other people in the hall loosely gathering around us. One of the Guard delicately picked the brooch from the floor, and walked off to return it.

"I hope you know the consequences so we don't have to tell you," the remaining Guard spat on me from over my head. I turned onto my side as he continued, "Her jewelry is worth more than you anyway."

"I didn't steal it," I whimpered before I realized I wasn't allowed to defend myself, even though it would be pointless regardless. Responding to my voice, the man forced me to my feet, and spoke next to my ear,

"Say that again."

I sucked in my breath, closing my eyes, trying to detach myself from what was happening.

"I said say that again," he jostled me, and I choked,

"I didn't steal it."

A humph of disbelief came from the man, and I felt his fingers on both sides of my neck. He practically threw me around and against the wall, though I held my head forward so it wouldn't take another impact. Before my senses returned, the man slammed his hand right beside my head. As I wondered why the stone wall didn't send some kind of shockwave up his arm, he snarled,

"Stand there. If you try to run, I'll personally make it worse for you."

My knees buckling, I looked down, and remained silent. The Guard didn't take more than a few steps away from me before he stopped. I couldn't see why immediately, though I heard the occasional, quiet breath of pain as she limped quickly over to us.

"I gave it to her, you imbeciles!" the girl shouted, stunning the room and the Guard. She walked past the man, and stopped in front of me.

"Are you okay?" she asked. I only looked at her, still struggling to breathe deeply enough to get air.

"There is no need to protect her," one of the Guard told her, and she spun on her heels.

"Read my lips. I... gave... it... to her. You're lucky I don't have you turned out of the manor for this."

"Might I ask why you gave something of this value to one of the workers?" they asked, still unconvinced.

"Because I wanted her to have it. Is that alright with you?"

The Guard looked at each other, and then to her.

"If that's all, I suggest you go find something else to do," the girl's voice lashed at them. With fake humility, they shortly bowed and grumbled,

"As you wish, Imperiess Arena."

As they left, they dismissed all the workers with harsh waves of their hands. Once we were alone, Arena came up to me, and I watched her with a new kind of surprise. I had questioned if there was a chance when I first heard her say 'my father,' but never thought to ask her name. One thing was certain, if the Etaira had seen her in the past eight years, I would have been shot without question the moment I claimed her identity. She and I looked very little alike: my short body and scarred, seemingly disproportionate features compared to her refined and natural beauty. Despite the fact that I hadn't known Arena, I couldn't help but feel like by assuming her persona so far away from her knowledge, I actually had stolen something from her. The moment I saw she was about to return the brooch to me, I opened my mouth, but nothing would come out. Arena wordlessly took my hand, placed it in my palm, and closed my fingers.

"No, please," I ripped away from her, and nearly threw the brooch across the floor, its running sound echoing up the walls.

"It's a gift," she frowned, turning her head over her shoulder, looking at the burnished bronze standing out against the plain stone.

"Don't make me take it. I have no use for it. It'll look nicer on you."

"That's not the point," Arena sighed like I couldn't possibly understand what her gesture meant. "Please, Arlie."

"I don't want it!" I screamed. She stepped away from me, taken aback. My eyes searched the airy foyer for some escape, and shot her the best apologetic look I could manage while running away.

I was thankful for the few people present in the kitchen when I found and slowly opened its door. Liam saw me, and watched me with an alarmed look as he weaved around the counters.

"You need to stop having all these confrontations with the Guard, hon," He assumed by my demeanor that something had happened again, and led me to the same chair at the same table with the same spice rack. I crawled up into the stool, and hugged my knees closely under his stare. Liam lowered his voice, "Especially if you and Bennett hope to slip out of here soon."

I was quiet, and he leaned against the table again, sighing.

"We've all had our fair share of black eyes," he touched the tender skin beneath my eye, smiling sympathetically. "The Guard are preoccupied with this verbal civil war, so it shouldn't be too hard to sneak you some ice in a bit. You want to tell me what happened or are you going to leave an old man wondering?"

Liam honestly didn't look that old. It was only his scar and bald head. As I relayed the past twenty minutes, he waved down another worker and asked him to go see if he could get some ice, gesturing at me. Still, as he spoke to someone else, he nodded occasionally to show he was listening.

"You must have impressed Imperiess Arena very much," his eyebrows rose in surprise.

"I don't know what I could've done."

"Well, she was raised mostly by us," Liam answered, frowning his disapproval as if the Imperial himself could see. "And after she was older, the Guard had her basically locked away except for when her father calls for her. She does not have many happy memories of anyone besides us since she began constantly trying to win his approval. Now she trusts some of us more than her own Guard, but still, she is a Lebon and that is irreversible. Arena is third in line for the throne, you know, after her two legitimate brothers. That is frightening to most. They think she is too fragile."

In spite of her appearance and high-pitched voice, I couldn't see Arena as internally fragile after what she had done, nor imagine her as any future, lone-ruling Imperia. When the man returned with the ice, Liam thanked him, and balanced it on my face, waiting for me to take it for myself. At first, the ice only branded a layer of cold onto the side of my head, though after a while, it nulled the pain and sensitivity around my eye from yesterday. I lay my head down on the surface of the table to block the light as Liam stood up to return to his work, gently telling me that I could only have a few minutes. Before my allotted time had passed, I could hear people nearly bursting into the kitchen. I worried it was the Guard, and sat up, dropping the wrapped ice in my lap. I heard their voices, but still couldn't pinpoint them until they came around me. Mom lifted my face in both her hands to look at her, though saw nothing new, as Bennett took the ice and held it for me to take. I only placed the melting rag on the counter.

"Amaryllis, what have you done?" Mom's voice, let alone her apprehensive face, was already accusing me. I only looked at her, betrayed. When I told her of the past eleven years, I never considered how she would interpret my confession. What if she now thought I had developed the mind, heart, and soul of a thief, as if I now couldn't help myself?

"I didn't steal anything," I answered, grumbling, forcing my head away.

"Then why was the Guard after you?"

"Leave the girl alone about it, Angela," Liam called at us from another counter as he relentlessly wiped down an already clean-looking surface. He thrashed the table with the rag, walking around to the other side to get closer to us. Though the room was now empty, Liam lowered his voice, "It was a bad misunderstanding, nothing more. You know very well how they try to make criminals out of us."

Mom was quiet, and backed off of me.

"How did you guys know?" I asked Bennett, turning myself around in the chair to look at him.

"Some of the people came outside and started announcing it. But by the time we got here, they were saying she came down here and said she gave it to you."

"That's what happened!" I exclaimed, trying to defend myself. After all we'd been through, I hoped he if no one else knew I wasn't just a petty thief. Bennett only picked up the ice, and insisted I hold it over my eye again.

"I believe you," he answered calmly. "What did you do with it?"

"I threw it back at her."

"You threw it at her?!" Mom returned to yelling. I felt like the perfect fantasy of reuniting with her and being happy again had been destroyed by the unfiltered opening of my heart. She said she wasn't upset with me, and I bought right into that, stupidly thinking I could finally forget that life.

"Quiet," Liam scolded us just as I began to defend myself. I was expecting a lecture, though he only closed his eyes and smiled thinly. "Hear that?"

I could tell Mom and Bennett heard nothing, but I barely distinguished the sound of the same instrument, now coming from what sounded like directly above us. Liam looked up and watched the ceiling as if he could envision an image that matched the light music, and eventually started toward the rear door, motioning for us to follow him.

We weren't stopped or questioned as we entered the floor above the kitchen on a different side of the castle. Music now drifted lazily through the halls, though the few people present carried on normally like they couldn't hear. Liam took us around the first corner, pausing in front of a wide open door. He turned around, silently telling us to remain quiet, and then moved on to stand in the middle of the doorway. The instrument's size complemented its large sound. A polished, blended brown body on three legs surrounded a long line of white and black keys, each one producing a different sound. It sat nearly center in the otherwise blank, empty room by the light of lanterns and candles. I could see only half of the player's face from where I stood. Standing over him was one Guard, and another, round man with tiny spectacles perched upon his bridged nose. Neither of them really seemed to be listening to the music, only judging it. For the remainder of the song, I tried to watch the man's face. Despite the complexity of the melody his hands played, it was relaxed, and it appeared his mind was someplace distant. But as if he already knew what the two behind him were going to say, he frowned deeper as he neared the quiet end.

"That one is... better," the round man spoke flatly, not entertained. The player didn't even turn around in response, only watching the keys closely like they would move. "He has gotten better," the man continued unconvincingly, speaking to the Guard. "But I tell you, taking this wretch and teaching him to play was like pulling teeth for the first several years."

He's not a Lebon? I thought, frowning. When both the man and the Guard looked ready to leave, Liam silently forced us all beside the doorway. They didn't even notice us as they passed, the sound of their conversation fading down the hall.

"Come on," Liam said, already half in the room. The man now had his head resting on his arms, leaning over the keys and onto the body of the instrument. As we neared him, I could see him stiffen, and he looked up at us with strained, tired eyes. His dark hair stuck to his skin with sweat, as did the neck and underarms of his white, collared shirt. He squinted like he couldn't quite see us, but sighed, slouching on the bench, when he saw Liam.

"They don't like to make it easy in here for you, do they?" Liam walked up behind him, slapping him once on the back.

"It's next to impossible to write music in a windowless room," the man leaned in to look at some kind of disfigured, foreign markings propped up on a stand in front of him. Now, standing right there, I could see he was much younger than what I originally thought, probably not even three or four years older than me. "Especially with one of them constantly leaning over you."

"They'll end up with a blind pianist one day if they don't get some real light in here," Liam shook his head, and then waved us closer. The man watched us strangely until we stopped beside the bench he sat on.

"You know Angela," Liam sat backwards on the corner of the bench. The man smiled uncomfortably and bowed his head. "And do you remember these two?"

I didn't think we'd ever meant him before, and didn't see how he could know us. But he nodded, looking up at Bennett and me, and said,

304

"I believe you introduced yourselves in line your first night. Bennett and Arlie, right?"

Bennett confirmed, though I couldn't catch myself in time to avoid staring at him. He was the man who sat beside Liam, wearing a typical, raggedy, yellow vest, who dropped pieces of bread in every soup bowl. *Welcome to Kieriana*, he'd told us, *where justice is spat upon, but law is worshipped.*

"It's complicated," the man uneasily answered to my expression alone. "I'm here during the day, but I'm back washing the pots and pans come evening."

"The boy came to us when he was so young," Liam started, and the man quickly feigned an interest in a nonexistent blemish on the wall beyond us. Liam laughed slightly, happy to embarrass him. "He had two run-ins with the Imperial himself. Before he played the piano, he played his Majesty's out of tune heartstrings, didn't you?"

"I was eleven," the man shot him a look. Liam didn't seem to mind.

"When they turned him over to us, he was such a little soldier. But no matter how much he set his mind to it, he was too skin and bones to do the work. I suppose he made quite the impression on his Majesty because instead of giving him some of the lighter jobs, he called him back in here, and commissioned someone to teach him to play the piano so he can entertain at the gatherings."

"It's sounds so pleasant when you say it that way," the man nearly snarled, and Liam backed away from the bench, still not intimidated. "I have to write every song I play, and last time the Council of Creaky, Gray, Loud-Mouthed Patriarchs didn't like one, one of them broke three fingers on my right hand. You know what the damn Imperial said about it? Nothing! And at the end of the day when I'm done entertaining these pig-headed murderers, I get thrown back like a fish. Everyone thinks it's so easy, don't they?! They practically accuse me of being part of them!"

"Relax, relax," Liam dared to put a hand on his shoulder. The anger seemed to leave, but the stress stayed behind. "I'm not accusing you of anything."

"I'm sorry," the man reached his arm over the keys, and leaned against the body of the piano. He picked up a fountain pen resting on the stand, and violently scribbled through a section of the markings written all over the page. "If they weren't up there spewing off right now, they'd probably have my head. I've been working on this song for a week, and I've only got until tomorrow's senseless peacemaking meeting to finish it. I don't see why we can't just give them all a fancy sword and have this poisoning scandal over with. There're too many others to keep track of."

The man clenched the pen until his knuckles were nearly white, staring hopelessly at the page. A few seconds later, he viciously pounded the keys in no pattern, sending a painful sound echoing down the hall.

"You need to get outside and see the sun," Liam told him, looking sideways at the page. Everything on it was well over his head, too.

"By the time I change and they let me out of here, the sun's gone."

Liam frowned, pursed his lips, and was quiet for a few seconds. His voice seemed to shock the man when he excitedly continued,

"Play the one you wrote for that girl last year."

"I got my fingers broken last time I played a song with any dimension," he answered, writing something new at the beginning of the page as he laid his fingers over four keys and silently stroked them. I could have sworn I saw him blushing, but not as if embarrassed, more like he was perturbed by the mention of 'girl'. "They only like their light and perfect stuff were every note matches. There is no depth in it."

"I didn't mean play it for them," Liam reached over the man's shoulder, and took the pages from his stand. He turned around to rip them away from him, but Liam had already moved out of reach. "Enough of this gobbledygook for right now. Play the one you wrote about that girl."

The man glared deeply in no one's direction. He stared at the ceiling as if trying to recall his song, all the while quietly pressing individual keys until he seemed satisfied with the group he'd found. When he suddenly struck seven keys at the same time, the sound seemed to penetrate the entire room. The melody was entirely different from the lighthearted, picture-perfect tunes he first played, and left an echo so real I thought we could reach out and touch it. I knew nothing of music, but I did know that this was by far better than anything he had been forced to write for the Lebon. Despite the emotion audible in the keys, the man sat as upright and still as a statue, in a state of intense concentration. Only a minute into the song, however, he shakily removed his hands, bracing his elbows against his knees so he could cover his face.

"I can't do it."

"What do you mean?" Liam dropped the paper on let it drift lazily on top of the piano's keys. "That was music."

"No, I mean I can't play that song. Not anymore."

"It's time you let it go, Bryn," Liam tried to put a hand on his shoulder again, though he quickly stood up and began pacing around the room. "It was eight years ago and it's still eating away at you."

"You try letting it go when all you see at night is the look on a person's face before they're murdered," Bryn stopped walked, his voice ice. But he seemed too afraid to storm out of the room, so without anywhere to go, he continued to pace in a circle.

"What are you doing in here?!" the round man's yelling voice returned to the room, though I was more concerned about the Guard in his wake. "Get out, shoo!"

It felt as if we were being forcibly ushered out of the area with a figurative broom. But before the door was slammed in our faces, I watched the Guard drag Bryn by one arm back over to the piano, and practically throw him down onto the bench. Liam steered us away from the light and openness of the hall into a darkened corner.

"I'm sorry about that," he moved a hand up and down his forearm as if dusting himself off. "I didn't think that they were close enough to hear him." Liam barely paused.

"You know, the boy was too scared to write down that song. He claims he has it in his head, though I've never once heard him finish it. He will always stop around the same time and say he can't continue. I feel so bad for 'im when the others give 'im a hard time for being a piano player for the Lebon. He was only nine or ten when they carted his family over here and it's not like he was given a choice."

"Where did he come from?" I watched Liam as if expecting horrible news. Both the song and the near confrontation with Bryn's overseers had shaken me.

"I wanted you to meet Bryn because of where he came from," Liam smiled as if he'd been waiting for me to ask. "He and his parents were caught in the Haritite State as Idrisans when he was a tiny thing. They dragged all three of them over here, but the Imperial couldn't execute a little boy, so he let him sit in the prison for another year or two until the next shipment of Idrisans came, and he went to the hearing again. He was eleven, and finally the big-hearted Imperial Acwel Aloysius decided to turn him over to us so he could work on the manor. I took him into the kitchen with me, and I remember him in such a panic over this girl. She was killed the following morning, and the poor boy just turned into a shell. Didn't take more than two weeks after that before the Lebon started him on the piano because there was literally nothing else he could do."

He's an Idrisan, I thought. *Now that he's older, the only thing that stands between him and execution is his ability to entertain the Lebon.*

"What girl?" I asked next.

"He hasn't said her name in years," Liam's eyes wandered around. "But I think it was Ruth something."

I stared wide eyed at the ground. I never knew her, and really my only connection to her was the fact that I was the only Stoleh who went to the Haritite State since. But there was something about Ruth that made me feel as if I'd known her so well, and I was grieving her death eight years later. Perhaps it was all the people from her life coming into mine that made her seem so tangible, like we would find her here alive any day now. Bryn was only eleven when she died, though she had left such an impact on him that he couldn't even say her name or finish playing a song he'd supposedly written for her.

"You look sad," Liam expertly deduced. "Did you know her?"

"I know of her," I answered. It was the truth, but I felt I was somehow rejecting her life by such a formal answer. Everyone in the Idrisan camp knew of her, left flowers at her empty grave in spring, and went about their business. Ruth had struck and stayed with me since the day of knew she existed. "When Bennett and I were on our way to the State, someone told us I was the first Stoleh the Idrisans had sent since Ruth," I paused, adding, "Her last name is Backenstose."

For some reason, speaking of Ruth brought back the haunting image of the distance in Joana's eyes last time we saw her. I couldn't immediately see any link, but a realization so apparent I'd paid little attention to it occurred to me.

"Bennett," I turned around quickly enough that the ends of my hair sharply licked the side of my face beneath my black eye. He seemed to know what I would speak of next, and already, it looked like he was trying to come up with a response. "If your dad and Lukas and Ellamae and Joana are still on the beach... there wasn't any food or water on the boat... they had to have run out of stuff to clot the blood with. We need to get out of here by tomorrow or they're going to die waiting for us."

"We will, okay?" Bennett shushed me, and I was reminded of where we stood. "Let's not talk about it here."

"We have to promise that we'll get out of here tomorrow no matter what happens," I repeated myself, and he widened his stare at me, shaking his head, trying to tell me to stop talking. "If they're still down there, then...."

Bennett placed his hands on my arms so I would be quiet, but he still smiled unconvincingly through his concern.

"If we have to dig under the manor's wall," he told me. "We'll get back to them."

An indistinct clatter reached us from around the corner. I separated myself from the group, and peeked out to see an empty hallway. I took a step, and something sharp poked a hole through my shoe and into my foot. I winced, quickly recoiling, only to see the culprit and immediately slip into a new panic. I squatted on my legs, picked it up, and dropped onto my knees right there.

"What's wrong?" Bennett came around and knelt in front of me. He wasn't looking at what I held, only at my face. "Amaryllis?"

"We're finished," I choked out, holding up my hand.

Bennett didn't need to have been there to know we had Arena's brooch.

Chapter Thirty Seven

Bennett and I spent the remainder of the day constantly jumping at shadows and looking over our shoulders, simply waiting for the Guard to start running after us. By the time night fell, no one had come for us, and I lay awake against the formerly comforting body heat of my mother. When I told Bennett we needed to get out of there no matter what happened, I wasn't considering that she had been standing right there, and that had gnawed at me since.

"Mom?" I finally asked. Her face frowned as she opened her eyes and looked down at me.

"What is it, my darling?" I felt her hand stroke sections of hair back. She accidentally touched my eye, and I grimaced, scooting away.

"You're coming with us, right?"

I became more and more nervous the longer her pause drew out.

"Of course I'm coming with you, Amaryllis," she answered. "Try to get some sleep, now."

Mom watched me as I forced myself into a sitting position, shaken. The cold ground was just as uninviting as it was uncomfortable, and the sickeningly familiar feeling of hollowness had settled in my stomach. Without saying anything, I stood up as silently as I could, and weaved my way around all the bodies packed together within the tent, accidentally stepping on one woman's fingers. Outside, the gathered tents were eerily quiet, the remnants of the fire and smoking cauldron filling the air with the smell of soup and burnt bread. I walked as if afraid of stepping on another person, watching my feet more than my path. The thought of going beyond the limited boundaries of the shanty town was intimidating, so I walked in a circle around all the tents, staring up at the looming, half-lit castle to the northwest, the fields in the southwest, and every other building and element of Kieriana west of where we were allowed to settle. As the wind began to cut through my skin and sting my eyes, I stopped in my tracks, and looked up at the manor's wall. By now, I struggled to not immediately think of it as the Wall I knew in my mind. *It is a rather easy place to get around if you know the blind spots*, Mr. Johansson had said back at the camp. I couldn't help but wonder if any of these so-called blind spots were tolerated in Kieriana. If only they were, I could go get Bennett and my mother and leave right now, only able to hope that when, if, we found the beach, the others would be there anxiously waiting for us.

I rounded the side of the small camp facing the L-shaped building where they had first taken Bennett and me. I suppose the wind and my distant thoughts drowned out the sound of their footsteps, because I didn't hear anything until they were near on top of me. It felt as if my heart entirely stopped when I sensed the presence before I heard the voices.

"What are you doing, little miss?" he asked, and I quickly turned around, staring nearly open-mouthed at the three. I didn't recognize them, but I figured it was only a matter of time we didn't have before I started running into Guard whom I'd already aggravated. The three laughed at my reaction. "Out for a stroll at this hour?"

"I-I couldn't sleep," I stuttered, not realizing the stupidity of what I'd said until it was too late. The apparent leader of the three brought me closer to them by the collar of my shirt, nearly picking me up of the ground.

"She couldn't sleep," his breath alone seemed to slap me across the face. "I'll bet the poor thing is just hungry."

He released me, and I stumbled backwards, barely staying on my feet.

"We're here to get two of you," he told me, taking a neatly folded piece of paper from another one of the three. "A girl by the name of Arlie, and a boy by the name of Bennett."

I considered telling the Guard I'd go find them, and then not come back, though I knew we'd end up caught one way or another. Their demeanor seemed too calm to know who we were, but that didn't mean the people wherever they would take us were the same way.

"Hello?" the man sharply snapped his fingers, and pointed me back in the direction of the tents. "Go get them."

"I'm Arlie," I felt like I was admitting something deeply personal.

"Well, you're making this easy enough for us, aren't you?" he laughed again with the others. "Go find your little friend and don't keep us waiting here half the night."

In a trance, I staggered back to the tent, and stepped over several people on my way to Bennett. I passed Mom on the way, and knew one of her eyes was on me as I lowered myself to my knees beside him. Bennett lay awake, and already looked at me with a concerned expression as he sat up.

"What's wrong?" he asked just above a breath.

"They're here."

Bennett's face turned ashen, and he looked beyond me and at the tent flap.

"They're waiting at the edge of the camp," I clarified. "What are we gonna do?"

I knew I'd put him on the spot for an answer neither one of us could possibly give. Bennett tried to smile thinly at me, and he took my hand to stand me up with him. As we left the tent again, I swore I heard Mom whisper my name.

The closer we got to the Guard, the harder I squeezed Bennett's hand.

"The most important thing is the others," he said beside my ear.

"We don't say anything," I agreed, though that made it no easier. Bennett didn't let go of my hand until we reached the Guard, who silently forced us in front of them and began to walk. They led us through a different entrance on the L-shaped building, and just as quickly held a door open. We jumped at the sound of it slamming and locking, looking at each other fearfully. The room was box-like and almost appeared to be shrinking, empty except for five chairs all loosely facing one another. I thought we were alone until I saw Bryn sitting silently in the chair farthest away from the door, his

311

head bowed, and holding his hand up. Four of his fingers were wrapped tightly together in gauze.

"You too?" he looked up at Bennett and me. I slowly walked into the room, and lowered myself into the chair next to him. "They're not broken," he waved the hand around in the air. "He just bent them backwards. I wrapped them like this so they would stay forward and I can play tomorrow."

"Are you sure you're okay?" I asked. Bryn smiled slightly at his hand.

"It was worth it."

Bennett quickly found the chair next to me at the door handle's jiggling. We watched in trepidation as the two entered the room, closing the door tightly behind them. A boy younger than me sat in the left chair, wearing a prim, white shirt and fancy, rippled, red collar. He incessantly, nervously, ran his fingers through one side of his black hair, watching the girl who comfortably sat beside him. Arena observed the three of us. Bryn seemed able to maintain eye contact, while Bennett and I struggled to find various points in the blank room we could emptily stare at.

"Why did you leave it there?" was the first thing she asked me. Surprised she would bring up the brooch again, I said nothing. She repeated herself.

"I can't take it. I don't want to be caught with it."

"Why are you here?" the boy demanded, dismissing the topic.

"Are you under the impression we want to be?" Bryn held up his hurt hand.

"Not you," the boy told him. "Them."

"I know what I heard," Arena quickly added. "Don't try to talk circles around me."

Bennett and I stared at each other like the answer was written on one of our faces. We didn't know exactly how much Arena had heard, and couldn't afford to give her more information than she already had.

"The Guard is suspicious that we told them to bring the three of you down here at this hour," Arena looked over her shoulder as if expecting to see one standing there. "We made something up, but the longer we're in here, the less likely they're going to believe it, even if it's me. Let's skip all the periphrasis. I know you two are Idrisans, and there are more of you on a beach close to here. Why did you come?"

Bryn, unmindful of them, jolted upright in his chair and began intently watching us.

"We were forced to stop here," Bennett carefully answered. "The man who stole the sword from the manor came to the beach and attacked one of us. We went up the mountain looking for a place to leave the sword for someone to find, were caught, and presumed to be the Stoleh workers who stole it."

The boy leaned forward as if studying us. By then, I assumed we were done, and only minutes remained before they sent for the Guard again. What I couldn't understand is why they had dragged Bryn, their former Idrisan piano player, into it.

"So you are Idrisans," he spoke like he hadn't believed Arena's story until then. Bennett and I didn't respond, but our expressions must have been validation enough. I watched, in shock, as a small excited smile spread across the boy's face. "I'm Alexander. You and Arena and I have a common goal."

There was little relief in knowing we would not be turned in that night. Just by the way he spoke, the three of us were hesitant of the conditions Imperien Alexander was about to establish.

"My father and his past several predecessors have shamefully degraded this land," Alexander began, and Bryn immediately stopped him.

"Don't try to make it sound like this is about us. You don't have but so much interest in everyone else. What do you want and what's in it for you?"

"As you probably noticed with the uproar the poisoning scandal caused," Arena continued, noting Alexander's speedily growing unpopularity with us. "There's a lot of unrest here, a lot of fake conspiracies, and a lot of real ones, too, all hidden behind the swords passed around at sham peace meetings. You have the standing Guard here who is loyal to the Imperial, and then you have all the other Lebon who would like to see his head on a platter. We want our father off the throne before he completely dismantles all the relationships here and starts an endless civil war. You know if one starts here, it's going to cause one on the main island."

"We have no common goal," Bryn said firmly. "And I know they can testify. I was never what most people here considered a real Idrisan because I was nine when my parents were captured. But I know just from what I remember about Baba that the Idrisans' objective isn't just to assassinate one Imperial and prop up another. Especially if it means working with Lebon who really don't have a thought about the island or its people in their heads."

Arena and Alexander stared blankly at him. I assumed none of the Lebon had ever heard Bryn affront anyone in any way for fear of his life. Now, he looked back at them as if daring them to threaten him, like Ruth's song had finally given him the courage to speak.

"You have every right to be bitter about what was done to you and your parents and your friends," Alexander gathered his bearings. "I know it means nothing to you, but it was wrong and a horrible display of injustice. You don't have to forgive us, but please listen."

Bryn frowned, and leaned back, cradling his right hand in his left.

"He didn't mean our common goal was to assassinate the Imperial," Arena said, lowering her voice. "If we did that, then the problem would continue when one of my brothers by the Imperia took the throne. What we want is to get somebody in there who can change something and not just ignore what's going on. But in order to do that, we need a complicated plot to degrade the Imperial and my brothers who are in line for the throne."

"I'm assuming you want it?" Bennett said as a question. To our surprise, Arena shook her head.

"I want Alexander to have it."

Several things immediately appeared wrong with the plan they had not yet told us. First, Alexander was not one of the Imperial's legitimate children. Second, he couldn't have been any more than fifteen years old. I also didn't think anything could convince the Lebon to put him on the throne, and nothing in what they'd told us yet seemed to line up with our supposedly common goal.

"Here's where we think you'll be interested," Alexander picked it up, encouraged by our expressions. "If I get the throne, we'll go."

"Go where?" I stared at him strangely.

"We'll all leave the island."

Bennett and I looked at each other, frowning in disbelief. A spiteful laugh left Bryn, and he began to slowly unwrap the gauze around his fingers.

"You must think we're very stupid."

"I do not think that at all," Alexander obtained a dead serious face as if offended by our doubt. "On the contrary, I think you three are our best chance."

"What motivation could you possibly have to pack up all the Lebon and leave? You don't think that's going to cause a civil war?"

"Here's how I see it. The island is in a state of glazed over revolution and that's why the Idrisans have grown so much. I can't possibly understand what goes on over there, but I know influential people get away with murder and beyond. As long as that continues, the Idrisans are only going to get bigger, the population is going to grow more and more resentful, and the massacres, tithes, roundups, and hierarchy system will get worse. The slow decay we're going through right now is going to spark one day with another incident like the poisoning, and when something erupts over here, the entire island goes down with us. If I can get us away from here now, we avoid the power struggle, have no resistance to worry about, and all the external things that cause half of the internal fighting are gone. And if you will help me, your home gets autonomy, and you can do whatever you want with it."

"We need to get off this manor," I added before any scheming that sealed the fate of the entire island could begin. "We have people waiting for us who can't wait any longer."

"Hear us out," Arena smiled slightly at me as if to affirm a promise. "And you'll be walking through the gates with no one pursuing you by tomorrow afternoon."

"Wait," I cut off Alexander before he could start, talking to Arena. "What's your part in this?"

"I'm the closest connection we have to my father," she answered coolly. "And all the time I've spent sitting in on these meetings and gatherings has only convinced me more that this is the best thing to do for everyone. And think about it. We're your only sure way out of Kieriana."

Alexander spent the following twenty minutes explaining his intricately designed and thought out plan to us. It had no margin for error, but many chances for it. If the execution involved only risking our lives, it wouldn't seem as unattainable and strange. However, the slightest mistake on any of our parts could result in the extinction of the entire Idrisan camp. Even if everything went smoothly for us, half the plan depended on the reaction we'd receive. As Alexander spoke, I looked at both Bennett and Bryn to see if I might tell what they thought. Bennett watched Alexander in a state of disbelief, like he couldn't accept that his lofty, dangerous proposal might be our only opportunity to get off the manor. Bryn spent the entire time slowly opening and closing his fingers with a subtle frown on his face. Long after Alexander had finished, he and Arena were still waiting for our reaction.

"What do you think?" Alexander spoke less like he was asking for our commitment, and more like he was seeking our approval.

"You're out of your mind," Bryn answered flatly. "But it's obvious you've been planning this for a long time. I just don't see why you're involving us in it."

"I need you three to be involved," he told us, frustrated. "I don't want to play this card, but you can force my hand."

He grabbed our attention with the threat. What seemed so frightening was that one minute he was practically begging our allegiance, and the next, threatening to hand our lives over to the Guard. I couldn't even tell from his face whether or not he had the capability to actually do it. But the truth was now that he and Arena knew, either one of them could end our lives with one conversation.

"Can we think about it?" I asked pathetically. I was only trying to buy us time before we had to make such a potentially earth-shattering decision.

"No," Alexander said in a scolding voice like he was speaking to a bunch of children. "There really is no decision to make considering it is your only way home and my only way to save my people. I only want your word."

"Alex," Arena shot him a glare, and he backed off slightly. "We will call for you tomorrow morning for your answer. Then we have a small window of time. Do you understand?"

They waited for each of us to nod vaguely before Arena stood, her long dress trailing behind her, and unlocked the door.

Bryn wordlessly separated himself from us when we reached the shanty town. The first thing I noticed when Bennett and I stepped through the open flap of our tent was the carelessly wrapped up blanket that lay in place of my mother. I figured she had gone out looking for us, and momentarily considered walking the circumference of the settlement again.

"She'll be back," Bennett whispered. "If she's not here in ten minutes, I'll go with you."

He lay on top of his blanket several feet away from me, while I tried to curl into a ball so I could fit under mine. With my back to Bennett, I looked from Mom's abandoned cover to the entrance of the tent, waiting for her to come back. I didn't realize how much I missed the warmth until she wasn't there. Minutes later, I turned over, trying to find a comfortable position and let go of the circulating thoughts and one option we'd been given. It took a while before I realized it, but Bennett was staring at me, frowning. *What are we going to do?* I mouthed. A look of confusion crossed his face, and I awkwardly adjusted myself closer to him.

"What?"

"What are we going to do?" I swallowed, looking down.

"What can we do?" he answered, sighing.

"I know it's our only way out, but what is Allyson going to say?"

"What can she say?" Bennett shook his head at the holed ceiling of the tent. I promised myself I'd go look for Mom in five minutes, but rested my head on one arm and fell asleep before I could convince myself to get up.

She was there the following morning as people began to walk around and shake everyone awake, though I was now closer to Bennett than her. We weren't touching, but only a foot of distance was between us.

"What happened to you two last night?" she frowned as we slowly sat up, looking at each other as if seeking confirmation that last night had been a dream. Bennett only followed the crowd outside so I could talk to her. Still, I could not find the words for a long time, and sat on my legs, obsessively folding my blanket smaller and smaller until it would no longer shrink. Mom stood up to crease the ends of hers together, but still kept a watchful eye on me.

"Do I need to know something, Amaryllis?" she eventually asked. Aside from a few, we were the only ones left in the tent. My initial belief was no, my mother didn't need to know anything more. She already thought I was a thief. But I told myself that I might as well say it now, because Arena and Alexander were going to have to make room in their plan for her if I was going to go through with it.

"Yes, I need to tell you something," I forced myself to look up at her. She sat down again to not tower over me. Before I could even begin to think of a way to express what we were going to do that day, someone poked their head in the tent, and said loudly,

"Poor Nik came back."

316

Chapter Thirty Eight

A mechanical wave of silence momentarily befell our procession as we neared a makeshift platform erected in one of the fallow fields. Aside from the Guard, the only thing we could see was a man on his knees, his arms chained behind him, alone on the stage. I couldn't tell if he was the same person or not. They had shoved a black bag over his head. But what was even more striking was the blood that stained the wood below him from previous executions. I must've asked Mom who 'Poor Nik' was five times before she hesitantly told me that he was the man who had stolen one of the Imperial's swords. *The person we almost died in place of,* I thought. *The one who could've easily killed Joana.* As everyone was ushered forward by the murmuring, sad crowd, I picked up only bits of conversation. It mostly pertained to Nik: who was only twenty-three, who had been in Kieriana since age seventeen. Nik: who had always kept his head down and mouth shut, never having any problems with the Guard. Nik: who had been acting

317

strangely, like he was hallucinating, the day before he vanished and took one of the Imperial's swords with him.

Bennett located me in the gathering, though neither of us could find anything to say, only watching this Nik. He sat there unmoving like a statue, as if he could not hear the whispers rippling through the crowd just in front of him. Once again, silence was induced by a Guard stepping onto the stage behind Nik. As I watched him load a small handgun right there in front of us, behind his victim's head so he could hear the resounding *click*, I felt physically sickened, cupping my hands over my nose and mouth as if I smelled something terrible. As the Guard took his time for the dramatic, lasting effect, I scanned the crowd, making out Liam and Ida a fair distance away, grimly shaking their heads at the ground. Mallory was watching nervously, and Bryn, with his back to me, stood unnoticed in front of us.

"Bryn?" I asked quietly, and he whipped around, staring wide eyed at me like I'd just screamed his name. A deeper state of horror seemed to grip him, almost as if he was the one on the Guard's platform. Bryn took a few steps to stand on the other side of Bennett and me, keeping his eyes on the ground. He eventually looked back up at Nik like he was forced to, watching the Guard, unblinking and seemingly squeezing his own arm tighter and tighter as the minutes passed.

"Have you anything to say?" the Guard behind Nik tilted the barrel upright behind his ear. Nik's head fell forward slightly, and the man roughly yanked it back up. Bryn emitted a soft, choking sound as he forced his eyes closed only for a moment. The voice from behind the black bag seemed detached and cryptic, like the area itself was speaking.

"It was only so the Imperial couldn't offer another weapon as a gesture of peace."

It suddenly seemed horrible that we even thought Nik could have run back here and announced he had seen a group of Idrisans on a beach. We knew nothing about him when he started to run, but now I couldn't help but feel a sense of debt. If he had told the Guard anything about us, they would have rewarded him for giving them information. Instead, he was quiet, more willing to accept death. The Guard was eager to get the execution out of the way. We had heard that they were going to do this in front of the other workers to set an example, but I somehow never thought Nik would return to the manor. He would have died either way. I just couldn't see why he would rather be executed by bullet than die alone in the woods and never be found. In the seconds that followed, I wondered if it was Nik, rather than the Guard, who was proving a quiet, though deafening point.

The nauseating feeling in my stomach only intensified, and I couldn't watch, impulsively turning to my left and hiding my face in Bennett's shirt before I realized what I was doing. Bennett lightly placed his arm around my back, and also looked down and away from this abysmal demonstration of the Guard's iron grip. I only heard the shrieking bang of the shot followed by the *thud* when Nik fell back to the platform. I shuddered at both, reminded up close of what actually happened every night at the Wall. The shockwave lingered for a long time, but I could not make myself turn around. The

Guard unfeelingly dismissed the crowd to their daily tasks, and Bennett's arm around me tightened as he swung us around. With our backs to the bloody stage, I thought it safe to look ahead. Around us were similar white, stone faces. Few people actually cried. I figured this must be a fairly regular event.

It took me a few minutes to realize Bryn was no longer beside us.

"Where'd he go?" I asked Bennett, slowly pushing myself away from him. He looked over his shoulder toward the castle, careful not to turn his head enough to see the gruesome scene that lay behind us.

"That way," he nodded in the direction. I paused, briefly watching Mom, who walked steadily and silently beside me.

"Come on," I cut across Bennett, heading against the flow of the crowd. No one tried to stop us as we half-walked, half-ran around the field, blocking our views of the platform, to a cellar-like door which led down into the hallway of the kitchen. We hadn't seen Bryn or which direction he'd gone, but I somehow felt like he would be forced to go that way because of the surrounding Guard.

The area was empty and poorly lit, but we could immediately hear the sound of someone climbing the stairs.

"Bryn?" I asked again as we ran up to the step below him. He didn't turn around, didn't pick up his pace, but continued forward with his arms pressed together over his chest. We followed him in silence for a few minutes until I realized where he was going. At the top of another staircase, we were barred by two Guard, who immediately recognized and scowled at me.

"What are you doing here?" one snapped at Bryn, who calmly answered,

"I must ask about a piano piece she wants."

They looked Bryn up and down several times, observing his clothes, not his face. Eventually one acknowledged him, and they moved to let him in.

"What about them?" they stopped Bennett and me, and Bryn turned around.

"We were told Imperiess Arena sent for them."

"You go," one of them put a hand behind Bennett's shoulder, and roughly forced him inside the double doors. "The tramp stays here."

"Both of them," Bryn tentatively repeated before Bennett had the chance to jump down their throats for the comment, which it looked like he might do. The Guard gave me a deep evil eye, and shoved me past them, snarling,

"Watch where your grubby fingers end up this time."

The corridor was not yet brightened by the slowly rising sun. Bryn paused in front of Arena's door. I saw his bloodshot eyes and the way he shook from traumatization, but said nothing as he knocked loudly.

"I was just going to ask for you," Arena barely opened the door, and spoke softly. "Have you thought about it?"

"I'll do it," Bryn looked down, nearly crying. Arena didn't bother to ask what had happened, and turned her attention to us.

"We need you in order to actually go through with it."

"Yes," Bennett answered quickly, and I was put on the spot. But regardless of how I felt, it was an obvious response, no matter how much we didn't like it.

"Arlie?" Arena prompted, impatiently waiting.

"On a condition," I said, and she frowned, surprised. "I'm taking some people with us."

"One person."

"Two people."

By the time Arena closed the door, she had harshly warned me to not bring any more, and to collect them quickly because we were to meet Alexander in four hours. Bryn recoiled as if in shock of what he'd just done, and leaned against the opposite wall with his hands in his face. As he tried to gather his composure, Bennett hesitantly approached him.

"Bryn..."

"I don't want your sympathy," he shook his head, breathed deeply once, and wiped his face though there were no actual tears. "I'm doing this for Ruth and Nik. Someone has to keep them alive."

After we passed the Guard, who made me show them my hands and shake my clothes, Bryn left to change and finish his song, as he said, though the plan we had just agreed to rendered that unnecessary. I figured he only wanted to distance himself from the possibility of the entire thing blowing up in our faces, and we watched him leave.

"Your mom and Liam?" Bennett asked as I set off for the kitchen again, assuming he would be there. I only nodded absentmindedly.

Relieved to see Liam alone in the flickering light dutifully cleaning the same counter, I began talking the moment we walked through the door. Startled, he held a finger over his mouth to quiet me, and gestured toward a bucket filled with water and submerged rags.

"Both of you get one of those, wring them out, and start wiping down the tables before people get here. Then we can talk."

I painstakingly did as he told us, aggressively cleaning the surfaces while trying to formulate exactly how I was going to tell Liam. Halfway across the kitchen from him, I panicked that by the time we finished, others would already be coming in. Lost in the swelling thoughts, I only came back to reality when Bennett slid a new, wet rag across the table toward me along with a look that could've audibly told me I needed to calm down. *How can I?* I mouthed back, irritated.

"Don't think about it too much. It doesn't change anything," he answered, no longer looking at me. "Just think about seeing Ellamae and Rose."

For some reason, *Rose* seemed like my name for her, and I felt a barrier go up. I had to tell myself several times that Bennett was only trying to make me stop freaking out lest I blow the operation before it started, and to let it go. Ten or fifteen minutes later, Liam brought the bucket over, and set it on the floor for us to return the rags.

"Thank you much," he signed in relief. Only then seeming to notice our grave faces, he leaned against the counter. "What's on your minds?"

I clammed up at the question, and Bennett took it from me. Liam's reaction wasn't as extreme as I thought it would be, though I watched him frown deeper and deeper with every sentence, once again nodding slightly to show he was listening as Bennett explained.

"Well, I'm not surprised Arena and Alexander want 'im off the throne," he took a long time to formulate a response. "But I still don't understand why they're willing to leave the island if this works."

"Liam, will you come with us?" I asked abruptly, and he quickly held his hands up, backing away from the table and retrieving the bucket.

"It's too much for someone like me," he said, and I felt something inside me deflate.

"But if this works then the Lebon are gone," I walked with him across the room. "You won't have to be a servant for them anymore."

"I'll have to wait here for that day to come. I'm not Idrisan material like you, Arlie. I don't think I could stomach that."

I would've hardly considered myself Idrisan material before I was sucked into it with Bennett. People in the camp came from everywhere, all with their different reasons and stories. The way I saw it, conditions in Kieriana were much worse than behind the Wall. We couldn't leave Liam here to endure the torment the Guard ruled by. To hear him refuse to come was crushing. I watched Liam eased the bucket down onto a stool, almost in tears as I followed closely behind him, begging him to come with us.

"Listen to me, hon," he looked like he was trying to carefully select his words. "It's not in my place to go back to the Idrisan camp with you. I know it's difficult for you to understand, but my place is Kieriana. Not working under the Lebon, but looking out for Ida an' the other people who work in here. I'd rather be the last one who's free, knowing there are people waiting for me on the other side, than leave first and have to hope and wonder if somebody filled my shoes."

I was quiet, my eyes wide. I hadn't expected Liam to stay here, and now the sudden thought of leaving him behind was overpowering.

"I admire you two," he tried to smile at us. "You've got that young courage all of us lost many years ago. Don't worry. I'll be right here when you come back one day."

321

I must have still looked unconvinced, because Liam then nearly picked me up off the floor in a hug. I didn't realize until then how gaunt he was beneath his baggy clothes. As I struggled to free my arms, he said,

"You two're goin' to be fine. You've got everything goin' for you. Sir Sordid and Sir Snob aren't gonna know what hit 'em, understand?"

I backed away, afraid to say anything else, and kept looking back at Liam over my shoulder as Bennett and I neared the door.

"You two take care of each other, hear me?" he called, watchful of his voice's volume. We stopped, and watched him for a little while under the dangling light bulbs. Something about this basement kitchen had grown on me, and I didn't want to leave. Only the sound of people coming down the hall forced Bennett and I to turn around. Still, I felt Liam's eyes on us as we left.

No physical remnants of the morning's execution were visible on the fallow field, though I could tell the workers were making a conscious effort to skirt around the sunken rectangle in the dirt left by the platform. It didn't occur to me until I saw so many people that I now had to find my mother somewhere on these few acres of land within the next four hours, and manage to pull her aside in a nook or cranny where the Guard could not eavesdrop. Bennett and I must have circled the castle and fields for over an hour, stopped several times and forced to come up with an excuse for walking around, as I desperately searched for a sign of Mom. The ticking clock in my head was thrown off by worry, and before long, I was certain three hours had passed and we had less than thirty minutes to find her. Bennett tried to tell me we had much more time than that, and she was around here someplace, but I refused to believe it until I actually saw her carting water back and forth for the people in the fields. When she caught sight of me, she indicated a small shed with a discreet nod, apprehensive about the Guard making their rounds while we spoke. Mom laboriously set the bucket down, and looked up at me. Once she saw my expression, she delicately placed her hands on either side of my face, mindful of my eye, asking what had happened.

"Nothing," I answered, and lowered my voice. "We're leaving today."

"Right now?" she leaned back to see the patrolling Guard just beyond the temporary safety of the shed. "Is that what you were trying to tell me this morning?"

"Yes. You need to be in front of the kitchen in two hours."

"What are we doing, Amaryllis? How do you plan on getting out?"

"Please don't ask me how right now," I frowned, still unsure about the logistics around Alexander's plan and if it was truly our sole option. "Just be there."

Bennett and I picked up the pace to get across the fields, waiting the entire time to be called down by the Guard. Of course by that point, it didn't seem to matter. They could threaten two helpless Stoleh workers as much as they wanted.

But they could do nothing about the two Idrisans preparing to abduct the Imperial in broad daylight.

Chapter Thirty Nine

We waited ten minutes later than we expected for my mother. I spent them pacing and panicking that she would not be able to get away from the Guard, only starting to breathe again when she silently rounded the corner. She asked again how we planned to escape the manor from beneath it. Bennett and I didn't answer as we started up the stairs toward the place where Arena had told us to meet Alexander.

In accordance with the plan, Bryn was not there. Both Arena and Alexander stood in a sectioned off, empty, dark hall near the staircase that led to Arena's room, frantically speaking in hushed tones. They didn't seem to notice us until we approached them.

"We can't wait any longer. Where's this second person?" Arena looked past me into the main hall, making sure no one had followed us. I only shook my head, telling her Liam had decided not to come. She appeared almost relieved, and I frowned deeply as she shoved a pile of clothes in my face.

"I forgot about these earlier. You have to look like you're supposed to be there. I could only get one outfit, and it's for a woman. So only you will actually go inside with me, Arlie."

I stepped back from the clothes, and looked up at her in dread. It seemed like such a small thing in the scheme of Alexander's planning, but to me, it already sounded like the plot was falling apart. Arena forced the folded skirt, blouse, and yellow vest into my arms, and ordered me to change right there. When I instead dressed over what I was already wearing, she looked me up and down several times, finally telling me that the stitched together moccasins looked strange with the fancier, loose-fitting clothes.

"It really doesn't matter," Alexander cut in, exasperated. He rubbed the side of his head with two fingers and looked past us again, nervous about our location. "The later Arena comes, the more he will have to be suspicious of, because she is usually early."

"Do you have the...." Arena began, frowning, stopping herself when Alexander barely lifted his shirt to reveal a short, unsheathed dagger attached to his belt. Alexander and Arena led us around a rear vestibule with a rounded ceiling, one that saw little to no traffic during the day. Before we even surfaced onto the next floor, I could hear the vulgar noise of a large gathering. It seemed to emit from behind another set of double doors located just beyond the partially hidden staircase. When he saw they were already closed, Alexander seemed to have a small heart attack, and fell back a step.

"Relax," Arena told him. "You know it hasn't started yet unless you can hear the piano. And if he'd already started playing, he would have been thrown out."

Alexander silently agreed, and stopped our group before emerging into the lighted hall above us.

"Stay out of sight," he told Bennett and Mom. She only stared in disbelief at our surroundings, and I almost forgot I hadn't yet told Mom how we were getting out of the manor, or who was involved. She probably didn't even know who exactly Arena and Alexander were, only that they were people of importance who were risking themselves to help us escape. I debated whether or not right now was an appropriate time to tell her that they were not in this to benefit us. They were here to remove their father from the throne.

Arena gently motioned for me to come with her as Alexander stopped outside the doors. Without Bennett, I felt I didn't know what the plan was anymore. *The piano's broken,* I told myself, running it through my head in an effort to reassure myself. *Alexander was supposed to make sure that the piano is broken so they throw Bryn out. He goes and stays with Bennett and Mom. I'm only here so Arena doesn't walk in alone, they would consider that strange, and all I have to do is stand there until the Imperial leaves, and then follow her out the back. Follow her out the back and meet the others at the bottom of the stairs.*

When Arena stopped, facing the plain, wooden door, she breathed deeply, and then looked at me as if waiting for something.

"You have to open it for me," she clarified. Before I moved, she quickly added, "And I apologize in advance."

"For what?" I asked in a panicked voice, thinking she was sharing her doubt about what we were going to do. She giggled at my apprehension.

"I meant for the people in this room. They will not be kind to you. Hopefully, we will leave in less than ten minutes. Also, if either of us is asked, you are my escort, for I am not supposed to walk around on my own because my father believes I am twelve. Don't say that part, though," she smiled slightly, quickly wiping it off her face as she realized I was too worried to see humor. "And I will have to pretend I don't know your name. If you have to say something to me, then you begin every sentence with your highness. That's the way it is around here."

I agreed, but I had no intention to speak at all once inside. Several seconds passed before I remembered I had to open the door for Arena, and awkwardly adjusted myself to prop it open with my back.

An airy, wide open corridor was made to feel claustrophobic by the tables set in two lines to face the empty center of the room. The men seated at them were all between sixty and eighty years old, though most of them appeared in halfway decent health. I momentarily frowned, remembering the pitiful state that half gripped Gregory Guise last I saw him, wondering why that couldn't have kept one of these vain Lebon home instead. As they sat there, half their conversations sounding like watered down arguments. I could see Bryn in the far left corner, mostly concealed behind another piano, dressed in his original, plain white shirt. He only sat on the bench staring at the keys, awaiting the order to play from the man on the large, upright throne.

There was something almost anticlimactic about the Imperial's ordinary appearance and stature. His black hair grayed at the ears and hairline, and was pulled back from his bored-looking face. He wore no crown and no gold, in contrast to the extravagant swords displayed behind him. On his left side was another, lesser chair seating who I assumed to be the Imperia. She was another naturally beautiful woman not affected in any extreme way by age, though she was hidden behind a colorless dress and a subtle frown. I closed the door as quietly as I could, watching Arena nearly silence

325

the room as she walked up the line of tables, bowed shallowly to the throne, and climbed two or three steps to her mother. The Imperia took her hand and smiled up at her, and I thought they looked like they got along fairly well. But as an outsider looking in, I could've probably said the same about her and the Imperial.

I quickly walked toward the side of the room where several other Stoleh workers stood with their backs to a large window. The person beside me discreetly tapped my elbow, and I looked up at Ida. Her eyes were big with concern, and she seemed to mouth, *what are you doing in here?* Without an answer, I bowed my head at the floor, staring at Arena out of the top corners of my eyes. As she calmly took her place on a bench next to her two adult brothers, the Imperial shifted his weight forward in the throne, and motioned at Bryn.

"Begin."

Bryn waited almost an entire minute like he was afraid to touch what he knew was a broken, or at least morbidly out of tune piano. Some of the men were staring harshly at him from over their shoulders by the time he started what would have been a light and flowing song, pretending he was oblivious to the screeching sound.

"Stop, stop," the Imperial held his hand out, wincing. One of the Guard standing near Bryn came up and harshly nudged him in the back. Bryn withdrew from the piano, looking up at him as if he didn't know what was wrong. The Imperial turned his hand upright, accompanied by a questioning stare.

"There appears to be something wrong with the piano," Bryn mumbled. The room laughed at him, and he shuddered as if reminded of a painful memory.

"We can hear as much, Bryn," The Imperial frowned, moving his arm again to unfeelingly eject Bryn from the room without so much as standing up. As he scuttled awkwardly across the floor, passing down the line, he briefly glanced up at me. I couldn't tell if his expression was meant to be reassuring behind the engrained look of worry. The door closed loudly behind Bryn, who was allowed to walk out unattended, and his part in the plan was over. He was almost free, which was more than I could say about myself.

Without anything to lead in to what Arena had called the Imperial's sham peace meeting, no one seemed to know how or where to start. One man thought it would be suiting to stand, his hand pressed firmly against the table, point his finger, and start accusing the person on the other side of the room for poisoning his brother. Amidst the resulting, room-wide argument, Ida and the other workers exchanged glances. They remained silent, though several of them held their forehead in their hands. I sensed they heard this often, and as I looked around the room, I couldn't help but liken these peoples' senseless squabbling, arguing for the sake of arguing, to that of my seven-year-old cousins.

"Gentlemen," the Imperia stood up, speaking down to them like children. They silenced, and watched her in surprise. Aside from Ida and I, who probably weren't even considered, she and Arena were the only women in the room. I assumed they were expected to only sit there. "We are not ignoring what occurred last time, and will determine who is responsible. However, you may be assured it will never happen again. Please, try to be civil."

Grumbling, the standing men all sat down, and waited for the Imperial to say something. He instead motioned again, this time at us, and all the others began to walk away from the window. I watched as they each took a pitcher from a nearby stand, and went to serve the Council of Patriarchs. I moved to follow, staring wide eyed when I realized there were no more, and I no longer had a place to inconspicuously stand. As I attempted to make myself blend in with the wall, slowly adjusting myself behind the three foot tall pedestal, I couldn't help but feel the Guard was staring at me. When I heard an accusatory voice from across the room, I looked up at the ones standing near the piano, trying to keep my expression from appearing too caught. One of them scowled at me, though it took me a while to realize he wasn't the one who had spoken.

"Why are you standing there?" the Imperial repeated, raising his voice. It was all I could do to keep my mouth closed, and my breathing under control. He frowned, annoyed, and leaned forward. Though he was on the other side of the room, seated, and far away, it seemed like his stare alone could reach out and slap me. Though I knew she could do nothing about it, I looked at Arena like she could intervene. "Answer."

"There-there are no more pitchers," I stammered quietly, remembering I hadn't called him 'your Majesty' only after I'd spoken. I glanced nervously at the Guard, expecting them come in my direction, though they seemed to be awaiting an order. I knew if I was truly stranded here like Ida, Liam, and Mallory, it would take years before I could swallow and address the Imperial like he deserved divine and absolute power over everyone.

"Why are you still here, then?" he pointed me out the door in the same way as Bryn. There could have been worse reactions, but I still shot Arena a horrified stare. She averted her gaze in an attempt to sever any obvious association we had, but the Imperial still traced the direction of my eyes, and watched her. We were saved by the loud, echoing sound of a silver pitcher hitting the floor, and the sweet-smelling wine sloshing out. It spilled into a pool beneath Ida, covering her almost from neck to knee. I stood on my toes to see her as she laid there in a vulnerable position with her arms half under her, and her face turned toward the floor. Her ribcage shuddered violently at every breath as if she was already silently crying, like she knew that the red, spilled drink might as well be her blood. I waited for her to stand, in shock that someone of her appearing grace and experience would simply fall over air. That was until I saw one of the men's feet move discreetly back underneath the table. I didn't know what Ida had said or done to make it right in his mind, but I still felt my face warm as two of the other workers tentatively came over to help her, sending ripples throughout the puddle of wine.

"Look at what you've done, you little lout," the same man's voice stopped the two in their tracks, and they retreated back against the wall as Ida stayed silent on the floor, in a position like she was groveling at the Lebon's feet. Even though the man didn't have any more than three drops of wine of the tails of his coat and she was dripping red, I knew he was going to capitalize on what the situation looked like for the sheer thrill of making Ida suffer. As she slowly sat up, I saw an alarm unlike anything I'd ever

327

seen behind her eyes, like she truly believed that her life now hung in the balance. The man raised his hand as if to smack her, and she infuriated him by crawling away, dragging the pool of red along to nearly the wall. Only after the Guard, without anticipating any executive direction, snaked around her did I realize that she might very well be right to fear for herself. But the Guard did not drag Ida from the room. They forced her to her feet, whispering something threatening in her ear, and gave her a different pitcher taken from another worker. The two left her to circle around the room with the bright red stain as a kind of loud badge of disgrace. By the time she was able to return to the window beside me, she was nearly in tears. When Ida saw me staring at her, she quickly lowered her eyes, and shook her head, dismissing the topic between us.

Leaving the wine unattended on the floor, the Imperial scanned the room, pausing at us, at a few of the men, and at Arena and his sons. Just when he appeared to be getting ready to stand and finally address the noisy gathering, the door cautiously opened as if in fear of hitting someone. I relaxed slightly to see Alexander, and watched a discrete smile barely curl the corner of Arena's mouth. He, on the other hand, stared into the rapidly quieting room like he was lost, or had forgotten what he was supposed to say. The Imperial frowned, waving him inside with two fingers. Alexander almost jumped out of his skin when the door shut behind him, but regained his confidence without too much falter, bowing similarly from his safe distance.

"What is it, Alexander?" The Imperial asked with a forced fatherly patience. I couldn't tell whether he was uncomfortable talking to him in front of a crowd, or if he was simply embarrassed to have one of his many illegitimate children show up right as he was about to speak. Alexander joined his hands in front of him, probably near where the hilt of his dagger was tied at his belt, and answered calmly.

"Your Majesty, the Guard asked me to inform you that they recently intercepted a treasonous letter."

Satisfied with the stirred reaction this fake letter yielded, Alexander continued. "They cannot yet say for certain, however we can only assume that someone sitting in this room is either directly responsible, or at least knew of it. The Guard apologizes that they must interrupt, but they would like you to come see this letter immediately so that they may make an arrest while everyone is still together in here."

A long, tense pause followed. It appeared as if everyone in the room had entirely fallen for the story except the Imperial. He didn't have any obvious suspicion against Alexander, but was still hesitant to step away from his throne and leave through the regular door. But as the subject of a new conspiracy threatened his control, he stood, not acknowledging the Imperia, Arena, or his sons, and held his hands behind his back as he walked. Alexander stepped aside for him, quickly taking note of the two Guard moving to follow.

"Please, stay to ensure no one attempts to leave. This is very serious."

Without much of a developed second thought, they bowed their heads, and politely agreed. As one of them stayed by the front door and the other moved to man another, single one concealed by the throne, Arena used the cover of the boisterous

328

gathering to slip from her seat. She passed behind her mother, and uncaringly motioned at me in the same way the Imperial had waved in Alexander. Turning my back to the others' questioning stares, I came at my call like a dutiful handmaid, and stood behind Arena as she spoke to the guard by the rear door.

"Please, I am worried," she looked anxiously over her shoulder at the Council of Patriarchs. I was surprised by how genuine she was making this look. When the man tried to graciously let her down, Arena's act replaced itself, and she told the man to get out of her way in a practiced, authoritative voice. We were met with no more resistance, and when the door closed behind us, we were compacted into a narrow set of stairs leading straight down into darkness.

"It's supposed to be only for an emergency," Arena explained quietly, taking the steep steps two at a time. The tapping of her shoes seemed deafening in the quiet as I tried to tell myself the Guard was not pursuing us. "However, this has been my father's grand exit for nearly every last peace summit in the past year."

I said nothing. Arena stopped abruptly on the last step, listening to the sound of people approaching from around the corner. I accidentally walked past her and into the same, rounded vestibule, and she quickly yanked me back into hiding by my shirt.

"Pay attention," she breathed, turning her head toward the dim, eerie light. As the voices rounded the bend, I could tell from the conversation between Alexander and his father that the dagger had not yet been shown. Arena waited until a precise time, seemingly counting down the seconds in her head, until she stepped into the open. Bryn, Bennett, Alexander, and the Imperial stopped short to avoid running into her, and took several steps back. I almost timidly followed out into the light, not sure at this point whether to stand behind or beside Arena. Still, my attention was divided between the anticipation and the penetrating, mortified look on my mother's face. It was like she was screaming at me in her mind, in total disbelief that I could involve myself in something like this. As if I was here by choice.

Alexander discreetly took several steps behind his father, and I watched unblinking as he relaxed his hand inches from his own belt. While the Imperial was preoccupied staring strangely at Arena, Alexander silently removed the dagger.

"Why are you leaving the room?" the Imperial demanded, oblivious.

"Because your reign is over," was her response. The look of confusion or even amusement on Acwel Aloysius's face was wiped away as he stopped breathing. He tried to lean forward out of the press of the dagger, though Alexander followed him, keeping it firmly against the small of his back. Despite the sudden change in demeanor, there was no shock or fear in his expression.

"Put your little toy away, Alexander," he instructed, and Alexander only forced the knife forward, making him take a step. "Put it away before you do something you'll regret, and we can forget it happened."

"We're done forgetting what's happened. It's time everything was thrown into the limelight. Walk forward and go left until the next case of stairs, then down, outside, and to the gate."

"I know you well enough," the Imperial chuckled in response. "You wouldn't have the nerve."

"You know nothing about what I'm capable of," Alexander mimicked his tone, only his dead serious expression and dagger heightened the stakes. "Let me put it to you this way. I have nothing to lose right now. We're leaving the manor, and either you're coming with us, or I'm leaving you on the floor with a knife in your neck."

Arena and I were brushed to the side as Alexander once again concealed the dagger, but forced his father forward. Not even two steps later, he turned to the seemingly weaker, easily swayed child who had tried so hard to please.

"How did he talk you into this, Arena? I am surprised at you. You were always a quiet young lady."

"You're out of your mind if you think you can try to talk to me now," her glare seemed to cut through him. "I spent years trying to appease you, and only got brushed off. When I finally stopped looking at you with rose-covered eyes, I realized that you're a weak, lying despot. We're doing you a favor. If you stayed here, you would have been assassinated any day now. All it would take is one more peace summit."

"Besides," Alexander added, pushing the Imperial to walk faster. "It was Arena's idea to begin with."

It seemed to dawn on Acwel Aloysius that they were actually serious. Still, he was overly confident in his abilities to make his way back to the throne, and continued to walk as if he was only humoring them and could return willingly. To avoid his eyes, Bennett, Bryn, Mom, and I fell back behind the three. The longer we walked, the more I wanted to say something to her, believing she must have thought I had betrayed her by dragging her with us. I looked up at Mom, moving my lips, though no words would come out. Finding she was already staring at me, I shut my mouth, and she struggled to contort her perpetually pained face into a partial, proud smile. Mom gently touched my shoulder, nodding reassuringly. I almost cried in relief that she was not mad. She was only just as terrified by all the variables in our plan as we were.

"Friends of yours, Bryn?" the Imperial's voice quickly separated us. He turned his chin onto his shoulder to see, eyeing each one of us thoroughly. When I felt his stare on me again, I blinked several times, but was determined not to shrink again. Out of the blue, Bryn seized his opportunity to tell the Imperial something he'd probably always wanted to say.

"You killed my friends, you bastard."

It appeared like the Imperial's sureness that his son would get cold feet eventually might carry us through the gate. It was wide open because of the peace meeting, but I hadn't thought about the Guard stationed there until we were nearly upon them, the Imperial having already drawn all their attention. I looked beside me at Bennett as if he had an answer, though he only returned my uncertain gaze. Arena was the one who fell back slightly, and whispered next to my ear,

"He's too proud, even if his life is in the balance. He'll keep trying to play with Alex's head. You'll see."

The four Guard looked from the Imperial to Arena, then from Alexander to us, trying to make something of our group. We probably could have kept walking through, but stopped in front of the path to safety as if the gate barred us.

"The meeting did not go well," Arena lightened her voice and spoke like a little girl. "We are going for a walk, and by the time we return, we want all of those people out of here."

The Guard looked at the Imperial for confirmation of her story, surprised that Arena was speaking while he stood right there. They still made no attempt to stop us as we passed, the sound of footsteps routinely following behind.

"We will go alone," Alexander told the two who had remained to accompany us. Though there was a hint of urgency in his voice, he covered it up with a gentle, courteous smile. "Thank you."

"Your Majesty?" one of them finally looked over his head to the Imperial, anxious. Despite Arena's certainty, I dreaded his response, and considered taking off up the steep, wooded mountainside with Bennett, Bryn, and Mom right then. The Imperial's voice was sweetly coated to appease the Guard, though it lashed out and seemed to physically strike Alexander.

"What is so dangerous about a walk with my son and daughter? If something happens, then that is why we are bringing these... attendants."

A heavy silence settled over our group as we headed into the woods. I watched Alexander the entire time, who only now seemed to be second guessing his entire plot. He kept his head ducked, but we were all unnerved by the pained expression that reflected his internal war.

"What do you say we actually go for a walk, return, and forget about it?" the Imperial jumped at his chance. Arena nearly snarled, went to Alexander, and placed her hands on his shoulders. He was much shorter than her, and so she squatted down slightly in her constricting, silk dress to look him in the eye.

"Don't let him get inside your head, Alex."

"Get off me," he shook his head side to side, removed Arena's hands, and fiddled with his belt to find the dagger. Everyone took a small step back as he forced it up against his father's back again. This time, a small blossom of blood from a shallow cut stained his shirt as Alexander sharply told him, "That's one time too many you thought you could manipulate me. Where's your Guard now?"

Acwel Aloysius was dead silent as we trekked up the side of the mountain. I constantly slipped and nearly fell down the steep face, lightheaded and unsure of where we were. At first, I almost didn't feel Bennett take my hand, and try to help me along beside him. He always kept several steps ahead of me, constantly looking back as if to make sure I was still walking. I tried to look at his face and smile, but there were rings of light blinking across my vision, hurting my eyes. Bennett and I didn't get very far until Bryn hesitantly came on my other side. They took my arms, and nearly lifted me up off the ground until the landscape turned downhill. It was now the entire group, including the Imperial, realized that we had no idea where to go from here. As Bryn released me, Bennett barely paused in taking my hand again, and walking to the front of the group to lead.

"Do you really remember how to get to the beach from up here?" I asked quietly. He supportively shook his arm, which in turn sent a warm vibration through my hand and into my shoulder.

"Yeah. I mean, I memorized going from the Dreary School to Rowana's."

Completely the same thing, I thought, though grinning slightly. It took over a long hour, and Bennett gave us a couple *it's this way... I think* scares, but the crashing sound of the waves reached us long before the view did. I looked behind us, beyond the Imperial, Arena, and Alexander, at Mom and Bryn. They shielded their sunken, tired eyes from the sun, in awe that we had actually managed to escape alive, and of the freedom that was now in their hands. Bryn more than anyone seemed almost sensitive to the sun's light, and tried to stick mostly to the shade of the trees for a while. I figured spending all those years locked in a room had made him nearly afraid of the daylight. Watching him closely, I waited for him to look up before I tried to extend my other hand in a gesture to bring him into the sun. He stared uncomfortably at me, shaking his head politely. Though as the terrain became vaguely familiar to me, he began to come out of the shadows, and walked alongside us. I recognized the actual path that swooped downward onto our beach before Bennett, and picked up my pace, walking ahead of him. Mom and Bryn stood around us, looking down onto the black gravel sand, though we couldn't see or hear any sign of life. For that moment, I forgot about Arena, Alexander, and the Imperial, and thought aloud,

"What if they're gone?"

"They're not," Bennett discreetly rubbed my hand, and then released it. As our prisoner was forced up behind us, I knelt on the ground, thinking I stood a better chance of staying on my feet if I walked backwards on all fours. Before I actually moved, I craned my neck up to look at Mom, Bryn, and Bennett, the sun casting halos behind their heads. I slipped down to the bottom, and immediately whipped around, running to the center of the beach where Ellamae had taught me how to play Sowing Seeds. The boat bobbed peacefully in the alcove, and I allowed myself to breathe again even though the area itself looked abandoned. Bennett quickly came up behind me, having a similar reaction. None of the others followed yet, and I assumed they were waiting to be given some kind of cue from us.

"Where is everybody?"

"Ellamae!" I shouted much louder than necessary at the boat. "Mr. Johansson!"

Nothing answered me, and I felt my heart sink into my stomach. A loud splashing sound from the stern of the boat lifted it slightly, and Bennett and I walked toward the noise, searching for a sign of life wading through the water around the boat. I had never seen Mr. Johansson look as feeble as he did, with dark circles under his bloodshot eyes and his arms, pressed against the back of the boat, nearly shaking. It took a few moments for me to realize that was not all due to weakness. I thought I saw him wiping tears off his face as he jumped awkwardly through the water, running to us like we would simply vanish into thin air before he got to the beach. What he did next, however, was the greatest shock. Mr. Johansson forced me to take several steps away from Bennett as he walked right up and hugged him. Only seconds later, he was extending one of his arms out to me. I couldn't help but feel like I was intruding on their time, but I still couldn't only stand there and watch. Mr. Johansson inhaled and exhaled deeply, and I felt his hand briefly come up and hold the back of my head. I knew since we first arrived at the Idrisan camp that I owed Mr. Johansson everything for looking past my patch and past the fact that I was the petty thief who stole from his fields, and despite the mess he had gotten us into in the Etairan Mountains, I respected him a great deal. But I'd never considered him to be a comforting father figure to Bennett, much less me. But as he let us go, stepping back and staring wide eyed at us, I knew there was no mistaking or ignoring that he had been crying earlier.

"We were about to leave you," he spoke like he still couldn't believe we were there. "We were sure you were dead. What happened, Bennett?"

Our response was interrupted when Bryn slid down the path, followed shortly by Mom. Mr. Johansson seemed jolted back into reality, and moved in front of us as if to protect us from them.

"Who are you?" he demanded.

"It's okay," I moved out from behind him. "This is Bryn, and-"

"Bryn?" he asked, recognizing the name. Mr. Johansson abandoned us, and walked slowly toward him. "Bryn Hendry?"

Bryn nodded slowly, reserved.

"You were over here with Ruth eight years ago," he continued. Bryn was suddenly interested by the mention of Ruth. "You couldn't have been any older than eleven."

"It was my age that made them feel obligated not to kill me," Bryn answered, looking up the path.

"What have they had you do for so long?"

"I was their entertainer."

Mr. Johansson looked genuinely horrified, like Bryn's life had been almost crueler than the death sentence handed down to the other Idrisans. As he made an attempt to explain our presence and how Bryn would be welcomed like a long lost family member back at the camp, I waded into the freezing water, and jumped to reach the ladder dangling down from the boat's deck. Sitting outside the cabin, Ellamae leaned against the mast, with her arms pressed over her stomach and her eyes closed. She either didn't hear me call her, or couldn't differentiate my voice. But as I dropped loudly to my knees in front of her, she jumped, and forced herself upright. Ella watched me almost suspiciously, like I couldn't possibly be real.

"Arlie," she sat up away from the mast. I stood on my knees and hugged her, overestimating the strength in my legs, and falling forward. Ella gently combed a short section of oily hair near my scalp.

"Where are Joana and Lukas?" I turned my head toward the quiet, closed cabin door, immediately fearing the worst.

"In there," she nodded. "She's hanging on by a thread. We have nothing to cover the wound with, and it's getting infected." She barely paused, trying to make her shaky voice gentler. "What happened to your hair?"

I sat back, and Ella frowned deeper. "And your eye?"

"I will tell you later," was my answer as I looked over my shoulder at the empty path. The lack of shouting below us indicated that Arena, Alexander, and the Imperial had not yet come. I wanted to get Ellamae down onto the beach before that scene erupted, and backed away, extending my hand to her. "Come on."

She hesitantly followed me down the ladder and back onto the beach, looking from Mr. Johansson to Bennett to Bryn. I watched her eyes briefly pass over who she saw as a strange woman standing behind them, not pausing. Mom assumed who she was by the way we stood together, and she only gaped for a moment as if shocked by how eleven years had changed her eight year old daughter. Once Ellamae noticed the tears welling up in this woman's eyes as she looked at her, she shifted her weight to her other foot, staring strangely. In response, Mom walked forward, through Bryn and Mr. Johansson, and wordlessly held her tightly in her arms. Ella stumbled, startled, and I walked around Mom's back to see my sister's face from over her shoulder. A more than freaked out expression met my smile.

Mom, I mouthed. Ella's eyes widened, and she shook her head at me as if I had just said something horrible. Mom felt her move, and released her, embarrassed.

"Ellamae, you're grown," she choked. I guessed imagining her as almost twenty years old and seeing her in the flesh were too very different experiences. Ella nervously laughed, still in disbelief as she tried to even consider the possibility that this could be our mother. Before she had the chance to say anything, Mom continued, "Are you okay, my darling? Amaryllis told me about... erm, Jason."

Ella stared past her and at me, her brow creasing.

"I'll always remember Jonathon, not Jason," she eventually answered, sounding truly like herself. "But I-I'm fine. I don't understand how you-"

"You two went into Kieriana?!" Mr. Johansson's shout crushed Ella's fragile voice. Bennett and I were standing almost ten feet apart, though he equally distributed the blame by quickly looking back and forth between us. It appeared Bryn was trying to tell him the part of the story he knew. He hadn't yet gotten to the best part, which sounded like it was on its way down.

"Bennett, answer me!" Mr. Johansson abandoned me, turning his entire focus on him. Bennett stuttered, searching for a response, and didn't get any further than *the Guard found us and the sword* before Arena slid clumsily down the path, unable to walk

334

in her heeled shoes, and ruining the side of her dress. Directly behind her, the Imperial stumbled downhill. Alexander followed closely behind him, using the natural rock wall beside the path to keep his balance. Mr. Johansson didn't have to recognize them or the story of the past two days to know who we had brought. He stood there at a loss for words for almost a minute, looking the Imperial up and down with wide, piercing eyes.

"You didn't," he spoke slowly, his voice still directed at Bennett. He took several steps toward the three as if sizing them up, and then suddenly cupped his hands over his face, running them back through his hair. They stopped and froze behind his head, and an entirely new look of dread and panic formed on Mr. Johansson's face. "What are we supposed to do with them?!"

"Arena and Alexander were our only way off the manor. We couldn't let you wait here for us until Joana died," I mediated from a distance. Mr. Johansson, more scared by the sudden power the Idrisans could wield than angry at us, continued to study the three.

"Arena and Alexander?" he asked no one in particular, though the two still nodded once in response to their names. "The Imperiess and Imperien you pretended to be in the Etairan Mountains?"

"Yes," I answered, glancing nervously at them. They seemed fairly surprised and curious, though not nearly as much as I would have been. Mr. Johansson looked back at the boat, deep in thought, only revoked by Alexander's hesitant voice.

"My sister and I mean you and the Idrisan camp no harm, sir. We are here for the same reason."

"You plotted to kidnap your own father, did you?" Mr. Johansson chuckled slightly, shaking his head. Alexander quickly shut his mouth, saving the rest of his 'common purpose' speech. "Why am I not more surprised by this? I suppose you also expected we would help you escape. You believe that you can hand him over to us as some kind of appeasement like the flimsy, decorative swords at your peace summits?"

"I have no intention of trying to appease you," Alexander stated firmly. "I have carefully planned out how this... agreement, if you will, shall work. Basically, all you have to do is pretend you descended upon the three of us in the woods, and took his Majesty and Imperiess Arena hostage."

"And you?" Mr. Johansson raised an eyebrow. Alexander seemed to just remember something, and momentarily relieved his dagger from its close pursuit of the Imperial. He examined it a long time, wiping a bit of his father's blood off on the hem of his shirt, and then began to cut ragged slits in his already disheveled clothing.

"I managed to get away. They will allow me into their court only if they believe I have information about the Idrisans that abducted the Imperial. That is my chance to expose him, and shame his natural heirs by taking charge of the situation. I've written out what I need you to do so my story appears valid."

Alexander took a neat, sealed envelope from his pocket, and set in politely on the black gravel, undecided about approaching Mr. Johansson.

335

"You've thought about this for some time, boy," he stared at the letter. "We see what you want, but why are you willing to work with us?"

"Desperate times. You should also be aware that if I succeed, I plan to leave and take all the Lebon with me. We will no longer try to impose any kind of rule over the people of your homeland," Alexander spoke as if it was nothing, knowing it meant liberation to us. Mr. Johansson seemed unable to answer to that. A loud, painful moan more than filled the silence, echoing from within the cabin and leaving an unsettled feeling behind on the beach. Though it only added to the uncertainty for everyone else, it seemed to affirm something to Mr. Johansson.

"Give me your knife," he held his hand out expectantly. Alexander paused, but eventually walked over and placed it lightly in his palm. Grasping the blade in one hand, Mr. Johansson abruptly seized Alexander's other arm, and spoke right in front of his face. "You will give me your word that no one has followed you."

"You have something better than the word of someone you don't trust," Alexander tried and failed to break free of his grip. "You know my motivation. I would have nothing to gain by setting you up."

Mr. Johansson said nothing, only pushing him backwards toward the path.

"Leave."

Long after Alexander had vanished above us, Mr. Johansson wordlessly retrieved the envelope, and stood closer to the Imperial.

"Say something," he snarled, only to be met by the same smug, condescending stare. The Imperial's manner was only changed when Mr. Johansson roughly pushed him forward by the blade. As he gave instructions, I saw a small flicker of excitement in the mixture of fatigue and apprehension.

"Bennett, keep him away from the cabin. Bryn, go get Lukas and tell him to come out. I'll need you two to help me get us into the channel. Amaryllis, Ellamae, stay on deck. You'll have to help sail the boat once we're out in the open."

He skipped over my mother's name, still unsure about who she was, but nevertheless included her.

"We have a dying girl aboard the ship and need someone to make sure she doesn't slip on the way."

Mom readily agreed, and everyone began to move to the boat, watching Bryn and the Imperial closely. When Mr. Johansson asked her if she was there willingly, Arena frowned, nodding.

"You're about to let yourself be kidnapped?"

"I wouldn't consider it kidnapping," she sighed, looking around her, and saying goodbye to her birthplace. "There has never been anything here for me, anyway."

On deck, the Imperial's unmoved silence continued as Lukas and Bryn carefully tacked our boat into the open. Mr. Johansson shouted directions at them, though refused to wander too far from where our prisoner sat. Arena was told to give up a thin fabric tied to the back of her dress so we could separate Joana's arm from the boards. If she wasn't still breathing shallowly and a thin, sticky layer of sweat hadn't formed on her face and neck, I would've thought she was already dead. The open skin around her deep wound was nearly black, rotting, and appeared to be spreading quickly. No matter what Mom did or said, nothing reached her. Still, she seemed to somehow know that Lukas had left, and her pained face appeared just slightly more bothered.

We could no longer walk on the deck without tripping over somebody. Three people were up and working at a time, switching off every twenty minutes or so as the exhaustion caught up with them. I knew the rotation was in order and fair, but I still felt as if my turn came more quickly than the others', and was dizzy after only ten minutes. I marveled at how Bryn, Bennett, Mr. Johansson, Lukas, and even Ellamae still appeared aware and able, at least during their shifts. While they kept the boat level and on course through the mouth of the channel, my second job was to relay all the events of the past two days, from how Arena first discovered who Bennett and I were to what had happened to my hair and eye.

I couldn't help but anxiously want to read the envelope Alexander gave us, though knew it wasn't at the top of our priority list as we sailed distantly past the Etairan Mountains, past the many short waterfalls where we first lost control of the camp's boat, and to the final, long stretch to the camp in time for night to settle. By that point, everyone was nearly stumbling around the deck, trying to be as productive as possible. I seriously felt as if I could throw up, and was strictly told by Mr. Johansson to just sit down with Bryn and Bennett to keep another eye on the Imperial. He hovered over us, concerned by our states even though he looked much worse. Mr. Johansson was about to return to his remaining, upright group: Lukas, Ellamae, and, occasionally, Arena, when he caught sight of our captive's haughty stare directed at him. He seemed to be silently ridiculing Mr. Johansson's captaining, and the fact that his crew was slowly dropping like flies.

"I'll wipe that look off your face, you dog," Mr. Johansson took the dagger out from under his belt, coiled his hand around the blade again, and held it above the Imperial's head. "You paint us like we create terror all over the island, so believe me, I'm not at all afraid to start living up to that name starting with you."

Just like that, the smirk fled, and a terrifying reality set in for Acwel Aloysius.

337

Chapter Forty

The soupy pink sky at half past six the next morning would have been more beautiful if any of us were aware enough to appreciate it. No one dared to sleep that night, the tension between us all running too high. Helping maintain the boat became the only excuse for not sitting on the deck in a steel, unnerving state of silence. Lukas took the first attempt to steer into the alcove too wide, almost smashing the side of the boat against the rock. He had to turn on a dime, line us up as closely as he could, and sail straight. The various twists of many interconnecting rivers confused me, and I wondered how Mr. Johansson could remember which way to turn. As we slowly worked our way through and the land became more recognizable to us, the Imperial sat there as if absorbing every direction we took, forming a map to the camp in his head. A person stood alone on the pier, not appearing to be there for any particular reason. The moment he saw our strange ship approaching, he ran off up the forested hill to the camp. He returned with four other deckhands, walking cautiously down the pier as we drifted in. Mr. Johansson poked his head over, and they seemed slightly less grave about the impending boat in their waters.

"Hurry and tie the ship," Mr. Johansson raised his voice nervously, and instructed us to throw ropes down to them. "Someone go get help, now."

Without any question, one of the five left. The other four quickly tied the boat down, two of them climbing onto the deck. They seemed startled by how everyone except Mr. Johansson sat slumped over below them as if too weak to get up, and even wary of the rough shape he was in as well. Though we were quickly forgotten about as all their mouths dropped open at the sight of Arena and the Imperial.

"Who-who are they?"

"Acwel and Arena Aloysius."

There was no answer, or any sound at all besides the lapping water for another five minutes. I leaned my head on Ellamae, wincing as the tender skin near my eye pressed against my skull. My eyes burned every time I tried to close them, and I eventually resorted to staring off into the distance, semi-conscious, watching as Mr. Johansson led the two within the cabin. Their panicked exchange immediately followed, forcing Mom from the room. As she slowly, distantly lowered herself beside us, I asked,

"How is Joana?"

"It doesn't look good, Amaryllis," she frowned, shaken. "If anything, I made it worse. She was only aware a few times, and she acted afraid because she doesn't know who I am."

Mr. Johansson exited the cabin, carefully carrying Joana, holding her wrapped arm over her chest. As the filtered, humid light shined in her face, she turned her head into him, opening and closing her fingers slowly like she was surprised to feel them there. Lukas abandoned the tiller, nearly running across the deck and through the people to get to her. She didn't react to his presence.

Before they reached the boat or even the pier, we could hear another procession of people coming down the winding path etched out in the woods. It was no surprise to see Allyson head them, with Emmitt beside her and Rose running ahead. Even from a distance, I could distinguish the deep, wide glare on Allyson's face, though she still didn't know what awaited her on that deck.

When they reached the pier, Mr. Johansson ordered Lukas onto his knees. He slowly set Joana in his lap, told him to hold her upright and keep her arm still, and stepped toward the gangplank to meet them. Mr. Johansson ended up being forced backwards to make room for both Allyson and the nearly tangible anger emitting from her expression and shaking fists. Even Emmitt kept a reasonable distance from her. Rose, on the other hand, plowed through them before anyone spoke and nearly tackled Ellamae and me. We held her together, though our arms were like slush and couldn't stay up.

Rose leaned back, not in tears, not happy or relieved, only with a frowning concern in her eyes.

"You guys look terrible," she spoke like we were young kids, holding her journal close to her chest in one arm. She slowly reached up, and traced her fingers down a thick strand of my hair with her free hand. "Where have you been? What happened?" she stopped for a moment, and then turned to Ellamae. "Where's Jonathon?"

"We'll tell you in a second, Rose," I whispered, pulling her back beside me and away from Ella, who cringed at the mention of the name. Though Rose was entirely oblivious, she was now also wedged next to Mom. She looked down at Rose with a curious, delighted look on her tired face. Still, Mom knew she had to contain herself and wait as Allyson's eyes darted from Mr. Johansson, to the two raggedy strangers, to the Imperial and Arena, and finally to Joana and Lukas.

"Joana!" she nearly screamed, stumbling over her feet and dropping loudly to the deck in front of Lukas. He stared back at her, grim as she gently turned Joana to look at her pained face. "Joana...."

For the first time, she opened her eyes and stared through Allyson as if she was not there. Still, a small sign of recognition crossed her face.

"M-m," her voice was raspy and faint, and she couldn't seem to quite choke out the word. "Mam?"

When she first said it, I thought she was calling Allyson, who had taken her off the street as a toddler, ma'am. It took the tears welling up in Idris's eyes as a response to the name to tell me otherwise, and that Joana probably hadn't called her mother in a very long time. Allyson nodded softly, stroking the side of Joana's sweaty, yellowish face as she gently lifted the wrap around her arm. I couldn't see the wound from where I sat, though the horrified look in Allyson's eyes was telling enough. She whipped her head around, and shouted much louder than necessary, "Take her back to the camp, now!"

Emmitt stepped forward to allow yet more people on the boat, dismally watching as they took Joana from Lukas, allowing her head to fall forward, and hastily walked down the pier. Several others followed them, leaving only the twelve of us, and a few odd, nervous people. Allyson sat in front of Lukas, wringing her hands and nearly crying. As she slowly regained her senses, touching several of our faces as if to affirm we were alive and real, Emmitt forced his divided attention away from us to Mr. Johansson.

"Where did you get these people?" he nodded at my mother and Bryn. Both of them frowned, squinting up at Emmitt's imposing figure, silent.

"Bennett and Amaryllis can explain what happened better than I can," Mr. Johansson spoke as if sorry he was shifting the attention onto us. "But please, we have a bigger problem."

"Two Etaira going missing will not alter the course of history," Emmitt waved one of his hands, dismissing the issue as Mr. Johansson slowly removed Alexander's envelope from behind his vest. "I left and I guarantee you no one even looked for me."

"Not Etaira. We had an issue leaving the mountains and were forced to stop again."

Mr. Johansson hesitantly extended the envelope toward him, and Emmitt, with a subtle worry behind his blank face, took it. As he read, his eyes moving quickly along the paper, that frown completely contorted his face until his mouth was nearly open. Meanwhile, Allyson left us, marched right up to Mr. Johansson, and pushed her hands sharply against his chest. She couldn't even make him stumble, but continued to snap at him.

"I think you must have lost your mind out there! Why in the world would you chase a mirage on the ocean, Gerald? You put all of these kids' lives in danger, and the crews that returned here with Emmitt weren't happy about it, either," she shook her head, her mid-length ponytail swinging side to side. "And tell me what happened to my girl. Her arm was almost severed from her body!"

"I *know* you must have lost your mind out there," Emmitt cut in, crumbling the paper in his fist. "We leave you in the Etairan Mountains, and you return with Acwel and Arena Aloysius?"

Allyson's eyes widened until I thought they might jump from their sockets, though the Imperial's face was unchangingly indifferent. He made no attempt to even sit straighter as he looked up at Emmitt, and spoke in a very matter-of-fact tone.

"How long have you been in contact with my son, Idris?"

"I know nothing of any of your sons," Emmitt spat back. "And I am not Idris, she is."

The Imperial looked with a blatantly raised eyebrow at the disheveled woman in between Gerald and Emmitt. Finally, she managed to say, "How did we escalate from searching the immediate area for a ship to abducting the Imperial from Kieriana?"

"A very impulsive and disorganized attempt at getting what you want. I hope you realize that when a war erupts in Imperiam, another will follow on the main island," Acwel Aloysius interrupted again with a returning smug smile on his face. Something within those two sentences struck a nerve inside Allyson.

"It would do you well," she took the gun Emmitt had forced her to carry with her from now on from beneath her shirt, and loosely pointed it at the Imperial's chest, "To remember that you are not the Imperial here. You are a murderer, a crook, and an oppressive tyrant. Once the news is out, there will be an extensive line of people longing to put a bullet in your head. Do not think that I won't do it myself if you cannot keep quiet," she paused, licking her lips, and absorbing his skeptical stare. "You've killed enough of ours with a wave of your hand. But you're our prisoner now, and you have a reason to be afraid in my camp."

341

She turned her face, but not the gun, to Arena, who stood almost unnoticeably on the opposite side of the boat. Before Allyson could say anything to her, Arena bowed her head as if to show respect.

"I wish not to be associated with my father. I am here willingly. My brother Alexander and I planned to remove him from the throne with the help of Idrisans."

Allyson slowly relaxed her hand, and looked over her shoulder at Gerald. She began to stammer, demanding an explanation, though he only held up his hands, motioning at us.

"I did not. Bennett and Amaryllis spent two days and three nights on the Imperial's manor because they were mistaken to be servants in the woods of Imperiam. Collaborating with Alexander and Arena Aloysius was their only way to escape, and they were right in doing so. Please do not lecture them now. We need to get them, Lukas, and Ellamae a bed and something to eat."

At a loss, Allyson frowned, bit her lip anxiously, and agreed. Bennett and I watched Mr. Johansson, surprised and thankful he had stood behind us. He briefly looked at us, smiling slightly, and nodded once. As Emmitt paced over and knelt in front of our group, Allyson slowly raised her hand, in a dream-like trance, and waved the remaining people onto the boat.

"Someone take him and guard him in a room deep in the Hall," she briefly paused, staring doubtfully at Arena. "For now, lock her up, too. Keep them separated."

Arena exhaled deeply like she had expected as much, and freely stepped off the boat and walked away from the pier with only one person following her. Three others were reserved for the Imperial, who was roughly yanked to his feet, and practically marched down the gangplank.

With only an empty space left on the other side of Bennett, I felt able to breathe again, and could see him also sigh in relief. Emmitt waited until they were gone to say anything to our huddled, sad-looking group. Even though he spoke like he was talking to them, his eyes stayed mostly on me, and the badge of shame upon my face. He asked Lukas and Bennett if they were able to walk, and they stood, Bennett bracing himself up by the side of the boat. Bryn joined them. Emmitt looked at him sideways, but said nothing. Bennett watched me from over his shoulder as Emmitt waved them to the pier, and I tried to smile as if to say *I'm fine, just go*. I couldn't tell if he understood as Mr. Johansson accompanied them toward the path, his hand firmly on Bennett's shoulder, their footsteps rapidly fading away. Now, with only Rose, Ella, Mom, and I left, Allyson swallowed her obvious impulse to chase after Joana and stood slightly behind Emmitt. They were unsure what to say about Mom, but very concerned between Ella and I.

"Who are you?" Allyson looked at Mom and the yellow vest she wore, seeming to recognize it. Mom froze like she had just been asked a very difficult question. But when she spoke, you could hear no fear in her voice, only an eagerness to get them away from us for just that moment. They were reluctant to give us the minute alone Mom asked for, and she only repeated herself with a degree of desperation in her voice. Emmitt and Allyson looked at each other, and retreated to the other side of the boat where Arena had stood, still within earshot.

"Rosalie, baby, is that you?" Mom wasted no time, and turned her body toward her. In response, Rose looked back at me, scooting away. Mom smiled kindly at her, and reached out with a shaking hand to push some long, bright red bangs away from her eyes. Like she thought this weird woman was trying to take her notebook, Rose held it tighter.

"What do you have there?" Mom attempted to lighten the conversation, and Rose stared down at it, peeking at the cover as if she herself didn't know.

"It's my journal."

"Do you like to write?"

I smiled slightly, and shrugged as Rose shot me strange stare.

"A little," she muttered, and Ellamae decided to finally put her out of her fidgety discomfort. She reached across me, and gently rubbed Rose's back until she turned around and faced at us again.

"Rose, this is our mother. She hasn't seen you since you were a baby."

Rose looked from me to Ella like we had just made a sick joke of the Cleansing from our childhoods.

"I thought they killed Mom. The Guard said they found her body somewhere in a mountain pass."

"They also said that all the people taken during Cleansings are eventually killed," I told her. "But they have thousands working as slaves in Etairan and Lebon homes. I found Mom on the Imperial's manor, Rose."

For a long time, there was no reaction from either of them. Mom reached out and took Rose's chin in her hand. Looking at both of them together, the resemblance of their facial features was remarkable.

"You have your dad's face shape," Mom smiled. "And his long arms. He liked to write too, you know. He used to be paid to write out notes and read to people who couldn't. But what your father truly loved was to write about fictional places. I remember when you were just ten months old, he would sit you on his knee and hold you there while he wrote. When you were a bit older, you wanted to hold the pen. He called you his little muse. Writing was always his second treasure."

Rose suddenly dropped her journal on the deck, stood on her legs, and wrapped her arms tightly around Mom. She smiled weakly, but shook as if about to cry. Mom gently rubbed her back up and down with one hand.

"I wasn't trying to upset you, honey," she whispered. "I just wanted you to know where you got it from."

"Was-was he on the manor, too?" she asked.

343

"No, Rosalie. Dad is in prison in the Etairan Mountains because he attacked a Guard with a pocketknife to save you and your sisters. I have not seen him since the day of the Cleansing eleven years ago."

I heard Emmitt and Allyson returning to us, probably having heard the entire exchange. As if it was a profoundly personal question, Rose lowered her voice, and asked, "What was his first treasure?"

"I asked him that once, too," Mom slowly sat back, gently picked up and brushed off Rose's journal, and placed it back in her hands. "He said his first treasure was his four beauties, of course."

Neither one of them appeared overly moved by our reunion, though Allyson smiled down at Mom, and extended her hand to help her to her feet.

"I am Allyson," she told her. "You are?"

"Angela."

"You are welcome here, Angela. I will personally make sure you and your daughters can see each other as much as you want. But for now, I will have to separate you. Eleven years is a very long time to slave for the Lebon, and you must rest."

Mom looked at us like she could never leave now that she'd found us, and Ellamae eventually had to tell her, "She's right, Mom. Please go."

As Allyson walked alongside Mom, keeping a gentle, reassuring hand on her upper back, she looked over her shoulder at Emmitt, instructing him to accompany us so she could go find Joana. He nodded slightly, kneeling down in front of us again. He told Rose to help Ella if she needed it, though I knew Ellamae would refuse any assistance our little sister tried to offer. I watched Emmitt closely, rubbing my eyes every so often, not even aware of what he was going to do until he had already picked me up off the deck.

"I can walk," I said, my legs swinging limply as Emmitt sat me like a toddler on his arms, and started down onto the pier. He still didn't put me down, and I pathetically kicked the air. I couldn't understand why I was being treated like I was so much worse off than Ellamae, Lukas, and Mr. Johansson, who hadn't eaten anything at all in almost three days, and even Mom and Bryn, who had been slaves for years. Emmitt paused, looking back at the ship for a moment. He turned his head to survey the limited view of the swampy area from the dock, observing it closely as if to check for any obvious change.

"I know you can walk," he told me. "But I don't want you to tire yourself going all the way back to the camp."

"But Ellamae-"

"Ellamae wasn't stranded on the Imperial's manor for two days: you've been abused enough. I want you to save your energy for my selfish reason, anyway. Everyone else is going to go lie down in a couple rooms in the Hall. But I am going to take you back into that place with the large map where I first met you and Bennett, do you remember?"

I nodded vaguely. He was only the guy with the graying moustache and temper to me then. Still, I refused to be carried like an infant, and argued until Emmitt hesitantly put me down, though walked stooped over, allowing me to lean heavily on his outstretched arm.

"I'll get you something to eat, too," he continued. "But I want you to describe to me as much as you can and help me understand this letter. You and Bennett will be a big part in what we have to do next."

"What is that?"

"I honestly don't know yet, Amaryllis. Don't worry anymore, not right now. We are not mad at you and Bennett, we are just concerned. This is a big deal. Idrisans have never done something like this before."

I was quiet. Emmitt sighed, and said next to my ear,

"But I think they needed someone like you to show them that it's time to step up and do something to let people know we're here."

Behind us, I could hear Rose walking slowly alongside Ellamae. As if expecting another person to soon follow us off the boat, Rose kept glancing back at it, only to be met by the empty gangplank and water.

"Where is Jonathon?" she repeated. "Wasn't he with you?"

"Something happened, Rosalie," Ellamae answered in a short voice. "I'll talk to you about it later."

Emmitt wouldn't allow me to walk entirely on my own until we stood in the Hall's foyer, and Rose and Ellamae left in the opposite direction. Suddenly balancing myself after tripping and falling my way to the camp made my head momentarily spin. Emmitt stood by, patiently waiting for me to come to my senses, and then gestured me down the hallway.

The table in this wide, window-lit room was still covered by the large map, which Emmitt told me to ignore, dragging a chair up to the other side. Only long after he left again did it occur to me that I was back in the only home I had left; surrounded not by Guard and a fake identity, but by my sisters, Bennett, Mr. Johansson, Allyson, Emmitt, and, now, Mom. I eased myself into the chair, and squinted at the intricate detail and writing all over the island. Looking once over my back, I leaned forward, and tried to remember where Allyson said the camp was located. A small indication and label reading *Home as of 1650* about half an inch from the coast, deep into a shaded area entitled *Southeastern Forests*, caught my attention. According to the date, the Idrisans had been here, in this exact location, for over 150 years. Seeing a broad view of how isolated we truly were possessed me to find out how far the camp was from the Wall, from my first home, from Aunt Clarissa, Uncle Graham, Niles, and Oakley. Tentatively sliding the northern part of the map forward on the table, I scanned the area I believed to have lived in for almost sixteen years. Instead of an outline and a simple label, I found

345

a blackened square over an inch and a half long, surrounded by abbreviated directions of sneaking behind it. I didn't know the map's scale, but it appeared I couldn't possibly get any farther away from my birthplace without leaving the mainland. I traced the Wall lightly with my finger as if my remaining family would feel my presence here, and know that I could never just forget about them. No amount of distance could make me feel unbound by that blackened square, and around eight o'clock at night, something within my head would always want to go on high alert, and jump at every loud noise.

Ten minutes passed, and Emmitt had not returned. I laid my head down over the bottom corner of the Haritite State, covering it entirely as I separated my head from the table with my arms. A watery, burning sensation remained behind my eyelids as I closed them, and I buried my face into my sleeve to block out the pulsing red that came from the window's light. I couldn't tell if I actually fell asleep or not, but was shaken by the soft tap of a bowl touching the table beside my head. As I peeled my arms off the map, suddenly concerned I had smudged the shading, Emmitt sat down in Idris's chair across from me. Any embarrassment I felt quickly disappeared at the sight of steaming rice, vegetables, and chunks of meat. I slowly took the bowl in my lap, staring at it until Emmitt prompted me.

"Eat first. Then we'll talk."

Even though Emmitt studied the map as he waited for me, I ate slowly like he watched my every movement. The pit in my stomach gradually closed, and was replaced with an ache that forced me into a half bent over position. When I set the bowl back on the table, Emmitt looked up at the remaining third.

"You don't want any more?" he moved the bowl to the side, frowning at the grimace on my face. I shook my head at the floor, and spoke like I was out of breath.

"I feel sick."

"I understand. When you feel like you can stomach it, you need to let us know so we can get you another meal. It's the only way you all are going to regain some strength."

Emmitt waited for my agreement, and gave me a small, concerned smile, which seemed huge for him. Looking past me and at the door as if to ensure it was closed, he readjusted the center of the map onto the table.

"Whenever you're ready, Amaryllis. Start from the morning after I left and tell me as much as you can."

Emmitt never interrupted me as I took ten or fifteen minutes to relive every moment of the past several days. He slowly nodded every so often to show he comprehended. As I watched his mannerism, I struggled to talk about Liam, reminded of the way he did the same thing while listening to me ramble in the kitchen. In the latter part of the story, my voice sounded almost panicked, like everything I spoke of was currently happening. My recollections turned into an almost incomprehensible mixture of defending Arena and apologizing for dragging the entire camp into possible disaster by bringing the Imperial back with us.

"Calm down," Emmitt put his hands on the edges of the table, and tapped his fingers in a random pattern. He took Alexander's envelope from behind him, and set it on the table. I thought he wanted me to read it, but he proceeded to summarize. "It spells out what needs to be done. Alexander Aloysius is very smart and most everything about his plan sounds on the level, however it is based mostly upon the Lebon's reaction and his ability to manipulate them, his half-brothers who are currently in line for the throne, and the Council of Patriarchs. He thinks he can slander his father so he loses popular support, but I believe that is going to be harder than he thinks. What will really count is if he can take complete charge of the situation and not allow the Imperia or the Patriarchs to question him, and then they will look to him for actual leadership in the negotiations he will fabricate."

My face must have shown that everything he had just said went completely over my head, because Emmitt lightened his voice and paraphrased.

"He wants us to send a threatening letter through our chain of correspondents to the Etaira, who will then forward it to Imperiam, saying that we kidnapped the Imperial and Arena and demand that the Lebon leave. Alexander will have to convince everyone that following that letter is the best option. The only thing I am concerned about is the Lebon are a rather divided race. Half of them would take Alexander as the Imperial and do as he says because they hate the current one. But the Guard is loyal to Acwel Aloysius regardless, and they would say or do anything to get us to return him, and then turn on a dime. Alexander must do what has been impossible for every Imperial in the past five centuries, and we have no easy task, either."

"What does he have to do?" I asked.

"Gather all the Lebon on the common ground that it is best to take the deal and leave because there is nothing left here for them. But that will only work if we can paint our group as a silent killer with more connections than we could ever hope to have. If the Lebon think they have a terror resistance group after them, they will be more inclined to take Alexander as the Imperial and leave to save their own skin."

"He doesn't necessarily have to get everyone to come to an agreement," a voice seemed to slowly open the door. I turned around in my chair to see Mr. Johansson, paler than ever, leaning heavily against the doorframe. "They are already on the brink of a civil war, and this will push them over the edge. The Guard is more equipped to put it down than anyone else, but without the Imperial there, they will turn to his oldest legitimate son. If Alexander humiliates him and takes control himself, support for the Imperial will fall. That's when the letter from a massive and influential group called the Idrisans arrives, saying they already have connections throughout the Etairan Mountains and across the channel. The Lebon will leave Capria Rodalia lest they want their Imperial returned in pieces, and our imaginary spies in Imperiam to come alive."

The corner of Emmitt's mouth was tugged to the side, his brow wrinkling as he considered it.

"Yes, I suppose you're right. But this is still a meticulous game."

"It's not a game anymore," Mr. Johansson answered. "Our correspondents will keep us informed as to the effects of the civil war on the main island, and then we will have to wait and receive some kind of communication back from Imperiam."

A familiar face passed behind him, and stared at him disapprovingly.

"Mr. Johansson, please," he gestured down the hall. "Everyone else is already in bed."

"I'm fine, Vince."

Vince? I thought. *What is Vince doing in the Hall?*

He gave a short sound of disbelief, and pointed in the direction more forcibly.

"With all due respect, you are going to make yourself even more ill, sir."

Mr. Johansson looked at the floor blankly, annoyed and possibly ashamed, until he nodded a goodbye at us and walked ahead of Vince.

"Vince and his wife were both trained to be doctors. After Serah's second miscarriage, they couldn't bear the confinement here anymore, and asked permission to start working outside the camp. The only things Theo could offer them were two horses and a cart, and having no idea what to do with either of them, they took it," Emmitt explained, noticing my expression. "Did you not know that?"

I shook my head slowly, staring back into the empty hall like I could still see them both. Emmitt, sensing he had said too much, stood up and walked around to my side of the table.

"Are you sure you can walk?" he asked. I also stood, pressing my hands against the table for support, as if that was an affirmative answer. "Then I'll leave you with Serah. She'll take care of you."

"What are you going to do with Arena?" I froze, unwilling to leave until he told me something.

"It is really not my decision, and you know that," he frowned at me. "I'll pass the story as well as the envelope on to Allyson later, when she leaves Joana's room. I will talk to the Imperiess after things calm down a bit so she might fill in some of these holes. But for now, Arena appears to be fine, unlike the rest of you, and she won't be hurt sitting in an empty room."

Emmitt left before I opened the door, telling me to be very quiet and that he would see me soon. There were two beds set far apart inside, and Serah sat on the corner of one of them, tucking blankets around a shivering, but sleeping Ellamae. An empty bowl sat on the floor beside her, and Serah nearly stepped on it as she turned around and watched me gently close the door. She warmheartedly waved me in, and met me halfway. Placing both her hands on my shoulders, she turned me around, and began to walk me toward the other bed.

"Do you feel any better, my dear?" she asked as I lay on my side. I nodded only slightly, still in pain. Serah removed my shoes, took a thicker quilt from a chest at the foot of the bed, and covered me. "I told him not to question you right now."

"It's not that," I turned my head into the soft mattress of cotton, and Serah dropped the topic.

"I want you to rest for a couple hours," she reached over me to adjust the blanket, placing one hand on my exposed, sunburned and peeling shoulder. I winced, and she moved her hand down onto my arm as she slowly sat down.

"Have you heard anything about Joana?" I mumbled, already half asleep. Serah continued to rub her hand up and down my arm.

"I was in there for a few minutes."

"What are they doing?"

"I don't know yet, Amaryllis. No one knows what will happen. The wound is already infected and rotting."

In an effort to keep that horrifying image from haunting my dreams, Serah lightly kissed the side of my head, leaned over me, and hummed next to my ear. Though I knew I didn't fall asleep for another ten minutes, that was the last thing I could remember.

I woke up on my own what appeared to be several hours later as the last of the sun was visible through the window above the bed. There was a presence hovering over me, and it took my eyes a while to see, and my mind even longer to recognize her.

"Rose," I choked in a raspy voice as I sat up, feeling a little stronger. She only smiled thinly at me, and stepped back as I swung my legs over the side of the bed.

"Serah had to go help with Joana," she said, looking at the empty bed behind her. "And Ellamae went to go be with Mom. You're the last one up, felon."

As I sat with hands clenching the mattress and my eyes on the floor, Rose squatted down on her legs, and leaned forward to look at my face.

"You know, I actually like it shorter," she said, and I couldn't help but laugh, feeling the ends of my straw-like hair. "It looks good on you. And the cut on your forehead is healing."

I had almost entirely forgotten about falling from the upper deck of the boat as it capsized in the Etairan Mountains, and traced along the hard scab with my fingers. I figured between that and the light purple ring surrounding my eye, I looked worse than I first thought.

"Bennett is really worried about you," she smirked, trying to embarrass me as she took a cup from the floor, submerged it in a tin pail, and set it lightly on the corner of the bed. I drank the water in one swallow, coughing uncontrollably afterwards. Rose only refilled the cup, and gave it back to me. I held it in my lap as she snickered. "It's kind of cute."

"Is he okay?" I asked.

"He's with his dad right now. Mr. Johansson won't listen to Vince, so Bennett went in and is trying to talk to him, I think." Rose barely paused. "Can I ask you something?"

"Sit up here," I patted the mattress, and Rose silently slinked down beside me. "You can talk to me about anything. You know that."

"How did you know she was Mom? You always said you didn't remember much about her."

"I didn't recognize her, no. But when someone said her name and how she always talked about her three daughters, I started wondering."

Rose nodded slightly, forming her walking man, and setting him on a path along her leg. She only stopped when I began to run my fingers alongside hers, and looked back at me.

"I'm glad you found her, but it seems weird," Rose sighed like she was admitting something terrible. "I can't help but feel bad that I'm not happier than I am. It's just unreal."

I wished I could say something to put her mind at ease, but I still felt the same way. There was something about an eleven year absence that sucked all the faith out of you. We hadn't been hoping and believing for all those years, we had simply accepted she was dead. Now, a feeling of guilt surrounded what should have been a joyous reunion. Guilt, and a lot of tears. The fragile set of circumstances we had found each in didn't help, either. Unable to continue the conversation, Rose stood up, holding her arms close to her body, and walked to the foot of the bed.

"Serah left these for you," she gestured at a pile of fresh clothes sitting on top of the chest. "I can't stay in this building anymore. I'm going to go walk."

Rose quietly closed the door behind her, and I wondered how she planned on slipping outside unnoticed. Judging by the noise coming from the window, there was a gathering of people out there waiting to bombard the first bringer of information. I assumed they'd all seen the Imperial and Arena be walked through the roads to the center of the camp. Even if they didn't know exactly who they were, their clothes showed they were definitely not Idrisans. And as the rest of us passed through looking the way we did, I was sure everyone now realized we were teetering on a crisis.

I changed as quickly as I could, though was still uncomfortable in my salty, sweaty, and sunburned skin, and couldn't wait to bathe later. The loose sleeves of the shirt rubbed painfully against the blisters on my shoulders, and I picked up and pulled back the barely breathable fabric several times to try to relieve the burning. Sitting alone, on the floor, lacing a new pair of moccasins, I couldn't make sense of the hushed tones the crowd spoke in, but listened to them anyway, almost not hearing the door as it cautiously opened. I expected to see Serah, and froze when Emmitt slowly poked his head in the room.

"A little bird told me you were awake and feeling better," he said, and I immediately assumed he had run into Rose on her way out. I nodded, uncomfortable, as Emmitt gestured me to come with him.

In the same room, the map had been rolled up and removed from the table. Allyson now seemed less like herself and more like her title as she sat there, leaning forward slightly, with her hands folded together on the surface. To the side, many of the important people I had been introduced to my first day at the camp stood with ripples of apprehension and excitement running through them. Arena sat with her back to me, facing the table, and explaining herself to Idris in a soft, child-like voice. When Allyson saw Emmitt and me in the doorway, she stopped her, and waved us in, motioning me into another chair beside Arena. As I walked around and saw her, I don't think I would have recognized the Imperiess in any other setting. She was dressed in normal clothes, with her very long, fine, white blond hair falling halfway down her back in a low ponytail. Her porcelain face looked sad, but she as willing and eager to talk to the camp's leaders. When I lowered myself in the chair beside her, she didn't seem to recognize me immediately. She eventually put a name to my black eye, and smiled thinly at me, happy I was there. I didn't return the gesture, disgusted by the metal handcuffs binding her wrists in front of her. Arena kept them discreetly in her lap, opening and closing her hands one at a time and nervously tapping the nails of her right hand in the palm of her left.

A large book sat open on the table in between us and Idris. It was open to a map spread over both pages, one that I couldn't recognize until I read the title squeezed at the top of the page.

Kieriana

"Did you think we lost it?" Allyson smoothed down the pages of the Atlas, half grinning at me. Her eyes were bloodshot, and the color was just beginning to leak from her face, so I assumed she had come from Joana's room. "I wanted to destroy the original, but we couldn't seem to perfectly transpose this map. I'm glad you talked me out of getting rid of it, Emmitt."

He grunted a response, looming behind Arena and me.

"Has she helped you update it?"

"It hasn't changed that much," Arena answered, looking over her shoulder at Emmitt. He avoided her gaze, but listened. "Only an extra building for the Guard to operate. My father felt threatened by the unrest and began keeping more of them around the area than he knew what to do with."

I wondered why Allyson was even paying attention to a map of Kieriana right then, as if she had plans to attack it. When I realized she was staring softly, sympathetically at me, I turned my head away from her and the other figures, staring at a vacant spot on the wall.

"If we are going to say we have spies throughout Imperiam," Allyson held up Alexander's envelope, tapping it approvingly with her fingers. She addressed the questioning stares amongst the group, asking the same question I had. "Then we must be able to prove we have knowledge of the area if we're asked. The Atlas is a bit outdated, but anything we are unsure about, we can ask her."

A short pause followed her explanation, and I felt her eyes on me.

"Amaryllis, dear, do you still not feel well?" she reached across the table as if to put a hand on my arm, but stopped midway. I forced myself to look back at her, and shake my head. My answer could have meant anything, and she frowned, motioning one of the unwilling people toward the table. "Would you go get her-"

"I don't need anything," I asserted, though Allyson looked at me skeptically. Seconds passed, and she dropped the subject.

"I only called you in here to let you know that Arena has told us her part of the story, Bennett told us his, and Emmitt told me what you said to him earlier today. But before we go any further, I want to hear it from your lips. You don't have to tell me everything. Just start from yesterday morning."

Sleep had obscured the timeline in my head, and I paused several times, trying to make sense of it myself. I felt the room's eyes on me, and shrank in my chair as I spoke. Allyson smiled kindly in an attempt to encourage me to keep going when I stopped, though I wrapped up the retelling quickly to remove myself from the center of focus.

"Everything appears to be as in order as it is going to get," Allyson set Alexander's envelope aside, and slid a blank, neat sheet of paper on the corner of the table closer to herself. Taking a pen from her shirt's pocket, Idris looked at the paper for a long time as if reading invisible words, and then started writing. Only seconds later, she slammed the pen on the table, sharply folded the sheet twice.

"Ivan, you write," she spoke in a demanding voice, and a man amongst the gathering approached her with an incredulous look.

"Why?"

His tone implied that she couldn't do it herself, and Allyson turned around in her chair with her nose scrunched and a piercing glare. She stood up, and pointed the man down in the seat.

"If we are sending this out into the public, I don't want people to be able to draw anything from the handwriting. Yours will be indistinctive."

As he took the pen in his hand and awaited both instructions and another piece of paper, Allyson walked up to another of the men, and held her hand out expectantly. Without any exchange, he sighed, and placed a small key in her palm.

"I'm very sorry," she said to Arena, standing beside her. She shook her head to dismiss the topic, and held her hands up so Allyson could unlock the manacles. Once they were off, Arena tenderly rubbed her wrists, looking around the room at the other, less than apologetic faces. "I hope you understand why we thought it necessary."

Arena said nothing, staring over her shoulder at the door.

"I would like you to help us write this letter. You know the people who shall receive it more than anyone else here," Allyson's voice turned her attention back to the task at hand. Arena agreed distantly, and Emmitt lightly tapped my shoulder to tell me it was time to leave them to their careful work. He tried to take me back to the room, but I knew I wouldn't sleep and didn't want to sit alone.

"Where do you want to go, then?"

"To see Abiona," I said before I even thought about it. Emmitt smiled slightly, and nodded toward the back part of the Hall.

"She's missed you, too."

He said it would be easier to sneak out through the rear door, and warned me to stay out of sight unless I wanted to be swarmed by questions. Idris had yet to address the thinning, but still present, crowd. There was no light in the narrow path behind the Hall, and I wondered if I could even locate the stable from there. Constantly stumbling over roots protruding from the ground, I kept one hand on the building nearest me as if to reassure myself that I was not lost. As I removed my fingertips from one cool, stone surface, felt the air, and then a log of splintering wood, I knew I'd found it. I pulled the loud, heavy door open just enough to squeeze myself inside, and replaced it as quietly as I could. The horses did not react to me, and I thought they may be asleep. Only the occasional snort told me otherwise.

Abiona was housed in the stall closest to the door, and I only stood there looking at her for a while. Her black, empty eyes again felt focused on me as I slowly climbed over the small gate, and stood under her towering neck. Unsure if she remembered me, I placed my hand in the center of her chest, and rubbed my fingers along her thick, warm coat. Her snort startled me, like she was asking why I couldn't saddle her so we could go out into the fields with Emmitt. Based on the way most everyone except those who cared for her referred to her as the too big, old, and virtually useless horse, I figured no one had taken her from this dinky stall since the day Jason ironically shot the unnamed spy. Now that we knew what he did to Ruth and who knows how many others, and what he had planned to do to us, I couldn't help but wonder if he didn't have some kind of prior tie to that man, and therefore had to get rid of him before he could be exposed.

I stood on my toes to wrap my arms around the bottom of Abiona's neck. But I couldn't keep my balance after a few seconds, and resorted to burying the blackened side of my face into her coat. She snorted again, and that was the most uplifting gesture anyone had offered me in a long time. With my eyes closed, I told Abiona in my head that I would come see her tomorrow, and get her out of this stable. As stupid as it sounds, I momentarily worried that if something came up or Idris wanted Bennett and me to stick around, Abiona would be upset that I didn't come fulfill my promise. I told myself I was thinking and acting like a child--to stand there hugging a horse and wondering about its feelings. I opened my eyes, separated myself from Abiona, and stood as tall as I could again to reach her head. She continued to study me as I lightly stroked the top of her snout, smiling up at her, feeling guilty I had ever thought riding her was repetitious.

I didn't pay much mind to the subtle clamor in the stall beside us, thinking it was only another restless horse. But as it continued, sounding more and more human, I eased my hand down Abiona's back, squinting to see. Evana appeared calm enough, and wasn't kicking or even moving her head, nothing to create noise. Swinging myself over the divider, I placed a hand gently on her back to let her know I was there as my feet crunched strands of hay beneath us. I accepted that as the source of the noise, and began to slowly move my hand down her sleek, gray body, turning around at her tail. I collided with someone in the darkness, nearly falling backwards not because of force but shock.

"Amaryllis," he breathed deeply, shuddering. "You scared me."

"I scared you?" I scoffed, and Bennett chuckled slightly, standing almost pressed against me in the cramped stall. "I thought you were with your dad."

"I was, but he didn't want me to stay," Bennett moved sideways toward Evana's head. I followed, feeling my way along, using the sound of crunching straw as a guide to the gate. Ignoring it, Bennett and I climbed over the side, and sat against the wooden partitions of the horses' stalls. Hay was still scattered everywhere in the aisle, and I took a fistful of it, breaking it into segments mindlessly. "He was just being difficult like he always is. But Vince finally got him to sit down and eat something, at least."

I nodded; glad Mr. Johansson wasn't still trying to run around dealing with people and the circumstances. Bennett watched as I continued to snap straw and throw pieces into the center of the aisle, and said teasingly, "You know, if you're still hungry, I'm sure we can do better than hay."

"You're not funny," I pushed him hard, but he barely swayed. Bennett smiled slightly as I looked up at him. He made a face to mock the annoyed, but laughable glare on mine, and I slowly laid my head in between his head and shoulder. Breathing deeply, I twirled a section of hair in front of my eyes, still unaccustomed to its length, and pulled my knees in closer to my body. There was a sense of familiarity in sitting there, though an unnerving feeling settled deep in my stomach sending anxious, prickling thorns up and down my skin. A minute passed, and Bennett adjusted an arm around my back, gently forcing me closer to him until our legs were against one another's. The feeling in my stomach spread, almost physically shaking me, until I became more focused on making that go away than Bennett.

"What are you thinking about?" his voice startled me. I cracked my neck once, and then placed my head back where it was.

"This is too much," I spoke distantly, like I couldn't even be with myself in that moment.

"What is?" he began to move his arm, thinking I meant I was uncomfortable sitting close to him. I turned my head into his shoulder to tell him that wasn't it. He replaced his arm, and slowly rubbed mine all the way down to my forearm and back, the needles on my skin following his hand.

"My mother suddenly appearing out of nowhere, abducting the Imperial and hanging the future of the island in the balance, Barney's still a slave and so are Ida and Liam, and I don't know what's become of my family behind the Wall...."

"Slow down," Bennett stopped his hand. It tightened as if to reassure me, though I nearly flinched. "If people went around listing all the bad things that could happen all the time, then we'd never get anywhere."

"I-I feel like I should be in there with Mom right now, but it's just so weird, and I don't know what to tell Rose, either."

"Are you somehow scared that because you found her, it's going to affect your relationship with your sisters?"

I didn't know what to expect. She had been absent my entire life, and now that she was back, I couldn't help but brace myself for even more drastic change. Rose and I were joined at the hip for years, and as selfish as it sounded, I didn't want anyone to take her away from me. There was also some kind of secret fear that told me simply because we found Mom, then something terrible must have happened to Niles, Oakley, Aunt Clarissa, and Uncle Graham. There was no logic to the paranoia at all, but it felt just as real and possible. Those four were my family. I figured in time Mom would become part of it, too. But I didn't want that at the expense of my uncle, who took me to his job when I was young and let me play with the all the trinkets, calling me 'little Mare' for a reason I never understood, who had always jumped down my throat about being early to the Wall and raced home after working fourteen hour days because he was so worried. My aunt, who would sit up with me at night when I woke with nightmares for years, who never withheld anything I wanted to know about Mom and Dad, who sewed every hole I ripped in my clothes, and always acted like she had five children, not two. And Niles and Oakley, all their mannerisms, their adorable birthday presents, and their occasional effort to behave like the tiny gentlemen Uncle Graham insisted they be. If we finally got out of here and realized they were gone, no matter what Mom did, nothing could fill that void.

"You're freaking out for no reason," Bennett told me, forcing me out of a long trance of memories which already almost had me in tears. The worst part of it was that I knew I'd neglected all four of them, showing no respect or appreciation in the years since I began to steal. "Rose spent her life looking up to you. She wouldn't forget about all that because of your mom. Maybe instead of viewing her as some kind of ill omen or threat, you should let yourself be as excited as you were when you first saw her. She obviously really missed seeing you and Ellamae and Rosalie grow up."

I became conscious of my loud breathing, and shut my mouth, thinking that I wanted to go see her after we left.

"As far as the camp goes, all we can do is send out the letter and wait for something to come back. There's no use in worrying so much about it as if it's your fault if something doesn't go according to plan. And when it's all said and done, I know one of the first priorities is going to be heading back to the Etairan Mountains and Imperiam to free Barney and Charleigh and Liam and all those people."

I nodded slowly, unconvinced. Only a few seconds later, I felt Bennett's hand under my chin. He lifted my face so I would look at him, and seemed to stare down into my core. My eyes and muscles itched to move away, but I couldn't make myself do it.

"I want you to stop panicking so much," he spoke in a serious tone, but still grinned slightly at me. "It's going to eat you alive if you let it. At least for right now, just relax. We're alone in a building full of horses. Nothing can bother you."

Bennett and I each had a small panic attack, jumping and separating like we were suddenly under siege, when Evana contemptuously grunted above our heads. I looked up at her imposing head for a while, trying to recover from the temporary burst of adrenaline. When we looked back at each other again, we were both breathing heavily as if out of breath.

"You're just as edgy as I am," I laughed quietly at him. "You're only better about hiding it."

Bennett raised his eyebrows, frowning slightly, and joined his hands around one bent leg.

"I'm serious," he said. "I worry about you. Please try talking to your mom and stop acting like everything else is riding only on your shoulders. We've been in everything together since they dressed us up for the Haritite State, and I'm not going to let anything change that."

I could almost feel the surprise radiating from Bennett when I scooted beside him again, and hugged him, burying half my face into his shirt. When his arms came around me and held me nearly up off the ground, I knew that this was more and better than anything Abiona or anybody else could offer. I sucked in my breath once in the quiet as Bennett moved his hand to the ends of my hair, and up to the highest point of my neck. Pulling back enough so I could see his face, and I closed my eyes as he lightly kissed the very top of my forehead.

"I would never want that to change," I whispered, never feeling so safe in the midst of both a real and a mental civil war. Bennett smiled, and stood up, taking me with him. Even after we separated and walked together toward the front stable door, the uncomfortable sensation in my stomach seemed to melt into a new hope and confidence.

We were either not recognized or disregarded by the sizable crowd murmuring in front of the Hall. Bennett and I were about to go in the back way until the front door finally opened, yielding Emmitt, with a little half smile beneath his thinning moustache, and Idris, with a deep stare and her arms crossed over her chest.

"If you want information," Emmitt raised his voice above the congregation. I could only pray this address would turn out better than his last. "Then you will stop acting like a pack of animals and back away from the building. There's honestly no need for you to hold everyone inside hostage."

The people took several wide steps away, forcing Bennett and I backwards with them. An indistinguishable mixture of "what happened?" and "who is that girl?" and "do we know where the spy came from yet?" loudly reverberated around the area and back to Allyson, who bore it with an air of patience and exhilaration.

"We've been given an opportunity," she summarized, noticing Bennett and me standing near the back. Idris fervently motioned us to come stand with them. It took the crowds' stares and Allyson's refusal to elaborate until we came to force me to walk through the clearing path. Bennett and I stood side by side in front of Emmitt, who discreetly placed a hand on my shoulder as if to keep me from running off as Idris continued. "Thanks again to these two young people, we've been given both an opportunity and a nearly failsafe plan to realize the once lofty goals of our predecessors: to dismantle Imperiam from the inside out until they are forced by fear and division into permanently leaving Capria Rodalia."

Excited disbelief echoed back to her from the crowd, though a single question or statement couldn't be heard amongst the noise. Eventually, one person managed to make himself heard when he asked Idris, "How are you going to do that before first dismantling us?"

"Easy," she answered, smiling widely in a way I'd never seen. "We're going to start the revolution that should have already come to pass. However, we are going to do it in such a way that the Lebon won't even know they are being insurrected."

Chapter Forty One

The ransom note went straight to the point, without any roundabout speech or additional information. Most importantly, it spelled out a choice for the Lebon. We return their Imperial and they leave, or we kill him if we don't hear back in eight weeks. Their response was to be sent to the Sturwaller Garrison, and someone would pick it up. This person wouldn't know where the camp is regardless, and if they tried to lay a hand on them, then the next thing that would arrive is the Imperial's head in a paper box. There was to be no negotiation.

After the letter was given to Vince to leave with a post in Nemirena, beginning the long chain of hands that would pass it onward, the Imperial's presence became a unifying force for the leaders of the camp. They spent the first week barely ever emerging from the Hall, debating and discussing all their possible responses to the loopholes the Lebon would try to take. "After the news arrives in Kieriana that there is an Idrisan presence at home somewhere, one that was clever and efficient enough to kidnap the Imperial and, as far as they know, me, that will start the panic," Arena once dared to speak without prompt. Being an unofficial, unbound hostage, she rarely did, so she held the entire room's attention. "The other Lebon shall want to disregard the Imperial entirely and let my oldest brother take the throne, but that feeling will change as Alexander steps up in front of the Council of Patriarchs and pretends he heard information when the Idrisans ambushed us in the woods. He tells them how well equipped and connected you are, and basically will try to frighten them into agreeing to leave, saying that you are prepared to start assassinating the Patriarchs. So here is what I see happening. They will agree to the terms and, because of the loyal Guard, they will ask you to return my father. But once we get there, you must be able to personally live up to the terrifying image that has been made of you because they will try to talk their way out of it. Then, you must have something that prevents them from returning later and reclaiming their control."

It seemed simple enough in theory, though there were so many elements that could alter the course of the transitory civil war Alexander had prophesized. The fact that all we could do was await correspondence from the posts, and eventually a response from Imperiam only added to the nerves. As the heat blanket quickly gave way to a constant, chilled, almost flooding rain, the atmosphere in the camp was more eager and restless for communication than anything else. The Imperial was kept in a sealed, guarded, windowless room downstairs in the Hall, and Arena was unofficially restricted to the building. Everyone inside had accepted her, though it frightened the rest of the population to know we were working so closely with an Imperiess. Arena appeared to have no interest in dealing with the reception she would receive if she made a habit of strolling outside, and was content to watch the rain from the windows. Rose and I felt badly for her, and made a point to always include her in conversation, and at least invite her outdoors.

The first time Joana emerged from the room was almost two weeks later, with Lukas at her side helping her along. I realized my wide stare, and quickly replaced it with a small, encouraging smile. She appeared a little disoriented, but was alive, walking, and vaguely aware. She also no longer had to worry about the spreading infection which would have killed her had it been left alone. After a long discussion with the other people caring for her, and an even longer one with Allyson, Serah had decided to amputate her arm, leaving a currently messy stub no more than three inches from her shoulder. But Joana did not grieve over the loss, acting as if it was only a minor setback. She was more concerned about what was going on with Imperiam, bombarding Lukas with questions. At first, he was in more agony over the amputation than she was. But as Joana started to recover, respond to people, sit up and walk again, he began treating her like nothing had changed, which was exactly what she wanted. Though Joana didn't seem any happier, she seemed maybe freer as the days passed. When I started to come see her as often as I could, she would always ask me to read to her. I felt terrible as I stumbled over the paragraphs, trying to sound out every other word in her eloquent, complex stories. Joana, staring blankly at the ceiling, would say everything I pronounced incorrectly, and sometimes finish the sentence as if she had already memorized the book. Once when I quietly opened the door, Serah was helping her dress to go outside in the rain. I had never seen her so eager, with a glint in her eye like a little kid. Emmitt took her, Lukas, Bennett and I around the back to avoid putting Joana in an overly public situation right then. We took her to see Darius, where Joana fervently asked Emmitt to help her learn to ride with one arm.

"It won't be easy," he told her. "But you can do it if that's what you really want."

And despite the rapier which cost her a limb, the second thing she asked was to learn to swordfight again.

Mom's presence and recovery helped Ellamae through the realization of Jason and loss of Jonathon almost overnight. It seemed like a weight, in a way, was lifted from her shoulders, and she and I now spent most of our time learning how to have a mother. Rose eagerly accepted her and showed her new stories she'd written on a regular basis. To my relief, nothing in between us changed. She still slept with me at night, though we would typically stay up and whisper about how we were going to find Uncle Graham, Aunt Clarissa, Niles, and Oakley as soon as this was over.

The abrupt transition between seasons seemed only a few days long, and it took no time before the rain turned into layers of slush in the roads, freezing everyone's feet through their shoes. Still, a sense of warmth lingered in the stable, and Bennett and I spent a lot of time there with Abiona and Evana, talking across the dividers. It seemed that night had solidified something between us, like I now truly had a friend whom I could tell anything. Who, as best as he could, tried to understand me and where I came from. It was almost like we were back to our talks from opposite sides of the cell bars, when we figured we would soon never see each other again so nothing really mattered, but in a more comfortable and personal setting.

"Amaryllis?" He asked me once while I stood on the other side of Abiona, standing as tall as I could to try to brush her back. I couldn't see him, but I still made a questioning sound as a response. "Did you ever think about where you wanted to be in a couple years?"

I paused for a long time, and walked around Abiona's happily swishing tail.

"Not really. I used to tell Rose that one day we'd all get together and topple the Wall."

"That's not a bad idea," he said, coming from Evana's head to where I stood hunched over, bracing my elbows against the low barrier. "A lot more important than what I thought about for a long time."

"What?" I watched him as he copied my method of leaning, both of our arms barely fitting on the surface of the divider.

"I liked the fields and the animals," he shrugged halfheartedly. "But after a while, it gets sort of...."

"Boring?"

"Just monotonous. You feel really isolated."

"What did you want to do, then?" I asked.

"I don't know. Just get off the farm and do something where I could be around people. But there wasn't really a lot of opportunity."

My mind shifted to the kinds of occupations behind the Wall. Some people had real jobs, but most only traded things they didn't need for things they did, and those like my uncle who could read, write, or perform basic calculations kept books for shop owners or were paid to write notes for people. Everything depended on which borough you lived in. Often, after a Cleansing, food shortage, or some other crisis, people would drift in between them looking for somebody who could pay them to do pretty much anything. They were always turned out before we became any more overpopulated than we already were. I couldn't imagine anyone from another class saying there was little opportunity in comparison.

"Nemirena is all about production," Bennett continued at my silence, and probably dubious stare. "You have to be able to do something with your hands, whether it be farming or working in a quarry, or you're useless. Everybody's expected to somehow work to help meet the tithe. There was a time not too long ago when, if you didn't, then your area had to pick someone to put the blame on, and they could end up in jail for ten years or better. It was insane. There was literally a list my father had to give to the Guard of people he would turn over if we ever had a bad season. That thing hung over his head constantly, and that was why he was always jumping down peoples' throats about working. My mother taught me at home, and then he started showing me how to operate the fields when I was twelve. I couldn't just tell him that I wanted to leave one day. Besides, no matter where I went, the tithe's still there. It's not like it would've been any different."

"But think about what's going to change after the Lebon are gone," I tried, though I wasn't as optimistic as I would've liked to be. "You can do whatever you want."

"It's going to take a long time for anything major to change," he frowned slightly. "We can get rid of all the patches, but the divide between them is too much to go away overnight. Besides, all the Nemirens, they only know how to work with their hands. Even if they aren't bound by law to do it, most of them will probably stay because that's all they've ever done."

There wasn't much I could say to that, and I moved away from the divider, kneeling down to take handfuls of the crushed straw beneath us.

"But I guess neither of us really have to worry about where we want to be in ten years anymore," he continued. "Or at least I don't."

"Where exactly do you think I'm going to go?" I laughed to myself, stopping when I thought about how I truly did have little outside the Wilds besides my family. Bennett shrugged slightly, and moved to return to Evana. "I'm just as bound to the camp as you are."

"Don't you want to be there to see it when the Wall comes down?"

"Yes, I'll be there, with you and all the others, in twenty years when they finally pound away enough to make it tremble," I jokingly threw the straw in one of my hands at him. Bennett quickly turned around, scooped some from Evana's stall, and tossed it back at me. "Can we wait until we run the Lebon out before we talk about that?"

He agreed as we picked the straw off our clothes, and dropped it back to the floor, just noticing Serah standing there. She stood in the aisle, her arms folded over her chest, half smiling at both of us. Since Joana was up and walking again, she only checked on her once or twice a day, freeing up her time to come work in the stable where she seemed happiest. Serah turned her head to the side, and took a section of hair near the back, shaking it and looking at me. I didn't understand what she meant until I felt the same area on my head, and pulled out another thin piece of straw.

"You two remind me of Vince and I years ago," she said, laughing. "But if I were you, I wouldn't be touching that straw. We've been rather busy, so it hasn't been changed in weeks."

It felt strange and a little uncomfortable being compared to Serah and Vince, but I knew she meant it in a harmless way. Three weeks had passed since Vince's departure, and he was due back a couple days ago. With each passing hour, Serah anxiously walked by the path he was supposed to return from for any sign of him, always retiring to the stable to drown her worry in caring for the horses. Part of the reason why Bennett and I spent so much time there was to keep her from panicking too much in his absence. As Bennett left Evana's stall and I lightly dragged my hand up Abiona's back, the door to the stable opened, sending the freezing air and mist inside. Emmitt stood in the way, but failed to block the sudden rush of cold wind invading one of the only warmer places left in the camp. Unbothered by the weather, he breathlessly gestured for Serah to follow him. A sudden paleness befell her face as she squeezed past Emmitt through the door, and all but ran off to the same road she'd diligently inspected for days. Watching her leave, Emmitt propped the door open wider with his back, and told us,

"Gerald and Idris are already down there. Apparently, something's changed in the mainland."

I knew it didn't have anything to do with our threatening letter. The Lebon probably didn't even have it in their hands yet. For a moment, I thought in the three weeks since the Imperial and Arena's sudden disappearance, Alexander might have already lost his voice in the Council of Patriarchs. The civil war could easily be out of the making and into its snowballing ruin.

Several people filtered in and out of the area where the path officially fed into the camp, emptying the back of the cart and unhitching its two horses. Mr. Johansson joined the line that passed down boxes, lifting ones that must have weighed fifty pounds with ease, as Idris stood among a few other figures, still keeping her lukewarm, protective sentry eye on Arena. Lukas stood slightly behind and against Joana to keep the wind against their backs from sending the empty sleeve of her jacket flapping around wildly. She still looked pale to me, and didn't appear at all thrilled by the presence of so many people, much less appreciative of their encouraging comments and sympathetic stares.

Vince's cheeks as well as the tip of his nose were red and raw from the sharp kiss of the wayward storms, and as he stepped down from the driver's perch of the cart, he rubbed his hands together, stuffing them in his pockets. Serah stood almost unnoticed off to the side, waiting for him to come down, and seemingly giving him a hard time about being so late. But the moment he touched the ground, she threw her arms around him and held onto him like a ragdoll for a moment, almost in tears. Surprised, Vince reacted slowly, folding his arms around her waist, and whispering inaudibly to her as Idris reluctantly approached them. Emmitt took that as his cue, and followed.

"Come on," he told us over his shoulder. "You two can lead the horses back after they get the cart off of them."

We stepped up in time to see Vince respond to Idris's presence by ripping a Nemiren badge from beneath his jacket, and holding it out to her in one hand, keeping the other arm around Serah. Allyson held it in her fist as if to keep a monstrosity out of sight, and patiently waited for a halfway decent time to speak. But the company of more people had already spoiled the time for Serah, and she shamefully separated herself from Vince. Before she could walk away and impulsively tend to the horses, he reached around her back and pulled her back into the conversation in an attempt to make her feel less embarrassed.

"Everything short of hell's broken loose in parts of the neighborhoods, Nemirena, and especially at the Wall," Vince shook his head solemnly at the ground. "I got out of the Wilds and into the roads easily, but spent at least four days trying to get back in. Some streets are entirely closed, and others are so full I couldn't drive the cart. The Haritites are pointing fingers at the Nemirens, and in response, there's been at least three workers' riots in Nemirena. The Guard got a grip on the situation, but there's something breaking down within them, too. They don't seem able to function efficiently at all. There's been another Cleansing in a distant borough, and according to the rumors, it left several people dead. The prisons are too full with Stoleh and now Nemiren workers. I don't know how long this can last, or what level it will soar to when word of the letter circulates. I handed it off to Eric two weeks ago. It should be on its way to the Etairan Guard by now."

"So the Haritite Guard already knows the Imperial is missing," Idris bit her lip. "Then the news that we are behind it will spread like wildfire. We can only hope Alexander retains his influence long enough for the Lebon to come up with their response."

"That won't stop the chaos in the streets," Mr. Johansson returned to us. "I doubt the Etaira will breathe about it, but word that the Lebon might be retreating from the island for good due to Idrisan activity will be equally monumental. For the Haritites, that is, and it will trickle down to everyone else through the Guard."

I noticed the people standing there waiting to hand the horses off to us, and tapped Bennett on the shoulder, indicating them. As we awkwardly walked through their conversation and took hold of the horses' reins, Vince told the three of them,

"Based on what I saw, if we hope to set up any kind of non-divisive structure for the years ahead, our first priority needs to be getting a group in the top tier of the Guard to regulate it. But we also must have people posted at places like the Wall and the crowded area of Nemirena to ensure these riots do not continue, or we will never get anywhere."

"Agreed," Emmitt held his hands behind his back. As Bennett and I led the horses around the group and down toward the back road, we purposely slowed down to hear one last bit of the discussion. "However, we first need to make sure the Lebon are actually leaving and find a way to guarantee they will not return in a few months. Receiving a response that supposedly admits defeat is half the fight at best."

The beginning of the fifth week since the letter left brought widespread anxiety that said response would never arrive. I could only imagine the thoughts of the Lebon as they weighed the options: either to accept Alexander and retreat into the uncharted ocean or to oust him and face years of power struggle at the ascension of one of the Imperial's legitimate, inept sons. The constant threat that the Idrisans who supposedly lived among them could animate at any moment had to be just as compelling, though I couldn't help but worry nothing would be motivation enough to force the Lebon to leave their home of multiple centuries. "Of course I'm not worried about where they're going to go," Allyson snapped at one of the posts. "They came from somewhere. If they're smart, they'll go back and stay there. Imperiam is part of Capria Rodalia. If they ever try to take it back, the only thing we'll be exchanging is gunfire."

As Mom started to emerge from the Hall, Ella, Rose, and I spent most of our mornings walking with her around the camp. She huddled inside a huge, woolen shawl, always cold, but she had more color in her face and strength than before. At first, Bryn stayed almost hidden to the point where many people forgot about him. Though once he was recognized by his last name, the others graciously tried to take him under their wings. He got along well with Emmitt, but seemed to be lost and without purpose with no piano, and lonely no matter how many people were in the room without Liam. Just as the rain let up enough to allow me to take Abiona out in the fields again, rumors of an arrived response of Imperiam excited the entire camp, though the Hall hadn't yet come forward with anything. When I finally worked up the nerve to ask Emmitt after he left the room in the Hall, the frown and worry riddled in his expression made me fear the worst.

"It's not from Imperiam, Amaryllis," he answered my questioning in annoyance. "You know we aren't trying to hide anything from you or the others. The moment we hear something from them, you, Bennett, Lukas, and Joana will be the first ones to know. This was only a letter from one of our posts in the Haritite State."

"What's happening?" I asked lamely.

"So far, it's in decent shape compared to the rest of the island. But banks are closing down due to the riots in Nemirena and unrest is high because most of the Guard have left to go control the outside situation."

At night, Mom would stay in our room very late, with all but one oil lamp turned off, and either talk to Ellamae or lovingly undo the braid in Rosalie's hair, running her fingers through it the way I used to. I generally slipped in, and acknowledged them, wordlessly getting into bed facing the wall. Any conversation they tried to pull out of me I answered in only a few words. I wasn't trying to be rude to any of them, but lying awake for half the night seemed to be the only time when I could let my mind wander from place to place, trying to envision what was lost and what was to come. Feigning sleep the entire time, I would always close my eyes when I heard Mom walking around the foot of the mattress, and try not to move when she lightly kissed the side of my head. Several times after the gentle sound of the closing door came from behind me, Rose rolled over, tapped my shoulder, and whispered something to the effect of "you know that she's not trying to replace you, right?" Surprised she had figured out so quickly that I was faking, I only answered "I know," in a partial trance. Her words couldn't have convinced me of anything, but the way she still curled up beside me before she fell asleep always made me feel as if nothing had changed, like we were at home years before when she was still just a little kid, and would crawl into bed with me when the shots rang out against the walls in the latest hours of the night.

But that day was different. Instead of kissing me and scuttling for the door, Mom slowly lowered herself onto the corner of the bed beside me. Though I tried to disguise it, my breathing momentarily picked back up to normal pace, easily telling her I was awake.

"Amaryllis, sweetheart," she whispered. I still took several seconds to stop clinging to my act, and opened my eyes to look at her. Even though my black eye had long since healed and the scabbed cut on my forehead was only a faint, red line, I still couldn't help but feel that when anyone looked at me, they were actually staring at one of the two. "Are you alright?"

I nodded slowly, looking away.

"You've been very quiet," she breathed deeply. "Did something happen between you and Bennett?"

"No. We're fine," I answered. The way she continued to frown at me suggested my response was lacking. "I'm just worried about Uncle Graham and Aunt Clarissa and the boys. And I can't help but feel like the Lebon aren't going to leave and stay away so easily."

"It's not your job to be concerned about the Lebon."

"I helped bring the Imperial and Arena over here," I turned my head into the mattress. "It's partly my fault if we return them and then get arrested for treason just like any other Idrisans they've ever gotten their hands on."

Mom only shook her head down at me, and resumed rubbing my exposed arm until I fell into a gray, dreamless sleep.

Probably the most unpleasant job anyone in the Hall could be given was to bring food to our prisoner. It was only a daily reminder that he still lived in our home, and we still had no letter in hand accepting our ransom and begging us to return him to Imperiam. Idris generally sent Emmitt down the dull, empty corridor to the guarded room, strictly prohibiting anyone else to accompany him. Not that he could pay somebody to do so. Five minutes later, Emmitt would return with an infuriated air about him. When finally asked what the Imperial had said, he would always answer,

365

"It's the same thing every day. He says he would bet his life that Alexander couldn't convince the Council of Patriarchs of anything, much less ascend to the throne in a matter of eight weeks. The bastard's still not visibly concerned. He believes we are bluffing about the threat to kill him, and that the Lebon are going to wait until after our deadline to see what happens before any rash agreement to leave the island."

Days afterwards, officially one week away from the Imperial's originally marked execution date, winter temperatures and weather had frozen many connections the camp had beyond the drop off. There was talk about actually cutting off one of the Imperial's fingers and sending that through the chain of correspondents in pursuit of the threat letter, made even more frightening by how dead serious some people were. His pointer finger, plus the signet ring he wore upon it, would certainly grab their attention. Idris squashed the idea before it spread outside the room when she pointed out that by the time the finger reached Imperiam, it would be shriveled and decomposed, hardly recognizable and not worth the risk of sending a human appendage on a four hundred mile journey.

We hadn't heard anything about the progression of the civil war in Imperiam or on the mainland since the final message from the Haritite State. A sense of doubt stalely replaced the excitement as people began to wonder if it was still happening, or if the Lebon had united under one of Arena's older brothers and already quelled the situation. The Imperial certainly became more vocal about our desperate state, openly mocking our brainless decision and asserting that the only thing that would become of this was the eventual locating of the Idrisan camp. We would have only ourselves to thank for it. It escalated to the point where we could hear Emmitt shouting uncouth equivalents of 'be *quiet!*' through the door to his holding room, and in the final days of our clock, he flatly refused to take him food anymore.

"Because," he told Idris in the hallway in front of the main room, "if you let me in there, I will strangle him so quickly, he won't feel any pain."

At that, Allyson decided to deal with him herself for the first time since we pulled into the alcove's dock, taking the tray sitting within the room in one hand and slamming the door behind her. It slowly creaked back open to reveal the questioning stares on everyone's faces as she disappeared around the corner. Emmitt watched until she was gone as if he suddenly felt remorse for sending her, but returned to the room, speaking to me over his shoulder.

"Go and find something to do. You aren't obligated to stay around the Hall. It's not healthy for you, and it won't make a response get here any faster." Emmitt briefly paused, and gestured in the direction Allyson had gone. "But don't get any ideas, alright?"

I agreed, barely waiting until he closed the door before I tentatively stalked toward the corner. Despite the sickness reflected on Emmitt's face at the same time every day when he knew he was about to be asked to enter the room, my curiosity over what Allyson was going to say to the Imperial overwhelmed my former judgment. I also figured that the unlucky souls guarding the door would follow Idris inside the room, and the area outside would be a safe place to listen in on the two opposing forces that had held the future of Capria Rodalia hanging in limbo for almost two months. Following

366

the sound of echoing footsteps, I kept probably a longer than necessary distance, stopping at the bottom of a staircase well for cover, and watching her dismiss two people standing in front of the door. Allyson received a key from one of them as they left, thankfully, in the other direction. She left the door wide open after she had gone inside, and I was about to get closer when I heard someone walking slowly down the steps behind me. They seemed to freeze and stare for a moment, and I forced myself to turn around. Rose stood several feet higher than me with her hand delicately on the railing, and a look that asked what I was doing crouching behind the wall as if planning a heist. I only motioned her toward me, worried that someone would come around and see us.

"He's in that room," I nodded in the direction of the door. Rose knew immediately who I was referring to, and looked away from me, straining her neck to look beyond the wall. "Allyson just went in."

"You're going to eavesdrop?" she blinked. I was afraid she would frown and lecture, but a small, crooked smile and a glint in her eye I so missed stared expectantly back at me as Rose held her notebook closer to her chest. "I want to come."

Rose and I slowly lowered ourselves near the wall on the right side of the doorway, just out of the light, and pressed silently against each other. For a while, it didn't sound like either of them was speaking, and we only stared blankly ahead.

A shadow thrown down the far hallway quickly caught my attention. I nudged Rose and took her hand, thinking it would be one of the people who had just left, and preparing to take off up the stairwell behind us at their dirty look. I relaxed as Bennett passed by, purposely turning down this hallway, keeping one hand dragging along the wall as if lost in the dark. I knew by his demeanor he had seen Allyson, assumed where she was going, and decided to follow around the back way to avoid running into her. Smiling slightly, we watched him as he felt his way along, walking slowly with his eyes on the floor. He didn't notice us until he stopped on the opposite side of the doorframe, almost jumping backwards. Our mutual purpose for being there slowly dawned on him, and he returned my shaky smile. As Bennett sat against the wall, the quiet, though taunting voice of the Imperial came from inside. He didn't utter more than a word or two before Allyson's shout seemed to shake the building.

"Don't say anything. I cannot stand the sound of your voice!"

"How many weeks has it been now, Idris?" Acwel Aloysius said her title like it was some kind of monumental laughing stock, like he still couldn't believe that a woman as harmless-looking as Allyson could possibly stand in the shoes of such an elusive and threatening visage. "Seven? I don't think your plot is quite panning out the way you envisioned."

"Either you do not realize what's on your head right now, or you're hopelessly stupid," she spat. I tried to picture the way they were positioning themselves in the room, far apart and perhaps circling each other like prey. "If we don't get a letter next week, we're going to do to you what you've done to so many of ours outside for everyone to see. You took the lives of so many people: whether they be the Idrisans you murdered or the Stoleh you violently ripped from their homes. You never had a direct hand in it,

367

but sitting on your figurehead throne and gesturing their lives around and away is a worse crime than being the mindless triggermen or the armed overseer."

"The kind of drastic change you wish to enact has no chance for stability or lasting. You spend all your time planning offenses against society that you have yet to fabricate a plan for what you will do once you have control."

"I would think you'd know this, but I, my father, and all of his predecessors never once attacked any area of the mainland, or Imperiam, for that matter," Idris spoke like she was explaining something he had no hope of ever understanding. "We have posts and correspondents everywhere, though, because people from every class and walk in your twisted society have begun to refuse to participate anymore. Truthfully, if this had never happened, you would've eventually been dealing with a revolution. All it needed was a spark. It was always there. You'll wind up assassinated if you and the other Lebon don't leave, so I do not see any reason for you to want to stay. What we do after you're gone, after we liberate all of your slaves, help all the innocents in prison find their way home, and get some relief the tens of thousands of people you keep behind a twenty-foot wall like a diseased population, is for us to worry about. Thank you for your concern."

In listening to her, Rose continued to squeeze my hand tighter and tighter. She mindlessly took her arm away from the journal held upright on its spine in her lap, allowing it to fall to the floor in the light of the doorway. The loudness of a resulting *thud* seemed much greater in the silence and circumstances as she scrambled to retrieve it, as if that could undo what happened. I looked past her at Bennett, debating whether or not it was a good time to run. Before I made the decision, Allyson's voice said calmly from within the room,

"I know you're sitting out there, Rosalie."

We saw her hand clutch the frame of the door, and she swung into the hallway, stopping short when she realized we were at her feet. Allyson didn't seem surprised or even angered by our presence, only exasperated. Behind her, Bennett sat in silence against the wall, looking up at her and wondering if he should say anything or retreat.

"I know Emmitt told you not to follow me," she looked disapprovingly between us, but stepped back almost on top of Bennett, as if inviting us within the battleground. Both of us must have looked horrified at her as she nodded inside again with a wide, serious stare. As we reluctantly stood against the wall, Allyson briefly, dubiously glanced over her shoulder, and spoke in a sigh.

"Hello, Bennett."

"Hi," he mumbled, following us without instruction.

I barely paid attention as Allyson closed the door behind us, only staring at the state the Imperial had been reduced to. He wore the same clothes as the day he was abducted, though they were almost unrecognizable with the untied ruffle collar and dirt stains. I swore he had several new wrinkles in his face as well as sunken, tinted circles under his eyes. Despite nearly two months bound to the same, windowless room, his demeanor was no feebler, and his long hair, weighed down by oil, was still tied away from his cutting expression.

Allyson stood behind the three of us, keeping us together, with one hand on my shoulder and the other on Bennett's. Rose stayed in between us, allowing me to keep holding her hand more for my sake than hers, and glared the man before us, disgusted. Acwel Aloysius didn't seem to see her glare at all, looking back and forth between Bennett and me in recognition.

"Yours, Idris?" he asked with a mocking sneer. The idea that the Idris could be a mother seemed to only further degrade her hostile image in his mind. Allyson eased us closer together in front of her, and retorted in an equally disdainful voice.

"No, they are not mine. Bennett is the son of one of our most important posts in Nemirena. Amaryllis and Rosalie came to us under different circumstances."

"Yes, I remember those two," he said flatly, and I struggled not to avert my eyes.

"I want to make one thing to you very clear," she patted my shoulder approvingly, then did the same to Bennett. "You were overthrown by Stoleh and Nemiren teenagers working hand in hand with your own children, not a powerful group of Idrisans. These two here first found the Atlas all on their own in the Haritite State before they even knew who had sent them, and then fooled a group of Etaira into thinking they were an Imperien and Imperiess before they managed to help outsmart you and your Council of Patriarchs. That fact alone should tell you the holes in your own system, and make you not feel as badly about its demise after you are gone. And we'll see what your own race does with you once they have you back again. My guess is they will not be kind after all that has been said and done and changed in the absence of an intimidating figurehead."

"And I wish to make something very clear to you and your child insurgents," he countered. "You are ignoring too many complications of your plan in order for it to succeed. We are not afraid of you or anyone else in your useless insurrectionist group."

"Who is 'we'?" Allyson cocked her head slightly. "You're alone here. No one is coming for you. Your most trusted daughter has been gladly giving us information and helping us work out the kinks in the framework. It was an unexpected venture for us, sure, but it is long overdue.

My father passed away this year after more than fifty years as Idris. He always told me as a child that if I ever looked you in the eye, then I was to feel pity, not anger, because you are one in a series of hopelessly debauched men who were born into the idea of accepting your system as functional and unflawed, and to pay little mind to what occurs beyond the Etairan Mountains. It honestly disturbs me to think that you believe we do harm to our own people while only cursing yours, and that we are not serious about any of this. I would say you are in denial. I honestly think you still have this belief that you are somehow going to end up lining us up in front of your firing squad, as you've done for years to so many others, and then return to your throne. What you fail to realize is that you have been finished for a long time. We were only needed to make the rest of the Lebon realize that. But whether you believe it or not, you helped us come to our own realization. We were sitting around a table bickering with each other instead of focusing on the real problem and ways we could actively address it. After Bennett and Amaryllis here returned home with you, we stopped and started cooperating like we had before my father died."

"It does not matter," Acwel Aloysius folded his arms, and then spun a finger around in the air as if gesturing nonexistent Guard toward us. "You are awaiting a letter that will never come."

"And when we go back over there and they're trying their hardest to talk their ways into some kind of sham peace agreement between our parties," Allyson entirely ignored him, and turned her body sideways to head for the door. On the way, she passed an otherwise empty table where it appeared the Imperial's tray of food had been violently slammed down. "Keep in mind that we have our own swords and have no use for yours."

Allyson stopped in the doorway, seemingly experiencing a kind of rush after what she had said, waiting for the three of us.

"You know, both of my parents were kidnapped in a Cleansing eleven years ago, and they found my mom working like a slave on your manor," Rose planted her feet firmly in the floor as Bennett and I slowly retreated. When I realized Rose was speaking, I quickly returned and put both my hands on her shoulders, trying to walk backwards with her. She unemotionally pushed me away, continuing to stare through the Imperial. He looked from her journal to her face, from her height to her scowl, outwardly amused by her attempt at confrontation. "Do you order the Cleansings, or do you just let them happen?"

"Rose," I tried to force her back to the door again. "He's not worth it. Let's go."

"No, I do not plan the Cleansings, child," he answered, pulling her back into the conversation. I glared deeply at the Imperial as if daring him to upset my sister, which of course he didn't take seriously. "The Haritite Guard handles that. They are random and occur no more than once a year. Under normal circumstances, they do not leave children orphaned."

"That is the most barefaced lie I've ever heard!" she nearly shouted. "They happen all the time in every borough behind the Wall. They kidnap as many people as they can fit in their cart! Children all over the place are orphaned and turned out on the streets because of them!"

"Then one of the parents must have fought."

Something about his indifferent, dismissing tone struck a nerve in me somewhere, and I injected myself between them before Rose could say anything.

"Because we're supposed to just stand there and watch our family members as they're carted away? My father pulled a knife on one of the Haritites, and I couldn't be more proud of him for that. I stole almost every day because I thought as a child that I could bail him out of jail with a jar of tin coins. As stupid as it sounds to you, you know you don't have that kind of bond with anybody, not even your own family. And it's funny how little regard you give to any of the people you claim as your own until your livelihood is on the line."

Satisfied, I turned around, holding Rose beside me as I left.

"So you're sending Stoleh petty thieves off the streets on your important missions now, Idris?" his contemptuous voice came from behind me, and I whipped around, preparing to get close to his face and let loose to the entire Hall what I thought of him. Rose halfheartedly held me back as Bennett moved in front of us, shaking his head at the Imperial.

"Better than a murderer," he said. "The so-called scum you pretend litters your streets are worth so much more than you, it's not even ironic anymore. It's only sad."

As if surprised by what he'd just said, Bennett turned on his heels, and placed a hand on my back to lead Rose and me from the room. We passed in front of Idris, who proudly smiled at us as she sincerely told the Imperial to enjoy his meal, slamming and locking the door.

Acwel Aloysius's sureness that we were going to waste our time until our imminent death as a camp only gave us the faith that something must have been on its way. And the morning afterwards, furious knocking startled Ella, Rose, and me from sleep. It couldn't have been any later than five, and I knew I couldn't entice either of them out of bed at this hour. Stuffing my feet in my shoes, I opened the door with my eyes still half glazed over to stop the pounding.

"Bennett?" I rubbed one eye, and saw his smile. "What's wrong with you?"

"It came," he told me, and I was suddenly awake. "We've got them."

I left the door cracked open behind me as Bennett and I paced quickly down the hallway. I didn't realize my shoes were on the wrong feet until after we began to run. Allyson, with only Emmitt and Mr. Johansson looking over her shoulders, held a neat, cream-colored piece of paper in both her hands. It wanted to curl at the edges, and she pressed it flat against the desk, reading and rereading the words. The three of them didn't try to stop us as we forced our ways among them. The first thing that stood out to me was not the scribble of slanted calligraphy, but the small, colorless peacock feather at every corner of the paper.

We agree to your terms. Please return Acwel and Arena Aloysius to our main dock.

The letter continued after that, though I only continuously reread the two sentences.

"Go and gather a crew again. Prepare one vessel," she told Emmitt, pointing a shaky finger out the door.

371

"At five o'clock in the morning?"

"Yes, we leave in three hours, wait the night out in the channel out of the dock's sight, and then deliver him this time tomorrow morning so the Lebon have today to get their act and fleet together."

After Emmitt left, she turned to Mr. Johansson.

"Please go wake Arena. I must talk to her about something important before we leave."

"I will. But shouldn't you consider sending more than one boat? That way we can send one that does not actually have the Imperial aboard and see if they try to capture and take control of it."

"I am not worried," a grin spread widely across her face as she angled herself in her chair toward us, dragging her finger along the words *Acwel and Arena Aloysius* with her finger. "Don't you see?"

"I don't understand," I said, and Allyson gestured me closer as if that would help me see her hidden meaning.

"They didn't call him his Majesty, Amaryllis," she spoke almost giddily. "That means Alexander must have succeeded to some degree in destroying the last shred of his reign."

Chapter Forty Two

The rising sun cast shadows of mountainous Imperiam away from the dock, illuminating the congested area in a yellowy pink light. Our ship's size paled in comparison to even the smaller Lebon vessels, all expectantly bobbing in the water, waiting to carry away an entire race of people made foreign royalty. Despite the near half mile of beach on the northern face of Imperiam scattered with strongly built piers, it was easy to locate where we were to dock. Lebon stood on an uncountable number of boats, watching harshly as two Stoleh workers tied our skip to the pier. It led to a wider platform raised a foot above the dark water, where several men from the Council of Patriarchs and other Lebon stood. Behind them, a murmuring group of Etaira waited for the Guard to join the Lebon on the dock, seemingly thinking this whole attempt at reclaiming the island would pass in a matter of minutes.

Idris asserted she personally be there to see everything this time, but forced Joana and Lukas to stay behind. While she argued with them, Mr. Johansson insisted that Bennett and I come, eventually forcing Allyson to agree just so we could leave the camp on time. The Imperial was kept alone in the cabin, and Arena was only forced in there with him as we drew near Imperiam. She had remained in a state of shock since her short, one-sided conversation with Idris the day before. Arena did not seem bitter toward any of us for the decision, and was so accepting of her fate that we thought she probably had been preparing for it the entire time.

Bennett and I leaned dangerously over the ship's thick, wooden railing, watching and listening to Mr. Johansson's heavy footsteps as he walked alongside Allyson to face the Lebon. I felt the deep, nervous pit in my stomach close as Rosalie came beside me, slipping one of her hands in mine, and Bennett covered my other clenched, nearly shaking fist. He rubbed it gently on top of the railing until I relaxed, opened my fist, and squeezed his hand tightly. The three of us kept our eyes trained on Mr. Johansson as he held his hands behind his back, wringing them uneasily, and stopped short before the pier merged with the wider dock. He took the Lebon's letter from inside his jacket, and turned it around as if to show them we had proof of their surrender. Mr. Johansson then folded it twice before their eyes, and dropped it on the dock, allowing the breeze the lazily blow it a bit closer to them.

"We have your Imperial," Mr. Johansson' voice spoke gruffly, carried away from us by the wind. "Board your ships and we will put him on the nearest one."

"Who might we speak to about this matter? I am sure we can settle this like adults and come to some kind of agreement," one of the elderly men said, his voice cracking with age and sugarcoated to appease us. The others looked at him harshly, indicating a peace summit between Idris and a fallen Imperial was not part of the plan this morning.

"You may speak to me," Allyson answered, folding her arms, trying to stand as tall and speak as vehemently as possible. "I am Idris. But I am not interested in negotiating with you. We have already settled this, and you will do it our way. Otherwise, the rest of the camp has been ordered to send a letter to Imperiam instructing our correspondents to start assassinating Patriarchs if my ship and crew do not return tonight. You murdered enough of ours that we will not grieve any blood shed on your part when you had ample opportunity."

A cloud of tense silence befell the group, not expecting such a response to come from Allyson. We knew from Alexander's envelope that one of the points he would make was that the Idrisans would start assassinating Patriarchs, so the Lebon had to have heard it before. But to listen to the very real-sounding threat come straight from the horse's mouth seemed to entirely blindside their party. To be honest, I expected the Lebon to put up a bit more of a periphrasis battle before allowing themselves to be run out of Capria Rodalia by one crew of Idrisans. Though it appeared no one else had the courage to test us for fear of Idris waving magic wand and animating her personal squad of cutthroats right there on the dock in the hazy light of early morning. Nevertheless, without prompt, six Guard surrounding the Lebon advanced toward Mr. Johansson and Idris. He in turn stepped back, but Allyson held her ground and said in a sing-song voice,

"Remember, if we aren't back by tonight...."

"We would like to see proof of the Idrisans you say you have posted here."

"Of course," Allyson half bowed graciously, and gestured at the long line of piers and ships. "Unfortunately, they never disclosed their names to us. If you'd like to walk around and ask everyone, please feel free. I would love to meet them."

He scowled as if he could intimidate her, but quickly stepped back behind the other Lebon at her unafraid glare, daring him to keep pressing. To replace him, and unrecognizable version of Alexander took command of the conversation. It wasn't that he wore different clothes or had physically changed since he ran off from the beach, but the way he uprightly stood and seemed to hold attention and control over the dock made me momentarily forget that Alexander wasn't even my age. Despite the unlikely circumstances, both the Guard and the other Lebon seemed somehow indebted to and almost dependent on the kid they had once scorned as a bastard.

"We should not trust that these people are capable of keeping their word anyway," he indicated us. I momentarily frowned before I realized it was all part of the show. "If we do not leave willingly today, then these spies will show themselves."

The Guard and Patriarchs seemed believing of him, though how Alexander planned on keeping the Imperial quiet after they had him back, I still did not understand.

"I can assure you that after you leave our connections with your people will be severed in the same way your connections with ours already are," Allyson quickly picked up the ball, speaking detached and in the same way as she addressed the other Lebon, even though she must have inferred the identity of this boy. Alexander did little more than nod in obligatory acknowledgement. Had it not been for his envelope, I wouldn't be able to differentiate his behavior from that of his father.

From the safety of our ship, the noise from our cabin startled me. I didn't realize Emmitt had gone inside until he brought the Imperial out onto the deck. Acwel Aloysius impulsively looked down to turn his eyes away from the light, staring at the thick, rusty irons clamped over his wrists that forced his shoulders uncomfortably forward into a slouch. The dramatic difference between the man from the throne room, the man holding everything from the executioner's baton to the Guard's whip to the book of names at the Stoleh Wall, and the man Emmitt now roughly forced down the gangplank was incredible. With the pier to serve as Acwel Aloysius's final, long walk of shame, I stared into the Lebon gathering for any reaction to his presence. The only thing amongst them appeared to be a lasting feeling of contempt. We were not returning their Imperial. We were returning their deposed prisoner. Idris and Mr. Johansson backed dangerously close to the narrow pier's edges to allow Emmitt and Acwel Aloysius through. With the harsh grip on Aloysius's arm serving as a third shackle, Emmitt surveyed the group as if awaiting a response. When another of the Guard began taking steps toward him, Emmitt unemotionally took the pistol from beneath his admiral's jacket out in one, swift motion. He spun it around in his hand and held it comfortably beside him. His bushy eyebrows rose at the man, who only growled,

"You have no nerve."

The shot rang up the mountainside, seemingly stifling the progress of the sun itself as Acwel Aloysius's painful, choked shout echoed back to the boat. I tried to turn my head away from it, though couldn't resist watching as one of the former Imperial's legs gave out from under him, and he was held upright only by Emmitt, leaning vulnerably over the water after he had been shot through the thigh.

"I have more bullets," Emmitt said as matter of fact. Even though the Guard easily out-armed his one pistol, something in his voice and demeanor froze them. Now, they were awaiting our instruction. But before Mr. Johansson, Idris, or Emmitt could say anything, Acwel Aloysius, desperate by the sound of his voice, apparently believed he could alter the imminent by exposing Alexander. As he attempted to explain away that he had worked alongside us, us meaning he named Bennett and I as we watched from the deck, he entirely left out Arena's part in the dealings, continuing on an angry roll over his son's treason. What was more intriguing than his account was the cold stone reception he received in return, like they were hearing and promptly disregarding everything he said. I sensed Alexander exercised no filter when he finally gained the Council of Patriarchs' courtesy, and stripped his father down to the foul core to get through their divine image of him. Now, the Imperial seemingly meant next to nothing to his own people. Once Acwel Aloysius realized the blank, unsympathetic expressions looking back at him as he struggled to keep upright with shackled hands and one usable leg, his voice slowed to a painful halt.

"Even so," one of the Patriarchs dismissed the topic with a short wave. He only continued to humor their estranged ruler, obviously thinking he was making this up as he went along in a last effort to restore his name and influence. "It is no worse than the treason committed by you."

At that, everyone seemed to come to terms with the fact that the Imperial's reign was finished. The Lebon didn't view his execution of Idrisans and kidnapping of so many Stoleh as criminal or even wrong, so I couldn't help but wonder what else this man had done to add to his famous repertoire of murder and enslavement.

I hadn't noticed Arena's timid hovering in the cabin door until she walked slowly across the deck, leaning over the side of the boat on the other side of Rose. Her face seemed pained, though she watched the gathering as if disappointed in them, not grieving over Idris's order. As her long, signature white-blond hair hung down over the dock with her leaning, one of the Patriarchs seemed to recognize it, and then her face.

"Give us her as well," he pointed a shaking finger at our boat, and Arena shamefully retreated out of sight. Sitting against the doorframe of the cabin, she looked up at Bennett, Rose, and I apologetically. At the same time, she seemed to realize that if she was allowed to return to the other Lebon, she would have been taken as a prisoner just like her father. Alexander would be powerless to do any more than make her comfortable, but locked away, just as she had spent her life before. The thought was powerful for her, and a sense of relief crossed her face. Perhaps she was just as happy to stay here on Capria Rodalia as the last Lebon in disguise.

"The Imperiess will stay here," Idris said spitefully. Though we knew she truly did care for Arena, it surprised us to hear her speak that way.

"That was not part of the agreement!" the same Patriarch hissed. He thought nothing of Arena's safety or happiness, only that the Idrisans simply could not tell the Lebon exactly which terms they would be granted.

"We are keeping her as collateral, and there is no discussion to be had. You all will stay away from here lest you want to see a bullet in her head," Idris continued.

Alexander looked around at the three of them in shock. By altering his infallible plan, Allyson said she was showing him that he didn't hold all the power in this situation. "It is necessary to instill a little fear in the boy," she said. "So he will keep the Lebon away from here. If he thinks we're holding his beloved sister hostage with a gun at her head, he will pass down his warnings to his children. Even after we're all gone, they or anyone else will not return to Capria Rodalia with all the legends of ruthless Idrisans surrounding it. Eventually, our memory will die with this group of Lebon."

A nearby, shrieking voice from the nearest Lebon ship pulled Arena from the shadows of the cabin, walking backwards with an arm shielding her eyes. She stopped walking at the tip of the bow, tilting backwards to see the taller deck. We could barely make out a woman's form leaning over the side of the nearby ship, though the sound of her voice bordered on hysterical. Arena recognized it, and appeared near tears as Guard aboard the boat surrounded the woman, and began to pull her away from the railing.

"Let my daughter leave with us, and we will never come back!" the fallen Imperia shouted through her tears, fighting uselessly as the Guard forced her backwards. When she realized she was addressing an unwilling crowd, she changed her plea. "Please don't hurt her!"

"They haven't treated me badly, Mother," Arena's frail, barely raised voice answered. I questioned whether or not the Imperia could hear the last words her daughter would ever say to her. "I'll be alright...."

Arena sat down exactly where she was and buried her face into her knees. Rose left us, trying to comfort her. Meanwhile, in spite of a heightened discomfort between us and the Lebon, Alexander seemed to agonizingly cut his loss, and agree to the new terms. In response, Emmitt suddenly dropped Acwel Aloysius, causing him to shout in pain again and almost fall off the pier. The Guard made no move toward him until Emmitt, Mr. Johansson, and Idris stepped back, walking backwards little by little to the ship. The exchange looked about over, and Bennett slowly shook my hand back and forth on top of the railing in assurance as they neared us.

But what about.... I mouthed, staring wide eyed at all the Lebon boats, imagining Liam, Ida, and Mallory cramped with so many others on the lowest decks. I hadn't mentioned them to Idris, but I thought that one of their first priorities would be to make sure these people didn't sail away with a thousand kidnapped Stoleh. Panicking they had forgotten about them in the stress of the moment, I pushed myself away from the dock and past Bennett. He followed right behind me, asking what I thought I was doing as I stumbled down the gangplank and toward Mr. Johansson, Emmitt, and Allyson. Emmitt noticed me first, and stopped their group, his stare demanding I return to the boat before I ruined something.

"You're going to let them take the Stoleh workers?" I asked, exasperated as the three seemed to just remember them. More intimidating than returning up the pier was the number of people we were about to rescue with absolutely no idea as to how we were going to return them home. Allyson looked down the line of boats as if she could see through their hulls, and then faced Mr. Johansson. He momentarily watched as the

Guard finally came toward the Imperial, and then carelessly motioned Emmitt and Idris back toward the boat.

"Come on," he placed one hand on Bennett's back, the other on mine, and led us in front of him back to the wider dock. "We'll get them out."

When they saw us returning, I heard a murmur of disbelief, and couldn't help but think they were dubious of Bennett and me. With us in front, I felt unprotected against the Lebon, wanting to turn around before we reached them. Progress stopped, and the Guard retreated beside the Patriarchs, leaving Acwel Aloysius unattended. Mr. Johansson halted us before we neared him, and gently nudged me forward before removing his hand.

"You're their voice, Amaryllis."

I tried to wipe the look of horror from my face as I realized I held their attention. Everything about that one moment would have been surreal months ago, when the Lebon were more powerful, foreign objects than very real nightmares. I could never have thought I would eventually stand on their beach and demand they free my people. But as they waited impatiently for me to speak, I realized my window of opportunity was closing.

"Release your slaves," I sounded much more composed and forceful than I expected, and I briefly paused as if taken aback by my own voice. They looked at me like I was joking, and before Mr. Johansson could take over for me, I vehemently repeated myself. "Release your slaves. They are natives to our home and will not leave with you."

"Also, you and I both know you do not have the resources aboard to carry you and a thousand workers over miles of ocean," Mr. Johansson said flatly, taking the issue from me. "You will have no use for them, anyhow. Every single one of them is to be let out onto the beach now."

"You cannot keep changing the terms of your...." one of the Patriarchs began, stopping at the sound of footsteps behind us. Emmitt and Allyson returned and stood behind us. Before I saw their faces, I turned my head and looked at the same pistol in Emmitt's hand, pointed carelessly back at the Imperial.

"The land is ours regardless. You are not giving us anything," he told them. "Your slaves committed no crime. Every last one of them was violently abducted from their home and made a prisoner, so you cannot say we have done anything worse than you rather you care to admit it or not. And you are still giving us nothing by releasing them. They are free people, or your significant war prisoner is a dead man."

It was a slow, tense process as a sea of yellow vests fled the ships in silence and confusion, filling the beach quickly. I frowned deeply as the second half of the people, even slower and sadder than the first, appeared to fall down the piers and toward the rocky sand. Several of the healthier ones had to return to carry smaller people, and before the crowd had thinned, everyone was backed to the paths leading up the mountainside. As I realized exactly how many peoples' lives had been ruined by a Cleansing, I felt terrible for ever thinking my case was somehow special. And in a way, these people were the fortunate ones. Luck of the draw had brought them here, while the other two thirds of the missing were either rotting in prison or dead in mass graves. Still, in all their years of imprisonment, all those years of being treated like dogs, they kept straight, steely faces until the very last of the sick and wounded was helped down the path, fearful of the Guard that harshly watched them emerge into the light until the very last minute.

Mr. Johansson took the overwrought time to press even farther and tell the Guard that if they had any Idrisan prisoners, now was their time to release them as well. Alexander didn't seem to have much of a reason to lie as he falsely retorted if there were any in prison, they would be in the Etairan Mountains, not in Imperiam. Mr. Johansson took a personal blow from the news, and I sensed he had a secret hope his wife was still alive in a cell somewhere. I couldn't belittle or feel sympathy for any such unfounded fantasy. I had done the same thing for the past eleven years with my father, even though a sad voice of reason had begun to tell me that he was probably gone by now.

With all the Stoleh workers on the shore, looking expectantly between their former masters and us as if expecting the war to turn violent right there on the beach, the Patriarchs gave us one final, deep stare and boarded the nearest ship with four Guard following closely behind them. All of us stepped back as the remaining two dragged Acwel Aloysius to his feet, and the Etaira, forced forward by the infectious disease now plaguing the beach, stepped onto the dock.

"You are going to release your slaves as well," Allyson snapped at them. They didn't appear surprised by the order as much as the forthrightness. "We are sending ships to come for them within the week. Until we get there, you are to take the sick and wounded into your homes. After we get everyone out, you'll have to leave your manors for a couple months. I expect you to be active participants in rebuilding your own home and make an effort to reach out to the other classes you have spent so long pretending don't exist. We are not going to try to take what you have from you so long as you do not disappear and become the new Lebon. If that is your intention, go find space on one of their boats. Am I understood?"

She received a short series of stutters before a reluctant agreement. The Etaira had the ability to take over the island and keep it almost exactly the way it is. Part of what would prevent them from doing so revolved around keeping our image as a insurrectionist group intimidating enough as connections between the population rekindled.

The sun was in full glare, though the shadows of Imperiam's mountains hadn't yet consumed us. In the still, peaceful noise of the rolling water whitecaps, Alexander motioned the Guard to haul his father aboard the ship. He stared piercingly at us as he passed, like he was itching to say one last mocking comment, and Idris felt compelled to ask him the ultimate irony.

"Have you anything to say?"

"Your beloved island," Acwel Aloysius spoke in an even, removed voice, as if he had thrown his hands up to remove any responsibility from his person, "was in the midst of total breakdown, a powder keg, a corrupt despot in itself before we arrived.

Without Imperiam, I give you thirty years before the remaining Guard and citizens turn on you, and your Capria Rodalia returns to the same state."

Allyson more than anyone heeded those parting words as the Imperial was taken up the gangplank to the deck, and was gone with the last of the Lebon Guard. Before he boarded his ship with the people he now had believing solely in him, Alexander approached us, and held out his hand to Idris. She stared at it for a while, and then pushed her way in front of Emmitt to shake his hand. Looking down at him, she frowned slightly as if sensing something was wrong.

"I am glad this was settled without bloodshed," Alexander said formally, and was completely thrown off his guard by her response.

"Bloodshed has riddled this island for centuries, boy."

"I'm sorry. I did not think about that," his tone drastically changed. "But please promise me you will not harm Arena."

"Arena is safer here than on that boat, and you know as much. It would not be fair for you to ask her to become a prisoner. So long as you keep the Lebon away from here and ensure they never return, she will be treated well. Aside from that, the only thing I ask of you is that wherever you end up from here, do not grow into your father. You sound like the kind of person these people need as a leader. My only fear is that time will change your intentions."

Alexander nodded once, silently affirming a promise. With little more than a nod of recognition at Bennett and me, the gangplank was kicked away from the boat following the ascension of the first genuine Imperial in centuries.

Emmitt sailed alone in our skipper-sized boat around Imperiam, following the large fleet as they slowly approached the far left, milky horizon. I cupped my hands around my eyes as they evaporated into the settled fog. Minutes later, Emmitt's three fired casings into the air signified they had entered the open ocean away from the island. On the pier, Allyson and Mr. Johansson watched the blank waters, in awe of what had just happened, while Rose and I kept our arms around each other, squeezing tighter and tighter as Emmitt's boat returned to us, the fleet of Lebon forever lost. As he drew closer to us, Mr. Johansson and Allyson moved to help him dock again, and I looked at the yellow covering the side of the mountain: huge expectant eyes watching us in disbelief. There was no rejoicing, and I sensed there would be nothing but straight faces until they could see and hear and touch the loved ones they'd left behind.

A single, yellow vest lazily drifting downward from a sharp overhang captivated everyone as it sank gracefully on the winds, casting ripples on the water in the empty docks of Imperiam. I squinted to see the tiny figure atop the cliff, leaving Rose and walking up next to Bennett. Ida stood triumphantly, having climbed up there from the beach to dispose of her chains, with her hair blowing around her face and an almost crazed look in her eye. No one climbed up there with her, but the riddance of vests commenced down on the beach as everyone dropped theirs plainly on the ground, and began to clap loudly. Not for us, but as if cheering the Lebon onward as they sailed into the open depths around the other side of Imperiam. In the midst of the skyrocketing noise, I turned my head toward Bennett, smiling in a way that had never felt so free. I found he was already looking at me, and only felt better about the future ahead for the island. Too many things were still left in the dark, but what happened there on the beach was what would tie these people together for the rest of their lives.

"I have an idea!" I was forced to scream at him over the sudden outburst of cheering and activity.

"What is it?!" he answered, leaning closer to me to hear. I placed my hand on his shoulder, pushing down as if to bring him to my height, and began to whisper a notion, a real and authentic one, to unite people through the years ahead. He smiled broadly at me by the end of it, and took my hand again as Mr. Johansson, Idris, Emmitt, Rosalie, him, and I walked down the dock and onto the dark, rocky sand littered with remnants of yellow to address the liberated slaves. We all stood on what would later become a dock famous for the event we had incited, the first thing we wholly took back from the Lebon.

Chapter Forty Three

Forty: the number of round trips it took with every boat the Idrisans owned to carry all the Stoleh workers from Imperiam home. I never found Mallory, though Liam and Ida rode the boat Bennett, Bryn, and I sailed with Mr. Johansson on the twenty-fourth passage. I had longed to see them again, and to hear Liam's strange but delightful way of speaking was wonderful. We never got to see the reunion part of their journey, only dropping them off with more Idrisans waiting for us in the Etairan Mountains, and waving our goodbyes before Mr. Johansson turned us around to go pick up more people. Though both of our expeditions were far from over, I knew as I watched them walk up off the beach that when I saw Ida again, she would have found her two children and husband, none of whom she had seen in six years.

Enough time had passed that everyone knew the Lebon were gone, but it wasn't quite long enough for us to get a total hold of the situation. Idrisans had managed to get into the top tier of the Guard to freeze their activity as planned, ordering they only make arrests or accusations in the case of actual crime and judge all classes on equal ground. As much as I would have liked to hope it was actually happening, I knew it would take a long time to erase the severely unbalanced scale. Allyson knew this as well, and had multiple people sent to the Wall. With help of the Haritite Guard, acting only under orders and not a sense of compassion or duty, the gate was permanently propped open, the book of Stoleh numbers was confiscated, and the Wall became only a functionless monument. As riots in Nemirena settled and the Haritites passively accepted their barely changed way of life, the patches still sewn upon all clothing as well as all minds became a barrier to melting down the mental walls. I figured then was a good time for me to run my idea by Idris, and she wholeheartedly agreed.

People from all classes worked together to haul kindling and dry shrubs into a vast, fallow field in Nemirena. Few Haritites from the State had made the journey, though most everyone in the nearby neighborhoods came with bags of clothing. The red patches immensely outnumbered the rest of us, and also came with their entire family's clothes. Most of the Stoleh, those who were not currently at home awaiting the sporadic arrivals of carts full of the long missing and dead from Imperiam and the Etairan Mountains, emerged from the surrounding woods as if in fear of being lynched. Skirmishes between bitter Haritites and Stoleh commenced almost immediately following their arrival, though most were settled by the bystanders without any intervention from the Idrisans. A starting point for acceptance began only with the start of the ceremony just at eight o'clock.

The tips of flames cut through the winter air, the array of warm colors both blinding and warming. Family by family, people ripped sewn patches from every article of clothing they had brought with them, ended by the one they were currently wearing, and threw them into the fire. As the night wore on, it spit unrecognizable, colored remnants into the air, which rained down on those of us in the front. Ellamae, Rosalie, and I were some of the last ones to go. I had nothing: my last yellow-patched shirt sequestered in Nemirena a long time ago, but took one from the Idrisan camp's collection to symbolically discard with my sisters. The fire burned late into the night, and by the time only a foot of its original height remained, a large portion of the crowd was still there, most of them Nemiren. When the remaining group of Stoleh decided to leave as a pack of twenty, still rightfully timid about separating to walk the streets, I felt forced to accompany them without finding Bennett, Mr. Johansson, or Idris and Joana. Stumbling tiredly through the woods, I thought that Aunt Clarissa, Uncle Graham, Niles, and Oakley should have been at the bonfire. I had walked around in circles studying the crowd for an hour to find no trace of them. In the streets, as we turned around to return to Nemirena, Mom held my head on her shoulder, and told me not to worry about them.

"We'll talk to Idris and go home tomorrow," Rose added, and we returned to the extra, empty storehouse on the industrial side of Nemirena where half of the fifty Idrisans who'd left the camp spent the nights. Early the next afternoon, Mom, Ellamae, Rose, and I were stopped by old friends so many times on our way to the house. Though they couldn't know the full story, it seemed to have gotten around that at least I was somehow involved with the Idrisans, and I only smiled slightly, breathless, and tried to hint that we wanted to get home. The only person receiving more attention than me was Mom, and Ellamae stayed behind with her as she struggled through the reunions, horrified that she could remember no one, and deeply saddened by everyone's questions about Dad. Rosalie and I rudely ignored everyone else and ran the rest of the way to the house. Its still silence and three broken windows caused a balloon of horror to swell in my heart, and I couldn't make myself open the door for fear of the absolute worst. Rose went in front of me, and we walked slowly and painfully into our familiar life: long settled in the dark.

"Aunt Clarissa! Uncle Graham!" she shouted, opening and promptly slamming the door to their empty room. Without shouting their names, she passed the sheepskin bench and provisional oven to the boys' area. The lingering smell of dirty clothes and matches assaulted my senses, and I used it as an excuse to cry. The home was so preserved, I could close my eyes and almost hear Niles and Oakley tumbling around the living room. I could hear Aunt Clarissa hunched over scrubbing the oven as clean as she could, and see Uncle Graham sitting at the table until the early hours of the morning, painstakingly doing calculations for his work. I would've given anything to listen to one of his long talks about always being early to the Wall, Aunt Clarissa's scolding voice, or the constant 'it's mine' and 'I saw it first!' exchanges over rocks and sticks between my young cousins. As Rose ran up the steps, audibly hitting her head on the protruding wooden beam, I slowly lowered myself onto the sheepskin bench. When Ellamae and Mom came inside, the door lightly closing behind them, I was staring off into space, petting the seat beside me as if waiting for Niles and Oakley to start jumping up and down on it: the way they used to startle me awake when I came home from beyond the Wall and fell asleep on the arm of the sofa. I buried my face into its softness, shaking as Ella and Mom approached me. I heard Rose returning from upstairs, and how she ran to Ellamae and started blaming herself again for not finding and taking Oakley with her to the camp to begin with. For at least the next twenty minutes, we sat there and silently cried.

In the sunken circle in the center of town, small, tent-like shelters were set up for the people arriving from Imperiam and the Etairan Mountains who had no home, and the children who had lost their parents in the most recent Cleansing. Amongst the sea of heads, I picked out one face I recognized who was there to help out with all the dislocated people.

"Stella!" I called out to her, and she looked up, not actually seeing me until I had picked my way through most of the crowd. I hugged her tightly, and she seemed divided between happiness, painfully explaining Barney's absence, and asking a long chain of inquiries that would require a longer chain of answers. Stella frowned at my red, swollen eyes and the dry paths of tears on my face when I pulled away, and only asked,

"Did you go home?"

"It still looks like they should be there...." I choked out, and she only half smiled sympathetically at me. I felt I'd seen more than my breaking point of those looks, and thought Stella knew that by now. But I still watched and listened as she pointed over her shoulder, and then looked back at me.

"Does that little blond kid over there playing with pebbles with another little blond kid look familiar at all?"

Without another word to her, I ran off in the other direction just as Rosalie, Ella, and Mom caught up. The two didn't pay any attention to me until I dropped to my knees beside one of them, and nearly picked him up off the ground.

"Oakley...."

"What the-" he scrambled away from me, looking up at my face for a long time before a smile managed to creep its way across. "Arlie!" he said excitedly, though the delight quickly melted into annoyance. "Wait a second. I'm *Niles.*"

I halfway apologized as the actual Oakley stood up, and they nearly tackled me together, doing the same to Rose when she managed to find me, and Ella as if she had never left. As they looked strangely up at Mom, she knelt in front of them, but couldn't seem to find the words to say. She was saved as two more figures came from a nearby tent, and froze when they saw our group. I had assumed the excruciating truth that the boys' presence here meant Uncle Graham and Aunt Clarissa had been taken the most recent Cleansing, and it would take a long time to get back if they were even still alive. But apparently the four of them, like Stella, were only part of the borough efforts to help with the homeless and displaced. Toward the end of the long, tearful event set right there in the center of town, between Aunt Clarissa's crying over the three of us and her long dead sister, Mom's slurred string of thank you's for taking us in so long ago, and Uncle Graham's fervent, but relieved and caring questions, Aunt Clarissa finally got enough of a grip to turn around and answer the boys' questioning stares.

"Niles, Oakley, this is your Aunt Angela."

For weeks, I never left the house. Mom was astounded by the fact that Rose, Ella, and I still had her quilts, and argued with us for a long time when Rose tried to give her hers to sleep with on the sheepskin bench downstairs. Aunt Clarissa, despite Mom's assurance that she was fine, tried to take care of her, never allowing her up off the sofa for days afterward. Eventually though, she let her begin to adjust to a normal rhythm of life: letting her help cook and walk to the center of town with Ellamae to buy some new shirts for Niles and Oakley. At first, they didn't seem to appreciate having another person intrude upon their family, though they took a special liking to Mom when she began happily playing their simple pretending games with them.

All connections we had to the continued Idrisan activity inside and outside the Wall seemed lost. As often as I told myself I would go find Allyson soon, it never happened. I began to miss being part of something bigger, even if only carting liberated Stoleh back to the mainland, and quickly grew tired of waiting around for news to arrive. On top of a growing fear they had all disremembered me, I longed to see Bennett much more than the others. I could fade away into nonexistence within the Idrisan community, but nothing frightened me more than the idea of Bennett either forgetting about me or thinking I had intentionally left the bonfire that night without any goodbye.

"Do you want to go see him?" Aunt Clarissa asked me, sitting across the table from Uncle Graham and me after I had finally worked up the courage to tell them the story. While my uncle watched me with widened eyes, listening to my part in overthrowing the Lebon, she seemed more interested in the way I spoke about Bennett, and how he'd always been at my side. "No one is stopping you. I think we can manage for one day so you can head to Nemirena to see Bennett, and find Idris so she knows you're alright."

I eagerly agreed, and stood from the table, my hands pressed against the back of the chair.

"I'm really sorry I lied to you for so many years," I said, thankful they hadn't asked me to elaborate on how I snuck around outside the Wall and stole half our dinner for seven years. I couldn't avoid telling them the truth, but felt a heavy weight lift from my heart. Uncle Graham turned around in his chair and looked up at me. I stared back at him as if expecting terrible news as he scratched the lower right side of his face: now covered in a short beard from weeks of neglect.

"Thank you, Amaryllis, but we aren't fools. We've known for some time."

"You have?" my mouth dropped open. He chuckled at my reaction, gently taking my arm and sitting me back down.

"You were a smart little thing to come up with your own plan so young. Of course it was wrong, but it gave you a sense of purpose, and times were very hard at the shop. I worried I would get laid off any day back then."

"We were going to tell you we knew after things improved a little," Aunt Clarissa leaned forward with her elbows on the table, smiling slightly at me. "We just never did."

"How did you find out?" I asked, thinking of how careful I thought I had been over the years.

"I found the jar of tin coins in your drawer when I was folding clothes, along with your fake Haritite patch and cut-out book," she answered. "I was going to take them and confront you about it, but then I saw you had written *Bail* on the lid of your jar. You were only ten, and if you needed to believe that somehow fifty of those could help your father, I couldn't take that hope away from you."

The following day, I was later waking up than I planned, and couldn't manage to get out the door until halfway through the afternoon. The moment it closed behind me, I noticed a poor, out-of-place individual walking down the quarter, looking around as if hopelessly lost. Smiling broadly, I weaved my way across the street toward him. Bennett barely had the chance to see me emerging from the crowd before I was standing on my toes with my arms around his neck. He remained still for a moment, but I soon felt his hands on my back and shoulder. We stood there for almost a minute until I had to return to my feet to keep balance.

"I've been lost since nine this morning walking around place to place looking for you," he said. "It's my luck you live in the outskirts of the first borough."

386

"You walked all the way over here without even knowing where I live?" I asked, not sure if I thought it was sweet or stupid.

"I was worried about you, and so are Dad, Emmitt, and Allyson. You just kind of disappeared after the bonfire."

"I'm sorry. It's been hard to get away. But I was just on my way to see you."

"Then I'm glad I caught you. It would have been difficult for you to get out. A lot of people from the Etairan Mountains are just now coming in today. It was hard enough for me to get in, and I can't help but feel like everyone's staring. Even without the patches, I guess I sort of stick out."

"Like a sore thumb," I grinned, motioning for him to follow me. "Come on. I want you to meet the rest of my family."

Everyone was still downstairs, and looked up as I propped the door open for him. Rose's cheery 'Hi Bennett,' announced his identity to my aunt, uncle, and cousins.

"It's nice to meet you," Uncle Graham shook his hand politely. "Amaryllis told us the story. You and your father have helped her a lot, and we're very grateful to you for that."

"Speaking of my father," Bennett dug deep into his pocket for a small envelope. "He asked me to give this to you, sir."

"What is it?" Uncle Graham stood up and took the envelope, slowly unsealing it with his thumb.

"I hope you don't mind that I told him all seven, now eight of you were living under the same roof. When he was in this borough to help after the last Cleansing, he said he saw the size and condition of your home."

As Uncle Graham read and reread the letter, his face went pale, and he practically fell into the chair again.

"Clarissa," he waved her over. Standing behind him with her hands lightly on his shoulders, my aunt squinted in the poor light to read the handwriting.

"That-that's very kind of him," Uncle Graham continued before she had the chance to finish, though her eyes were already big. "But he shouldn't feel obligated. Things are starting to look up a bit around here. We'll be alright."

"He told me to ask you to please consider it. I know he's not doing this out of obligation, either," Bennett answered, grinning. "We have plenty of space and supplies on the farm, enough to eventually build you your own house. It really isn't a problem, and it would be easier for Idris to keep in contact with us as time goes on than if you lived so far away. We would love for you and your family to come live with us."

Uncle Graham sat in shock, running his fingers through his hair and once again rereading the offer.

"We couldn't just ask him to take in our entire family and do nothing to help."

"There's a good amount of former Nemirens leaving us, as well as the markets. Dad's already found a shop owner that buys our produce not too far from the farm who needs a new clerk. He'll pay you twice what you make now to work eight hours a day, six days a week. It'll be in a cooler building and you will get to do much more than sit and perform calculations. And if and when they're ready, there's plenty of work available for your wife and Mrs. Carter too. And there's a primary school down the road for Niles and Oakley. Everything's already set up, but only if you're interested. He said to take as much time as you need to discuss it and think it over."

A grand total of five minutes passed, and the easy decision was made.

That night would be our last behind the Wall.

Chapter Forty Four

The farm was a lot bigger than I first thought, though it didn't seem that way at first with everyone on top of each other in the main building, functioning as both a home and a storehouse. Just enough people to keep the farm operational stayed behind, and the realization that Mr. Johansson had been working for the Idrisans for decades didn't appear to bother them. Niles and Oakley spent half a day, five times a week at school, and though they complained about it almost as much as their teacher complained about them, I knew they were happy to have something to do and other children to play with. Nemirena's surrounding woods also gave them many opportunities to go exploring. Without a Wall to enclose them, the boys managed to build makeshift rafts in which to drift around in the lake and rivers. Niles and Oakley's days of bickering over rocks were over. Mr. Johansson even let them build a swing on his land.

I couldn't remember another time when Uncle Graham was as content as he was now in his new job. His boss treated him well, and kept his word about the pay and the hours. Returning home while we still had daylight was a wondrous thing for him, and spending that time with his sons and the rest of his family was priceless. The biggest difference, besides the treatment and money, between the two jobs was the opportunity he now had to advance as opposed to always being stuck in a rut and taken advantage of. The shop owner told him after only his first week that his extraordinary work ethic could easily give him his own shop over the next five years. And once she realized Niles and Oakley were in good hands throughout the day and didn't need her to watch them like a hawk anymore, Aunt Clarissa got up one day, and randomly said she would like to learn to be a nurse. With both of them gone during different parts of the day, Mom refused to 'be useless,' as she said. Mr. Johansson told her several times that she didn't need to rush back into normal life, and we really didn't need the money. But Allyson in her frequent visits seemed to understand how she felt, and told her there was always something local she could do for the camp whenever she needed to get off the farm.

On the other hand, Bennett and I, and occasionally Bryn, didn't seem to have a choice when it came to our constant travelling with Lukas and Joana. Often, I wouldn't see Rosalie or Ellamae for ten or more days. The first thing we did was clean out the jails in Nemirena, releasing those who had been arrested during the riots. It went simple and fast enough, though the prisons in the Haritite State were an entirely different story. Our reception ranged from brownnosing, hearty welcomes to Emmitt's refusal to let us leave our temporary housing alone for fear of someone assaulting us in the streets. We began in Sturwaller: a bigger, more modern version of Rochonnell, working our way south and then west. We freed a large group of Stoleh caught in Cleansings, some of whom had sat in the same cell for forty years and couldn't even walk outside unaided. After some of them had begun the journey home, though one of the other Idrisan posts took almost two thirds of them to a nearby clinic, Emmitt demanded the Guard present him with some kind of document showing who all these people were. They looked at him dubiously, then at each other. I will never forget the pages and pages of Stoleh numbers they gave us, with many of them already crossed out, each sickeningly thick, black line marking the end of a life. During the course of the short civil war alone, the Guard had executed almost a hundred people. The five hundred we released couldn't seem to compensate for their lives in my mind, and I barely kept myself from crying as we left Sturwaller.

On our last stop in the Haritite State, passing down the line of cells, I stopped at the front of each door, asking a reluctant, short, and rude member of the Guard to tell me who it held. I couldn't bear to look these people in the eye considering most everybody in prison outside of Sturwaller actually deserved to be there. As we walked down the last row, the second to last cell, I accidentally caught the eye of a young man sitting on a thin, dirty mattress on the floor.

"Stephen Laurie," the Guard said flatly, waiting for me to nod and move on. "Suspicious activity."

"Laurie?" I asked, coiling my hand around one of the bars. The man looked up at me, surprised, and unnerved that I knew his name. "Are you-?"

A voice called out to me from the final cell. Leaving the Guard wondering what had possessed me all of a sudden, I abandoned the young man, and shouted at Bennett. He just about ran over, probably thinking something was wrong, only to see Rowana carefully pick herself up off the dusty floor, and walk to the front of her cell with her hands cupped over her mouth. Emmitt tried to tell her that she was welcome to come live at the camp if she feared for her life in the State, though she subtly shook her head. After a long goodbye and a promise to come back to see her, she and Stephen acted like they could simply turn around and walk home like nothing had happened.

"Are you sure you don't want to at least see a doctor?" Emmitt made another attempt to stop them.

"We are alright," she smiled slightly, winking once at Bennett and me. "We're going to just put this behind us, and I am going to Sturwaller in the morning to find my daughter."

Before we left for Nemirena again, Joana insisted we stop by the clinic where so many of the newly freed were being kept until they were well enough to return home. She said what little accommodation they had available in the mountains to offer their sick and wounded was spread thinly, so they also sent many of theirs over to the State. Walking by the open doors in a building set up strangely like the Drierie school, I tried not to be overly hopeful that Barney could be in one of these rooms. But tucked away in the corner of the second floor, a lanky boy with straw-like, yellow hair lay asleep on a cot beside a window. I hovered in the doorway, afraid of waking him or the three other occupied beds in the room. *Idiot Barney,* I mouthed as if he could hear me, chuckling silently to myself. *I can't believe you ran away three times. Thank you for not trying that again.*

Another familiar face on the first floor on the opposite side of the building caught my attention. She sat with her legs crossed on the bed, looking distantly out the window, and didn't seem to notice me until I lowered myself onto the corner of the bed. I was shocked when she spoke.

"I promise I didn't tell anybody you and the other girl were Idrisans."

"It wouldn't matter if you did. It's all over with now," I smiled. "It'll take a while to rebuild the island and get everyone home. But we're going around releasing all the people who were taken in Cleansings, and I know they must have reached all the manors in the mountains by now. It's a start, anyway. How are you feeling, Charleigh?"

"I feel strange, but in a... good way," she answered in a voice so child-like, one who didn't know her would think nobody ever taught her how to speak at all. "But you know Charleigh isn't my name. It's Odette. I remember it. I can still remember it."

Idris never let anyone get too excited or comfortable without sternly reminding them that our work wouldn't be done until the names of the Lebon are forgotten, and a permanent government was set up. *We aren't going to hold power forever. If we tried, we would be no better than the tyrants we just overthrew,* she said to us many times until we could recite her dictum.

The next several years were to be spent blurring lines between the classes. The plan for doing so consisted of helping former Stoleh get to the point where they could stand on their feet: putting them to work and getting them out of the slums, and keeping close connections and watch on the former Etaira and the Guard. Allyson was adamant on not taking anything from those who had it, saying that giving redistributed handouts would make the people dependent on the government again after it was set up. Only relief supplies could be used for the first several months as Nemirena shifted its system to sending produce and goods to different areas of the island based on population, and not the Guard's tithe. People would be free to move around anywhere, and the Haritite State would have to open up its borders.

All Guard whom had worked to their position stayed to operate under the new terms, but a different Cleansing of sorts swept through its ranks: washing out as many cheats and corrupted officials as they could find. The next time we were in the area, long after Odette and Barney had gone home, I learned that because there were no more intimidator Guard lurking in the background of the State, Mrs. Cromwell retired and Gregory Guise was allowed to return to the organization for small, local work in between his crippling spells.

Emeline had also finally gotten out of Rochonnell. But instead of moving to Sturwaller, she moved to the Wall to help with the slow process of relocating families. And Arena, eventually growing tired of sitting around the drastically reduced camp in the isolation of the woods, took the simple name of Kyna, a former Nemiren, and never truly lived in one place as she happily jumped at every opportunity the Idrisans had for her.

The proposal was to strip the Wall down until only the gate remained, and leave that as a monument to the Stoleh who had lost their lives in prison, after eight o'clock, as slaves, or as victims of the random violence the Guard had once been prone to. For now, Lukas and Joana came up with the idea of what they called a graveyard for the missing. Short slabs of stone were engraved with the names of those who were still unaccounted for, but not proven dead, and placed in long columns on a bare spot of land by a river. As more and more people returned home, a family member would come and retrieve the stone from the yard. The idea was to give those of us with still-missing loved ones a sense of hope as we watched the number of stones shrink with the passing months.

On occasion, I would pass a sad, lost name with an unlit candle resting on the ground below it. It was a symbol of mourning: a symbol that this man, woman, or child was now confirmed dead by the Guard's scarcely kept execution records or some other evidence. I cringed every time I saw one of these candles, my eyes always terrifying me when they manifested one before my father's stone. It felt too cold and unfeeling to stand for a life, and one night, I walked out there with Rosalie, Ellamae, and Mom to bury a small chest of things we thought best stood for him. Mom painfully wrote out the words to a song he teasingly sang to her before any of us were born. Ellamae contributed a small handful of copper and tin rings, saying her most vivid memory of

392

Dad was how he would make similar trinkets for her as a little girl, and told her that they would turn into gold when she fell in love for the first time. Rosalie ripped her Shattered Glass poem from her journal, folded it, and tucked her favorite pen inside, insisting that even though I taught her to form letters, he taught her to write.

Mom said that of the three of us, I looked the most like Dad. If we never found him, I wanted a piece of me in his emblematic grave. So I cut my hair again to my shoulders, tied a lock of it with a ribbon, and placed it inside the small chest. The next morning when I returned alone to the site, I plucked a weed flower from the ground, and tucked it gently within the tiny mound of upturned dirt that held our faith, hoping that we would one day be able to exhume his box. Rose once asked Mom if, after twelve years, she still loved our father. Mom paused for a long time, not as if debating but like she had to think about how to phrase her answer.

"I will always, always love your father, Rosalie," she finally said, hugging her beside her on the sofa. "He was the first and only man I ever loved. He gave me so many precious memories that carried me through the years in Kieriana. And above everything else, he gave me you, Amaryllis, and Ellamae. He loved the three of you more than life itself. Never forget that."

I repeated these words over and over again in my head, standing in front of the stone one year from the insurrection of Acwel Aloysius. The biting wind felt as if it could leave scars on my face, and chilled my spine as I shoved my hands deep into Uncle Graham's thick, comforting jacket. The flower I picked had gone from wilting to brittle to brown-stemmed, and finally I admitted to myself that it was dead. The prisons all over the island had been emptied of Stoleh, though his name was not written on any execution record we could find. Something about not knowing hurt even deeper than death. My hope grew staler every time I looked at the trees surrounding us, and they were different than what seemed to be only weeks ago. Kneeling down in front of the stone, I stared deeply into the neatly carved name of my father, and shakily took a half melted, wax candle from my pocket. I dug into the sunken, wet mound of dirt until I felt the hard surface of the chest with my fingers, and gently placed the candle on top of it. As I replaced the dirt, I felt something that seemed to elude me for a long time: peace.

I heard the footsteps behind me, and looked over my shoulder to see Bennett walking amongst the stones. He came from finally placing a candle beside his mother's memorial, and seemed to have the same kind of reaction as I. As he drew closer, I forced myself to my feet, though couldn't take my eyes off of the unchanging name, the pair of almost human eyes staring back at me.

"Are you okay?" he stopped beside me, also looking down at the stone, and knowing what I had done with my candle. In response, I leaned against him, turning my head away and forcing my eyes closed. Bennett's arm slowly came arm my back, his hand gently running up and down my arm.

"I feel terrible," I swallowed, determined not to be the one to cry again. "I can barely remember him."

Bennett easily turned me toward him, and we continued to stand there in a silent hug. Despite how much I trusted him, I momentarily tensed, but relaxed slowly as the seconds passed, burying my face into his coat.

"They were willing to die for us," I felt his warm exhale on my neck. "It doesn't make it any easier, but at least we know they were thinking about us until their last breath. The least we can do is keep their memories with us until ours."

I lifted my head, and looked at him with wide eyes as if expecting him to keep talking. With our faces only inches apart, he pushed my hair behind my ear, and unconvincingly tried to smile.

"How can I keep his memories if I don't remember him?" I asked, knowing he couldn't have an answer. I just wanted to know what he was going to say.

"You don't have to remember to know how much you meant to him. What he did for you is all the proof you'll ever need."

With nothing else to say, we only listened to the sound of the wind. It blew relentlessly around us, though I felt balanced and safe where we stood, resting my head just below his chin.

"It looks like your flower is finally escaping," he said, and I looked below us at the dead weed tumbling out of the dirt and along the ground. I all but scrambled after it, skidding on my knees and snatching it violently in my hand before it got away. In the process, the stem entirely severed from the flower, along with almost half its petals, rolling silently past the other stones like dust. I stared at the little I had left in my hand, aghast, and slowly turning my body around to face undoubtedly the only proof my father had ever lived. Cupping the dejected remains in my hands to protect it from the cold, like it was still alive, I didn't pay much mind as Bennett knelt behind me. He slowly lifted one of my hands, causing the flower to fall into my palm, and guided it back down to the dirt. Together, we tucked the bottom loosely below the earth.

"It's time to let it go, Amaryllis," Bennett said softly next to my ear. "Never forget about him, but don't let this haunt you anymore."

I knew what he meant, but my hands shook as I gently covered the colorless petals. I felt the biting breeze suddenly morph into a ton of rocks, and turned back around into Bennett, shaking, but still not in tears. In his awkward half-sitting, half-standing position, he continued to try to comfort me. When he kissed the top of my head again, a warm, soothing shudder ran through my bones. As we helped each other stand, he asked,

"Is there anything I can do?"

I shook my head, standing taller on my toes, and kissed him. I hadn't thought about it beforehand, but I couldn't say I regretted it as his arms around my back tightened to raise me higher. Ten seconds later, we separated and looked down at the same time, backing away slightly as if shocked by what we had just done.

"I-I'm sorry," I offered meekly, though Bennett only smiled, and reached for my icy hand. He took a few steps backwards, waiting for me to start walking with him away from this graveyard. He didn't speak until we reached its boundaries.

"I'm not."

The news waited for us at home, and everyone decided to come. I had never seen the atrium of a clinic so congested, but recognized almost every face in the room as an Idrisan. Allyson greeted us, and motioned down the hall.

"We've already seen her. Serah looks healthy, but the doctor said only one person besides Vince can be in the room at a time."

By some unspoken, unanimous vote, I tentatively moved down the hall, and knocked lightly on the door. A few moments later, with no answer, I opened it myself.

The color was drained from her face and she appeared fairly tired and weak, but all things considered, Serah had done considerably well. Vince waved me closer to the bed, and motioned me down into a chair beside her. The eight pound infant rested comfortably in her arms, wrapped tightly in a small blanket, sound asleep. When Serah and Vince renounced their philosophy about children and gave it a second chance, we were all happy for them, though the pureness of their child's unmarked skin and light brown ringlets was something else beautiful. They had kept the name a secret until now, and seemed to want everyone there to hear it. When Vince later emerged from the room and announced his newborn's name with a broad, almost goofy grin, I thought the entire room was brought to tears.

Vince and Serah had named their daughter Ruth.

Epilogue

Chapter Forty Five

The sky has stopped raining for the first time in what feels like years on this morning. I know I was not the only one who could not find sleep last night, and whether or not my shaking hand, sunken eyes, and brittle, beaten body show it, I am at peace internally. The one thing I find fascinating about knowing death approaches with the ascension of the sun is that I did not wish it would return below the horizon once it began to rise. I cannot feel the same penetrating fear that used to shake me to the core, nor the grief that once shackled me in tears. I said my final words yesterday, and I want that to be my legacy. I have no interest in giving them their standard, barely audible '*the dreams of the people live on*' patter before they put a bullet in my head. Today, I will be silent.

But that is today. Last night, the obligatory decency so lacking amongst the Guard scarcely presented itself when the same people who were thirsting me to death beforehand unlocked the door to my individual, gloomy room. They told me that they were here to listen to any wishes they could fill before I died.

"Paper and a pen," I answered quickly, ashamed that I was asking anything of them. Surprised by my strange request, it took ten nerve wracking minutes before several sheets of paper and a fountain pen were slipped carelessly under the locked door. By the light of this barred window, I feel compelled to write my story. It is not of my life, which no one will remember after this day, but everything that has led to this moment in Kieriana. While the Lebon Guard prepare a wagon in which to carry us to the public execution stage they erected in the night, I will fold my papers together, and force them between the bars in the high window. I have every reason to believe that a Guard will later find them, laugh, and incinerate my last testament in the shaken sparks of a measly cigar. But I am hoping that a slave, one even less fortunate than I, might receive it first, and keep it hidden until they are freed. I ask now that when the day comes, you give my letters to Theo. I want him to know that I was here, I know about Jason, and that I am not afraid, nor do I ever regret leaving the Wall for the camp. It is better to die with a sense of purpose, even if I only tell myself there is indeed resolve for the sake of comfort, than to live and grovel to your betters in hope they might spare your pitiful life for a bit longer. I know the camp will carry about its business just as well without me and the others, though my wish for the Idrisans is that they stop hiding in the shadows. What are our lives if spent squatting alone in the Wilds? If we allow ourselves to only talk about the day we are free, then nothing differentiates us from our traitors, or the Lebon themselves.

There is no more to say. I am worried they will come soon, and I will not have the time to slip my paper through the window. But at the end of this entry, at the end of my life, I have one last thing I feel must be written if not spoken. I will repeat it to myself as I am taken from this hell, marched onto the stage, and as they force the black bag over my head. It will remain on my tongue and in my heart until after the trigger is pulled.

3-1-16-18-9-1 18-15-4-1-12-9-1 2-5-12-15-14-7-19 20-15 21-19.

About the Author

Sidney is a junior in the Math and Science High School at Clover Hill High School, located in Richmond, VA. She began seriously writing in the eighth grade, and developed a passion for the written word. She is also a pianist, and performs with her high school's award-winning show band and show choirs. This year, Sidney is excited to be part of the National English Honor Society, Writers' Guild, and French Club. She and Jessica have been close friends since age ten, and have a plethora of embarrassing photos to prove it. Sidney enjoys spending time with her dog, Phoebe Louise, adores her four marvelous cousins, and is fortunate to live just down the road from her beloved Nana. This is Sidney's second novel, two years following her first release, *Seven Summits: the Magical Talent.*

About the Illustrator

Jessica has taken creative classes every year since elementary school, but her real love for art started seven years ago when her brother introduced her to drawing anime. It began as a small hobby, but eventually she would find herself always doodling in class, where she developed her own style. She is currently enrolled in AP Studio Art as a junior in high school in Richmond, VA. Jessica and Sidney have been friends since fifth grade, and she fondly remembers the night of June 25th, 2013, when they locked themselves in Sidney's house, frantically writing/drawing until eleven at night. They currently attend math class every day in power suits. Just kidding.

DSP Books and Information

If you like this story, you'll also enjoy these Deep Sea Publishing (DSP) books in the same genre:

Seven Summits: The Magical Talent, by Sidney McPhail

Hardt's Tale, by Gwendolyn Druyor (DSP 2013 Author's Contest Winner)

The Good Fight, by Ophelia Hu (DSP 2013 Author's Contest Winner)

Other DSP books that your family will love, include:

Let Sleeping Dragons Lie, by Tyrone Burson (DSP 2013 Author's Contest Grand PrizeWinner)

The Gallivan Legacy, by Sable Lewis (DSP 2013 Author's Contest Winner)

Not Myself, by Faith Miller

The Bryant Family Chronicles: Death and Gold in Zara Zote, by Eddie Hughes (Readers Choice Winner 2011)

The Bryant Family Chronicles: Homicide in Honolulu, by Eddie Hughes

These award-winning works are available in paperback and eBook form at Deep Sea Publishing's Online Store, Amazon, Apple's iBookstore, and BarnesandNoble.com. The website also lists the shops and bookstores that carry the books. These books can be ordered from any bookstore as well.

Deep Sea Publishing (DSP) is a Florida-based company that sells novels, young adult/teen fiction, children's books, photography books, and reference guides. The website mentioned below supplies details on all DSP publications and the expected release dates of new material.

www.deepseapublishing.com

www.ingramcontent.com/pod-product-compliance
Lightning Source LLC
Chambersburg PA
CBHW060145260626
47160CB00001B/123